# Echoes *of* Grace

Caragh Bell

POOLBEG

Published 2018
by Poolbeg Press Ltd
123 Grange Hill, Baldoyle
Dublin 13, Ireland
E-mail: poolbeg@poolbeg.com



1

A catalogue record for this book is available from the British Library.

ISBN 978-1-78199-8045



Typeset by Poolbeg

Printed by CPI Group, UK

www.facebook.com/poolbegpress
@PoolbegBooks

**www.poolbeg.com**

# About the Author

Caragh Bell lives in West Cork with her husband and five children. When she isn't writing romance novels, she teaches English and French to teenagers.

She has previously written the *Follow Your Heart* Trilogy: *Indecision, Regrets* and *Promises.*

You can connect with Caragh on Facebook (Caragh Bell-Writer), on Twitter (@BellCaragh) or on Instagram (@caraghbellwriter)

Also by Caragh Bell

**The *Follow Your Heart* trilogy**

*Indecision*

*Regrets*

*Promises*

Published by Poolbeg

# Acknowledgements

This book was such a joy to write.

Thank you to Dan McCarthy, the 'Dan' in the dedication. Without you, I wouldn't be where I am today.

To Fódhla, Aoibhe, Lughan, Oscar, and Feidhlim. I'm so lucky to be your mother.

To Mum and Dad for your constant love and support. You've helped me through so much. I appreciate it every day.

To Kathleen and Eugene. I couldn't have asked for nicer parents-in-law.

To Louise, Ian and Freyja. The planned ones!

To Gaye, Paula, Kieran, David, and all those at Poolbeg. Thanks for all your help and advice.

To all my colleagues at school for your encouragement, especially those at my table.

To Daniel O'Driscoll for believing in me.

Finally, to my husband John. Here's to the next chapter . . .

*For Dan*

# PART ONE

## Cornwall 2002

# Chapter One

The rain beat against the window pane, causing rivulets to fall down the old lattice at tremendous speed. The Big House of the estate had weathered many a storm; for over three hundred years it had faced the wrath of the Atlantic, its grey granite stones defiantly protecting its inhabitants within. Its sheer size was enough to stop any wind in its track. The fourteen-bedroomed mansion stood regally on the cliff's edge. Today, its strength was being tested; the sky was dark-grey and the sea a murky green with waves crashing against the rocks of the Cornish shoreline.

Aurora picked up her Barbie and bent the doll's rigid body into a sitting position. Then she carefully placed it on a dining-room chair in the banquet hall of her large doll's house. The little girl's dark-brown hair fell down her back, the long tresses tied with red bows. Her large brown eyes, fringed with black lashes, dominated a pretty heart-shaped face and her slim frame was dressed in an old-fashioned plaid frock, chosen as always by her nanny that morning.

'Now, Princess Grace,' she said sternly to her doll, 'eat your broccoli so you'll grow to be big and strong.'

The doll stared into space, her back straight and her blonde hair carefully pulled back into a ponytail. Aurora always christened her dolls 'Grace'. It was the name of her dead mother. The game never varied either: Princess Grace, the beautiful blonde heroine, was rescued from her lonely tower by a handsome prince. She had lived all of her life alone and was desperate for company. Then her prince would arrive and take her away in his red Barbie Ferrari to a new life.

Aurora sighed. She was just so bored. Being nine was hard enough without being bored stiff as well. Her father, though attentive, was just too old to play. He was nearly sixty-two and constantly complained of a bad leg. 'Not today, my darling,' was the habitual reply when she begged him to play ball with her or take her to the beach. He was always sitting in his study, writing on paper and frowning. He refused to have a TV in the house and so she had to content herself with making up stories and singing to her teddies. Maggie, her nanny, would explain that her father was writing plays and must not be disturbed. Aurora understood that he was famous. Her teacher at school always talked about the great playwright Henry Sinclair, but Aurora had no interest in reading his books. The words were too long and she didn't understand any of it.

Her older brothers lived in London, not that it made a difference. In fact, they tended to ignore her. They were the product of Henry's first marriage – their mother Marcella had died of breast cancer fifteen years before. They had no interest in their half-sister, from what they deemed Henry's unsuitable marriage. Nor did they lament Grace's death – her dark beauty and mane of wild hair had made her unconventional and they resented her association with their upper-class father. In their eyes, she had pounced on Henry when he was grieving for their own mother and, despite being almost thirty years his junior, had trapped him into marriage by getting pregnant with Aurora. To top it all off, she had been an actress – in their opinion a two-bit singer. This, for George and Sebastian, was just lurid icing on the ghastly cake. Her death during childbirth had been tragic and they had helped their father through his loss, but it definitely was in their favour when it came to inheritance and the estate.

Aurora got to her feet and stretched. Her tummy rumbled so she bounded down to the big kitchen where Maggie was rolling out pastry for an apple pie.

Maggie was an elderly lady of about sixty-five with a shock of white hair. She was small and wiry with sallow skin. Her wise eyes were as blue as the sky and her hands were rough from manual work throughout the years. She had worked for the Sinclair family since the age of fifteen, just like her mother before her. She still cycled around the Cornish countryside as she had never learned to drive.

'Alright, little 'un,' she said lovingly as Aurora took some orange juice out of the fridge. 'Daddy 'as visitors comin' today.'

Aurora drank thirstily and wiped her mouth with her sleeve. 'Is it that Gloria lady?' she asked, her brown eyes wide.

'It is, my lovely,' said Maggie. 'It's the third time this month. She must like your daddy to drive all the way from London.'

Aurora tilted her head to one side. 'Are they kissing, Maggie?'

Maggie started. 'I don't know about that, my darlin'. Don't be worryin' about things like that.' She started to slice cooking apples into the waiting pie dish. 'Your father needs friends, that's all. It's lonely down 'ere without company.'

Tell me about it, thought Aurora, frowning.

She was still too young for boarding school so her father had hired a tutor to teach her every day. He was a stuffy man of fifty-five, a Latin scholar with a love for the classics, and so Aurora was an expert on Dionysus and Ariadne, but had problems with basic mathematical problems.

Oh, how she yearned to play with children her own age! There was only Freddie, Maggie's nephew, who visited on weekends. He was a farmer's son from the village and was a whole year older than Aurora. He had sandy-brown hair, a ruddy complexion and sea-blue eyes. He took her to the beach sometimes and explained in his Cornish drawl about periwinkles and sea-monsters. He related tales of smugglers and pirates and showed her the dark caves beneath the cliff where treasure was supposedly hidden.

Aurora adored Freddie. Not only was he a year older and infinitely more sophisticated, he was also kind and didn't mind that she was a girl. They had become firm friends and she craved his company. His visits were more frequent in the winter, as the summer and harvest were busy times at the farm. He would arrive around noon and they would run off down the road, making the best of the limited daylight.

'Freddie,' said Aurora once, as they sat on the rocks and trailed their fingers in the lukewarm water of the rock pools.

'Yeah?' he answered, splashing her gently.

'You'll always be my friend, won't you?'

He nudged her. ''Ere, why do you ask?'

'Because you're *my* best friend,' she said seriously, sitting up and brushing her hair back from her face. 'Without you, it would just be me and Daddy and Maggie. Don't ever leave.'

'What about Seb and George?' he asked playfully. 'Your dearest brothers?'

'*Ugh!*' She made a face. 'They're horrible and you know it.'

'Look,' he said, grabbing her shoulders and staring into her dark eyes, 'you're cool, as girls go. I'll be your friend forever. Do you believe me?'

She stared back. 'I believe you.'

'Now, come on. Auntie Maggie has 'ot chocolate for us when we get back.' He pulled her to her feet. 'I'll race you, Sinclair!'

'*Aurora!*' Henry Sinclair's booming voice resonated down the corridor. '*Aurora, darling! Come and say hello to Gloria!*'

Aurora sighed and put a bookmark in her worn copy of *Harry Potter and the Chamber of Secrets*. She was just at the good part. Now, she would have to smile and pretend to be interested in grown-up conversation that she didn't understand.

This Gloria lady seemed nice enough; she always brought sweets and smelled like lavender. Her blonde hair was short and wavy with streaks of grey, her blue eyes merry and her tall frame dressed beautifully in couture. Aurora could tell she was nearly as old as her father, by the lines on her face. Maggie had mentioned that she was a widow and that she had pots of money. Why did she visit then? Surely she and Daddy were too old for kissing and hugging and things?

She could hear laughter from the drawing room as she trudged down the stairs. The oak staircase dominated the main hall and had a threadbare red carpet on the steps. The house, though majestic, was badly in need of refurbishment. The paint was peeling in some parts of the walls and the heating was Victorian. Aurora was quite accustomed to seeing her breath as she exhaled on cold winter nights. Her bed had two duvets and she had fluffy socks for her feet. Her hot-water bottle was her favourite possession and she cuddled it each night, luxuriating in the heat it emitted. Sometimes she wished she had a house like those people in the village: a small, warm terraced house with double-glazed windows and central heating.

She entered the drawing room quietly, shutting the old door with a click. Maggie's apple pie was on the dresser. A jug of cream stood near it and a stack of china plates.

Her father, Henry, was standing by the old fireplace, his handsome face smiling down at their guest. He was a striking man with his tall slim frame and grey hair. His blue eyes were warm and he had a soft voice that was rarely raised. Gloria looked as groomed as always, her legs crossed elegantly at the ankle.

'Aurora, darling,' said Henry, gesturing for her to come closer. 'Gloria has brought you a gift.' He pointed to a bag on the coffee table. 'Come and say thank you.'

Aurora approached the smiling lady and gave her an awkward peck on the cheek. Then she picked up the bag and peered inside. It was filled with sweets and chocolate bars.

'Oh!' she said in delight. 'Thank you!'

'You look lovely today,' said Gloria, brushing a long tendril of dark hair from Aurora's shoulder. 'Such a pretty child,' she added to Henry.

'You look nice too, Gloria,' said Aurora dutifully.

Gloria squeezed her hand. 'You're so good to say so,' she said with a laugh. 'It was such a long journey, I was sure my hair would be flat on arrival.'

'Did you drive, ma'am?' asked Maggie, appearing out of nowhere with a tea tray in her hands.

'No, my son James brought me down. He's nineteen and desperate to practise his driving.' She smiled. 'His Volkswagen Golf is his pride and joy. Any excuse and he's off. The opportunity to drive hundreds of miles was too tempting so he came along.'

Maggie poured two cups of tea and placed them on the coffee table with a jug of milk. 'Sugar, ma'am?' she asked Gloria, knowing that Henry preferred his tea without.

'Not for me, thank you,' replied Gloria, smiling.

'Where is James now?' asked Henry, accepting a cup of tea from Maggie.

'He's just popped down to the beach to take some photographs,' said Gloria, adding some milk to her cup.

'Photographs? Whatever for? The weather is frightful.'

'He's studying photography as you know,' she said, placing her cup and saucer carefully on the small mahogany table near her chair. 'He saw the stormy sea as he was dropping me off and scooted down to take a few shots before he loses the light.'

Maggie placed a plate with a slice of apple pie and a fork on the table by Gloria's chair. 'Cream?' she asked politely, holding up a small jug.

Gloria nodded. 'I shouldn't but I will.'

Henry refused a plate of pie and sipped his tea.

'Have you other children?' asked Aurora politely.

'Yes,' she replied. 'I have three children: James, William and Laura.' She smiled. 'Laura is only a few years older than you. She's thirteen.'

'Did she come today too?'

'No.' Gloria shook her head. 'She was at a friend's house last night and she stayed over.'

'Oh,' said Aurora in disappointment. 'Will I ever get to meet her?'

Henry's eye met Gloria's and he cleared his throat. 'Well ...'

Suddenly, the front door banged loudly and they all jumped. Maggie scuttled out to the hall and reappeared seconds later with a young man, drenched to the skin.

'James!' exclaimed Gloria, jumping to her feet. 'You're saturated! Oh, for goodness' sake!'

He pulled back the hood of his jacket to reveal dark hair and eyes. His skin was sallow and he had light stubble on his chin.

Maggie took his soaking jacket from his outstretched hand and held it at arm's length.

'I'll put this by the Aga,' she said, walking out of the room. 'It's bleddy soakin', it is.'

'James! You said you would take those photos from the car,' his mother fussed. 'You'll get pneumonia, being out in this weather.'

'Relax, Mum! It was worth it. I can't wait to develop them.' He ran his fingers through his hair and droplets flew everywhere.

Henry held out his hand. 'Good to see you again, son.'

They shook hands formally and James smiled.

'Did you see the rugby yesterday?' he asked. 'It was a close one. Will nearly blew a gasket when that Kiwi kicked the drop goal.'

Henry nodded. 'I thought we had them. It was a tragedy in the end.'

Aurora sidled behind an armchair and gazed at Gloria's son. His eyes were warm and he winked at her. Blushing, she smiled back, unsure of how to react. He was the opposite of her stern haughty brothers who habitually ignored her completely.

'This is Henry's daughter, Aurora,' announced Gloria, gently pulling her into view.

James held out his hand. 'Charmed, I'm sure,' he said, shaking hers firmly. 'Are you a princess with a name like that?' His brown eyes crinkled in amusement.

Aurora giggled. 'Sleeping Beauty was called Aurora.'

'Is she the one who ate the apple?'

'No!' She shook her head furiously. 'That was Snow White. Aurora hurt her finger on a spinning wheel and fell asleep.'

James scratched his head. 'I'm pretty sure my sister Laura has subjected me to every Disney film that has ever been made, yet this does not ring a bell.'

'She sleeps and sleeps and then the prince kisses her and wakes her up.' Aurora's brown eyes were wide. 'He saves her and takes her back to her real family.'

'Is she happy?' he asked softly.

'At the end,' she sighed. 'She's happy at the end.'

James winked at her again. 'Sounds like a great film.'

Henry cleared his throat. 'Gloria, darling, will you two stay the night? That storm is going to get worse before it gets better.'

Gloria got to her feet and looked out the window at the black sky and incessant rain beating against the pane. 'Well,' she began, glancing at her son, 'James has a date later with this girl ...'

James shrugged. 'It's not that important. It was only a few drinks.'

'I would really prefer if you didn't travel.' Henry's tone was firm. 'Wait until morning.'

'I didn't bring anything ...' Gloria gestured to her clothes.

'I'm sure Maggie can produce a nightgown for you,' Henry said with a smile.

Aurora put her head to one side. She was unaccustomed to seeing her father behave like this. His head was always intent on a computer or a page; now he was beaming and speaking in a strange voice.

Maggie bustled back in and poured a cup of tea for James. He gratefully accepted it and took a sip. Then, placing the cup and saucer on the coffee table, he sauntered over to the bookshelves that lined one wall. 'Are some of these first editions?' he enquired, running his finger over the faded volumes stacked closely together.

'Why, yes,' answered Henry. 'My father flirted with being a writer at times. He loved Thomas, Eliot and Frost in particular. He was also a good chum of Teddy Hughes.'

'I really enjoyed your play about Cocteau.' James pulled out a worn copy of *La Machine Infernale*.

Henry shrugged. 'It was in my head for years. I just had to take the time to write it.'

'I went to see it with Dad that time. Do you remember, Mum?'

'Yes, I do,' she answered sadly. 'I took Laura to see *Toy Story* at the Odeon. We had ice cream afterwards.'

'Master James,' Maggie interrupted, 'your apple pie's 'ere on the table for you.'

'Thanks, Maggie,' said James, moving back to the coffee table.

Henry took Gloria's hand in his own and stroked her wrist. 'It's odd how it can hit you sometimes – the grief. It's almost ten years since Grace passed, but sometimes it feels like only yesterday.' He gestured towards a huge portrait by the bay window. It was of a beautiful dark-haired woman wearing a white dress with a faraway look on her face.

All the occupants of the room gazed at it for a moment.

'She looks just like you!' exclaimed James, his eyes moving from Aurora to the painting. 'It's uncanny!'

Aurora said nothing. She was used to people saying that: she strongly resembled her mother. She often wished she could see her and touch her and hear her voice: just once.

'Yes, Aurora looks exactly like Grace,' agreed Henry sadly. 'I can't quite believe it sometimes.'

'She was very beautiful,' concluded Gloria.

'Right,' interrupted Maggie. 'Are you two stayin' for a bit of dinner? I 'ave stew and dumplins, followed by cherry puddin' and cream.'

'Sounds great,' said James, smiling. 'I'm famished.'

# Chapter Two

James scraped the bottom of his bowl with his spoon and groaned.

'Maggie, you're an absolute wizard in the kitchen,' he said, patting his belly. 'Mum, I love you, but your cooking skills are not your greatest attribute.'

Aurora sprinkled Smarties on her ice cream. She didn't like pies and puddings. Instead, Maggie always gave her two scoops of vanilla with sweets on top.

Henry sipped his cognac and grasped Gloria's hand. 'It's so lovely to have company,' he said. 'This old house needs a bit of life.'

They were seated in the banquet hall. Maggie had set four places around the far end of the long mahogany table and the remainder of the polished surface stretched interminably into the darkness. Large paintings dominated the walls: Henry's ancestors in different period costumes, all with the same expression. Aurora hated the banquet hall; she much preferred eating her meals with Maggie in the warm kitchen.

James turned to Aurora and whispered, 'Do you like reading?'

She nodded fervently. 'I love it. At the moment I'm reading *Harry Potter and the Chamber of Secrets* and I'm at the best bit.'

'When will the new book be released?' he asked seriously.

'J.K. Rowling said 2003, so next year, I hope. I can't wait!' She sighed. 'I just loved *The Goblet of Fire*, but this one seems to be just as good.'

'Laura's very excited too. She keeps telling me that it's Levi-*oh*-sa, not Levios-*ah*!'

Aurora laughed. 'You're funny.'

James refused a second helping of pudding from Maggie. 'As delicious as it was, I'm absolutely stuffed.'

'Ah, go on, my lovely,' she said. 'You're only a skinny little thing.'

'Oh, go on then.' He held out his bowl and Maggie piled it high with two heaped spoonfuls of cherry pudding and a huge helping of cream.

'I'll pop,' he whispered conspiratorially to Aurora before taking an enormous bite.

Aurora giggled.

'So, why were you called Aurora?' he asked, chewing. 'It's a cool name.'

'I don't know,' she answered truthfully.

'Henry?' pursued James. 'Why did you call her Aurora?'

Henry sipped his brandy. 'It was her mother – she chose the name.'

'Why?'

'She was named for the Goddess of the Dawn. Her birth was a new beginning.' He sighed. 'Well, that was how it was supposed to be.'

Aurora looked stricken for a moment and James nudged her. 'Hey, you're a princess and a goddess. Pretty impressive.'

Her face changed immediately. 'I'm also stars. Daddy says that I'm up in the sky.'

'Of course!' James clapped his hands. 'Aurora Borealis! The Northern Lights.'

'I suppose ...'

'Or Aurora Australis, the Southern Lights.' He rubbed his chin. 'We should stick to our own hemisphere, I think. Borealis it is.'

'What do you mean?'

'That's it! From now on, I'm going to call you that.' His eyes twinkled. 'You're hereby christened Aurora Borealis Sinclair.'

Aurora gazed at him in delight. 'No one has ever given me a nickname before.'

'Well, that has now changed.' He took another bite of pudding. 'I can't believe that you've lived this long without someone calling you that.'

'I'm only nine!'

'You're an old lady, Aurora Borealis!' He shook his head. 'Practically a pensioner.'

'You're silly.' She giggled and picked a yellow sweet off her now-melted ice cream.

The storm ceased later that night. Henry and Gloria busied themselves playing gin rummy by the dwindling fire as the windows stopped their rattling and peace descended on the clifftop.

James showed some of his photos to Aurora who observed them intently.

'I really like this one,' she commented, pointing to an old woman in a black cloak, standing still under the neon lights of Piccadilly.

'Yes, that's rather good,' agreed James. 'The crowds are blurry around her yet she's stationary. I love the expression on her face; she seems so ...' He paused.

'Wise?' Aurora suggested.

'Yes,' he exclaimed, surprised. 'That's exactly it. The rat race surrounds her and she realises that it's all utterly pointless, that rushing and running serves no one and that we should stop and enjoy life.'

Aurora frowned as she considered this.

James laughed. 'Sorry, Aurora Borealis. I get carried away sometimes.' He closed his portfolio. 'So, what do you like to do? Besides reading *Harry Potter*, of course.'

'Me?' She bit her lip. 'I don't know. I suppose I play with Princess Grace a lot.'

'Princess Grace?' He raised an eyebrow. 'Is she your neighbour?'

'No, silly!' She punched him playfully on the arm. 'She's my doll.'

'Oh! Well, may I meet her?'

'My doll?'

'Why, yes. Why not?' He got to his feet. 'I've never met a real princess before.'

Aurora jumped up in excitement. 'Oh, she's beautiful. I did her hair today and she looks so pretty.'

'Sounds great,' he said, smiling. 'Right then, lead the way.'

Aurora bounded up the stairs and led him down the dark corridor to her bedroom. Maggie had lit the fire in the grate and the flames danced merrily in the darkness.

'My God, this place is stuck in the Dark Ages,' observed James, staring at the old-fashioned décor and the four-poster bed. 'I feel like I'm in a gothic ghost story.'

'Yes,' agreed Aurora. 'It can be scary sometimes. That's why I have Grace here with me. She looks after me.' She pointed to her doll who was sitting on a deck chair by a plastic palm tree. 'Isn't she lovely?'

James went down on one knee and kissed the doll's hand. 'Charmed, I'm sure, Your Highness,' he said solemnly.

Princess Grace stared blankly back at him, her face frozen.

'She has a lovely home,' he continued, looking at the doll's castle. 'Is she married?'

'Well, the prince rescues her and takes her away in his Ferrari,' explained Aurora, pointing to the Barbie car parked by the bookcase. 'But, the next day she's back again, stuck in the house all alone.'

James said nothing. He watched the little girl smooth her doll's hair sadly and his heart constricted. What a life for a young girl: isolated and lonely in the back end of nowhere with only an elderly woman and her father for company. It was no wonder that she lived in a fantasy world with her dolls. He thought of his own little sister, Laura. She was the total opposite to Aurora: she played volleyball and hockey, had tons of friends and a hectic social life.

'So, where's this prince?' he asked and Aurora looked up.

'He's sitting over there,' she said, pointing to the toy chest by the window. 'His name is Prince Ken.'

'Oh, it is,' said James with a smile.

'That was on his box when I got him,' she explained.

'So why did you call her Grace?' he continued, gesturing to her doll.

Aurora's face tightened. 'It was my mother's name,' she said softly.

James wanted to kick himself. *Of course, it was.*

'Look, let's go back down,' he suggested. 'We could watch a film or something.'

Aurora shook her head. 'We don't have a television. Daddy doesn't like them.'

'No TV?' gasped James incredulously.

'Nope,' she confirmed, shaking her head. 'The only time I get to see anything is at Freddie's house.'

'Freddie?'

'My best friend.'

'How about internet?' he pressed on. 'Surely you have a computer.'

'Daddy has an old one in his study but he doesn't let me near it.'

'What?' James ran his fingers through his hair.

'But Freddie has one. He lets me play games on it sometimes.'

James felt slight relief. At least the child had someone to play with. He felt momentarily angry with Henry Sinclair for subjecting his daughter to this medieval upbringing. From the way his mother was talking, it was likely that a wedding would be on the cards. He had been pretty indifferent to it up to now – he wasn't bitter about her moving on after his father's death and Henry seemed like a nice enough chap. Now, it seemed like a great idea. Aurora could grow up normally with a proper family. Laura would be a perfect companion with her army of friends and hectic social life.

'Let's go downstairs,' he said, holding out his hand. She inserted her little one into his immediately and he led her out onto the landing.

The next morning Aurora woke up and stretched, momentarily disorientated. The wintry weather gave little light, so the morning was the best time to see the surrounding countryside. She pulled open the heavy drapes and rubbed the condensation from the window pane. Their house boasted huge gardens and a pathway down the cliff to the beach. The ocean glinted in the pale sunlight and a huge ship was visible on the horizon. She put on her slippers and padded over to her robe which was hanging on an ancient brass hook by the dresser.

She and James had played Scrabble until after ten and then she had been sent to bed by her father.

'You'll see him again in the morning,' Henry had assured her as she protested. Gloria gave her a small hug and told her to sleep well.

James had winked and given a small wave. 'Night, Borealis,' he mouthed with a wide grin.

Maggie was in the kitchen when she burst through the door.

'Mornin',' she said warmly, kissing Aurora's head. 'I'm makin' drop scones.'

Aurora took her usual seat at the large table and watched Maggie drop batter onto the skillet on the Aga. It sizzled and she expertly swirled it to create a round shape.

'Is anyone else up, Maggie?'

'That nice young man was in a while ago.' She flipped the small pancake over in the pan. ''Ee was like a toad on a 'ot shovel, 'ee was. Drank a cup of coffee and off out to take some photographs down by the water.'

Aurora's face creased in disappointment. She would have loved to have gone too. The only time she got to go to the beach was with Freddie.

'Did he say when he'll be back?'

''Ee'll be back dreckly, little 'un.' She slid the pancake onto a plate and passed Aurora the honey. 'Now eat up. It'll get cold.'

The little girl half-heartedly nibbled on her breakfast, her countenance gloomy. Why did he have to go out? She was hoping that they could play a game together before he had to leave.

As if on cue, the kitchen door opened and James walked in, all wrapped up in his coat and scarf. His camera was slung casually over his shoulder and his eyes were blazing.

Aurora sat up straight the minute he walked in and beamed.

'This place is incredible,' he enthused, placing his Nikon carefully on the table. 'It's so rugged and wild. I got some amazing shots of the sea crashing against the cliffs.'

'Did you go to the beach?' she asked.

'Not yet,' he answered, hanging his coat on a wooden chair. 'You mentioned last night that you loved to go there, so I decided to wait for you.'

Aurora glowed with pleasure.

'Breakfast, sir?' asked Maggie, her pan poised. 'You need to eat in the mornin'. I 'ave some drop scones, I do.'

'I'd love one,' he replied, sitting down opposite Aurora. 'And call me James, please.'

'Okey-dokey.' Maggie pushed a plate in front of him. 'I'll get some coffee now.'

'Any sign of the olds?' he asked, munching loudly.

'The olds?' repeated Aurora, confused.

'Mum and Henry,' he explained. 'You've got to learn the lingo, Borealis. This is what having no TV and internet does to you.'

She giggled. 'They're not down yet. They probably stayed up really late.'

'Great. You go and get dressed and we'll head down to the beach.' He accepted a cup of coffee from Maggie. 'We'd best hurry – I know Mum will be anxious to leave – it's such a long journey and she wants to be home before dark.'

'Okay!' Aurora jumped up. 'I'll be down in a few minutes.' She scampered off in excitement, banging the kitchen door behind her.

Maggie crossed her arms and observed James thoughtfully. 'Ere, 'ow old are you?'

'Nineteen,' he answered. 'Since last week, in fact. I'm the eldest.'

'You're very good to take Aurora out. She gets so lonely.'

James nodded with his mouth full. 'I get that. I mean, she's like a Victorian child. I swear to God, if you met my little sister Laura you'd think they were from different planets.'

'Her older brothers never make an effort with her.' Maggie's face hardened. 'They don't visit very often, but when they do they are nasty so-and-so's.'

'Where do they live?'

'London. They work in the banks, they do. George is thirty-two and Seb is thirty.'

'Married?'

'Just Seb. He brought 'er 'ome last Christmas. She complained from the minute she arrived. The water was too cold – the rooms were too dark.' Maggie couldn't hide the disdain in her voice.

'Really?' James shook his head. 'They won't want to move back here then.'

'I 'ope not.' Maggie shuddered. 'She even 'ated my cooking! She don't eat bread and meat and such things.'

James stifled a smile. 'Did she have your cherry pudding?'

'Nope.' Maggie snorted. 'She don't eat no puddin', she said. 'Skinny little thing she was too.'

James scraped his plate and sat back. 'Well, there's no fear of me rejecting your food, Maggie. I think you're a genius.'

Maggie blushed. 'Ah, get out of 'ere, you!'

'I'm serious,' he said seriously. 'My mother is many things but she's not a great cook. I know KFC's number by heart.'

'Do you live at 'ome?' Maggie enquired, taking a seat herself.

'No,' he said, shaking his head. 'I'm sharing a flat near Tottenham Court Road with two other blokes. It's safe to say there's not much home cooking in our place either.'

'You need a girlfriend, you do,' concluded Maggie.

'I'm working on it,' he admitted. 'She's a waitress in our local caff but she doesn't seem that interested.'

Maggie looked disbelieving. 'I'm surprised to 'ear that, Master James. You seem like a lovely young man.'

'I'll wear her down,' he said cheerfully. 'Now, where can I get more coffee?' Maggie moved to get up, but he waved her back down. 'I can get it myself,' he insisted. 'Would you like some?'

'Well, why not?' Maggie beamed at him. ''Ere, I could get used to this.'

'Oh, I'm buttering you up so that you'll bake me more puddings.'

He winked at her and filled a cup. When he had resumed his seat, his expression became more serious.

'So, tell me about Aurora,' he said.

'Aurora?' she repeated, her expression guarded. 'What do you want to know about 'er?'

'What happened her mother?'

Maggie sighed. 'Oh, Master James, there's a tragic tale if ever there was one.'

'Please,' he pleaded. 'I want to know.'

''Ere, you got to be quiet.' Maggie got up, opened the door and poked her head into the corridor. There was no sign of Aurora so she sat down again. 'We don't ever talk about that time, Master James.'

'But you've got to,' he insisted.

'You can't tell anyone, mind,' warned the old lady. 'The master can't abear to 'ear about it. You 'ave to promise me,'

'I promise, Maggie.' James crossed his heart. 'I won't tell a soul.'

Maggie took a deep breath. 'Well, back-along, the master was married for years to Lady Marcella. They got married when 'ee was only twenty or so. She was the daughter of the neighbourin' Big 'Ouse, so it was all arranged. They were 'appy enough, don't get me wrong. He 'ad his writin' and she 'ad her 'orses, but then she got the cancer and she died.'

'So, George and Seb are her children?'

'Yep,' she confirmed. 'They were spoilt rotten all their lives. She doted on 'em, she did.'

'What was Marcella like?'

Maggie frowned. 'Not the warmest, I 'ave to say. She was bossy and had a short temper. She could've been nicer, let's leave it at that.'

'So, where did Henry meet Grace?'

'Well, 'ee writes plays, 'ee does. You know that, my lovely. Grace was an actress 'erself – she could proper sing too. She was born in some small village in Ireland and when her parents passed on, she moved to London. It seems that she 'ad no family – she was all alone. Mr. Sinclair saw 'er play Salomé on stage and that was it, so they say.'

'Salomé?' queried James. 'You mean, Oscar Wilde's play?'

'I do,' said Maggie, sipping her coffee. 'I read it afterwards. It's about this woman who demands John the Baptist's 'ead on a platter in return for a Dance of the Seven Veils.'

'Wow,' said James, impressed. 'A master chef *and* a literary buff!'

'Well, it was all the master could bleddy talk about: this Irish girl who had danced on stage with a voice like an angel. George and Seb were jumpin', I can tell you. They didn't want no incomer takin' their money.'

'Go on,' urged James, fascinated.

'Well, Grace were only twenty-five or so, just a young little thing and suddenly they were married. He brought 'er back 'ere and she was already with child. She was so bleddy sick. I remember making 'er ginger tea and wiping 'er brow.'

'Was she nice?'

'She was,' Maggie paused, 'but she were quiet. She seemed sad.'

'Really? That doesn't sound like someone newly married.' James rubbed his chin thoughtfully. 'Maybe she wasn't wild about being pregnant.'

'Nope, that weren't it. She wanted the baby. She would knit clothes and talk about the little 'un every day. She wanted the baby, as sure as the sun is in that there sky.' Maggie sighed. 'She 'ad melancholy, that's what it was.'

'So, how did she die?' he pursued. 'In this day and age of medical advancement?'

'The baby was due to come in February or so. She wanted Aurora for a girl as it was a new year and a new beginning. Then, on New Year's Eve it was, there was a big storm, far worse than last night. All the electricity went and it was just me and the missus – the master and the boys were on the way back from a party in London.'

James sat up, enthralled.

'The lights went out and suddenly I could hear the missus calling and crying. I jumped like a mackerel and rushed upstairs. There I found 'er in a pool of blood on the ground. My 'eart nearly stopped beatin', Master James, I can't abear blood, you see. She was crying and callin' out. I grabbed as many towels as I could and tried to stop the bleedin'. The phone was disconnected because of the storm so I was in a proper state, I was. I couldn't leave 'er but she needed the doctor.'

'What happened?'

'Well, my brother Conny called over, only by chance, to see if the old generator out the back was workin'.' Maggie made a Sign of the Cross. 'It was a miracle, Master James. I couldn't believe it when I saw 'im. I told 'im to run to the village and get Dr. Roberts and 'ee did, but by the time they came back, it was too late.' Her face fell. 'The missus 'ad died and the baby was in my arms.'

'You delivered Aurora?' he exclaimed in wonder.

'I did. I pulled her from Grace and it was just in time.'

'So, why did Grace die?' James looked confused. 'Why all the blood?'

'She 'ad a 'aemorrhage, they said. It was amazin' that Aurora survived at all. She was born on the stroke of midnight. The first baby of the year.'

'What happened then?'

'The master was inconsolable, 'ee was. ''Ee cut 'imself off from the world and I took care of the little 'un.' Maggie's face softened. 'She's like my own, Master James. I promised 'er mother that I would look after 'er and I 'ave.'

James took a deep breath. 'That's some story,' he concluded.

'You mustn't mention it,' she insisted, glancing at the door.

'Nobody talks about it, do you 'ear? The master blames 'imself – he feels 'ee should've been 'ere and not at that party in London.'

'I promise,' he said solemnly. 'Hand on heart.'

Aurora burst into the room at that moment, dressed in a fur-lined jacket and a woollen hat. Her eyes shone as she zipped the coat right up. 'Are you ready?' she said breathlessly.

'I am,' said James dutifully. 'Let's hit the beach.' He put on his jacket and pulled a beanie over his dark hair.

# Chapter Three

The waves crashed on the shore, sending short bursts of spray aided by the wind. Aurora had led him down the cliff path: a treacherous manmade trail over clumps of heather and natural gaps in the rocky surface. Beneath the majestic cliff there was a vast sandy beach which was isolated and untamed. James watched Aurora skip ahead and prance along the sea's edge, narrowly avoiding the waves as they flooded the sand inches from her feet. Her long dark hair flowed in the wind as she had discarded her woolly hat. She screamed in delight as the sea almost caught her out and raised her arms up to embrace the gusts of wind as they whipped past her.

This was the first time he had seen her like this: young and carefree. It warmed his heart and he was reminded of a poem he had read once by WB Yeats about a child dancing in the wind. His old English teacher, Ms Manning, would be proud that he remembered. He could still see her reciting it at the top of the classroom, her glasses perched on her nose.

He didn't know why but he wanted to help Aurora. Her obvious loneliness coupled with Maggie's tale of her birth only added to his sense of duty. She had to be saved. Henry and

Gloria's marriage was on the cards and the sooner the better in his opinion. Aurora needed normality. He had heard Henry mention a tutor and boarding school last night. That had to be vetoed. Laura went to a good local school and was quite happy – why then should Aurora be different?

He had always been a sucker for the needy. Years ago, he had trudged into his mother's kitchen with a bedraggled puppy he had found by the river's edge. Gloria had been firm: under no circumstances was she taking on another dog. They had two already: Labradors called Rosencrantz and Guildenstern. He, however, embarked on a crusade to save the little terrier and, in the end, he succeeded. So, Bilbo the dog had joined the Dixon household, named for his tiny, hobbit-like size and in honour of James' favourite book at the time.

A bitterly cold gust of wind caused him to pull his jacket tightly around him. Looking at his watch, he tried to calculate how long it would take to drive back to London. Maybe if they left soon, he could chance his arm at asking Rosie out for a drink as she left the caff after work. She liked him; he was pretty sure of that. He wasn't vain but he knew that the opposite sex found him attractive. With his dark looks and athletic frame, he had never had a problem in the girlfriend department. Rosie was proving difficult, but that was because she had just broken up with her long-term boyfriend. It would just take time.

'*James!*' Aurora called breathlessly, twirling around and around. 'Let's try and run out as far as we can without getting wet! When the sea comes in, you have to run like mad to beat it.'

'Are you *crazy*?' he called back, laughing. 'I only have one set of clothes.'

'*Scaredy cat!*' she taunted, her cheeks glowing. 'Freddie always plays this game.'

She looked so young and happy, he hadn't the heart to refuse her.

'Oh, okay,' he conceded, joining her on the shoreline. 'Right, let's wait for the next backwash. Right now … *Go!*'

Henry and Gloria were in the drawing room when they got back. Aurora burst into the room with an animated face and told her father how James had fallen on the sand and a giant wave had washed over him.

'He's absolutely drenched!' she said, laughing, her cheeks pink.

'Again,' James added drily from the door. 'However, I don't think the Aga will dry my things in time.'

'Not to worry, son,' said Henry, getting to his feet. 'I'm sure Seb and George have some old clothes you could borrow. Back in a sec.'

Gloria ushered James down the hall to the warmth of the kitchen. 'You'll catch your death,' she scolded. 'It's November, you know. Not July.'

James winked at Maggie, who was making bread, and mouthed, 'Mothers!'

She wagged her dough-covered finger at him. 'Now, now, Master James. No matter what age you are, mothers will always worry.'

'Spot on,' agreed Gloria. 'Now, change your clothes, get your bag and we'll depart.'

She closed the door of the kitchen and walked back to the drawing room. Aurora was standing by the fire, warming her hands. Gloria paused for a moment. She really was a stunning child. Henry had mentioned that she could sing like an angel, proudly telling the story of how she sang 'Silent Night' in the local chapel the previous Christmas to rapturous applause.

'Poor James,' she said, resuming her seat on the chaise longue.

'I hope you're not cross,' Aurora said in alarm. 'It was my fault. I mean, I asked him to play. I didn't know he was going to fall.'

'Of course I'm not cross,' Gloria assured her gently. 'Not at all, in fact.' She smiled warmly. 'So, you must come and visit us in London,' she added, changing the subject.

Aurora gasped. 'London? I've never been there.'

'Well, that settles it then. You must come and stay. Laura would love to meet you and there's so much to do for a child of your age.'

'Will James be there?'

Gloria smiled slightly. 'I'll tell him to call home to see you. Chances are he'll pop in anyway to leave his bag of washing or fill up a box with food.'

Aurora beamed. 'Shall I see the Queen?'

'That I cannot guarantee, but you can see where she lives.'

James arrived back at that moment in a blue shirt, black pants and a tweed jacket. They were too small for his tall frame and he made a face.

'Pretty cool, huh?' he quipped. 'This is all down to you, Borealis. You and your game.'

She giggled. 'I think you look lovely.'

'I've never worn tweed before,' he reflected. 'Maybe it's a new look for me.'

Henry followed him into the room. 'Right, I suppose you'd better be off,' he said regretfully. 'If you want to be back in London before dark.'

Aurora felt a rush of disappointment but she suppressed it. She knew they had to go. It was just that it felt like James had been around for ages. He had been such a novelty and now he had to go.

'Goodbye, Aurora,' said Gloria, giving her a peck on the cheek. 'See you soon, my darling girl.'

'Goodbye,' she said in a small voice.

Gloria linked arms with Henry and they vacated the room.

James regarded Aurora thoughtfully. 'Did Mum mention a trip to London?' he asked.

Aurora nodded. 'Yes, she said I should come up. I might see the Queen!'

'Yes, you might,' he said, laughing. 'Thanks for showing me the beach, even though you tripped me and I fell.'

'I did not!' she protested hotly. 'You're clumsy, that's all.'

'Whatever you say.' He held out his hand. '*Adios*, Aurora Borealis Sinclair. Till we meet again.'

She shook his hand firmly and stared up at him. 'Please come back,' she said softly.

He nodded. 'Of course I will. Mum needs a chauffeur. There's no way she can drive all this way unchaperoned. Now come and wave us off.'

# Chapter Four

'Two weeks to Christmas, Freddie!' Aurora hugged herself in delight. 'Are you excited?'

'Suppose,' he answered. 'If it means no school, I'm okay with that.'

They were on their weekly walk to the market at the village square. Maggie had given her a list of ingredients for dinner and strict instructions about which stall to visit.

'Look for Ricky the fisherman, not Mike, do you 'ear me? I don't want to pay through the nose for the 'alibut, I don't.'

The frost had melted on the sunlit sections of the small road leading down from the cliff. In the shady areas, its white tinge still remained on the branches and bushes, giving a Narnia-like feeling to the children as they skipped along.

Freddie whistled a Shakira tune and pulled his fleecy hat down over his ears. 'It's bleddy cold, Sinclair. We best move faster.'

They increased their pace. Corey Jones passed in his ancient Land Rover and honked, waving madly. Freddie waved back and said in an undertone, 'He owes me dad forty pounds. It's no wonder he's so friendly.'

Aurora giggled. 'Has your father killed the turkeys yet?' she asked, knowing that Conny had fifty birds ready for sale.

'Not yet,' said Freddie as they crossed the road. 'Next week, I reckon. They 'ave to hang for a few days.'

Aurora shuddered. '*Yuk!* I can't bear to think about it.'

'You can bear to eat it though!' he mocked.

'I suppose.' She blushed. 'Daddy is taking one to London as a gift.'

'So you're going then?'

'Yes. It was confirmed last night. We'll spend Christmas and Boxing Day with the Dixons and then back here for the New Year.'

'Your birthday,' he finished.

'Yes, my birthday,' she repeated gloomily.

Freddie said nothing. Her lack of enthusiasm was only natural. Aurora's birthday was also the anniversary of her mother's death. It had always been bittersweet. More often than not, Henry would retire to his room with a bottle of cognac after Aurora had blown out the candles on her cake. Freddie always made sure that he was on hand to distract her. Together they would go to his house and play video games or watch a film. His own mother, Mary, would bake cookies and light the fire in the front room. Maggie would come later in the evening, have a cup of tea with her younger brother and his wife, and then take Aurora home.

'Do you think they'll get married?' he enquired casually.

'Who?'

'Your dad and that woman.'

Aurora paused. 'Maybe. They see each other a lot.'

'Will she move down 'ere?' Freddie kept his tone normal.

'I expect so.' Aurora brightened. 'Maybe her children will come too. She has a daughter, you know. She's called Laura. I can't wait to meet her.'

Freddie felt his chest tighten. He didn't want things to change. He liked life the way it was – just him and Aurora, best friends forever. Now, he would have to share her with those incomers. She constantly talked about someone called James. Freddie's expression darkened. He didn't want anyone invading his turf.

'Look, who knows what will 'appen,' he said then. 'Grown-ups are weird. One minute they're in love – the next, it's all over. Look at Britney Spears and Justin Timberlake. I was sure they'd get married.'

They rounded the corner and onto the main square which was bustling and noisy.

'Right, do you have the list?' Freddie asked, all business.

Aurora nodded. 'First, the bread stall.'

A man watched them from behind a telegraph pole. He wore a black hat and a grey cashmere scarf, his trench boat buttoned right up. All you could see were his eyes: his brown cycs fringed with dark lashes. He moved slightly as the girl headed in his direction. Her arms were laden down with bags full of bread and cheese. Her companion, a sandy-haired boy, brought up the rear, two parcels balanced on his right arm.

'Let's get a mug!' Aurora squealed as they passed the hot-chocolate stall. 'With marshmallows on top!'

Freddie put the shopping down on a low wall and counted out the change in his pocket. 'I think we 'ave enough,' he said. 'Let me 'aggle with Antonia and see what she says.' He ambled up to the red-haired lady serving the hot beverages and winked at her playfully. 'Can you spare a couple for two freezin' kids?' he pleaded. 'But we only 'ave enough for one.'

Antonia's green eyes crinkled in amusement. 'Go on then,' she laughed. 'You're a right charmer, Freddie Thompson.'

He smiled broadly. 'Marshmallows too if you can.'

'Does your dad 'ave my turkey ready?' she asked as the

machine hissed and spluttered. ''Ee knows I want a big one this year?'

'Yep,' answered the boy.

'With the giblets,' she added.

Freddie nodded. ''Ee 'as a nice eighteen-pounder, 'ee does. I 'eard 'im talkin' about it yesterday.'

Aurora turned around to gaze at the lace hanging from old Mrs. Stephens' stall. Reaching out, she fingered it lightly, her brown eyes fixed on the toile design of the fragile cloth.

She didn't notice the man staring intently at her face. She didn't see him back away slowly, his face ashen. She didn't even react when he fell backwards off the step, knocking over a bucket of ice by the fish stall.

'Sinclair!' called Freddie. 'Come and drink up! We need to get back.'

Freddie's mother Mary was emptying the tumble dryer when they arrived back to the farmhouse. Their kitchen was small and homely, with a large dresser in the corner filled with plates and books.

'Where do all the socks go?' she muttered to no one in particular. 'Every bleddy time.' Sighing, she rummaged around the drum of the machine, trying in vain to locate the second of a green pair.

'Hello, Mary,' said Aurora in her clear voice.

Mary started. 'Aurora! You gave me a fright, you did. I didn't 'ear you come in.' She straightened up and smiled. 'You must be frozen – would you like a 'ot drink?'

Freddie appeared behind her. 'We're okay, we had 'ot chocolate at the market.'

'Oh, you did.' His mother winked. 'It kept the life in you then.' She had strawberry-blonde hair that was streaked with grey. Her blue eyes were crinkly from smiling so much.

Measuring at about five-foot seven inches, she was a head over her small husband. Like his sister Maggie, Conny was of a small build.

Aurora took a seat at the large kitchen table and petted the family dog, Milly. The radio was playing in the background – someone was being interviewed about their Desert Island Discs. Freshly baked muffins stood on a wire rack on the countertop, their tops crusty from being in the oven for a minute too long.

She loved Freddie's house as it was the antithesis to her own: it was small and warm, with just enough room for everybody. Freddie's parents were like family to her also – she had visited with Maggie since she was little.

Freddie had been a surprise. Conny and Mary had been in their forties when she had become pregnant. Born a year before Aurora, he had a smattering of sandy hair from birth. He and Aurora had been inseparable since she was old enough to play, despite coming from separate worlds. He had an open and honest face and was proving to be a great help on the farm. Conny was delighted that he showed such an interest in the animals and the everyday running of their small holding. He loved how Freddie asked intelligent questions about farrowing and understood that a sow could lose up to three piglets per litter. His young son accepted it as nature's way; he had learned from a young age that only the strongest stood to survive.

Aurora often cried when he told her of the stillbirths. 'The poor little piggies,' she would sob. 'That's so sad!'

He would pat her back dutifully, allowing her to grieve. It amazed him how she would weep for the dead piglets yet would tuck into a bacon sandwich without a second thought. She loved coming to the farm with him and he loved explaining to her about the different breeds of animal under his care.

'So, Mr. 'Enry is up in London a lot,' said Mary, stealing a glance at the young girl.

'Yes, I suppose he is,' reflected Aurora. 'I know he has a new book coming out so I suppose he's busy with that.'

'That must be it.' Mary started to fold the newly washed clothes. The whole village was talking about His Lordship and his new love interest. Speculation was rife that he would marry again. Mary hoped it was true. Aurora could do with a mother figure. Maggie had done an admirable job, but she was feeling her age. Caring for a young girl required energy.

'Susie left you a tape,' Mary announced, pointing to a cassette on the bookshelf. 'It's the recordin' of that show you wanted – *The Phantom of the Opera*?'

'Oh, wonderful!' Aurora clapped her hands in delight. 'I want to learn the songs. Tell Susan that I'm ever so grateful.'

Mary nodded. 'She's 'appy to do it, little 'un.'

Susan was twelve years older than Freddie and away at university in Bath. Aurora loved when she came home for the weekend as she allowed her to play tapes on her old stereo. She also let her experiment with eye shadow and lipstick. She and Freddie were very close, despite the age difference. Conny, though adoring of his daughter, was delighted to have a son to work the farm. It had been obvious from an early age that Susan was more interested in science. She was now doing a physics degree and loving every minute. Tall, like her mother, she shared her fair hair and blue eyes. A cluster of freckles were visible on her nose and she hated them. Freddie teased her about them constantly, saying that they were the mark of the devil. 'Isn't it funny that you have them too?' she would reply, sticking out her tongue.

'So, 'ow's Maggie?' asked Mary. 'She mentioned that 'er back was nippin' 'er.'

'She's very well,' answered Aurora in surprise. 'I've never heard her complain.'

'Well, that'd be Maggie – never one to moan.'

Freddie nodded in agreement. 'She's a gem, she is.' Reaching out, he picked up a muffin. 'Can I 'ave one?' he asked, the cake almost at his lips.

'Go on then,' ginned his mother. 'Offer one to Aurora too, Fred. Be mannerly.'

Aurora accepted the warm bun eagerly. It smelt of cinnamon and had nuts sprinkled on the top. She sank her teeth into the side of it and groaned. 'Oh, it's banana cake,' she said in delight. 'It's heavenly, Mary.'

Freddie had wolfed down the first one and was about to launch into his second.

'You won't eat your dinner,' warned Mary disapprovingly, wagging her finger at her son. 'I made a chicken stew from one of our broilers.'

Freddie put the muffin behind his back. 'I'll save it for later,' he lied, backing out of the room. 'Come on, Sinclair,' he hissed, gesturing for her to follow. 'Let's watch some TV.'

# Chapter Five

'So, who is this girl?'

Laura sipped her smoothie and regarded her mother shrewdly. Her blonde hair was tied in a ponytail, which swung from side to side as she moved.

'Well, she's Henry's daughter. She has grown up all alone down in Cornwall and I want you to be kind to her when she arrives.' Gloria sipped her carrot juice.

'How do you mean, kind?' Laura looked alarmed. 'Please don't say she's bunking in with me!'

'Now, Laura,' her mother warned, 'you've got to be charitable. The house will be full, what with the boys and Henry. Oh, by the way, I'm pretty sure Henry's sons are calling too.'

'Sons?' Laura nearly choked on her drink. 'How many children are there exactly, Gloria?'

'Don't call me that,' her mother berated her mildly. 'You needn't worry about George and Sebastian – they are grown up and hardly see their father.'

'So why are they coming to our house?'

'It's Christmas, darling. Families are supposed to be together for the holidays.'

'So, I get to play sleepovers with a child.' Laura crossed her arms petulantly. 'What did I do to deserve this? I mean, really!'

Gloria smiled to herself. Her daughter was thirteen going on thirty. She had always been candid and her sharp tongue often got her in trouble.

'She's a sweet little thing, Laura. She won't be any trouble. Plus her mother isn't around.'

'If she touches my Pink CDs ...' She looked fierce for a moment.

'She won't. I don't think she's even heard of Pink, to be honest.'

'What?' Laura sat up straight. 'Are you mad? Everyone has heard of Pink. She's the greatest singer in the world. Don't be barmy.'

'I doubt she has,' argued her mother. 'Aurora has led a very sheltered life. You'll have to be gentle with her. As I said, her mother is not on the scene.' She drained her juice and decided not to elaborate. Grace was no business of the children. Not yet anyway. 'Now, shall we mosey on then? I want to go to Sainsbury's on the way home.'

'Look, I'll be nice for you, but only for you, got it?' Laura slung her bag over her shoulder. 'I like being the only girl around the place. I don't want anyone cramping my style.'

'Noted,' Gloria laughed.

'*Aurora! We're leaving in five minutes!*' called Henry up the stairs.

'Okay, Daddy!' she answered, snapping her small suitcase shut. She had packed two party frocks, her cosy pyjamas, everyday clothes including cardigans, warm tights, underwear and two books. Maggie had advised that she pack for the snow that was forecast.

'Goodbye, Princess Grace,' she said solemnly, placing her doll in the Barbie Ferrari next to Ken. 'I shan't be gone for very long. Look after my bedroom for me.'

The doll's face stared straight ahead, unresponsive as always. Aurora got to her feet and hurried over to her dressing table. Perched on top was a small wooden jewellery box; it had belonged to her mother and was filled with small trinkets. Maggie had given it to her on her eighth birthday and she loved rifling through the different bits. Opening the heavy lid, she surveyed the contents. There was a coloured friendship bracelet with frayed edges, a brass coin commemorating the Pope's visit to Ireland in 1979 and a black-and-white picture of a man and a woman outside a large Georgian house. There was a letter from someone named Kathleen, all about the summer holidays in a place called Castlebar, and a picture of Bob Dylan holding a guitar.

'*Aurora!*'

'*Coming!*'

Henry was shoving the last bag into the boot of his vintage E-Type and slamming the lid, just as she appeared at the door.

'Righty-oh, my darling, let's get going!' His green waterproof jacket coupled with brown pants and boots made him look the quintessential country gentleman. He didn't look his sixty-one years; it was hard to believe that he had two sons in their thirties.

Aurora flung herself into Maggie's arms and clung to her. 'It will be our first Christmas apart,' she murmured into her shoulder. 'I'll miss you.'

'I'll miss you too, little 'un.' She kissed her dark hair. 'Now be a good girl and don't get up to no jiggery-pokery in the big city, you hear?'

'I won't,' promised Aurora solemnly. 'I'll be on my best behaviour.'

'Goodbye, my lovely. Give me a ring when you get there.'

Aurora kissed her soft cheek once more and squeezed her tightly. 'Bye, Maggie. I love you.'

Henry hooted the horn. 'We must go, Aurora! Come on, my darling!'

The little girl ran to the passenger door of the old car and wiped a tear from her cheek. She hated leaving Maggie and venturing off to a new world where she didn't know anyone. She had just inserted her seatbelt into its clasp when there was a rap on the window.

'Bloody hell!' said Henry in exasperation. 'Will we ever get on the road?'

Aurora peered out and saw Freddie's face smiling back at her.

He motioned for her to put down the window. 'You never said bye, Sinclair,' he chided playfully, 'so I decided to come and say it myself.'

'Oh, Freddie,' she said apologetically, 'I called over this morning but Mary said that you had gone to the abattoir with your father.'

'Yep, but I'm back now,' he said with a grin. 'Did you get your turkey, Mr. Sinclair?'

Henry pointed to the white lump on the back seat. 'Thank you, Freddie. It looks like a fine bird. Now, if you don't mind ...'

'See you when you get back,' whispered Freddie, squeezing her hand. 'Don't get up to no good up there.'

She blew him a kiss. 'Bye, Freddie. Happy Christmas.'

The car sped off in a cloud of dust. Maggie watched it disappear down the road, her heart heavy. She was no fool. She knew what was coming down the line. It was only a matter of time.

Her nephew stood motionless, thinking the exact same thing.

It was only a matter of time.

James trailed his finger down Rosie's bare thigh. It had taken him three weeks exactly to convince her to have a drink with him. Then, one week later, he had brought her back to his dingy room and the rest was history. She really was pretty with her blonde curls and her blue eyes.

They lay entwined on his single bed as the sun set over the high-rise buildings of west London. The wallpaper was stained and peeling on the walls of his room; his clothes were strewn all over the ground. Student life wasn't glamorous but he saw it as a rite of passage: an inevitable experience before the dreaded nine to five. Rosie was training to be a nurse and worked in the local café to subsidise her rent. It was there that he saw her, serving tea to local customers who came in for their Full English every morning.

His Nokia buzzed on the chest of drawers by the door.

'You have a message,' she said sleepily.

'I'll get it.' He got up, his muscles rippling as he stood.

She admired his naked body as he padded over to the phone and accessed the screen.

'*Fuck!*' he shouted, banging his head with his spare hand. 'It's from Mum. Henry and Aurora have arrived.'

'Who?' she yawned, stretching her white arms over her head.

'Mum's new boyfriend and his daughter. Damn, Rosie, I wanted to be there when they arrived.' He started to rifle through the clothes on the chair, searching for his jeans and a passable shirt.

'Whatever for?'

'She knows me, you see. The little girl – Aurora. She'll be nervous enough as it is.' He yanked a fleece over his least wrinkled shirt and pulled a pair of odd socks from a box beneath his bed.

'Blimey, calm down.' Rosie positioned the pillow under her cheek. 'I'm sure someone will thrust a selection box into her hand and all will be well.'

'You don't understand,' he argued, tying his laces. 'She's not like other kids. I've got to hurry.'

'Well, my shift starts at six thirty in the morning so do you mind if I crash here?'

He bent down and kissed her hard on the lips. '*Mi casa es su casa*,' he murmured into her jaw. 'I'll be back later tonight.'

'You will?'

'I will,' he repeated firmly. 'I told Mum that I wouldn't be home officially until Christmas Eve so I have another twelve hours of freedom.' He kissed her forehead. 'I'll be back before you know it.'

Aurora clung to her father's hand, her large brown eyes wide. They had arrived ten minutes before after the long drive. The Dixon's sitting room was adorned with garlands and lights. The large fir tree sparkled in the corner and there was a log fire burning merrily in the grate. The dogs were running wildly around the sitting room, chasing a rubber ball that squeaked.

'*Bilbo!*' shouted Gloria as the little terrier nearly knocked her over in his haste. '*Calm down!*' She bent down and picked up the offending ball. '*Who the bloody hell brought this into the house?*' she yelled, seriously frazzled.

'Not me,' said her second son William, whistling innocently as he strode by. He winked at Aurora and watched in amusement as the Labradors pounced on his mother in an effort to relieve her of the desired ball.

'Rubbish!' said Gloria sternly. 'This is exactly the kind of thing that you'd do.'

William threw his arms up. 'Out of order, Mum!'

Aurora stared at the young boy in fascination. He was about sixteen, with slicked-back blond hair and a cheeky grin. His Eminem T-shirt hung from his slight frame and his jeans were far too big with a chain hanging off them.

'Hi, I'm William – you can call me Will,' he greeted, holding out an arm covered with leather bracelets. 'You must be Aurora.'

'Hi,' she answered in a small voice.

'Have you met Laura yet?' he asked, glancing around. '*Laura? Laura!*'

A blonde girl appeared from the kitchen, the phone in her hand. 'What?' she barked. 'Can't you see that I'm on the bloody phone?' Suddenly, she stopped short. 'Oh!' was all she could muster. She looked warily at Aurora.

Gloria ran her fingers through her hair as Rosencrantz jumped on Guildenstern and they started rolling around the carpet.

'Henry,' she cried, 'what must you think of us?'

Henry smiled beatifically. 'Don't mind us, my love. We're just not used to big families.'

Aurora shrank back behind her father, hiding her face behind his jacket. This house was noisy and busy and completely alien to her. William had secured the squeaky ball and was taunting the terrier with it; Laura had her hand over one ear and was trying to continue a conversation on the phone, while Gloria was trying in vain to pull the Labradors apart.

Laura eventually hung up the phone. 'That Simon is a right no-hoper,' she informed her mother. 'If I have to hear Ella moan about him once more!' She reluctantly turned to Aurora and held out her hand. 'Hello,' she said as amiably as she could. 'I'm Laura. You must be Aurora.'

Aurora smiled and shook her hand shyly. 'Hello,' she whispered.

'Have you got a bag?' Laura enquired matter-of-factly. 'You'll be bunking in my room, I'm afraid. There's not much space but we'll manage.' She gave her mother a pointed look.

'Just a small case.'

'Good. Follow me then.' Laura walked purposefully out of the room. 'I'll show you the den and the loo. Then, you should be all set.' *I mean, why do I have to baby-sit this child?*

Aurora picked up her suitcase and ventured out into the vast hallway. A huge staircase dominated the foyer with marble steps and a mahogany bannister on both sides. Lugging her case, she mounted the stairs after the older girl.

Laura's room was covered in posters ranging from Justin Timberlake to Pink. A giant bookcase by the main window was filled with *Sweet Valley High* books, CDs and magazines. Her dressing table was covered in powders and gels and her wardrobe was filled with dresses and tops. The walls were pink and the bed was festooned with cushions and teddies. It was the total opposite to Aurora's out-dated bedroom at home. It screamed '*Girl!*' and she felt her mouth drop open.

'Now, put your bag over by the dresser there,' Laura ordered, 'and fold up your blankets when you're not using them. I don't want my room to be a tip.'

'Okay.'

'My CDs are out of bounds. Under no circumstances are you to touch them, okay?'

'Okay.'

Laura opened her wardrobe and pulled out two spare pillows and a blue sheet, muttering under her breath.

'Do you wear all of this?' Aurora asked, pointing to the make-up.

'Of course not,' said Laura briskly. 'It's forbidden at school for a start. Plus Gloria would have a canary.'

'Do you call your mother Gloria?'

'Sometimes I do, yes. What's so strange about that?' Laura rounded on her. 'I suppose you call your mother 'Mummy' or something.'

Aurora's face fell and she shook her head. 'My mother's dead,' she said quietly. 'She died when I was born.'

Laura immediately felt terrible. No one had told her that. Gloria had been deliberately vague about the girl's mother. All she had said was that she 'wasn't on the scene'. That could mean anything. She had thought that they were divorced.

Her expression softened and she pulled Aurora into her arms. 'Hey now, I didn't know. My bloody mother forgot to mention it. No hard feelings?'

Aurora shook her head.

'Good.' Laura patted her back. 'Now, I'll put a couple of duvets on the ground as a mattress and you can sleep there by the bookcase. Will that be all right?'

'Yes!' answered Aurora, beaming. 'It sounds absolutely perfect.'

James' Golf pulled up outside his mother's house and screeched to a halt. He was kicking himself for forgetting that the Sinclairs were due to arrive.

'*Mum?*' he called, opening the front door with his key. '*Mum?*'

Gloria appeared out of the sitting room. 'Hello, darling. I'm so glad you could make it.'

'Where's Aurora?' he asked, glancing around. 'Is she okay?'

His mother smiled. 'She's perfectly fine, James. William and Laura are looking after her upstairs.'

'Oh, are they,' he said dubiously. 'I'd better check.'

He bounded up the stairs and down the corridor. A sign saying 'ENTER IF YOU DARE' was stuck to Laura's door, along with stickers of the Backstreet Boys and the Spice Girls. But the door was slightly ajar and he could hear the murmur of conversation inside, so he paused.

'Well, the school dance was epic,' came William's voice. 'Nigel Brown smuggled in some of his mother's vodka and Mary Jane Andersen asked me to bonk her.'

'You?' came Laura's voice incredulously. 'That's a bit rich.'

'What's bonking?' asked Aurora in her clipped tone and James fought the urge to laugh.

There was a pause and James cautiously peered inside.

Laura giggled. 'Well, it's when two people love each other and ...'

'They take off each other's clothes and …' added William.

'Roll around the place, I guess,' finished Laura.

'It's how babies are made,' added William helpfully. 'But you must be in love, isn't that right, Laura? You don't just bonk anyone.' He looked at her meaningfully.

'Oh no,' she agreed, trying her best to be serious. 'You must be in love.'

Aurora raised an eyebrow. 'Oh, so bonking is like having sex. A bit like Freddie's pigs. '

'Freddie? Who the hell is Freddie?' said Laura, laughing.

'He's my best friend and he's a farmer,' she explained calmly. 'I saw the daddy pig jump up on the mummy pig and then they had babies.'

'Well,' concluded William, 'that's it exactly. The pigs were bonking.'

'So, is this Mary Jane girl in love with you, Will?' asked Aurora logically.

'Probably,' admitted William. 'I mean, I'm a serious catch.' He stood up and fixed his hair in the mirror. 'Laura?' he asked, pouting slightly. 'All the girls in my form are mad for Enrique Iglesias. Should I paint a mole on my face? Right here?' He jabbed his cheek.

'No, Will,' his sister assured him. 'That would be a disaster.'

'You're sure?' He stepped back and resumed his seat on the bed. 'He's the number-one guy around school because of that *Hero* song.'

'I'm sure,' affirmed Laura, patting his arm. 'Quite sure.'

Aurora stared at them in fascination. 'You two are funny,' she said, sipping her Coke. She was rarely allowed have the famous fizzy drink and she could feel it flowing through her veins. It made her feel good.

'Thank you,' said William, bowing. 'We try our best.'

James decided he'd had enough and knocked on the door.

What with bonking and pigs and his siblings' attempt at morality, it was time to interrupt.

'*Entrez*,' called Laura, who was learning French at school.

'James!' gasped Aurora, spilling her drink in excitement. 'You're here.' She jumped up and catapulted herself at the young man, hugging him fiercely. 'I'm so glad!' She buried her head in his chest.

'Well, hello, Borealis,' he said fondly. 'I see that you're getting on just fine without me.'

'I'm having the best time,' she said, pulling back. 'Laura is letting me sleep on her floor and she said she might give me a makeover later and Will gave me Coke to drink and –'

'You really need to get out more,' reflected Laura, shaking her head. 'So, James, where's Rosie?' She looked at him innocently. 'Ella said she saw you two at the cinema the other night and you didn't see much of the film by all accounts.'

'Butt out, little sis,' he warned good-naturedly. 'I won't be bringing her home to Gloria just yet.'

'Who's Rosie?' asked Aurora, looking from Laura to James.

'The love of James' life,' William informed her, getting to his feet. 'He's been chasing her for months and she's finally caved, the poor sod.'

James calmly covered Aurora's ears. 'Enough of this, siblings. She is yet a child in this world.'

Aurora pulled his hands down immediately. She had never been part of such a grown-up conversation before and she didn't want to miss a minute.

'Fine, fine.' Laura stuck out her tongue. 'Well, at least you're getting some action, Jiminy Cricket.'

James grinned. 'Enough of the Jiminy. I'm the nickname person around here, Laura. Don't you forget it.'

'Jiminy Cricket? That's so funny.' Aurora giggled and James ruffled her hair affectionately. 'Why does she call you that?'

'Jim is a pet name for James,' explained Laura, turning towards her mirror and practising a pout. 'Should I dye my hair like Posh Spice then, Will?'

'Blondes have more fun, I reckon,' he answered thoughtfully. 'Still, a change is as good as a rest, so they say.'

'Well, I suppose I'll hold off,' she decided, releasing her blonde mane from its bobble. 'I'm saving myself for Mr. Right anyway.'

'Who?' asked Aurora, wide-eyed.

'You know, my soul mate,' the older girl said. 'He has to be tall, handsome, well-dressed and filthy rich.'

'Laura,' said James shaking his head, 'you're incorrigible.'

'You see, Aurora, love will only get you so far in life,' Laura continued, ignoring him. 'I want to shop and travel and stay in nice hotels.'

William snorted. 'Then get your own job, freeloader. My word, what has happened to feminism?'

'Well, men are paid more than women, yeah?' Laura rounded on her brother fiercely. 'Why not take a slice of the cake? Little Laura Dixon isn't going to change the world all by herself.'

James stood up. 'I've had enough of this conversation,' he announced. 'Borealis, do you want to come and watch a movie or something?'

'Okay,' she beamed, scrambling to her feet. 'May I choose the film?'

'You may,' he said, winking. 'Nothing too scary though. I'm not very brave.' He ushered her out in front of him.

Aurora turned to Laura, just as she was on the threshold.

'I'm going to marry for love,' she said clearly and the occupants of the room stopped dead. 'A prince is going to come and rescue me and we're going to live happily ever after.'

William opened his mouth to scoff but James glared at him. 'Shut it,' he mouthed warningly.

William understood and said nothing. Laura didn't dare look at her brother in case she'd laugh.

'Okay, see you later!' Aurora skipped away, energised by her Coke.

# Chapter Six

Gloria stared at the turkey.

'Good Lord, Henry. This is enormous! Will it fit?' She glanced in panic at her built-in electric oven and then at the huge bird on the countertop. Conny Thompson had proudly boasted that all his free-range birds were at least eighteen pounds in weight.

He laughed. 'We'll make it fit, my darling girl. Now, come over here and kiss me.' He pulled Gloria towards him and kissed her full on the lips, just as Aurora and James walked in.

'*My eyes, my eyes!*' mocked James, taking a beer and a Coke from the fridge. 'Please, no hanky-panky in front of your children.'

'Daddy!' exclaimed Aurora. 'Why were you kissing Gloria?' She stared at the older woman, who was looking flushed.

Henry smoothed his grey hair and smiled. 'Because I love her,' he answered simply.

'Love?' repeated Aurora. 'Does that mean that you two are bon–?'

James yanked her by the arm before she could finish and hauled her out of the room.

'Is that your word of the day?' he whispered loudly, half-laughing. 'I'm sure Henry wouldn't appreciate that kind of language from you.'

'Do you think they are?' she pursued, following him into the sitting room.

'I don't want to know,' he said. 'That is not an image I want in my head, to be honest.'

He picked up the remote control and activated the television in the corner.

'I'd love one of those new flat-screen TVs,' he said, pressing the AV button. 'They look so cool on the wall.'

Aurora shrugged. She had no knowledge of such things. Any TV was exotic to her, even Freddie's ancient twenty-inch in his sitting room.

'Right then, choose a film,' said James, gesturing to a mixture of VHS tapes and DVDs on the shelf. 'Laura has most of the Disney ones.'

Aurora bounded over to the brightly coloured titles and peered closely. 'Oh! You *do* have *Sleeping Beauty*,' she cried in delight. 'We must watch it! It's about Princess Aurora.'

'Sounds brilliant,' said James as enthusiastically as he could. 'I'll go and microwave some popcorn then.'

'You're sure you won't be bored?' she asked.

'Not at all – bring it on,' he replied cheerfully. 'I just love singing animals and all that jazz.'

'Really?' She looked doubtful.

'No.' He grinned. 'But I'll do it for you, Borealis. Now, grab the sofa before Will gets it.'

Maleficent was in dragon form and was trying to kill Prince Phillip as he raced to save Aurora. James kept one eye on the screen and the other on his phone as Rosie had been texting him. He had planned to go back to the flat, but a thick frost had descended outside and Aurora's head was heavy on his arm.

Earlier, Will and Laura had walked in and out in one movement when they saw what was on the screen. 'Disney?' Will had mouthed in mock horror, backing away. James had presumed they retreated to Gloria's room to watch a film on her computer.

Finally, the prince defeated his nemesis and found the sleeping princess.

'This is the best part!' squealed Aurora, jumping up in excitement.

James placed his phone on the coffee table and tried to look attentive. He watched the screen and then his eyes strayed to the little girl on his right. Her face was rapt and her eyes were shining as she watched the events unfold. He could see why she was so childish for her age as she had been denied crucial social contact with her peers. He couldn't see Laura getting excited about Prince Phillip saving Aurora, unless she saw his bank statements first. His own sister was the complete antithesis of his film companion and this made him slightly uneasy. Aurora's innocence was endearing but it also rendered her vulnerable. He didn't know why but he wanted to protect her.

The end credits came up on the screen and Aurora sighed. 'I just love that film,' she said. 'I've only seen it twice.'

'It was fantastic,' lied James. 'Thank you for letting me experience it. Now, I think it might be bedtime for you, Borealis. It's past eleven.'

'Oh,' she said in disappointment.

'It's Christmas Eve tomorrow – you need to get all the sleep you can before the Big Man comes down the chimney.'

'What's Father Christmas bringing you?' she asked, clapping her hands. 'I asked for a CD of *Greatest Songs of the West End.*'

'You asked for what?' He started in surprise. 'Aurora, you're *nine*!'

'So? I love to sing. Freddie's sister Susie has seen all the great musicals in London. She lets me listen to her tapes when I call.'

She sighed wistfully. 'That's what I want to be when I grow up: a singer like my mother.'

James shrugged. 'Fair enough. Well, I asked for money and a large bottle of Jack Daniels. That's about it.'

'Have you been good?' she asked seriously.

'Oh, an angel,' he replied.

'Then, you should get what you asked for, Jiminy Cricket.' She burst out laughing and ran upstairs.

'*Don't call me that!*' he yelled, chasing her. '*I'm the nickname guy!*'

Laura appeared down the corridor with William in tow as Aurora slammed the bedroom door. 'We've been watching *Meet the Parents*, James,' she said. 'It's absolutely ace! We laughed and laughed.'

'Ace,' repeated William. 'That scene with the ashes.'

'Why did she bang my door like that?' asked Laura, straightening the 'ENTER IF YOU DARE' sign on her door with a frown.

'I was chasing her,' answered James. 'No harm done.'

'So, did you enjoy *your* film?' said William, grinning. He opened his own bedroom door. 'I admire you for your sacrifice.'

'It was great. She loved it which is the main thing. Right, you two, see you in the morning.'

He headed in the direction of Gloria's room and, walking in, closed the door behind him. Her computer stood on a wooden desk by the window. Laura had forgotten to shut it down, so he activated the screen immediately. In two seconds, he was typing 'Grace Sinclair' into Google. Immediately, links popped up. Newspaper articles about her death, pictures of Henry and then theatre reviews of Grace Molloy. He clicked on one and found that it was from *The Irish Times*, dated the tenth of July 1991.

**Grace Molloy dazzles in the title role of *My Fair Lady*, playing Eliza Doolittle with such style that her fellow countryman, George Bernard Shaw, would be proud. The popular musical was given a makeover by pioneering director,**

**Silas Walsh, who wanted to stay true to its *Pygmalion* roots ...**

There was a picture of a beautiful young woman with cloudy dark hair and huge brown eyes, dressed as a flower-seller. James drew in a sharp breath. She was the absolute spitting image of Aurora, even down to the heart-shaped face. Henry had no claim to the child when it came to appearance.

He exited out of the article and scrolled down further. There were pictures of Grace in various roles ranging from Christine in *The Phantom of the Opera* to Desdemona in *Othello*. She was smiling and radiant in most of the pictures, not like the sad image Maggie had imprinted on his brain. Her wedding to Henry was documented and immediately he could sense the change. Her once smiling face was morose and her large eyes were haunted.

The front door slammed and James jumped. He exited out of Google immediately and deleted the search history.

Back in his room his phone buzzed in his pocket and he knew immediately who it was. *Rosie.* He really ought to reply but he wasn't in the mood for flirty texts right now. Back and forth coquettish messages that were amusing when at a loose end, but annoying when busy.

Throwing his Nokia on the bed, he frowned. Something didn't quite fit. He yearned to know more about the enigmatic Grace Molloy. He didn't know why, but he could sense a story. There was more to this woman's life and death than people thought.

His photographer's eye had ascertained right away that the camera loved Grace. She had it all: perfect skin, chiselled cheekbones and big dark eyes. Her cloudy hair framed an exquisite face and added drama and depth. She fascinated him and he vowed to find out more about Aurora's mysterious mother who had lost her life so young.

The next morning and the radio was blaring non-stop Christmas songs.

William sang along in his baritone, buttering toast.

Rosencrantz and Guildenstern were sitting on two kitchen chairs, watching every morsel of food that was being eaten.

'Lolly, pass the jam!' William called from the top end of the kitchen table.

Laura, who was sitting nearly at the opposite end of the table, tore her eyes away from the newspaper. Extending her arm, she handed her brother a pot of blackberry-and-apple conserve. 'Did you make me a slice?' she demanded, watching William deposit a huge dollop of jam on his toast.

'You didn't ask,' he said.

Aurora sauntered into the kitchen in her pink pyjamas and bare feet. The tiles felt warm as she walked and she luxuriated in the underfloor heating. She could never walk around her house at home without two pairs of socks on at least. Gloria's house was double-glazed and comfortable, with working radiators and smaller rooms.

Sleeping on the floor had been a pleasant experience. The two duvets had served as a soft mattress and she had fallen asleep as soon as her head hit the pillow. It was strange to sleep in the same room as someone else – every so often she would tune in to Laura's breathing and jump.

'Morning,' she said uncertainly, unused to a crowd around a breakfast table. It was normally just her with Maggie serving. Henry rarely joined them at breakfast time.

'Good morning,' greeted William, blowing her a kiss. 'Lolly was just about to make some toast so if you're hungry ...'

A slice of bread came flying through the air and hit him on the head.

'Well, as a certain someone didn't make it for *her* ...' Laura scowled at her brother. 'So, Aurora, would you like some toast? Or we have cereal too. I'm not sure about porridge, but I can check.'

'I'd like some toast,' said Aurora, beaming.

'Coming up,' said Laura, popping two more slices of bread in the toaster. 'What would you like on it? I like Nutella on mine, but there's jam too.'

'Nutella?' asked Aurora, confused.

'*Nut-ell-a*,' repeated William slowly. 'Please tell me that you've heard of it.'

Aurora shook her head. 'I'm afraid not.'

'Nutella,' said Laura briskly, 'is a chocolate spread with hazelnuts. I spread it on toast or pancakes and it's quite yummy.'

'I'll have that then,' said Aurora in delight. 'It sounds wonderful.'

She took a seat at the table and Bilbo the dog licked her feet. Bending down, she scratched his ears and hugged him against her legs in contentment.

Laura pushed a plate with two slices of toast in front of her, along with a knife. 'Knock yourself out,' she prompted, pointing to the jar.

Aurora spread a thick layer of Nutella onto a slice and took a bite.

'Wow!' she sighed in delight. 'This is so nice.'

'Good,' said William. 'There's plenty more where that came from.'

'Tea?' asked Laura.

Aurora shook her head. 'I'd like some juice, please.'

William pushed an empty glass towards her and pointed to the carton of Tropicana. 'Help yourself.'

The kitchen was warm and cluttered, dominated by an island unit in the middle of the tiled floor. Aurora drank in the rows of cookery books stacked by the larder, the magnets on the fridge and the dresser filled with Delft ware. Framed photographs lined the shelf by the window: ones of Gloria and Andrew, her late husband, three of James, William and Laura at different stages of their childhood and one of an old lady blowing out candles on a cake. Aurora got to her feet and approached the shelf, anxious to see what James looked like as a little boy. Sure enough, there was a shot of him on his mother's knee, smiling madly with dark curls and grubby knees. He looked almost the same except that he didn't have stubble. She moved along the pictures until her gaze rested on Gloria and her dead husband. He resembled James in colouring: both men were dark and had brown eyes. Laura and William looked like their mother with their fair hair.

'What did your daddy do for a living?' Aurora asked Laura, resuming her seat at the table.

'Our *daddy*,' William mimicked.

Laura glared at William. 'That's okay, Aurora. Our dad was a doctor. A paediatrician, in fact.'

'Do you miss him?'

'Sorry?' Laura stiffened.

'I mean, he only died a few years ago. Was it terribly difficult?' She took another bite of toast and chewed thoughtfully.

Laura regarded her for a moment and then spoke softly. 'I did at the beginning. I was only nine when he died – the same age as you now. I was his little girl, his pet. He would come home from work every day and I'd jump into his arms.' She bit her lip. 'Then after a while, I started to forget him. I changed schools and made new friends and suddenly it was hard to remember his face or the sound of his voice.' She looked stricken for a moment. 'Mum said it was natural, that time heals and the pain fades.'

William twiddled his teaspoon. 'I miss him,' he said quietly. 'I miss him a lot. James is cool, but he's not my dad. No one will ever replace my dad.'

Aurora munched on the crust of her bread. 'Well, you're lucky to have memories. I have none of my mother. I sometimes wish that I could meet her – just once. Just to smell her perfume or touch her skin. Daddy showed me videos of her singing but the quality was too bad. Then he would get sad and we always ended up turning them off.' She sighed. 'I'm sorry your daddy died but at least you got to know him.'

'I guess you're right.' Laura sipped her tea gloomily. 'Well, that's the festive spirit well and truly ruined. Cheers, Aurora.'

William pulled himself together. 'It's time for me to sing then,' he proclaimed as Mariah Carey came on the radio. '*Oooooh, babeeee!*'

Bilbo started to bark frantically when William began to sing.

Laura put her head in her hands. 'Listen to the dog, Will. Put a sock in it.'

Aurora giggled. William, rather than take his sister's advice, was now standing on his chair using his spoon as a microphone and screeching at the top of his lungs.

'What the heck?' James appeared, wearing a pair of sweatpants and a black T-shirt. His feet were bare also and his stubble was even more pronounced. 'William, singing Mariah Carey at this early hour is completely out of order!' He ruffled Aurora's hair as he passed. 'Hey, Borealis, did you sleep well?'

'Yes,' she beamed. 'It was really comfy on those duvets.'

He smiled at her and took a bottle of milk from the fridge. Pushing Rosencrantz off the kitchen chair at the head of the table, he sat down.

'Laura's snoring didn't disturb, I hope?' he grinned, pouring some muesli into a bowl.

'Ha, bloody ha,' his sister replied. 'We all know who the Snore King around here is.'

'Not me, surely,' mocked James. 'I've never had complaints in that department.' He poured some milk into his bowl.

The winter sunlight streamed through the kitchen window, highlighting the dust particles floating in the air. The sink was full of dishes from the night before and two empty wine goblets stood on the counter, waiting to be handwashed. Gloria and Henry had obviously had a nightcap when they returned.

'So, what's Father Christmas bringing you?' asked Aurora, drinking a glass of juice.

Laura glanced at William who stifled a laugh. *Father Christmas? Really?*

'Lots of things,' said James meaningfully, glancing at his siblings. 'Right, guys? Lots of nice things.'

'Oh, of course,' said William. 'I want a new PlayStation and Lolly there wants more make-up to hide her ugly face.'

'At least I attempt to hide my ugly face,' Laura shot back. 'You subject us to yours without a second thought.'

'Have you been good all year?' continued Aurora, ignoring the bickering. 'I made a big effort this past month.'

'I've been positively angelic,' said William seriously. 'In fact, I've been so good I'll probably get extra presents.'

Laura made an '*ahem*' sound. 'Right, all. I'm off for a shower. I'm meeting Ella down the High Street later.'

James jerked his head in Aurora's direction and stared pleadingly at his sister.

Laura sighed. 'Aurora? Would you like to join us?'

'You mean, meet your friends?'

'Why, yes. If you like.'

'I'd love to!' she squeaked. 'Oh, thank you, Laura!'

James felt his heart swell. He loved to see her happy. Even though she had only been in his life for a short time, he felt like she was part of the family. It was a Bilbo situation all over again. He would rescue Aurora in the same way. Now, if only Henry would pull his finger out and propose.

# Chapter Seven

'*Ella! We're over here!*' Laura waved frantically at her friend.

They had arranged to meet by the fountain on the square.

Laura and Ella had been best friends since nursery. Both blonde and outspoken, they could easily have disliked each other and competed. However, they became firm friends as they shared similar outlooks and opinions. Make-up, boys, Justin Timberlake and gossip were what they lived for, in that order.

Ella saw and started to push through the crowds of Goths who habitually loitered around the square in packs.

'All right?' she said, kissing Laura on the cheek. 'Happy Christmas!'

'Happy Christmas to you too!'

Ella looked older than her thirteen and a half years. Her blonde hair was mostly covered with a purple woollen hat and her black coat was zipped up to the chin to keep out the cold. Slung over her shoulder was a brown-leather bag with a logo of a bush on the front. Aurora had seen Gloria carrying the same type of bag.

'Who's this?' asked Ella, turning to Aurora. She regarded the dark-haired child in wonder. Dressed in a red coat and black woolly hat, she looked like a little doll.

'She's Gloria's boyfriend's child,' said Laura. 'Remember I mentioned her yesterday?' She glared meaningfully at her friend, urging her not to repeat the negative things she had ranted about before the Sinclairs' arrival.

Ella nodded and winked. Sure she remembered. This was the usurper, the threat to Laura's position in the family, the burden that her best friend did not want to take on, the thorn in her side. Why then was she present on their shopping trip?

'I'm Aurora,' said the little girl, holding out her hand.

'Like Sleeping Beauty?' said Ella, raising an eyebrow. 'I loved that film when I was a little girl.'

Aurora nodded.

Laura linked arms with her. 'We're great friends now,' she said meaningfully to Ella. 'In fact, we're sharing a room.'

Ella nodded knowingly. 'Well, that's super news,' she said warmly. 'Aurora! That's some name. It's far better than boring old Ella or Laura.' She rummaged in her bag and pulled out a box of cigarettes. 'Want one?' she offered, holding out a box of Marlboro Lights.

Laura shook her head. 'I've given up. James smelt the smoke off me last weekend and nearly blew a gasket. He threatened to tell Gloria and everything.'

'Bloody square,' her friend scoffed. 'Honestly, since your dad died, he has become so boring.' She lit a cigarette and inhaled deeply. 'Having said that, he's pretty fit. I still definitely would.'

Laura pretended to vomit. 'Stop that right now, Ella Taylor. Out of order!'

'What?' she questioned innocently. 'He has a great body, that's all I'm saying.'

Aurora gazed at her. 'How old are you?' she asked, wide-eyed.

'Thirteen,' Ella replied. 'However, I don't broadcast it. Life is hard for under-agers, therefore I try to look as old as I can. How old would you say I am? Just looking at me now?' She put her shoulders back and posed with her cigarette.

Aurora bit her lip. 'About seventeen? You definitely look older than Will.'

'I like you,' Ella said with a grin. 'That's exactly what I wanted to hear. Now, let's get on. I have to find a present for my mother and she's virtually impossible to buy for.' She started to walk in the direction of the shops. 'Plus, I've bugger-all money. That school dance cleaned me out. What a disaster! Nigel Brown charged me ten quid for a smidgen of vodka and Mary Jane Andersen was slavering over Will for most of the evening ...'

'She wanted to bonk him,' Aurora informed her authoritatively.

Ella stopped short. 'Say again?' She burst out laughing. 'Blimey, Aurora, you hit the nail on the head.' She shook her head. 'He was having none of it though. I mean, she's the school bike anyway – did I tell you how she was all over Simon in the canteen last Tuesday, Laura? I mean, come on. As if he would.'

'Who's Simon?' asked Aurora.

'The love of my life,' said Ella with a sigh. 'He's a god, a perfect being. I absolutely adore him. He's fifteen and plays rugby. Oh, Aurora, he's all I want!'

Laura shrugged. 'Boys have no standards, Ella. That's why I'm saving myself for a real man.' She pointed to a massive billboard with a poster of David Beckham. 'I mean, he's perfect. Pots of money, great abs and did I mention he's loaded?'

Ella stared at his image. 'He's not the worst,' she admitted. 'However, Simon plays drums in a band, did I mention that before?'

'Once or twice,' smiled Laura. 'Oh, Ella, you're in dire straits.' She paused outside Starbucks. 'Who would like a hot chocolate to heat us up?'

Aurora immediately thought of Freddie. How she missed him. Then she banished that thought from her mind. She would be back at home in a few days and all this would be a dream.

'Yes, please,' she beamed. 'With marshmallows.'

'Come on,' laughed Ella, 'Lord knows what they'll write on Aurora's cup. They never get the name right.'

They got home around four. Henry and Gloria were sitting on the sofa when the three girls entered the sitting room.

'*Daddy!*' cried Aurora, catapulting herself on her father. 'We had the best time! Ella took me to a shop called Claire's Accessories and I got this.' She showed him a silver bracelet with a star. 'Then we looked for a present for her mother and then we got ice cream and –'

'Ice cream?' said Henry. 'In this weather? Are you barking mad?'

'Oh no, Daddy, it was delicious.' Aurora was glowing. 'I had cookies and cream with chocolate sauce.'

Ella stepped forward and held out her hand. 'Hello,' she said formally. 'I'm Ella Taylor, Laura's best friend.'

'Delighted,' he replied, shaking her hand.

'Happy Christmas, Gloria,' she said then. 'Mum said to thank you for the card.'

'Are you all set?' asked Gloria, smiling.

'Pretty much.'

Laura tapped her foot impatiently. 'Ella? Let's go upstairs.'

'Oh right, of course.' She backed away. 'Aurora, would you like to join us?'

The little girl jumped up. 'Oh, yes, please.'

'So, your daddy is pretty old,' observed Ella, painting her nails on Laura's bed. 'He must have been a fine age when you were born.'

Aurora shrugged. 'He's always looked the same to me. My mother was his second wife.'

'Let's listen to some music,' Laura suggested, popping open

the CD compartment on her stereo. She inserted a Destiny's Child CD and pressed 'play'.

Suddenly, the door swung open to reveal William wearing a blue woollen jumper with a giant Santa on the front.

'Ella Taylor!' he said, stopping dead. 'No one told me that you were in the house.'

'Well, here I am,' she replied, blowing on her nails.

He flopped down on the bed.

Ella held up her hands and inspected them. 'Did you escape from Mary Jane after I left the last night?'

William shuddered. 'You bet. There was no way I was letting her near me.'

'I don't blame you,' said Ella. 'I hope Simon was as well-behaved.'

William said nothing. He knew that Ella was bordering on obsessed with his classmate. She didn't need to know that he had got off with Tina Sheeran behind the bicycle shed. As girls went, Ella was cool. He had known her since she was four years old and she wasn't your typical whiney girl. You could have a laugh with her and she always knew the gossip at school. He sometimes bought cigarettes for her, but only sometimes. James would kill him if he knew.

James appeared at the door and knocked to announce his presence.

'Henry's son Sebastian has arrived,' he announced. 'Mum wants you to come down and say hello.'

Aurora shrank backwards. 'Seb's here?'

'Yes – he and his wife. They've just joined Henry in the lounge.' He grinned. 'Mum didn't expect them until later so she's been caught on the hop.'

'Is George here too?' Aurora's voice had a slight tremor.

'No. He rang to say that he's sick and sends his apologies.' James focused in on the little girl. 'Hey, Borealis, are you all right? You've gone as pale as a ghost.'

Aurora nodded wordlessly, her brown eyes huge. Her brothers filled her with trepidation. All her life they had treated her like an annoying insect that they would like to swat.

James held out his hand and she gladly took it. 'Right, get a move on, gang. We have to appear polite.'

Sebastian Sinclair surveyed the room. So, this was the home of his father's intended. It was the complete opposite of his birthplace with its pastel colours and common prints of famous paintings on the wall. Three dogs roamed freely and the result was hair all over his expensive suit. His wife, Cressida, sat rigidly beside him, clearly uncomfortable. She smiled politely when Henry handed her a glass of wine. Her dark-brown hair was cut in a stylish bob and her slim frame was dressed top-to-toe in Chanel. Not once did she open her mouth except to greet the family. Sebastian didn't like it when she talked; he made it quite clear that she was to be seen and not heard.

Sebastian was similar in height to his famous father; both were tall, slim and had blue eyes. However, where Henry's eyes twinkled with warmth, Sebastian's were cold. He swirled his whiskey around the glass and watched his father laugh uproariously at something Gloria had said. She flicked her hair and her bracelets jangled. They really were the epitome of a loved-up couple, holding hands and laughing at each other's jokes.

Sebastian pursed his lips. With this bourgeois environment, he was pretty damn sure that this Gloria Dixon had an ulterior motive. Of course she had her sights set on his wealthy father. Marriage to a famous playwright would do wonders for her credibility at the bridge club. Oh, why was his father such a fool when it came to women? That Grace had been the same: a no-good gold-digger who was after the family fortune.

Suddenly there was a thundering sound from the hallway as

the children came downstairs. William burst into the room, followed by Laura and then Ella, all laughing loudly.

'As expected, I beat you all,' boasted William, puffing out his chest. 'Losers!' he added, making an L-shape with his fingers.

'You had a head start, Will,' argued Laura breathlessly. 'Bloody cheat. Plus you have much longer legs.'

Gloria cleared her throat and gave them a pointed look. 'William, Laura! We have guests. This is Sebastian, Henry's son, and his wife Cressida.'

William held out his hand amiably. 'Welcome to the madhouse,' he quipped, winking at Cressida. 'Happy Christmas.'

Sebastian forced a smile. 'Delighted,' he muttered, shaking William's hand loosely.

Cressida smiled but it didn't meet her eyes. She had no interest in meeting Henry's lover's family. Especially the children. She loathed children. That was the one saving grace of the pre-nuptial agreement that Sebastian had forced her to sign. They both shared the same opinion when it came to procreating: it was to be avoided.

'Hello, I'm Laura, good to meet you.' Laura half-waved but remained next to Ella by the door. She could sense their lack of interest and so she kept her distance. She regarded the blond man with his aloof stance and unfriendly eyes. Then she sized up the woman on his right. She looked like she was sitting on something pointy. Laura inhaled sharply. She had these two pegged already; they were not the type of people she was interested in being friends with at all.

The couple nodded at her and Sebastian turned to Henry. 'Where's Aurora?' he asked. 'I presume that you brought her here?'

'Why of course,' said Henry in surprise. 'I'd hardly leave her with Maggie.'

Cressida sipped her wine and tried not to look bored. She was due to meet Alexis, her best friend, at a wine bar in Kensington at eight. She hated being late and this wine was just vile. It tasted like a sharp New Zealand Sauvignon Blanc, a wine that assaulted her delicate palate.

Suddenly James strode in with Aurora trailing behind. 'Sorry we took so long,' he apologised, surveying the room.

Aurora waved shyly at her older brother, who was glaring in her direction. 'Happy Christmas, Seb and Cressida,' she said in a small voice, shrinking behind James.

Sebastian sipped his whiskey slowly and deliberately, his cold blue eyes trained on her face. Then, he turned to Henry, ignoring her greeting completely. 'So the stocks are up,' he said.

James stiffened. Maggie had mentioned that Aurora's brothers were a bit off, but this was just rude.

'So, do you work in the stock market?' he interrupted coolly, causing Sebastian to turn around again.

'Yes,' he said curtly. 'It's too complicated to explain.' He turned to his father once more, clearly put out at having been interrupted.

'And you?' asked James, directing his question at Cressida.

Before she had a chance to speak, Sebastian turned again. 'Work? My wife? I'm afraid you're barking up the wrong tree there, old chap. She just spends my money.'

Cressida blushed crimson and took a frantic sip of wine.

James could feel his hackles rise. Gloria, sensing his anger, waved him away. James understood her silent message but there was no way that he was leaving Aurora with these people.

'Come on, Borealis, let's go and make some hot chocolate,' he said, holding out his hand.

She grasped his fingers and smiled gratefully. It felt good to be protected.

'What did you say?' asked Sebastian with a snide smile. 'What did you call her?'

'He calls me Borealis,' explained Aurora in her clear voice. 'It's a nickname.'

'Bore being the operative word,' said Sebastian nastily,

laughing at his own joke. 'How clever.' He turned to Cressida and snorted. 'Why did I not think of that before?'

'What did you say?' asked James in a dangerously low voice.

Gloria stood up in alarm. 'James, darling, could you get some more wine for Cressida here? She's almost empty.'

James ignored her and stared contemptuously at Sebastian.

'I said, what did you say?' His brown eyes flashed.

Laura and Ella glanced at each other in excitement. Maybe James would punch Sebastian.

William, sensing the same thing, walked over to James and grabbed his arm. 'Your phone is ringing,' he lied, pulling him towards the door.

James tried to resist but William was firm. Laura and Ella walked out too, ushering Aurora in front of them. You could cut the air with a knife.

'Well, it's certainly quieter now,' said Gloria lamely, shocked at Sebastian's behaviour.

Henry said nothing; he just hung his head and sighed.

Cressida placed her glass on the coffee table. She looked at her watch pointedly and nudged her husband. Sebastian nodded, drained his whiskey and stood up.

'Well, enjoy your day tomorrow, Dad,' he said, patting Henry's shoulder. 'We're off to Cressida's place. Her brother is back from Moscow so ...'

'Enjoy!' cried Gloria in relief, jumping up. She had been terrified that this vile young man would come back the next day.

Cressida gave her a tight smile and picked up her fur jacket. 'Goodbye,' she said, nodding formally. 'Thank you for the drink.'

'No offense, Aurora, but your brother is a total arsehole.' Laura folded her arms. 'He's just awful.'

Ella nodded in agreement. 'That was tense.'

James circled the island unit in rage. How dare that snob

come into their home and treat people that way? How could anyone be so cruel to a motherless girl?

William peeled a clementine. 'Now, Lolly, I don't seem half as bad.'

'I've got to agree,' she answered, shaking her head. 'Good lord, Aurora, what was it like growing up with that pig?'

'He was away at university,' she said in a small voice. 'I didn't really see him.' She bit her lip. 'George is far worse. He's older and much nastier.'

'You poor thing,' exclaimed Ella. 'You've really had a rough time.' She rubbed her shoulder comfortingly.

Aurora shrugged. 'It's not too bad. I don't see them a lot and I have Maggie and Freddie.'

'Maggie and Freddie?' repeated William. 'As in Freddie the pig farmer?'

Aurora giggled. 'Yes, that's him. Maggie's my nanny. She looks after me. She's our cook too.'

James opened a can of beer viciously. 'Why does Henry let him treat you that way?' he asked angrily. 'It's completely out of order.'

'Daddy doesn't like shouting,' she answered simply. 'He just pretends it doesn't happen.'

William spat out an orange pip. 'Tell your pal Freddie to call his next two piglets George and Seb,' he suggested.

'Maybe.' She giggled.

'Right,' said Laura, all business. 'It's Christmas Eve, you lot. No more negativity. Let's play a game and sing some songs. Father Christmas will be here soon so we'd better get a move on.'

# Chapter Eight

The turkey was delicious. They toasted Freddie's father for rearing it and Gloria for cooking it so well. She had stuffed it and roasted it slowly for five hours. After the clean-up, the whole family retired to the sitting room to watch the Queen's speech which Gloria had recorded.

Aurora clutched her new Barbie doll possessively. Father Christmas had brought it, along with the CD she wanted and chocolate sweets. She was the same size doll as Princess Grace but she had long brown hair instead of blonde and two different outfits: a ball dress and a jumpsuit. She would fit in quite nicely at the doll's house.

'What will you call her?' asked James, stretching out his long legs. He was sitting on the sofa eating Quality Street and flicking through the channels.

Aurora kissed the doll's forehead. 'I'm not sure yet,' she said seriously. 'It's a very big decision.'

'Yes,' he nodded gravely. 'You're absolutely right.'

Gloria stood at the drinks cabinet and poured Henry a cognac. 'It's Remy Martin,' she said, putting the cork back in the dark-green opaque bottle. Walking over to the sofa, she handed it next to him. 'You're probably used to far more expensive brandy but –'

'It's perfect,' he interrupted, grasping her hand.' Now, for goodness' sake, sit down. You've been slaving all day.'

She sat down next to him, still holding his hand.

The fire blazed merrily in the grate and the room felt warm and cosy.

Laura and William were playing chess on the coffee table. Every now and then, William would shout in triumph. 'Strategy, Laura! You've just got to have strategy.'

Henry stroked Gloria's wrist. 'You know, today has been so wonderful,' he said softly. 'It's usually just us, isn't it, Aurora?'

She nodded. 'You and me and Maggie.' She sighed. 'Freddie invited her over this year as we weren't there.'

'If they had a turkey half as good as ours, she will have had a great time,' said James. 'I'm absolutely stuffed.'

'We would normally have goose or something like that,' continued Henry, 'and then sing carols by the fire.'

'Shall we sing?' suggested Gloria. 'Then it will feel like home.' She kissed Henry tenderly. 'I want you to feel at home,' she added in an undertone.

He smiled broadly. 'That sounds wonderful. Right, I'll start.' He got up and turned off the television. 'Any requests?' His tall frame blocked the light from the fire and James squinted.

'*Eminem!*' yelled William.

'Who?' Henry scratched his head.

'Take no notice,' giggled Laura. 'Try something like "O Come All Ye Faithful".'

'Righty-oh.' Henry cleared his throat and began to sing in a baritone.

Gloria joined in and tried to harmonise. James' eye met Laura's and they smiled. Singing carols was definitely a first in their home.

The song came to an end. Aurora clapped and beamed at her father.

William stood up and wagged his finger at Laura. 'Pause the game, little sis. I want to beat you properly in a sec.'

He took a deep breath and started to sing 'The First Noel'. Henry and Gloria joined in and, despite himself, James started to hum along. He couldn't remember the words but he knew the air from primary school. Aurora watched him in delight and he winked at her.

Laura threw her eyes to heaven. 'Good Lord, family mine, can we please stop behaving like *The Brady Bunch*?'

William bounded back to the game of chess. 'Laura should sing next,' he suggested cheekily.

'Not a chance,' she retorted. 'Now hurry up and take my pawn. This is getting tedious.'

Henry pulled Aurora to her feet. 'Let my darling girl have a go. She has a lovely voice.'

Aurora blushed. 'No, Daddy. I can't.' She backed away slightly. 'You sing again.'

'Go on, Borealis,' urged James. 'Sing "Jingle Bells" or something. Please?'

She pushed her hair back from her face. 'Oh, all right. I'll sing something.'

Gloria smiled encouragingly and sipped her wine. The shadows danced around the room and the light from the fire served as a makeshift spotlight.

William whooped as he took Laura's rook. '*Get in!*' he shouted, punching the air.

'William!' chided Gloria sternly. 'Aurora is about to sing. Please be quiet.'

Aurora took a deep breath and started to sing 'O Holy Night'.

Gloria nearly dropped her glass. William and Laura whipped around in shock. James sat up straight, his dark eyes widening in surprise.

Aurora's voice was sweet and true and it soared over them all. With closed eyes, she projected her voice and every word was clear.

James could feel the hairs stand up on his neck. He had never heard anything like it. The child was only nine years old, yet she possessed a voice more akin to that of a trained soprano. It was simply beautiful: rich and melodious. He gazed at her in wonder.

William nudged Laura and whispered, 'Blimey, can we exploit her? We could make a fortune.' He gazed at Aurora in awe. 'We should definitely sign her up for *Pop Idol.* I could be her manager.'

Laura said nothing. She just stared at the younger girl in astonishment.

The song ended and for a moment Aurora kept her eyes closed. Then she came down to earth and curtsied.

Henry clapped and opened his arms for a hug. 'You were simply wonderful, my darling,' he praised. 'Simply wonderful,' he repeated, kissing her forehead.

James couldn't hide his amazement. 'Where did you learn to sing like that?' he asked.

'I don't know,' she replied honestly. 'I just can.'

'You could be on the West End,' chimed in William. 'Have you ever considered getting an agent?'

Aurora giggled. 'You're silly.'

Gloria stroked her hair. 'That was absolutely amazing, darling. You are just terrific.'

Aurora glowed with pleasure. Singing was her drug. It relaxed her and made her feel good. When she closed her eyes, it was like she disappeared and got lost in the music. Even as a baby, she had picked up melodies very quickly. Maggie taught her local folk songs and she listened to Freddie's tapes as much as she could. Laura had played her Pink CD over the past couple of days and she already knew the notes. It was very different to what she normally listened to, but it was definitely good. Maybe Laura would copy some songs for her to take back home.

James sipped his beer and stared at her speculatively. 'Your mother could sing,' he said quietly. 'She was very good, right, Henry?'

Henry looked wistful for a moment, his lined old face sad. 'I thought she was an angel the first time I heard her sing. It was in Dublin. She was simply exquisite.'

Gloria put her arm around his shoulders. 'Well, she lives on in your daughter,' she consoled him. 'Aurora is the angel now.'

'Stars, a princess, an angel. What next?' mocked James, grinning. 'You're a remarkable little lady.'

'Thanks, Jiminy,' Aurora said with a laugh.

Henry clapped his hands for attention. 'Gloria and I want to make an announcement.'

Laura choked on her Coke. 'Mum?' she squeaked. Her mother winked.

Laura glanced wildly at William and then at James. They had discussed a possible proposal but had not expected it so soon. Aurora smoothed her doll's hair, seemingly unperturbed by Henry's call to attention. Gloria beamed at them all, her face young and hopeful.

'Well, we would like you all to join us,' said Henry, 'on New Year's Eve in Cornwall. I would like to host a party for you all to show my gratitude for your wonderful hospitality.' He smoothed his grey hair back from his forehead.

'A party?' gasped Aurora in delight. 'Oh, Daddy, that sounds fantastic!' She jumped up in delight. 'We've never had a proper party before. May I invite Freddie? May I stay up late?'

Henry smiled. 'As the birthday girl, you may do what you please.'

'Birthday?' echoed William. 'Your birthday is on New Year's Eve?'

Aurora nodded. 'I was one of the first babies born after midnight.' She blushed. 'Well, that's what Maggie says.'

James said nothing. He could tell that Aurora knew little of her birth and that was a blessing. Maybe a party wasn't such a bad idea. Laura and William would be fascinated by Henry's house and he wouldn't say no to Maggie's cherry pudding. Plus, he could take more photos of the landscape; the ones he had shot that last day were truly stunning. His professor had given him a distinction for his image of a wave crashing on the jagged rocks of the beach near Henry's house. Maybe Laura could advise Aurora on how to modernise her Victorian bedroom. Rosie was heading home to Norfolk so he was at a loose end. Plus, he could stand up for Aurora if her nasty brothers turned up.

'I'm in,' he said definitely. 'Tell Maggie to start baking, Borealis. I've been dreaming of her cherry pudding for weeks.'

# Chapter Nine

Maggie held her arms out wide and waited for Aurora to hug her. She was standing at the main door of the old house, dressed in a long tweed jacket to keep out the cold. The frost still had its icy grip on the Cornish countryside, its white mark glistening on the stark trees and frozen fields.

'I'm so glad to see you, my lovely,' she said tenderly, kissing the child's forehead. 'Did you 'ave a nice Christmas in the city?' She cuddled her close.

Aurora nodded. 'Oh, Maggie, it was so much fun. I met lots of new people and I went shopping and I had Nutella!' Her cheeks glowed and added much-needed colour to her pale face. She was dressed in her red coat and black hat.

Henry deposited two suitcases on the flagstones. 'It's a long drive, Maggie,' he muttered. 'My leg isn't the better for it.'

'Was it slippery on the roads, sir?' she asked, taking Aurora's hand and rubbing it. 'I 'eard there were black ice up near the cove.'

'No, we were quite fortunate in that respect,' he said, shaking his head. 'I drove slowly just in case.'

They went inside and took off their coats and hats in the hall.

Aurora was delighted to see that Maggie had lit the fire in the drawing room. The large room was cosy for once with the flames in the grate dancing merrily.

'Did you enjoy your time off?' asked Henry, sitting in his favourite chair by the fireside. 'Tell Conny that our turkey was quite something.'

'Our bird was good too,' she agreed. 'I spent the day with Conny, Mary and Freddie.'

'How was the pudding?' asked Aurora, referring to the Christmas pudding they had made together two months before.

She always helped Maggie with the Christmas baking. A large bowl would be filled with dried fruit, suet, sugar, apples, orange rind, spices and a good splash of brandy. 'Stir it and make a wish, little 'un,' Maggie would say, handing her the wooden spoon. 'Wish and it will come true.' Aurora would close her eyes and wish with all her might, stirring the thick mixture simultaneously. It was always the same: that she would get a new brother or sister. Oh, how she craved company! She would prefer a girl so that she could play dolls and do her hair. However, a boy would be fine too. They could go to the beach and chase the waves or go for picnics in the woods.

Henry rubbed his hands together and warmed them over the flames. 'I certainly missed your baking, Maggie,' he concluded. 'Gloria is a wonderful woman, but the pudding was definitely from Waitrose.'

'*Lawks!* That sounds awful, that does. Lucky I kept a spare puddin' for the New Year party you've sprung on me.' She took Aurora's coat and hat from the little girl's hands. 'I'll put these away and you warm yourself up. I made an apple pie this morning. The kettle's boiled. I'll just make some tea.'

Henry beamed at her. 'That sounds wonderful. Apologies again for the late notice regarding my little soirée.'

'Don't give it a thought,' she replied. 'If they're all as nice as

Master James, then it will be a pleasure.'

William punched Laura in the arm. 'Move over, you hog. This back seat is cramped enough.'

'You're too tall,' she grumbled. 'Now, stop pushing me or I swear!'

'Shut up, you two,' said James cheerfully, hopping into the driver's seat. He repositioned the rear-view mirror and saw the reflection of his mother locking the front door of the house. Her head was wrapped in a scarf and her handbag swung from her arm.

Laura patted James' shoulder and handed him a CD. 'Please play my music, Jiminy,' she pleaded. 'Please!'

William pulled her backwards. '*No way!*' he yelled. 'It's going to be the real Slim Shady, I'm afraid.' He thrust a CD over James' shoulder.

'*No!*' she shouted venomously. 'I'm sick of him. James, why does Will get to play CD commando? We're listening to the Spice Girls! End of.'

'*Never!*' William grabbed the CD from James' hand. 'There's no way I'm driving to the end of the country listening to that.'

Gloria sat into the car. 'Pack it in, you two,' she ordered. 'No more arguing.'

'But, Mum!' cried William.

'Gloria!' Laura protested.

'Not another word!' Gloria was firm. 'I have a CD I would like to play.' She rummaged in her bag. 'Ah, here we are: Doris Day.'

'Say again?' William looked alarmed.

'A movie icon.'

James smirked. 'Doris Day it is then,' he said, slotting the CD into the stereo.

'*Mum!*' wailed Laura in despair. 'I really wanted to hear "*2 become 1*".'

'Drive, James,' said Gloria, ignoring her daughter completely. 'We need to get on.'

Aurora gazed longingly out of her bedroom window. The drive up to the house remained empty. There was no sign of the Dixons. She had been waiting all morning for them to arrive.

'What time is it?' she asked Maggie for the tenth time.

'Still too early, my lovely,' said Maggie, smoothing the duvet on the bed. 'Not long now.'

Aurora sighed. She couldn't wait to show Laura her doll's house and the beach. She couldn't remember the last time they'd had proper guests. Sebastian and Cressida's wedding had been in London so the old house had not seen a celebration since Grace and Henry's wedding ten years before. There had been no big christening for Aurora; Henry had deemed it inappropriate so close to Grace's death. Instead, a short ceremony in the chapel had taken place with just Maggie, Conny, Mary and Baby Freddie. A bemused Henry had held the small bundle and cried silently as the priest poured holy water over her dark head. George and Sebastian had opted to stay at school, claiming that they were too busy revising for exams.

Aurora wiped the condensation from the old pane and bit her lip. *Please arrive!*

'Seb wants some drop scones, little 'un. I got to get me back to the kitchen.' Maggie paused at the door. 'Are you 'ungry?'

'No, Maggie. I'll keep watching,' she answered, placing her chin in her hands. 'I've nothing better to do.'

The sky was a dark grey with a thin cloak of cirrus clouds. The winter did not afford much light, so she craned to make out a black dot in the distance. It gradually got nearer and nearer, its engine noise growing louder as it came.

'Oh!' she exclaimed when she realised that it was James' car. '*Oh!*' She scrambled to her feet and raced down the stairs.

'*Daddy! Daddy!*' she yelled. '*They're here!*' She jumped down the steps, two at a time, nearly crashing into the giant plant at the base of the staircase. '*Daddy!*'

'*My God, can you please shut up?*' George appeared at the top bannister, his hair tousled. 'Some of us are still asleep.' He glared at Aurora who cowered backwards at the sound of his voice.

'Sorry, George,' she mumbled, red-faced.

He scowled and turned on his heel.

George Sinclair was thirty-two years old and had mourned when Thatcher left Downing Street in 1990. He was of medium height with dark hair, a slight paunch and a large nose that was slightly too big for his face. Where Sebastian resembled Henry, he took after his mother Marcella. Unmarried, finding a wife was not high on his list of priorities. George Sinclair thought only of himself. He didn't do romance or flowers. He certainly didn't do nice.

He ambled back into his childhood bedroom, the belt of his tartan dressing gown trailing on the floor. His room reeked of stake cigarette smoke and half-empty glasses of whiskey were discarded here and there. He glanced at his gold watch and decided to go back to bed for a while. There was no point getting dressed too early. No doubt the ground floor would be overrun with that family and he didn't want to engage with them.

A banker by trade, George's life was filled with corporate events and meetings; long hours in the office and an unhealthy diet. He disliked the gym and preferred instead to follow the racing from the comfort of his flat in Chelsea. Smoking was his greatest pleasure and he was known to have the odd cocaine-fuelled night after a long week. He had successfully avoided calling to that woman's house at Christmas, feigning a flu and staying at home. Seb had done his duty and for that he was grateful. Now, he had to meet them but at least he was on his own turf. He could disappear upstairs and avoid them as much as possible.

He climbed back into bed and pulled the blanket over his head. Another few hours of sleep was just what he needed.

Aurora burst into the study to find her father typing.

'They're here, Daddy!' she said breathlessly. 'I saw the car.'

He brightened immediately. 'Ask Maggie to put the kettle on. I expect that they'll be peckish after such a long journey.'

'Okay,' she said.

Sebastian didn't even acknowledge Aurora when she burst in announcing their guests' arrival.

Maggie had filled the kettle right away. She had scones and homemade jam ready to serve.

'I'll have another couple of those pancakes, Mag,' ordered Sebastian. 'Just cook them for longer this time. I thought they tasted quite doughy.'

'No problem, Master Seb,' she said mechanically. 'Comin' right up.' She poured some batter into the pan and swirled it. 'Will I make some for your wife too?'

Sebastian snorted. 'Good God, no. You know she doesn't eat flour. She will probably have that apple in that bowl. Perhaps a grape or two.'

Maggie said nothing. Cressida's eating habits were alien to her, but incomers were always a bit strange. She found Seb's wife cold and haughty; however, she wasn't paid to like these people. Cressida reminded her of Marcella, Henry's first wife. She had been a cold woman and had passed this hauteur on to her sons.

Henry pushed open the heavy oak door and stepped out into the cold air. He was wearing brown slacks, a cream Aran jumper and a peaked hat over his grey hair. His blue eyes creased when he smiled in salutation.

'*Welcome to you all!*' he shouted over the roar of the engine.

Aurora appeared at his side, her long hair braided, wearing a navy mini-dress with black tights.

James turned off the ignition and hopped out. 'Happy New Year, Sinclairs! Great to be back.' He shook Henry's hand vigorously and, picking Aurora up, he swung her around.

'Put me down!' she squealed in delight.

'*Wowee!*' said William, craning his neck to look at the huge house. 'This is like a National Trust house.'

'Crikey,' said Laura, equally shocked. 'I didn't expect this.'

Henry ushered them inside. 'Go and warm yourselves by the fire. I'll tell Maggie to bring the tea.'

Laura's eyes widened as they entered the drawing room. The walls were lined with books and the carpets were like tapestries. Huge portraits hung on the walls – most of them looked like stuffy old men in suits but there was one of a woman. Laura peered closer. It was a stunning image of a beautiful dark-haired lady wearing a white dress.

'Will,' she whispered loudly, nudging him. 'That must be Aurora's mother. Blimey, they're like twins.'

William nodded in agreement. 'Twins,' he echoed.

Maggie arrived in, laden down with a large tea tray. James jumped up the minute he saw the old lady and offered to carry the tray.

'Thank you, Master James,' said Maggie gratefully, handing it over to him. 'I'll just get the scones, I will.' She scurried off and closed the door behind her.

'They have a real maid,' whispered William, wide-eyed. 'Imagine that at home!'

'Imagine,' repeated Laura, equally astounded.

It felt like they had entered another world: a world from years ago. Laura gazed at the expensive art and ancient books. Even the chairs looked antique – embroidered armchairs with golden legs. Henry looked right at home in the old house – it suited him. He had seemed out of place in the Dixon household – his old-fashioned clothes and plummy accent just didn't fit. However, here he was in his proper surroundings.

James placed the tray on a sideboard and began to unload its contents, admiring the beautiful tea set and the silver cutlery.

'My sons are here,' said Henry. 'Seb and his wife Cressida . . .'

'Yes, we know them,' interjected Laura, making a face at Gloria who glared at her.

'And my eldest son, George.'

'That's great, isn't it, kids?' Gloria forced a smile. 'Let's all muck in and I'm sure we'll get on very well.'

'What time is the party starting?' enquired James, looking out the huge drawing-room window. 'I'd like to take some photos before we lose the light.'

'Around eight,' answered Henry. 'Maggie has help coming from the village and we are to have a sit-down meal in the hall.'

'Have you invited many?' asked Laura.

'No,' answered Henry. 'Just Marcella's brother Gordon and his wife Helena.'

'Marcella?' William looked confused.

'My late wife,' explained Henry. 'She was from these parts.'

Aurora skipped over to Maggie who had reappeared with a plate of golden scones, already spread with homemade jam and clotted cream.

'Shall I serve, Maggie?' she asked.

'You may, little 'un,' answered the old lady. 'Let's give Master James some right away – 'ee looks famished, 'ee does.' She winked.

James laughed. 'I've been dreaming of your cooking, Maggie. I won't say no.'

Sebastian appeared just as they were finishing their tea. Laura and William smiled tightly. James just nodded curtly and turned his back. Gloria made the biggest effort, holding out her hand to greet him. His blue eyes narrowed as he regarded her. He found it hard to disguise his dislike. Her London home had been bad enough, an apt reflection of her social class. He still shuddered at the thought of that cheap Van Gogh print framed in the hallway and the dog hair plastered over every available surface. Predictably, she looked out of place in his ancestral home.

'Cressida has a headache,' he began stiffly, shaking her hand limply. 'She wants to sleep it off upstairs.'

'Oh,' said Gloria sympathetically. 'I have some Panadol if she'd like some.'

'She's fine,' he said curtly. 'Every time we come down here she develops some sort of ailment. It's becoming quite a bore.' He strode over to the fireplace, his hands in his pockets.

'Tea?' asked Henry. 'I can ring for Maggie and get a fresh pot.'

'No, I'm sick of tea,' he retorted.

There was an uncomfortable silence. James glowered and focused on the branches of a larch tree that were bending slightly in the wind. He couldn't hide his dislike for Henry's son. Gloria had warned him to keep his temper in check. They were on Sinclair turf now and she would not abide rudeness of any sort.

'Where's George?' asked Sebastian, taking a seat by the fire and crossing his long legs. 'He took a bottle of Glenfiddich from the bar last night. I warned him to take it easy but when has George ever listened to anything?'

'I saw him,' said Aurora helpfully. 'He told me to be quiet.'

'Maggie is waiting to make him breakfast,' continued Sebastian, ignoring her completely. 'Is it me or has the old thing gone a bit gaga?' He threw his eyes to heaven. 'She seemed a bit distracted this morning – not that she was ever that scintillating.' He swept an imaginary piece of fluff from the chair. 'I had forgotten how much her accent and that dialect annoys me. Anything but the Queen's English is just so frightful for one to engage with. If I hear 'my lovely' once more!' He shook his head.

Aurora's face grew dark and she watched her older brother intently. Was there any limit to his nastiness? How dare he speak about her beloved Maggie that way? She was probably subdued because she found him intimidating. She could just imagine him sitting at the big scrubbed oak table, demanding his breakfast rudely.

James sensed her anger and walked over. 'Come on, Borealis,' he said quietly. 'Let's go for a walk. I want to take some photographs.'

Laura and William jumped up too. 'Why don't we all go?' they suggested in unison. Anything to get away from Sebastian. The atmosphere had become decidedly cold since his arrival.

'Yes, let me show you the beach,' said Aurora, brightening. 'There's a cave where the smugglers hid years ago. Freddie showed it to me before.'

'Right, get your jackets,' said James, taking Aurora by the hand. 'Let's get going.'

Sebastian examined his manicured nails. The house would definitely be more peaceful with all those children out of the picture. Again he despaired over his father's lack of foresight. This Gloria was just not suitable. Nor were her overbearing family. He had expected a proposal over Christmas and was gratified when it didn't come to fruition. Maybe the old chap had seen sense. He doubted it, but it was a possibility. He and George had their speech all planned out. They would convince their father in no time that any notions he had about Gloria Dixon were unsuitable and inappropriate. Henry needed to learn that you could have fun without having to put a ring on a finger. His secretary had taught him that. She was the perfect distraction and Cressida had no idea. Her voluptuous body was a welcome change from the thin angular shape of his wife. She didn't tell him what to do and was incredible in bed. Fun.

Henry needed to understand that he could have fun without expectations.

# Chapter Ten

The waves crashed on the shore and sent salty spray into the air. Laura squealed in horror.

'My hair!' she wailed. 'I straightened it this morning.' She tried in vain to keep her blonde locks contained.

William picked up a stone and tried to skim it on the water's surface. His hair blew into his eyes and his jacket billowed out behind him.

'*This place is ace!*' he yelled over the wind.

James knew what he meant. It felt like they were on the edge of the world. The sea stack he had photographed the last time stood steadfastly in place, bracing itself against the power of the relentless sea. When the sun began to set, it created a silhouette against the silver horizon – a giant piece of rock cut off from the mainland.

Aurora raced out to the water's edge and screamed as the sea nearly caught her out.

'Come on, James,' she shouted. 'Let's play again.'

'Are you having a laugh?' he laughed. 'I ended up like a drowned rat the last time.'

Laura grimaced as the wind whipped past her. 'Is my eyeliner running?' she called to William, pointing to her face. 'I mean, do I look like a panda?'

William shrugged. 'You look as scary as ever,' he replied seriously.

'Bite me,' she retorted, sticking out her tongue.

'Come on!' cried Aurora. 'Let's go to the cave.' She ran off in the direction of the cliff, her long hair streaming out behind her.

Laura shoved her hands in her pockets and followed. William was already halfway there, his long legs loping after the little girl. James focused the lens of his camera on ripples of sand near the water's edge. He snapped repeatedly, taking shots at different angles. The film in his camera was black-and-white which would work well with the fading light.

Aurora stopped outside a big craggy entrance at the base of the cliff. The rough sides of the cave glistened with seawater and were covered in sporadic green lichen and periwinkles. The sand was darker in the shade; it had a waterlogged appearance and their feet sank down into its depths as they walked in.

'This is a very long cave,' Aurora said seriously. 'No one has ever gone right in.'

'Yeah, right!' scoffed Laura.

'No one has ever tried,' insisted Aurora, her brown eyes wide. 'Smugglers would hide in here and some say that there's lots of treasure buried in there too.' She could almost see Freddie as he told her about it the first time they had ventured inside.

'Treasure?' said William. 'Now we're talking.'

'Come on!' Aurora disappeared into the dark depths.

William plunged after her.

'*Come on, Laura!*' Aurora called.

Her voice sounded far away. Laura shivered. There was something unnerving about the lack of light. The cave seemed like an eerie place. Slowly she put one foot in front of the other. The daylight was sucked out as she advanced, leaving a damp, cold feeling and a smell of rotten seaweed.

'*Where are you?*' she yelped fearfully as she stumbled slightly.

'*We're just in here!*' came Aurora's voice from the recesses.

'*I can't see!*' cried Laura in panic, feeling her way along the cold wall. '*Will? Aurora?*'

There was a strange silence within the high black walls. The sound of the waves had diminished and all that was left was a trickling sound as water escaped from the rock above. She could hear voices but they seemed to be miles away. The acoustics in the cave were strange and the weirdest sounds were amplified. Her foot sank down into a hole in the sand and she jumped backwards, terrified. Her sock was sodden and she could feel the water in her black ankle boot.

'*Boo!*' came a deep voice from behind her and she let out a bloodcurdling scream.

James grabbed her arm and laughed. 'Calm down, Laura. Bloody hell.'

'Oh, James,' she gasped, falling back against him. 'You nearly gave me a heart attack.' She turned and collapsed into his arms, stifling a sob. 'I don't like it in here – it's scary. Please take me back out.'

James nearly pinched himself. He had never seen his sister behave this way. Laura was always cool and confident. She mocked weakness and could handle any situation.

'Okay, come on,' he said. 'Lean on me.'

He guided her gently into the daylight, stalling her fall as she tripped on a rock.

'Are you all right?' he queried in concern when they were safely outside.

Her face was pale and her lower lip was quivering. 'I don't know what happened,' she said in a shaky voice. 'I just panicked. I don't know why, but it felt like death in there.'

James shook her gently. 'Blimey, Laura, that's a bit morbid. It's only a cave.'

'No,' she shook her head obstinately. 'I hated it – it was awful.' She exhaled slowly. 'I never want to go in there again.'

James rubbed her back. 'Hey, you'll be fine. I'll call the others and we should get back.'

Laura nodded numbly and wrapped her arms around her upper body protectively. She couldn't explain what had happened. Was she claustrophobic? Maybe the enclosed space had caused her to panic. The rational side of her brain kicked in and she felt her cheeks redden. Thank God it was James who had found her and not William. James would never broadcast her meltdown. William, however, would tell everyone at school.

James reappeared with Aurora and William in tow. They seemed unperturbed. In fact, the little girl looked exhilarated. This only added to Laura's mortification.

'That was so cool,' exclaimed William with flushed cheeks. 'It was so spooky.'

'I love it in there,' said Aurora.

'We should get back,' suggested James, winking at his sister. 'I'd love another cup of tea.'

'Yes, let's,' agreed Laura. 'The sun has almost disappeared anyway. I don't fancy being down here in the dark.'

'Let me show you my room,' suggested Aurora when they were back at the big house.

Sebastian had disappeared, as had Henry and Gloria.

William took a seat on the armchair closest to the blazing fire.

'I'll just wait here,' he said, holding his hands over the flames. 'No offense, Aurora, but I hate Barbies.'

Aurora pulled Laura's arm. 'Come on, you have to meet Princess Grace.'

'Who?' the older girl asked reluctantly.

'My favourite doll.'

Laura raised her eyes to heaven and James grinned. 'Give my

regards to the princess,' he said gravely.

Aurora nodded and skipped out of the room.

'Do I have to?' muttered Laura, making a face.

James nodded and waved her away.

She emerged out into the hall and shivered. Without the heat of the fire, the cold air of the main hallway was sharp and hit her immediately. Sighing, she followed the younger girl up the old staircase. The carpet was worn and pinned into place by large brass rods along the length of each step. She trudged up and tried not to notice how dark and gloomy it was. It was the opposite to her own home which was warm and cheerful. The sombre dark oil paintings of Sinclair ancestors loomed over her and their eyes seemed to follow her everywhere. She shivered again.

'*Down here!*' called Aurora, beckoning from the end of the corridor.

Laura trudged down and turned into a large bedroom. A four-poster bed dominated the right side, covered in a lace bedspread. A fire burned in the grate and a large doll's house stood in the corner. Bookshelves lined a wall.

'So, do you like it?' Aurora beamed.

Laura forced a smile. 'It's lovely,' she lied.

'Let me show you my favourite doll.' Aurora pointed to her Barbie doll who was sitting at the miniature dining-room table. 'Her name is Grace.' Then she pointed to the doll she had received at Christmas. 'And that's Juliet. You must remember her from London.'

Laura dutifully '*oohed*' and '*aahed*' at the wardrobe full of small gowns and the rows of plastic shoes designed for dolls' feet.

'Your room is right next door,' Aurora informed her. 'Our rooms are connected, look!' She bounded over to an old oak door and yanked it open to reveal a room almost exactly identical to her own. Laura's leopard-print suitcase was already at the foot of the bed. A fire blazed in the small grate.

Laura shivered. She didn't know why, but this house gave her the creeps. It had a darkness about it: an eerie aura that assaulted her senses and made her tremble. It was similar to how she felt in the cave: uncomfortable and frightened. Gloria planned to stay for two days and initially she had welcomed the idea, deeming it an adventure. Now, she couldn't wait to go back to her own house and her own room, to listen to her CDs and paint her nails. It was no wonder that Aurora seemed like a child from another time.

'Would you like to play?' the little girl asked, holding up her new brunette doll.

'Why not?' said Laura, closing the connecting door with a bang.

Anything to distract her from the creeping darkness that was threatening to engulf her.

Later that afternoon, Aurora was sitting at the kitchen table, drinking juice as Maggie put the finishing touches to her birthday cake.

'Do you like it, my lovely?' asked the old lady, swirling the last of the chocolate icing on top. It was to be sprinkled with Smarties: Aurora's favourite.

'It's wonderful, Maggie. I can't wait to have at least three slices.'

'You'll be sick, little 'un.'

'Not at all. Everyone knows that you can eat as much cake as you like on your birthday.' She sipped her juice. 'I wonder what Daddy got me as a present? I'm really hoping for a new Ken doll for Juliet.'

Maggie regarded her for a moment and licked her thumb which was covered with chocolate buttercream. 'As it 'appens, I 'ave a present for you,' she said after a moment. 'I think you're old enough now.'

'Can I open it now?' The little girl clapped her hands in delight.

Maggie nodded and disappeared into the pantry. 'It's only small but I think you'll like it.'

She reappeared and held out something on her palm. Aurora gasped. It was a pendant with a silver flower on the end.

'Oh, it's so pretty!' she said in wonder, lifting it gently from Maggie's outstretched hand. The flower pendant was an unusual shape, the petals like a ballerina dress and the multiple stamen looking like tiny legs.

'It's a fuchsia,' said Maggie. 'Grace wore it constantly. I kept it after she died until you had come of age.'

'Grace? My mother?'

'Yes, it was hers.'

'Did Daddy buy it for her?'

Maggie's face was impassive. 'I'm not rightly sure. I think she 'ad it before she met 'im.' She opened the clasp and put the chain around Aurora's neck.

Aurora admired the pretty flower pendant. She didn't have much jewellery, just a gold cross from her Communion and pearl earrings from Aunt Helena when she was born.

'I love it!' said the little girl. 'I'll wear it all the time, just like Mummy.'

'You do that,' said Maggie wistfully. 'She'd like that.' Her lined old face looked sad and she turned away. Resting her hands on the edge of the sink, she hung her head for a moment.

'Are you quite all right, Maggie?' asked Aurora in her clear voice.

'Of course, little 'un. Of course.'

Freddie kicked a stone and it hit the old wall behind the servants' entrance of the big house. He was debating whether to knock on the door or not. He knew Maggie was inside in the big kitchen, preparing food for the party that evening.

The day before, Aurora had asked him to come, saying that it was her birthday and that she wanted her best friend there. He had nodded, vaguely saying yes, but now he didn't want to go at all. Her horrible brothers would be there for a start and those incomers were around too.

Freddie frowned. Those Londoners made him uneasy. Aurora spoke about them constantly and when she did her face shone. She had arrived back after Christmas on a strange high, relating tales of a world he didn't understand or feel part of. He couldn't compete with this new exciting life that she was experiencing and this made him anxious. He had heard his mother talking to his father about Mr. Henry and this new woman. He got the gist: a wedding was expected and then they might move away.

He traced his finger along the old stones that were slotted together so artfully so as to form a steady wall. Pieces of moss grew between the cracks and offered a soft silky texture amongst the rough granite.

He didn't want Aurora to leave.

She would move to the big city and forget all about him. How could his tales of smugglers and pirates compete with Madame Tussauds and Starbucks?

He took a deep breath. He had come to tell her that he wouldn't make it to the party. He would suggest a walk to the village in a few days where they could go for hot chocolate. He knocked on the door.

'*Come in!*' called Maggie.

He pushed open the heavy oak door and stepped into the big kitchen. The air smelt of cinnamon and cloves. There was a pot bubbling on the hob and a large cake on the sideboard. Maggie was alone and up to her elbows in flour. Expertly, she rolled out some pastry into a circular shape.

'I'm makin' a lemon tart, I am,' she announced, swatting her hair out of her face. 'Mr. 'Enry wants a few different types of puddin' to choose from.'

Freddie took a seat at the old scrubbed table. 'Will there be a big crowd?' he asked, peeling the label off a jar of honey. 'Aurora said that there'll be the whole family plus those incomers.'

Maggie nodded. 'They're nice people, my lovely. Especially that James. Right good and ordinary, they are. No airs and graces like other people.' She threw her eyes to heaven.

Freddie knew that she was referring to Aurora's brothers and Cressida, who were snobby and more often than not treated his aunt terribly. Maggie had been with the Sinclair family all her life and was certainly not just a servant. She had become part of the family and had earned their respect.

'Aurora asked me to come tonight as it's her birthday,' he began reluctantly. 'But . . .'

'You won't come,' she finished. She stopped her work and regarded him thoughtfully. 'Why not, Fred? You're 'er best friend, you are.'

He shrugged. 'I won't know anyone and I don't like all the posh food and grown-up conversation. I don't like her brothers neither.'

'Is that all?' Her eyes were shrewd.

'Yep,' he answered, not meeting her eyes.

Maggie knew exactly why her nephew was reluctant to go to the party. He felt out of the loop and unsure of how to behave. He was intimidated by these incomers and slightly jealous to boot. She could sense a change coming and she knew that he did too.

'Just explain to the little 'un,' she advised, resuming her rolling. 'Maybe you two could do something special when everything has calmed down.'

Freddie nodded with a faraway look on his face.

He wasn't sure that things would ever calm down again.

# Chapter Eleven

'Thank you all for joining us on this special night!' Henry raised his champagne flute and nodded at the occupants of the table who raised their glasses in response.

The party was in full swing. The long banquet table was covered with a white lace cloth and Maggie had unearthed the crystal claret glasses. Silver cutlery gleamed and a large flower arrangement stood in the centre.

Laura shivered in her silver party dress. The air was cold despite the roaring fire. William was uncharacteristically smart in a shirt and tie by her side. He had a Gameboy surreptitiously hidden beneath the tablecloth and was biting his lip in concentration as he played. James sat by Aurora on the other side, wearing a dark-grey suit with a white shirt open at the neck.

Gloria glanced at him and was jolted by how much he looked like his late father. She was seated at the head of the table, to Henry's right side. Her blonde hair was wound up into a chignon and her bracelets sparkled on her wrists as she moved. She had chosen her dress very carefully. She wanted classy and demure and so had splashed out on a dark-blue silk mid-length dress with a golden trim. Laura had applied her make-up and she smelt of Chanel.

'That duck was superb,' said Gordon, taking a swig of wine. 'Henry, you must allow me to poach that chef of yours.'

Henry's face creased into a smile. 'Maggie is worth her weight in gold,' he agreed. 'Sorry, old chap, but I'm keeping her here.'

Gordon snorted. 'I'll pay her double,' he argued. 'That orange sauce was just wonderful.'

Gordon resembled his nephew George in looks. He was slightly rotund with a balding head and a large nose. Marcella, Henry's first wife, had been his older sister. However, he didn't share his sister's personality. Marcella had been haughty and cold, whereas Gordon was warm and kind. He loved two things: hunting and his wife Helena. After Marcella's death, he and Henry had remained friends and socialised together a lot. He had supported him through Grace's death and the ensuing heartbreak. He had treated Aurora like one of his own.

Helena was a tall woman with dark hair streaked with grey. She had borne Gordon three sons, all of whom lived abroad. Her broad frame was dressed handsomely in a dark-green dress and draped on her shoulders was a mink stole. She was polite and rarely expressed an opinion. Henry's guests had caused speculation, but she was not one to gossip.

Cressida had appeared for the meal, wearing a clingy black dress and silver Jimmy Choo sandals. It didn't take a genius to work out that she hated her husband's childhood home. She picked at her duck and sipped her wine delicately. Sebastian barely spoke to her, preferring to pontificate loudly about the state of the stock exchange. George wore a suit and a scowl. He hated evenings like this: ones where he had to engage with dull people that he had no interest in.

Narrowing his eyes, he focused in on Gloria. She was just so gauche. His father certainly seemed smitten; Sebastian had been quite right about that. Things were more serious than they had originally thought. She was here with her brood, sitting in his mother's chair with her hand on his father's arm.

His face tightened.

She would have to go.

'Why didn't Freddie come?' enquired James, eating a large slice of lemon tart. 'You invited him, didn't you?'

Aurora licked her spoon, making sure to rid it of all the ice cream that coated it.

'He didn't want to come. He hates dressing up and it was all grown-ups.'

'You two are pretty close, then?'

She nodded. 'Oh yes. We're best friends.' Her large brown eyes softened. 'He makes me laugh all the time. We're always going on adventures. He knows everything about the coast.'

'I must meet him,' said James thoughtfully. 'He sounds like a good guy to know.'

'Oh, he is,' she agreed. 'He definitely is.'

Laura refused lemon tart and opted for coffee instead.

'Coffee?' said Gloria with a disapproving look. 'You're only thirteen.'

'Oh, chill out,' her daughter retorted. 'It's better than whiskey or brandy.'

William had abandoned his Gameboy and was laughing uproariously at something Gordon had said.

Cressida sighed and shook her head when Maggie offered her some dessert.

George caught Sebastian's eye and jerked his head in Henry's direction. They needed to get their father alone. He needed to be told what was what: there was no way they were condoning another unsuitable marriage.

Henry tapped his glass with his bread knife. 'If everyone would quieten down,' he said, smiling. 'Gloria and I have something we would like to say.'

Sebastian looked at George in alarm. Surely there wouldn't be an announcement? Surely not?

James stared at his mother. She was flushed and excited, her chest heaving and her face radiant.

'Well, we would like to get some news out of the way before Aurora turns ten. We shan't steal my beautiful daughter's limelight.' Henry took Gloria's hand in his and held it to his chest. 'This woman has made my life so happy. I thought I had lost my way and now I'm writing again, filled with inspiration and hope.'

Gloria beamed up at him.

'So, we decided to make things official.'

Cressida looked up from her espresso and frowned. Surely not. This would make Seb even crankier than normal.

'Meet the new Mrs. Sinclair.' Henry kissed Gloria tenderly on the lips. 'We got married a month ago in secret.'

Sebastian spat out his wine and coughed loudly.

George didn't move, only a muscle flickering in his cheek. 'You did what?' he said softly and dangerously.

'We got married!' repeated Gloria in delight. 'We decided to do it in secret so as not to create a fuss. We didn't want a big thing at our age.'

'Been there, done that,' added Henry.

The Dixon children stared at their mother in shock. James was stunned. His mother and he were very close; she told him everything. Or so he had thought.

Only Aurora clapped her hands in delight. Her wish had come true. She had a family. A part of her was disappointed that she didn't get to see the big white dress or throw confetti, but the reality was that now she had instant brothers and sisters. Not just any siblings: cool siblings who listened to modern music and knew about bonking.

Gordon and Helena stood up and went over to shake hands. 'Congratulations,' they said in unison, masking their surprise well.

'Best of luck,' added Gordon, thumping Henry on the back. 'Never say never.'

'This means we'll be a family,' breathed Aurora, her pale cheeks rosy. 'This means I'll have a sister?' Her eyes sparkled and she turned to James in delight.

Laura's blue eyes widened as it dawned. 'Does this mean we'll have to live here?' Her voice started to rise. '*I can't live here – I hate it here!*' She jumped to her feet. 'Mum! Tell me that you don't want to move here!'

William pulled her dress. 'Sit down, for God's sake.' He made apologetic eyes at the table.

'*No!*' she yelled in panic, pulling free. 'My life is in London, Will. *Our* life is there. I don't want to live in this place. I have my school and my friends.' She turned to her mother wildly. 'Mum?'

Gloria hushed her. 'We'll discuss all that later, darling,' she soothed. 'Now, sit down.'

Aurora regarded Laura in confusion. 'But of course you'll live here,' she said logically. 'This is where we live, Laura. Now that we're a family ...'

'*No!*'

James got up and strode over to his sister. 'Come with me,' he ordered, pulling her towards the door. 'Bloody hell, Laura, there's a time and a place.'

'Shut up, James!' she seethed as he pulled her into the hall. 'It's fine for you! You've left home. I'm still a minor.'

'Enough,' he said through gritted teeth. 'You'll upset Mum.' He led her towards the kitchen.

Back at the table, George sipped his wine slowly, ignoring the scene between Gloria's brats. He had more pressing questions.

'This is certainly a surprise,' he said in his silky voice. 'Why the rush?'

'Well, I'm not getting any younger, son,' Henry said. 'I decided to take the plunge. I'm fed up with being lonely.'

'*Hear, hear!*' yelled Gordon, refilling his glass. 'Quite right, Sinclair, you old dog!'

Cressida glanced at her husband in alarm. He hadn't said a word since the big reveal and was viciously twisting his napkin around and around.

'Seb?' she whispered, placing her small hand on his arm.

'Shut up!' he hissed, shrugging it off violently. 'Not a word.'

William took the golden opportunity to fill his glass with wine. Turning sideways, he downed the red liquid greedily. No one took any notice, so he hastily refilled it. Gloria's marriage didn't bother him. He liked Henry and the bottom line was he wanted his mother to be happy. He agreed with Laura though; he couldn't imagine life as a country squire. Still, he was sixteen. Just a couple more years and he was a free man.

'I'm so happy, Daddy!' cried Aurora, running up to her father and hugging him.

'Me too, my darling,' he murmured into her hair. 'It will be a new beginning for both of us.'

Gloria reached out her hands for a hug and Aurora fell into them. 'I've never had a mother before,' she said shyly. 'Just Maggie.'

'Well, now you do,' said Gloria with a tender look. 'I'm going to look after you all.'

'Are you feelin' better, my lovely?' Maggie rubbed Laura's rigid shoulders in concern.

'No,' she said frankly. 'No offense, Maggie, but I can't live here. I just can't.'

Maggie glanced at James. She wasn't surprised by the news. It echoed the time Henry had married Grace: that too had been done in secret and had caused just as much furore. She had been initially as horrified as the boys about Grace. How could Henry run off and marry a girl half his age? So impulsively? However, when she met the beautiful young girl, her heart had melted. She was just so sad and lost. Her eyes were faraway and her spirit waned as her belly grew.

Henry's new wife would be a good thing. He needed companionship; he needed a friend.

'Master James,' she began. 'Did they mention anything about movin' 'ere?' She honestly didn't know what would happen. She couldn't see Mr. Henry living in a city but she couldn't imagine Gloria's little 'uns fitting in here either.

James shook his head. 'Nothing. I mean, they didn't have time before motor-mouth here started ranting.' He leaned backwards against the kitchen counter. 'It's early days, little sis. They're not going to uproot you right away.'

Laura started to sob. 'I won't do it! I just won't!'

James pulled her close. 'This is a big night,' he said softly. 'I'm just as shocked as you are. We can tackle all those questions tomorrow.'

Laura shook her head obstinately. 'This place gives me the creeps. I don't think that I'll be able to sleep.'

'You will,' he insisted. 'Just have some hot milk or something. That coffee you had a few minutes ago certainly won't help your insomnia.'

Maggie pulled some ice cream from the freezer. 'Would you like some?' she asked kindly. 'It always makes Aurora 'appy.'

'No, thanks,' replied Laura, wiping her nose.

James gave her a gentle shake. 'Right, chin up!' he ordered. 'It's Aurora's birthday in about an hour and we must not ruin it for her.'

Laura raised herself to her full height, her eyes flashing. '*Aurora, Aurora, Aurora!*' she spat, turning on him. 'It's like she's the only one you care about, James. I'm sick of it.'

'Hey now,' he said angrily. 'You're out of order.'

'It's true,' she continued, her eyes filling with tears. 'Since she's come into our life, it's all about her.'

Maggie watched this exchange with a frown. She could see why the girl was upset. Her whole life had changed in five minutes. Teenagers were a lot harder to please than children; she remembered her niece Susan and her shouty ways. Aurora was still a child and would adapt quite easily to the new situation. Laura, however, lived in a world where she was at the centre, surrounded by her friends, her school and her social life. Any slight shift in this was seen as a threat. Staring at the young girl's tear-stained face, Maggie felt sorry for her.

'Come on, my lovely,' she soothed. 'It will all be okay, it will.'

'Laura,' said James gently. 'Cut it out. You're upset over nothing. I just want to look out for her, that's all. She's not replacing you. Not in the slightest.' He pulled her close. 'You're my little Lolly. Remember? You're my baby sister and always will be.'

'Lolly?' echoed Maggie with a smile.

'Will called her that – still does,' explained James, grinning.

Laura sniffed, slightly mollified.

'It's just that Aurora needs me,' he continued. 'She's isolated and alone. She needs rescuing like Bilbo.'

'The bloody dog?' She stared at him incredulously. 'You're unbelievable!'

'Come on, let's help her celebrate her birthday,' he cajoled. 'She's only a kid.'

'Oh, all right,' she conceded. 'But remember, I'm never moving here, yeah? I'd move into your hellhole of a flat first.'

Sebastian banged the door of the library with a crash. Striding over to the decanter of scotch, he filled a glass with a trembling hand. George entered the room and closed it quietly.

'*The bloody fool!*' hissed Sebastian in fury. 'I sometimes wonder if he's all right in the head.'

George took a seat by the rows and rows of first editions. He rested his chin on his hand and stared at his brother speculatively.

'We've been here before,' he said in his soft voice. 'Remember the last time?'

'Do I what!'

'Well, it worked out quite fortuitously in the end,' he continued, pulling a loose thread from the upholstery of his chair.

'I don't think there's a chance of Gloria dying in childbirth,' scoffed Sebastian. 'The old bird is past all of that.' He knocked back his drink and wiped his lip. 'What I don't understand is how a man of his age could be so reckless. I bet you a thousand pounds he didn't force her to sign a pre-nup.'

George said nothing.

'Which means that she and her army of brats may be entitled to our fortune.'

'Perhaps.'

Sebastian banged his fist on the mahogany table. 'We should have cornered him months ago and stopped it. We should have knocked sense into his head long ago.'

'Hindsight is a great thing,' mused George. 'Look, Seb, there are ways and means. We need to ascertain what Gloria wants and go from there.'

'I think that's a *fait accompli,*' replied Sebastian bitterly. 'Someone like her is only out for one thing: our inheritance.'

'Well, I'll get some legal advice next week,' decided George, tapping his fingers on the armrest. 'If she's indeed after our money, it won't be a walk in the park.'

Aurora was sitting on Gordon's knee on an armchair by the fire. giggling as he tickled her.

'So, how old will you be after the clock strikes twelve?' he asked. 'Forty? Forty-two?'

'No, silly, I'll be ten.' She rested her head on his shoulder. 'I'll be so old,' she sighed.

'So, are you going to give us a blast of that glorious voice of yours?' he boomed. 'Henry, tell your daughter to sing us a song.'

Henry looked at his watch. 'We do have some time before the countdown,' he observed. 'Aurora, darling, would you like to sing something?'

She shrugged. 'I suppose so.'

James and a tear-stained Laura reappeared at that moment.

'What did we miss?' James asked the group, positioning Laura at the table.

'Nothing,' announced William loudly, hiccupping slightly. 'Tweedledum and Tweedledee left the company about ten minutes ago.'

Henry and Gordon were laughing loudly and didn't hear him. Helena, however, had been listening intently and a ghost of a smile appeared on her lips.

'And that Camilla,' continued William.

'Cressida,' corrected Laura, grinning.

'She went to bed with a headache.' He smoothed his hair off his forehead and tried to look alert. He'd had the most of a bottle of wine and was desperately trying to conceal it.

'Someone get Maggie,' suggested Aurora. 'She must be exhausted and she wants to ring in the New Year with us.'

'I'll call her now,' said Henry, shuffling over to the door. His bad leg combined with cognac had rendered him quite unsteady and he held onto the door frame for support. '*Maggie!*' he called. '*Come and have a drink!*'

'This is my chance to convince her to desert,' Gordon guffawed. 'I'll offer her a huge pay rise. She might just do it. *Desert* Henry so I can have her *dessert*!' He laughed uproariously at his own joke.

William paused and processed the pun. 'That's bloody brilliant!' he exclaimed. 'Gordon, you're a genius.'

James glared at his younger brother who was clearly

plastered. Luckily, the remainder of the group were staring at Aurora who was standing under her mother's portrait. She curtsied and held her head up.

'I'm going to sing a song from my new CD,' she declared. 'I love it because it's a little girl who sings it. Her name is Cosette and she is all alone in the world.'

Gloria put her hand to her mouth. She knew instantly what Aurora was planning to sing: 'Castle on a Cloud' from *Les Misérables*. It suited her perfectly with her cloudy dark hair and clear voice. The fact that she was motherless only added to it. Cosette, the little abandoned girl from Victor Hugo's famous novel, dreamed of having a mother and was isolated and alone.

Maggie ambled in, her small frame slightly hunched. Her back always gave her trouble in winter and she had been on her feet all day. James jumped up from his chair immediately and offered it to her.

'Thanking you, Master James,' she said gratefully.

Henry stood by the fire and gestured for his daughter to begin. There were only twenty minutes or so remaining before midnight. He wanted everyone to be in position with a glass of Dom Perignon, ready to toast the beginning of a new year. Not to mind his darling girl's tenth birthday. Her cake was waiting on the sideboard, the ten candles ready to be lit.

Aurora closed her eyes and began to sing, the candlelight flickering on her enraptured face. There wasn't a sound in the room.

Gordon closed his eyes and swayed to the music. '*Wonderful!*' he shouted and Helena put her finger to her lips.

James stared at her in wonder, again jolted at how good she was. It was like the young innocent girl was replaced with an accomplished performer. And she was truly happy when she was singing; he could tell that from a mile away.

Laura tried to focus on Aurora but instead her mind began to wander. What the hell was Gloria planning to do? How could she have married Henry without consulting her children? It was rash and unfair; she had betrayed them all. Her expression darkened. Her dad would not be pleased. Her darling, darling dad. Oh, how she missed him!

William rested his head on the table and closed his eyes. Aurora's voice had a soothing effect and he was suddenly so tired. Unused to large amounts of alcohol, he began to drift off. Images floated into his mind: the cave, James and his camera and then Ella. She was standing on the beach, smoking a cigarette. She blew a smoke ring in his face and winked. He smiled in his sleep.

Gloria felt a lump form in her throat. She didn't know if it was the song or the fact that Aurora was standing under her mother's picture, but she felt very maudlin indeed. Henry seemed unaffected; he was just staring in delight at his daughter as she sang.

James was feeling just as moved. He couldn't put his finger on it but Aurora pulled on his heart strings. He felt so sorry for her. It was unnatural for a little girl to grow up without a mother. The fact that it was the tenth anniversary of her death only added to the atmosphere.

The song came to an end and Laura shivered. She could not wait to go home. Back to normality, back to reality. She felt like a heroine from a ghost story. Any minute now and she expected Grace herself to make an appearance.

Maggie clapped loudly. '*Bravo, my lovely!*' she cried, her eyes shining with tears.

Henry held out his hand. 'Wonderful, my darling. Now come here and we'll serve the champagne. Where are the boys?'

'Oh, we're right here,' came a voice from the shadows. 'We wanted some coffee but it appears the hired help is part of the family now.'

George walked into the light, followed by Sebastian.

Maggie pulled herself up, her cheeks hot with mortification. 'So sorry, Mr. George. I'll get some right away, I will.'

James' eyes flashed. 'You will not!' he fumed. 'You have been slaving all day. I suggest that if you two would like a coffee, then go and get it yourselves.'

George started in surprise. 'What's the meaning of this?' he said to Henry.

'This is the upstart I was telling you about,' sneered Sebastian, pointing to James. 'He was frightfully rude when Cressida and I called at Christmas.' He narrowed his blue eyes and raised his head haughtily.

'With just cause,' retorted James, his eyes flashing. 'You were just as awful then.'

'James!' squeaked Gloria, pulling his sleeve. 'Enough!'

Henry went to stand by James' side. He realised that his sons could be difficult, but this was blatant rudeness. 'He's quite right. Maggie has done more than enough.'

George scowled and turned on his heel. Sebastian followed and banged the door behind him.

Aurora's eyes widened. She had never seen her father stand up to them before. All through the years, he had given in to their cantankerous behaviour. Her mild-mannered father preferred to bury his head in a book rather than confront them. She had just accepted it as normal; any nastiness she had experienced had gone unchecked and so she had thick skin.

Tonight she had a seen a new side to her father. Perhaps Gloria was having a positive influence on him. George and Seb treated Maggie terribly and he had defended her.

Her heart felt full as she regarded her silver-haired father sipping his champagne. Tonight was a new beginning in so many ways. This old house would be full again and Maggie could make drop scones for William and Laura every day. Perhaps Henry would allow her to go the local school with her new brother and sister. No more fussy old tutor. Laura loved watching soaps on the television – maybe they would buy one for the drawing room? A bright future beckoned: one filled with Nutella, family dinners, *EastEnders* and grown-up conversation.

'*Ten seconds!*' shouted Gordon, counting down loudly. '*Nine ... eight ...*'

Everyone got to their feet, except for William who was snoring.

'*Seven ... six ...*'

James grasped Aurora's hand and squeezed it.

'*Five ... four ...*'

Gloria put her arms around Henry's waist.

'*Three ... two ...*'

Laura nudged a dozing William. 'Get up, numbskull!' she whispered.

'*One! Happy New Year!*' Gordon kissed Helena and hugged her fiercely.

James whirled Aurora around and around. '*Happy birthday, Borealis!*'

Laura kissed her mother coldly and shook Henry's hand. She was not giving an inch until everything was sorted. A big conversation was looming and she had her argument all planned out. If Gloria thought that she had any intention of moving down here, then she was barmy.

William yawned and stretched. His mouth felt like sandpaper. For a moment he was disorientated, focusing in on Gordon's face and feeling confused. Then the events of the evening came back to him and he accepted a flute of champagne from Henry.

'Hair of the dog!' he mouthed to Laura, grinning.

'Happy birthday to my darling girl!' announced Henry, pulling Aurora close. He kissed her forehead tenderly and smiled. 'Your mother would be so proud of you,' he whispered.

The little girl beamed back at him. Gloria watched their little exchange. Maggie had mentioned earlier how Henry found this night hard, how the reminder of Grace's death rendered him gloomy and melancholy. Looking at his smiling face, she felt her heart soar. He looked genuinely happy and hopeful. She liked to think that she had given him that.

Maggie lit the candles on the enormous cake and beckoned for Aurora to come close.

'Blow 'em out, little un,' she said, taking Aurora's hand. 'Make a big wish.'

'I wish Freddie were here,' reflected Aurora. 'It's such a pity that he couldn't come.'

Maggie rubbed her arm. 'You'll see Fred tomorrow, little 'un. 'Ee 'as a lovely gift for you, 'ee does.'

James' phone started to ring and he glanced at the screen. It was Rosie, ringing from Norfolk. 'Hey, Rose,' he said joyfully, walking out of the room. 'Happy New Year!'

William nudged Laura. 'Jeez, Lolly, cheer up. You look like you want to murder us all.'

Laura scowled and didn't respond. She couldn't understand why William was so bloody calm about the whole fiasco. Probably because he was sixteen and only had a couple of years left. She had been worried about falling asleep in that awful room; now she *knew* she wouldn't sleep. Fear and panic threatened to engulf her. Plus that wind outside was causing the windows to rattle. She shuddered.

*Over my dead body am I moving here.*

George inhaled his Gauloise deeply and exhaled slowly, the cloudy smoke dissipating in the cool night air. He was sitting in the large gazebo in the garden, enjoying his second consecutive cigarette.

Henry's actions had surprised him, he couldn't deny it. George had always been more adept at hiding his feelings than Seb. His younger brother let his temper take hold and was prone to dramatic outbursts. No, he was the opposite. He thought things through; he planned his actions with precision and intelligence. Their father's unsuitable marriage would have to be dissolved. It was only a matter of time before the gloss would wear off. It was inevitable. No one could stand that cheap perfume and twangy accent for any length of time.

They had faced the same problem that time he had married Grace. He could still remember the utter shock when Henry had presented his new bride. She had only been a few years older than him at the time. He and Seb had cornered their father and ordered him to sign over their mother's fortune to them and them only. They didn't see why Grace's brat should be entitled to any of Marcella's legacy. Henry had agreed but had refused point blank to make them executors of his will. Aurora would inherit his own fortune, along with his sons. He had been quite clear about that.

He and Sebastian had sought legal advice after Grace's death. They needed to check if she had family and whether they would be knocking on their door looking for a share someday. Their solicitor had assured them that there was no risk of that. Only if Henry died and left guardianship of Aurora to a sibling of Grace or indeed, her parents.

Paranoia had taken hold and he had set about finding out all that he could about Aurora's mother. Grace Molloy, as she had been known, was difficult to trace. There was no birth record available – only evidence of an adoption in 1968, when she was documented as being six months old. A couple named Molloy, of a place called Westport, had raised her as they had no children of their own. George, gratified that there were no siblings, was also delighted to see that Mr. Jack Molloy was a doctor. There was less and less of a chance of any underhand behaviour. Further investigation revealed that both Jack and his wife, Maureen, had died of cancer within six months of each other in 1988, rendering Grace an orphan. It also revealed that Jack, although a kind man, had been a chronic alcoholic and had been bankrupt at the time of his death. This had explained everything to George. That was the reason Grace had pounced on their father; she had been on the make from the beginning. After months of research, he had closed the case. Aurora's Irish roots were of no threat to the Sinclair fortune.

Marcella's nest-egg, which he and Seb had secured as their own, lay untouched in a bank in London. He needed to check if her money was safe, now that his father had married again. Would those awful Dixon children be entitled to a share?

He blew a perfect smoke ring which was destroyed almost instantly by the cold wind.

Cressida had signed a pre-nup. There had been no argument. She had never caused any problems.

Gloria Dixon was another story. She could make things very difficult indeed.

# Chapter Twelve

Laura entered the kitchen the next morning with shadows under her eyes. As expected, she had tossed and turned all night. A combination of the ghostly atmosphere in her dark bedroom and the whistling wind outside only added to her unrest. As dawn broke, she had her argument all laid out in her head. Aurora and Henry would have to move to London. It was the logical move. They had far less to give up.

James was drinking coffee and laughing loudly with Maggie. She took a seat at the head of the table and took an apple from the fruit bowl.

'Can I make you a 'ot breakfast?' offered Maggie, gesturing to the Aga. 'I 'ave fresh eggs from Conny's farm, I do.'

Laura shook her head politely. 'An apple will do just fine.'

'Did you sleep well?' asked James, observing the shadows under her eyes and her tousled hair.

'No.'

Maggie, sensing tension, got to her feet. 'I'll just set the fire in the drawing room,' she informed them, leaving the room.

'Laura!' chided James. 'You've got to let this go. Wait until you hear what they've planned.'

'*No!*' She banged the table with her fist. 'It's out of order, James. She could have at least consulted us. I'm so angry.'

'I said to wait,' he repeated. 'Don't jump in head first.'

William appeared through the side door, rubbing his head. 'Keep the noise down,' he groaned. 'My head feels like it's about to break.'

'Well, you went on a serious bender last night,' said James matter-of-factly. 'I'm not surprised.' He got to his feet and filled a glass with some cool water. 'Get this down you,' he advised, handing the liquid to his brother. 'I'll ask Maggie for some painkillers when she comes back.'

'It was a good night, yeah?' William frowned. 'I can remember some of it at least.'

'Well, you sang "Auld Lang Syne" over and over again with Gordon,' Laura informed him, grinning. 'You kept calling him "uncle" and slapping him on the back. Thank God he was just as pissed as you.' She smiled, momentarily snapped out of her dour mood.

'He's a right laugh,' agreed William. 'I'm pretty sure he let me finish his brandy at some stage.'

'Looks like you mixed every drink available,' said James laughing. 'That'll teach you.'

'Now that we're all here,' began Laura seriously. 'I think we need to have a family meeting pronto. Has anyone seen Gloria today?'

William shook his head. 'I'm only up myself. At the rate she was downing champagne, my guess is she's still asleep.'

'Well, she needs to know what's what,' Laura declared firmly. 'We need to stand together, yeah? We need to veto any plans to move to this place right away.'

The door opened and a breathless Aurora arrived with Freddie trailing behind her.

'Morning,' she greeted them, her cheeks pink. 'I would like

you all to meet my best friend, Freddie Thompson.'

James held out his hand immediately. 'Good to meet you,' he said, smiling warmly. 'I've heard a lot about you.'

Freddie had a guarded look as he shook his hand. Aurora had to practically drag him to the house. He had tried every excuse in the book not to come. He just didn't want to meet these people. They were everything that he wasn't. He just couldn't compete.

'We should all get to know one another as we'll be living so close,' continued Aurora, sitting on a chair near William.

'Over my dead body,' muttered Laura with a dark expression.

'Hi,' said William, with a half-hearted wave. 'Overdid it on the booze last night, Freddie, so excuse my deathly state.'

Freddie grinned and softened slightly. 'You look pretty sick, you do,' he agreed.

James pointed to an empty chair. 'Take a seat,' he suggested. 'I'll make some tea or would you prefer a juice?'

Freddie shook his head. 'I just 'ad my breakfast.'

'Oh, have some orange juice or something.' Aurora raised her eyes to heaven. 'Let's be sociable.'

Freddie shrugged. 'Okay, then.' He sat down and brushed his sandy hair out of his eyes. James looked just as Aurora had described. He seemed pretty friendly too. William had his head on his arm and looked green. Freddie smiled to himself. He had seen Susan look just as bad after a mad night down the pub. The girl looked sullen, her blue eyes narrowed. There was tension in the air, there was no denying it.

'So, Mr. Henry and your mother are married,' stated Freddie frankly, accepting a glass of juice from James.

Aurora clapped her hands in delight. 'We're a big family now!'

Laura snorted. 'Calm down, for goodness' sake. We're no such thing. You can't just wave a magic wand and expect everything to be hunky dory.'

'Oh.' Aurora looked deflated. 'I just thought that ...'

'Laura!' James glared at her. 'Stop that at once.'

'Why?' She rounded on him fiercely. 'Little princess here thinks that we'll be moving to Cornwall. Not on your nelly.'

'Laura ...' His tone was dangerous.

'No! Stop protecting her, James. I'm sick of it. She's not some stray dog you picked up. She's well able to listen to the truth.'

'The truth?' Aurora's beautiful face looked worried. 'What truth?'

Freddie cleared his throat. 'I'd better be going,' he said awkwardly, getting to his feet. 'Maybe I'll see you again before you 'ead back up the country.'

'Don't go!' pleaded Aurora, looking around wildly. 'There's been a misunderstanding, that's all.'

'I'll call later, Sinclair.' Freddie was firm. The blonde girl looked mightily cross about something and he didn't want to be present when it all kicked off. Maybe the picture of the perfect family that Aurora had been painting was not so perfect after all.

'*Adios*, Freddie.' William gave him a thumbs-up. 'Get out while you're still alive.'

The door banged but Laura didn't notice.

'Aurora,' she said, turning to her, 'there is no way that I'm moving here, okay? My life is in London. You and your dad had better talk about this because I'm not changing my mind.'

'*Laura, for fuck's sake!*' James banged his fist on the table. 'You're thirteen. You're not in a position to make a decision like this.' He turned to Aurora and lowered his voice. 'Don't listen to her, Borealis. We must wait until Henry and Mum come down and tell us their plans.'

'What do you mean, plans?'

'You know, what they plan to do now that they're married.'

'I don't understand.' Her big eyes filled with tears. 'You'll all move here. It's a much bigger house and Maggie is here. I mean, Maggie looks after us.'

'*Shhh*,' soothed James, pulling her close. 'Don't give it a second thought. Everything will be okay.'

Laura flounced out of the room. How dared they act like it wasn't the biggest thing in the world? There was only one way to sort it out.

She climbed the stairs, two at a time, and marched straight up to Henry's bedroom door. Her face set in a determined line, she knocked three times.

'Yes?' came her mother's sleepy voice.

'Please come to the kitchen, Gloria,' she ordered. 'We need to have a meeting.'

There was a slight sound of shuffling and then footsteps. The door opened to reveal a scantily clad Gloria with dark smudges under her eyes and hair that was neither up nor down.

'Whatever's the matter?' she asked sternly. 'How dare you order me downstairs?'

Laura's eyes filled with frustrated tears. 'How dare *you* get married without telling us! How dare *you* throw our lives upside down without a second thought.'

'What?' Gloria stepped outside the bedroom and closed the door behind her. 'Explain yourself. I thought that you'd be happy for me, Laura. I've found joy again. I never thought that it would happen after your father died.'

'I don't want to move here,' sobbed Laura, falling into her arms. 'I hate it here. It's cold and dark and damp. I don't like the caves and I'm sure this place is haunted. I want to stay in London, Mum. Please don't take me away from everything that I know!'

Gloria rubbed her hair and kissed her forehead. 'We won't be moving here, darling. Not at all. Henry had agreed to move to our place. We're going to build an extension. That way he'll have an office to work from and a few extra bedrooms.'

'Say again?' Laura sniffed.

'Henry and Aurora will be living with us,' she reiterated

gently. 'He's planning to move in the next few weeks. Christmas was a trial run. When he saw how happy Aurora was with you and your friends, it sealed the deal.'

'Aurora thinks that we're all moving here.'

'*Hmm*, I know.' Her mother looked vexed. 'We're gearing up to tell her, to be honest. She's very attached to Maggie. One thing at a time.'

'Will Maggie not come too?'

'No, sweetheart. She's close to retirement and she would hate the city. We'll board up the house and she can continue to live in the cottage by the gate.'

'Oh.' Laura rubbed her eyes. 'I'm sorry for shouting.'

'It's understandable.' Gloria's expression softened. 'I know how self-obsessed teenagers can be.'

'Hey!' Laura tried and failed to look affronted.

'Now, go downstairs and I'll be down in a while.'

Aurora eyed her warily when she re-entered the kitchen.

'Where did you go?' she asked immediately.

Laura shrugged. 'Nowhere.'

William let out a sigh. 'Bloody hell, James. I need those pills off Maggie. Please find her, yeah?'

Aurora got up. 'I know where she is. I'll go.' She headed off in the direction of the drawing room and closed the door behind her.

'Mum has no intention of moving here!' declared Laura triumphantly. 'I totally overreacted. This day has just got so much better.'

'Keep your voice down,' warned James sharply. 'Aurora will be upset about moving away. Maggie is like a mother to her.'

'She'll be far better off,' rubbished Laura. 'I mean, look at this place.' She screwed up her nose. 'We'll be doing her a favour.'

'Laura!'

William took a sip of water. 'How will we all fit?'

'They're building an extension!' Laura clapped her hands in excitement. 'I may get a new bedroom, if I play my cards right. Aurora could move into my old one.'

James gave her a warning look. 'I said to cut it out!' he said. 'This should not be discussed until Mum and Henry tell us officially.'

'Fine, fine,' his sister replied. 'I'll keep my immeasurable joy to myself for the moment.' She punched the air. 'Get in! We're going home.'

George woke up to a loud knock on his door.

'Wake up, son!' came Henry's voice. 'Family meeting in the drawing room in ten minutes.'

George groaned. He had no intention of meeting that family again. Whatever could his father want?

He debated whether to get dressed but then decided not to bother. His robe would do quite nicely; plus, he planned on going back to bed after hearing whatever his hare-brained father had to say. No doubt it would be something else that would annoy him.

He eyed the half-empty goblet of whiskey on his bedside locker. He must have fallen asleep before he had finished it.

*You're slipping, old boy.*

Sebastian knocked on his door. 'George! Are you coming?'

'I'm on my way.'

When George entered the drawing room, Gloria was sitting in his mother's favourite chair. His face tightened immediately. Marcella was worth ten of this interloper. He just couldn't fathom what his father saw in her.

Henry was standing regally at the fireplace. 'Now that George is here, we'll get started.'

The whole family was seated, waiting expectantly. Aurora sat next to James on the sofa, her small hand in his. William was perched on the armrest with Laura on his right. Sebastian and Cressida were sitting rigidly on an antique two-seater.

'Last night was a shock for you all,' Henry began, smiling at Gloria. 'But we are blissfully happy and we hope that you will be too.'

George snorted and stared out of the window. Aurora blew a kiss at her father, clearly delighted that he was so happy. James had a pain in his chest. He could sense that she was about to get a real shock. In the long run, he could see that it was the better option: she would have lots of friends her own age, central heating and a hectic social life. She would attend a proper school and have a normal upbringing.

'The thing is, now that we are man and wife, there is the question of where we are going to live.'

Laura nudged William smugly. She knew what was coming next. She was so glad that she had cornered Gloria earlier. Otherwise, she would have been on tenterhooks.

'We are going to live in London,' continued Gloria. 'Henry and Aurora are going to move into our house and we will be a family.'

'London?' breathed Aurora, going pale. 'What did you say?'

'London?' repeated Sebastian in disbelief. 'But you hate the city.'

'London?' said George silkily. 'Whatever will happen to *our* house?'

'Yes, London,' affirmed Henry, taking Gloria's hand. 'We plan to extend her house to accommodate the extra people. I think it will be a new start for us both.' He winked at Aurora.

'Us both?' she echoed. 'But what about Maggie? She'll be coming too.'

Henry glanced at Gloria. 'Well, actually no, darling. Maggie was planning to retire and it would be too much of an upheaval for her.'

'*What?*' The little girl put her hand to her mouth. *Surely not.*

*Surely they wouldn't separate her from Maggie.*

'She would hate city life,' he pressed on. 'It's best that she stays here.'

'Forget about the maid, what about our house?' asked George in annoyance.

'But I can't leave her,' Aurora gasped, her eyes filling with tears. 'She's old now. Who will look after her?' A new realisation dawned. 'Oh, what about Freddie? I forgot about him. He's my best friend, Daddy. I can't just leave.' She got to her feet and clutched her hair, the panic rising up within her in waves. '*I won't go. I won't go!*' She began to scream at the top of her lungs.

James put his arm around her small shoulders. 'Hey, Borealis, you can visit. It's not forever. This is for the best.' He rubbed her hair soothingly. 'Don't be upset, please.'

'*I can't leave. I can't leave!*' She was openly crying now, big tears streaming down her face.

Henry looked on helplessly. He hadn't realised the impact this information would have. Gloria had said that children were adaptable. He had expected her to be slightly upset, yes, but certainly not this outburst.

James picked her up easily in his arms. 'I'm taking her to the kitchen,' he declared grimly as she showed no sign of calming down.

The door banged shut.

George turned to Henry. '*Now, what about our house*?' His roar reverberated around the room. 'How dare you seat your sons here amongst these people without warning? There are legalities and a certain protocol. I'm fed up of your childish whims and ridiculous behaviour. Are you planning to sell, is that it? Sell up and split the money between your gold-digger of a wife and her army of brats?'

There was a shocked silence. Sebastian stood up and joined his brother. The battle lines had been drawn. They stared at their father mutinously.

'Boys, we can discuss this later,' began Henry, flustered. 'Please don't raise your voices in front of the children.'

'We will discuss this now,' corrected George. 'Gloria should know what's what. She will not be entitled to any of our mother's estate in the event of your death. We need to be clear about this.'

'Nor will she have a claim to this house,' added Sebastian nastily. 'I think it's high time you signed it over to us. Go and play happy families in suburbia for all I care, but leave the Sinclair heritage to true Sinclairs.'

Henry ran his fingers through his hair, clearly mortified.

Laura, incensed at the 'gold-digger' comment, sprang out of her chair.

'*You two are just hateful!*' she shouted, her cheeks red with rage. '*How dare you insinuate that my mother is after Henry's money? We're quite well off ourselves and we certainly don't want a stake in this dump!*'

William pulled her back. 'Chill, Laura. Stay out of it.'

'I will *not!*' she fumed, her eyes flashing. 'These two are completely out of order, Will.'

'Enough, Laura,' said Gloria calmly. 'I'll handle this.' She stood up and straightened her blouse. Her blue eyes narrowed and she raised her chin. 'I appreciate your concerns, George and Sebastian. It has all been noted. I am one hundred per cent behind a legal document being drawn up safeguarding your inheritance.'

George looked at his brother in confusion.

'I married your father because I love him,' she continued. 'Not for his house and certainly not for his money. There will be no biological children between us so you're quite safe, I'd expect. There will be no claim from our side when the time comes.'

Cressida watched the older woman with wide eyes. Her voice remained steady and she exuded serenity. It was the perfect antidote to the outburst minutes earlier.

'This had been a huge shock for you, but you must realise that your father is a grown man and may behave how he pleases. Marrying a "gold-digger" may seem utterly abhorrent to you but he's entitled to do that if he so wishes. But it's fortunate that that is not the case.' She stared at them coldly. 'Now, if you'll excuse me, I want to pack my things. We have outstayed our welcome.'

'Gloria!' protested Henry, flummoxed. 'Please don't leave. I want them to leave instead.'

She shook her head. 'No, Henry. We have done what we came to do. It's time for a new beginning.' She turned to Laura and William. 'Pack up your things, kids. We are leaving in an hour.'

Laura couldn't mask her glee. William pulled himself up with supreme effort. He just wanted to go back to bed. This was officially his first hangover. Stuart Barnes at school had experienced three in his lifetime. His description in the school canteen had been inaccurate, by all accounts. It felt like absolute hell.

George and Sebastian watched Gloria's back as she exited the drawing room. They glanced at each other and self-satisfied smiles played on their lips. Who would have thought that the old bird would be quite so malleable? The fight they had expected had not come to fruition. Sebastian winked at his older brother and smirked.

Henry stalked out the other door and slammed it loudly. Climbing the stairs, he barged into his room to find Gloria folding her dress from the night before.

'I'm ever so sorry,' he apologised, hanging his head. 'There's no excuse at all.'

She held out her arms. 'Come here,' she requested, smiling. 'Money doesn't matter. All I want is you, do you understand? They're naturally worried as I'm a threat to them. Let's just move on.'

He buried his head in her shoulder. 'You're the light of my life,' he murmured. 'Thank you for saving me.'

# Chapter Thirteen

Aurora drew a moon shape in the wet sand with a stick. The water was grey and churning and the easterly wind whipping past them made their ears sting with the cold. James was sitting on the sand next to her in silence. He knew that she was desperately trying to process the news.

'I guess it won't be so bad,' she said softly, a big fat tear rolling down her cheek. 'I'm supposed to go to boarding school next year anyway.'

'Boarding school?' James started. 'Are you serious? He'll hardly send you now.'

'Oh, he will,' she said sadly. 'He put my name down when I was born.' She sighed glumly. 'Maybe it will be fun. Maybe I'll be like Harry Potter and put into a cool common room.'

James stared at the sea for a moment. He would have to nip that in the bud right away. Was Henry completely bonkers? He was planning to send away a small girl to school after her lonely childhood. Laura went to the local Catholic school; it wasn't a posh private boarding school, but it had a great reputation. He could see Aurora fitting in quite nicely. She could join the hockey team and perform in the Christmas play.

'I'll have a chat to him,' he announced determinedly. 'Everything has changed now, Borealis. He's not the only one who'll have to adapt.' Noticing her gloomy countenance, he nudged her playfully. 'Let's think of all the good things about you becoming a city slicker.'

Aurora sighed. 'I can't think.'

'Right – you'll have a TV in the sitting room for a start.'

'I suppose.'

'You'll have a sister.'

Aurora made a face. 'She's very bossy.'

'Yes,' agreed James, laughing, 'but she has a heart of gold. Her outburst earlier wasn't directed at you, Borealis. Underneath all that grown-up exterior, Laura is only a child.'

Aurora said nothing.

'You'll have lots of friends your own age and weekly shopping trips into town.'

'I've no money,' she said dolefully.

'Then earn it,' he suggested, tickling her. 'Earn some pocket money. Do some chores around the house.'

'Chores?' she repeated. 'Whatever do you mean?'

'Sort the laundry and empty the dishwasher, that sort of thing.'

'Dishwasher?'

'We have a machine that washes dishes,' he said with a laugh. 'Not a Maggie, like you.'

'Oh, I remember seeing it at Christmas time!'

'So, there you are, Princess Aurora. Earn some money and then blow it all in the shops like other teenagers.'

'I'm only ten.'

He made a face. 'You're being impossible. Now, cheer up. There's far worse going on in the world.'

She sighed. 'I suppose.'

'No more moping. We should go back. The others will be

worried.' He stood up and brushed the sand from his trousers. 'Race you to the cliff.'

'Okay,' she conceded, getting to her feet. 'I'd like to go somewhere first. Will you come with me?'

'If you like.' James frowned. 'Are you going to tell me where?'

She shook her head sadly. 'Just follow me.'

The gravestone was large and imposing, made of white marble with pillars on the sides. It stood amongst generations of Sinclair ancestors in the small graveyard adjacent to the chapel on the grounds of the estate. Carved into its face were the words:

*Grace Molloy Sinclair*

*1968-1993*

*Requiescat In Pace*

Aurora knelt down and pulled some stray blades of grass from the base of the stone. They marred its pristine appearance, making it seem unkempt with their sporadic clusters. She threw them to the side and they scattered in the lively breeze. The tiny pebbles strewn on the ground were white like the headstone and they hurt her knees as she knelt down. Maggie always warned her not to stand on the actual grave as she claimed that it was disrespectful. Aurora didn't agree. This was her mother; she knew in her heart that she wouldn't mind.

She traced Grace's name with her forefinger and then she reached out and rubbed the marble lovingly.

'Aurora Grace – that's my name, you know,' she said.

'It's beautiful,' said James. 'Truly beautiful. Suits you.'

She smiled at him and pointed to a blood-red rose by the headstone. 'See that rose? Daddy leaves it every year. She loved roses. Maggie told me.'

Henry had once told her that he had given Grace a dozen red roses after every performance until she agreed to have dinner with him. The rose was a symbol of love and beauty and he felt it was the perfect floral representation of her mother.

James put his hand on her shoulder. 'Why did you bring me here, Borealis?' he asked softly, his dark eyes filled with compassion.

Aurora sighed. 'She died on my birthday. I always visit her on New Year's Day.'

'Of course,' he said hurriedly, kicking himself. 'How crass of me. I didn't think.'

He stood back and let Aurora have a moment. Her long hair flowed down her back and her small frame was hunched as she knelt there. There was complete silence in the little enclosure. The only sound was the whistling wind as it whipped past them.

She wrapped her arms around her waist protectively. 'I suppose I wanted to tell her that I'll be moving away. I wanted to say that I won't be gone forever. That I'll come back and visit as much as I can.'

'I'm sure she knows,' he comforted. 'She knows everything that you do, I'm sure of it.'

'Daddy never speaks of her. I don't know anything about her.'

He rubbed her shoulder. 'It's probably painful for him.'

'But I want to know what she was like. I have no memories.'

'Maybe when you're older you'll find out more.'

'Will you bring me back here?' she pleaded, turning to face him. 'I can't come by myself. Will you bring me back?' Her brown eyes filled with tears. 'I don't want to forget, James. I don't want to forget.'

She started to cry and he pulled her close, rubbing her hair rhythmically.

'Of course I will,' he murmured. 'Anything you want, anything you want.'

Aurora let him hold her and closed her eyes. Everything she knew was about to change. Soon she would be living in a new house and have new friends. Her father was happy; anyone could see that. She was glad that he had found Gloria. She was perfect for him. It was just so hard to leave her home; it was the only link she had with her mother.

Pulling herself together, she rubbed her eyes and sat up straight. James looked at her in concern. Her pale cheeks were blotched with red and her nose was streaming.

'We should go back,' she said in an unsteady voice. 'Maggie will have tea ready.' Her heart felt heavy as she twisted her body around to stand up. She glanced at her mother's headstone again and made a silent promise. She would never be too far away; she would never abandon her.

He held out his hand. 'Come on then. I want at least two helpings of pie before I have to drive to London.'

She grasped his hand tightly and they walked away, her hair blowing in the breeze.

Maggie sat at the kitchen table, lost in memories. Henry had called her up to the drawing room to relate the news of their departure. She had been expecting something like this to happen, but it had still knocked her for six.

She remembered holding Aurora in her arms when she was a tiny baby. She would nuzzle into her breast, searching for milk and Maggie would chuckle. 'I don't 'ave no milk, little 'un,' she would say, holding her close. Instead she would fill a bottle of formula and heat it gently on the Aga, singing Cornish folksongs to the squirming baby as they waited.

She remembered Aurora's first steps when the little girl had been around thirteen months. One day she had let go of the kitchen chair and toddled unsteadily over to the dog's basket by the back door. Maggie had clapped loudly, singing her praises, and the little girl had beamed and clapped too, delighted with herself. Her dark curls bounced as she grew more adept at walking upright and soon she was up and down the great staircase at speed, causing Maggie's heart to jump.

She had been six years old when she had asked about Grace. Maggie had learned later that Freddie had been talking about his mother, Mary, earlier in the day and Aurora had asked him if Maggie was her mother. 'Oh, no,' he had answered. 'Your mother's dead.'

'What's dead, Maggie?' Aurora had asked later as they were walking through the apple trees on the south side of the estate.

'Do you remember Zeus the dog?' the old lady explained. 'Do you remember 'ee left us and never came back?'

'Yes,' she answered.

'Well, your mother did the same,' finished Maggie. 'She 'ad to go but I know she watches over you.'

'But why did she have to go, Maggie? I don't understand.'

'I don't understand either, my lovely. Sometimes God wants people around 'im. He wanted Grace to sing for 'im, I reckon.'

Aurora had accepted this explanation but there was many a day that Maggie found her sitting beneath her mother's portrait, staring up at the woman she had never met.

The kitchen door slammed and James strode into the room with Aurora in hot pursuit. Maggie wiped the tears from her eyes and stood up, a broad smile plastered on her face. She would have to be strong. She could not let her darling girl see her sadness.

'Hello, Maggie,' said Aurora, her cheeks pink from the wind.

'You look frozen, you do.' She gestured to Aurora to come close for a hug. Pulling the little girl into her arms, she squeezed her tightly. 'Are you 'ungry, little 'un?'

Aurora shook her head. 'I'm fine.'

'Coffee, Master James?' Maggie offered, releasing Aurora from her embrace.

'I'll make it,' he answered cheerfully. 'Sit down and rest your back.'

'You're real kind, you are.' She regarded him fondly. 'After all that walkin' you must be 'ungry. Would you like some pie?'

'You read my mind, Maggie.'

'I'll just get the pie, I will.' She got to her feet and opened the Aga. Using a thick tea towel, she heaved out a large pie. The pastry was golden and the apples had caramelised around the edge of the dish. 'Now, Master James, would you like some with custard?'

James blew her a kiss. 'Absolutely. I've been looking forward to it all morning.'

The Dixons left two hours later. Aurora watched James' Golf disappear down the road with mixed feelings. It didn't feel like the end, it felt like the beginning. Soon she would be part of that family, living in their house and abiding by their rules. She would no longer have free rein of the beach or the cliffs. Instead, she would be surrounded by concrete and traffic. James had winked at her before leaving, whispering that he would convince Henry not to send her away. It didn't matter to her any more. Perhaps boarding school would be the answer. A fresh start: away from everyone else.

She wandered into her father's study to find him ranting on the phone. His desk was as disorganised as ever: papers were thrown in messy piles around his computer and empty coffee cups lined the edge.

'*Good Lord, Gordon, how could you have been so stupid?*' he raged. 'Now it will be plastered all over the papers.'

Aurora sat on the leather chair by the signed print of *Portrait of George Dyer Talking* by Francis Bacon. She didn't really understand the funny-looking person in it, but she liked the pink and purple colours. Her father knew this painter quite well and often talked about him. She remembered telling Freddie about his surname: Bacon. They had laughed and laughed when Freddie had said, 'Imagine if I were called that in my line of work, Sinclair? Freddie Bacon, the pig farmer.'

She watched her father pace the room.

'I don't care how charming she was. All journalists are guttersnipes. Everyone knows that. She bought you a double gin? My word, it doesn't take much to buy you!'

He hung up the phone a minute later, running his fingers through his grey hair in frustration. His blue eyes looked troubled as he resumed his seat by his desk.

'What's the matter, Daddy?' Aurora traced the embroidery on the arm of the chair she was perched on with her finger.

'Your bloody uncle has gone off and told the papers about my marriage.'

'But why?'

'Because he's an idiot.' Henry picked up a random cup and took a sip. Realising that he had consumed cold coffee, he spat it back into the cup in disgust. 'Now the press will be here, asking questions and talking about Grace again. I could kill him.'

'Oh, don't kill Uncle Gordon!' she protested in alarm. 'He brings me sweets and he's funny.'

'Oh, I won't,' said Henry wearily. 'It's just sometimes he can be swayed by a pretty face and a free drink.'

'Daddy,' she began, 'I went to Mother's grave today . . .'

He cut her off absentmindedly. 'Where did I put my ink pen? I was sure I left it on the mantelpiece.' He scratched his head.

'But, Daddy,' she said, 'can you tell me about her? You never speak about her.'

'*Aha!*' he exclaimed triumphantly, finding the pen under a pile of papers. 'Good work, old boy.'

'*Daddy!*'

He stopped in surprise. 'Yes, my darling?'

'Tell me about Mummy.' Her cheeks were flushed and her expression determined.

'What? Why?' He shook his head. 'What do you want to know?'

'What she was like. What her favourite book was or if she could cook.' She shrugged. 'If she had a favourite chocolate bar, perhaps?'

Henry said nothing for a moment. Lots of emotions flitted across his face until eventually he spoke.

'She was bright and funny. She loved going for walks by the sea. She adored Romantic poetry and always said that she would have loved to meet Lord Byron.' He chuckled. 'She couldn't cook at all, not even an egg. Thank God we had Maggie.'

Aurora's face was enraptured. 'Maggie gave me this for my birthday. She feels that I'm responsible enough now. She says Mummy wore this necklace all the time.' She pulled out the silver pendant from under her blouse. 'Did you give it to her, Daddy?'

He shook his head. 'She had that when I met her. I gave her pearls and diamonds but she always insisted on wearing that.' His face became sad. 'She never told me why – it must have meant a great deal to her.'

'I love it,' said Aurora, fingering the flower pendant. 'Maybe her mummy gave it to her. Or perhaps her daddy.'

'Perhaps.'

Maggie appeared in the doorway. 'Master Seb and Master George have left, sir,' she announced. 'I prepared dinner for us three.' Without a word, she gathered the offending cups and threaded the handles through her fingers. That way she could carry three in each hand.

'Wonderful, Maggie,' said Henry gratefully. 'I'm jolly well glad to see the back of them for the moment too. Frightful behaviour all round.'

Aurora said nothing. George and Sebastian always behaved like that. However, this was the first time her father had seen it. Perhaps Gloria had had something to do with it. Yes, maybe she would change him for the better.

'Try not to worry, Daddy,' she soothed, pulling at his

cardigan. 'Your wedding news is wonderful. You know what they say: today's news is tomorrow's fish-and-chips paper.'

Henry smiled and kissed her forehead fondly. 'Now, where did you hear that?'

'Freddie, of course,' she replied. 'He knows things.'

'Is it true, Sinclair?' Freddie's freckled face looked stricken.

Aurora nodded. 'It's true. We're leaving tomorrow.'

They were upstairs, swinging their legs through the gaps in the bannisters.

Conny had mentioned the news the night before at dinner. Freddie had pushed his plate away, having lost interest in his stew. It was like a suspicion was being realised. He had expected this. However, it didn't make it any easier.

'Will you visit?' His voice was barely audible.

Together their legs moved in unison. One pair was pale and slim, the other muddy and sturdy.

'Of course,' she replied. 'I'll have to see Maggie, won't I? It won't be forever, Freddie. As soon as I'm old enough, I'll move back here. Wait and see.'

'What about the 'ouse?'

'Daddy's closing it up.' She sighed. 'My toys were packed away today along with my books and my dolls. They're on the way to London already.'

'Can I visit you, do you think?'

'Of course, silly.' She nudged him playfully. 'Daddy and Gloria are building an extension so there will be plenty of room.'

Suddenly there was a loud knocking on the old front door. It reverberated around the hallway and the children peered down in curiosity.

'I'll get it, Mr. 'Enry,' called Maggie, shuffling towards the main entrance.

'Not at all,' objected Henry, suddenly appearing in the hall.

He pulled open the heavy door and slammed it almost immediately.

Glancing behind him frantically, he hissed to Maggie, 'Where's Aurora?'

'She's upstairs with Freddie,' Maggie informed him, startled. 'Are you all right, sir?'

'I need to go outside. Keep the children indoors.'

He opened the door again and walked out into the cold breeze.

Freddie's eye met Aurora's and they scrambled to their feet.

'George's room will have the best view,' she said breathlessly. 'Let's go in there.'

They rushed into the room and pulled open the drapes that hung by the bay window. They could see Henry gesticulating madly and shaking his fist. A man stood opposite him, with his back to the children. He was wearing a black hat and a grey scarf.

'Who's that?' asked Aurora in wonder. 'Daddy looks furious.'

Freddie shrugged. 'Let's open the window and listen,' he suggested. 'It looks like a big fight.'

He pulled the latch on the heavy glass and tried to heave it open.

'Help me, Sinclair,' he said, pushing with all his might. Aurora tried her best, but to no avail. The window remained fastened shut, its ancient hinges in need of oil.

The man backed away from Henry and started to walk down the driveway, his hands deep in the pockets of his coat.

Henry shouted at him and he turned briefly. His face was tanned and his cheekbones were chiselled. Aurora felt a jolt. He seemed familiar somehow. She didn't know why but she felt like she had seen him before.

Then he turned on his heel and walked off.

'I'd better go,' he said, backing out of the door. 'Looks like a bit of drama in the making.'

Aurora nodded wordlessly. She had never seen her father react like that. She had to know why.

'Daddy! Who was that man?' Aurora stared at her father questioningly, her hands on her hips. 'Why were you so angry?'

Henry walked straight over to the decanter of brandy and poured himself a big glass. He knocked it back in one go and winced as it scalded his throat. Then his hands shook slightly as he filled another.

'Daddy!' Aurora tugged at his sleeve. 'Who was that man? Why were you so cross?'

Henry hung his head. It seemed like ages before he spoke.

'He's an old acquaintance from Oxford,' he said quietly. 'We knew each other years ago – long before you were born.'

'Why did he visit?'

Henry sighed. 'I don't know – I just don't know.' He took his glass and sat down by the fire.

Aurora sat at his feet and rested her head on his knee.

'Don't worry, Daddy. I'll protect you.'

He smiled slightly.

'If he comes back, I'll tell him to leave right away.'

Henry moved forward suddenly and grabbed her small shoulders.

'You are never to talk to that man, do you hear me?' He shook her slightly.

'Stop it, Daddy,' she said, frightened. 'You're hurting me.'

'Promise me, Aurora.' He forced her to look at him. 'Promise me that you'll never speak to him.'

'I promise.'

He released her immediately and resumed his slumped position. 'I think it's time for dinner, my darling,' he said in a defeated one. 'Ask Maggie if we should join her in the kitchen.'

Aurora stood up and kissed his lined cheek. 'Of course, Daddy,' she whispered. 'I love you.'

'I love you too,' he said fondly, stroking her cheek. 'More than you know.'

Later that evening, the rain began to fall once more. Aurora could hear the tapping on the windows as it deluged down outside. All her daddy's notes and manuscripts had been sent to London, along with hundreds of books. All the paintings and furniture were to be stored away.

Her gaze drifted to a portrait of Henry's first wife. Aurora knew little of Marcella, except what Maggie had told her. She knew that she had been quite snobby and mean, and that she had treated Maggie like a slave. She also knew that Seb and George had not liked Grace – they had always made that plain. All her life, she had seen Henry take a step back from their rude behaviour. Maybe he was guilty? Maybe he felt bad for marrying her mother without telling them first?

She frowned. The fact that he had gone off and got married again must have really annoyed them. She knew little of money but she realised that her father was rich. She had no interest in that, but she could see that the boys did. She admired Gloria for her speech about it; how she had told the world that she loved her father for him and not for his money. Maybe that would keep them quiet for a while.

When Aurora had asked about Grace's portrait, Henry had sighed. She wanted to hang it in her new room. He sat her down and took her small hand in his.

'It's just too large, my darling,' he explained. 'It simply wouldn't fit.'

'What?' she gasped in horror. 'I can't leave it here. I look at it every day.' Her eyes filled with tears. 'I can't leave it here, Daddy. I just can't!.'

'I shall have it covered up properly,' he hushed. 'Then you'll have it when you have a home of your own.'

'Where? You mean, here in the dark? But she'll be lonely in the dark. I know she will.'

He pulled her close and kissed her forehead. 'She'll be just fine, sweet child. She'll be safe in here.' He put his hand on her chest, just where her heart was located. 'Grace will live forever in you. Don't ever be afraid of forgetting her.'

'Just make sure that it's safe,' she beseeched. 'Don't let anyone damage it.'

'You have my word.' He shook her hand solemnly.

Aurora sat on the floor, staring at her mother's face. She looked like a princess in her white dress. She closed her eyes and willed her brain to memorise it. She understood that it would be a long time before she would see it again. Tears welled up once more, but she blinked them away. She would have to be strong. As James had rightly said, there was far worse going on in the world. That War on Terror for example. Daddy was always ranting about Tony Blair and George Bush.

Climbing up onto the armchair, she took a closer look at the portrait. Grace's eyes were brown like hers, but a slightly different shape. Her mother's eyes were like almonds whereas Aurora's were wide.

Maggie had explained that when Grace sat for the portrait she had been pregnant – so, she said, Aurora was in the portrait too but not visible. Aurora focused on the huge diamond on her mother's left hand – the engagement ring from her daddy. That was locked away until she was older. She couldn't imagine a stone like that on her small finger but it looked sparkly and wonderful all the same.

Aurora put her fingers to her lips and kissed them. Then she reached out and touched her mother's face.

'I'll never forget you,' she whispered.

Grace's face stared impassively back at the little girl.

'Goodbye.'

# PART TWO

## London 2015

# Chapter Fourteen

Aurora buttoned up her Mac and faced out into the grey London evening. The Tube had been as packed as ever, filled to capacity with commuters on the home run. Men in suits staring blankly ahead and women with their faces hidden behind magazines. Teenagers with earphones, tapping on their screens. The station was only a five-minute walk from her flat but even this short distance seemed interminable in the driving rain. She paused at the main door of the station and bit her lip. The one day she hadn't brought an umbrella.

It was the week before Christmas and she still had most of her presents to buy. She simply had not had time for shopping, what with the rehearsals and her part-time job at the florist's. The whole family were due home for the holidays. It had been years since everyone had been together. William, who had done medicine at university and was now a doctor at Great Ormond Street, worked long, unpredictable hours. Laura spent her time between London and New York, working for a PR company, and James' photography took him all over the world.

Aurora, though based in London, rarely went home to Oxshott. Gloria and Henry had the house to themselves, along with the dogs, Pyramus and Thisbe. Their predecessors, Rosencrantz and Guildenstern, had died six years before, followed closely by a heartbroken Bilbo. A devastated Gloria had gone to the Battersea Dogs Home the next week, with Aurora in tow, to choose two new canine additions to the family. Aurora had then named the two squirming puppies after the tragic story of Pyramus and Thisbe who were forbidden to wed due to their parents' rivalry. She had been studying *Romeo and Juliet* at the time and could definitely see how Shakespeare had been inspired by Ovid's sad tale. Henry had been delighted by Aurora's literary choice. He had half-expected her to call the dogs Beyoncé or Rihanna – certainly not classical names from a bygone age.

Aurora had not been a typical teenager. Instead of going out kissing boys and trying cigarettes, she had instead opted to join the school theatrical society and the chess club.

James had been around in the beginning to help her adjust and to defend her from Laura's sharp tongue. However, his job took him away a lot and Aurora had to fend for herself. She and Laura loved each other dearly but, like all sisters, they fought frequently. Aurora, being a girl, had usurped Laura's young-sister position in the family and it had taken her years to get used to it.

She paused to cross the road. A black taxi sped by and splashed her.

'Bugger!' she said as her black tights were now soaked.

Henry had set up a small trust fund for her when she had started university and she now used it to pay her rent. Despite having had two main parts in plays by an unknown playwright called Justin Debussy, she was barely making ends meet. Everyone had warned her about show business: there were five months of poverty to one month of champagne. Despite all of this, she adored it. It was in her blood. She never felt more alive than when she was on stage. Justin had a new play about to premiere and she had the main role. The theatre had been so busy practising for opening night in January that she had little or no time for anything else.

She arrived at an old Georgian house that was situated next to an Indian restaurant. It had a red door with peeling paint and a huge bay window jutting out onto the street. The flat was a two-bedroomed affair overlooking the main high street, boasting a small kitchen and living room. Her own bedroom was on the small side, but it had a bay window with red drapes and she loved it. She shared a flat with her best friend Ophelia Carter: a struggling thespian also. They had moved in together straight after graduation from RADA.

Shaking the excess moisture from her long dark hair, she took off her coat and hung it on the rack.

'*Lia?*' she called, using a pet name she had for her friend. 'Are you home?'

No one replied.

*Great. There'll be enough hot water for a shower.*

Kicking open her bedroom door, she threw off her shoes, one by one, and peeled off her wet tights. The ancient plumbing in their building was temperamental to say the least and hot water was a rarity. She'd had a long day reeling off lines for an increasingly demanding Justin and she yearned for the Christmas break.

There was no comparison between this bedroom and the one at home. As promised, Gloria and Henry had built an enormous extension twelve years ago. Henry's study had taken up most of the ground floor, with walls lined with shelves of books and papers. Aurora and Laura had been given huge adjacent bedrooms on the first floor. Instead of the four-poster bed in her old house, she had been given a brand-new double with a soft mattress protector and plump pillows. She had covered her walls with posters ranging from Oscar Wilde (her favourite writer) to Lea Salonga (her idol of West End fame).

However, her present bedroom, as pokey as it was, had real character. The ancient brass bed had a lumpy mattress and the walls were damp in places. All this aside, she loved its authenticity.

She sat on her bed and looked at the photos she had pinned to the wall. There was one of Maggie on the beach, her lined old face smiling. She barely saw her old friend now. In the beginning, she had made the long journey home to Cornwall every couple of months. James had driven her most of the time, keeping his word. However, as time passed, her notion of 'home' became blurred, and soon her new life replaced her old one. Maggie, though cherished, faded into the background.

Next to Maggie's photo was a perfect shot of her mother's portrait. James had taken it as a surprise, just before it had been covered up. He had presented it to her as a welcoming gift, when she had mutinously dragged her suitcase up the path, all those years ago. 'Now, Borealis,' he had said softly, 'a little bit of home.' It had been the most wonderful present anyone could have given her. Bursting into tears, she had hugged him fiercely and now that photo accompanied her wherever she went.

To the left of Grace's painting was one of the whole family at William's graduation. Gloria looked so proud of her son who had followed his late father into paediatric medicine. William, despite his laidback exterior, had been focused at school and had surprised everyone when he got top marks in his A-Levels. 'Who knew? Who knew?' Laura had repeated in disbelief. Now, almost twenty-nine years of age, William was a handsome man with blond hair and blue eyes. The only qualm Gloria had about her second son was the fact that he was a workaholic: it was all work and no play. As a result, he was still single. Aurora met him for lunch sometimes, regaling him with tales of her life at the theatre. More often than not, his pager would buzz and his ciabatta would be left untouched.

Then there was her much-loved eighteenth birthday photo. She was standing next to James and he was laughing. He had surprised her that night. She had received an email in early November saying that he would not be back for Christmas. Devastated, she had cried her eyes out. He had never missed her birthday, not since she had moved to London. During those first stormy months, he had been her rock. When she woke up screaming for Maggie, he was by her side straight away. When she had refused to go to her new school, he had cajoled her into it. Then, his email had knocked her for six. It was just unthinkable that her favourite brother would miss her birthday.

Then, just before midnight on New Year's Eve, James had appeared in the doorway of the conservatory. His dark hair was slightly longer and his face was covered in stubble. He had come straight from the airport and still had his camera slung over his shoulder.

'*Borealis!*' he called over the din.

She saw him in the candlelight and her heart had filled with happiness. Throwing herself into his arms, she hugged him fiercely, just as the clock struck twelve.

'Happy Birthday,' he murmured. 'Did you really think that I'd miss it?'

She barely saw James now. His work took him all over the world, but for the past year he had been stationed in Syria. He had started as a nature photographer, freelancing for the BBC, spending weeks perched on a rock to get one shot of a rare snow leopard. Then, he had branched out into journalism and decided to take the photos that no one wanted to see: horrific portraits of misery and death caused by senseless violence and terrorism.

Now, stationed in Aleppo, he travelled around interviewing locals and taking portraits of the terrified civilians. He was good to keep in touch, emailing every couple of weeks. He didn't want to upset Gloria as she was recovering from having breast cancer a few years before. He knew that she hated his line of work and worried constantly about his safety. All that aside, he couldn't imagine being anywhere else. The people had touched him; he wasn't ready to return to England and ignore the human suffering that was mounting every day. His friends gave him grief over his 'white knight' behaviour. He was a privileged white male from the West – why then was he involved in something that he couldn't possibly change or control? Risking his life every day for personal satisfaction and a sense of 'doing good'? James ignored their criticism. Far better to be on the front line, physically helping a family hide from ISIS. than a sofa-activist who posted pictures on Facebook and reacted to horrific new reports with an icon of a crying, sad face.

Aurora would get the odd Facebook message, entitled 'Hey, Borealis'. It would normally be a fleeting 'hello' with little or no news about his whereabouts. He deliberately shielded her from the horror of his quotidian life. Instead, he asked silly questions about Pyramus and Thisbe or enquired how she was coping with Justin's artistic temperament.

*Oh, how she missed him.*

He had kept his word. When they had first moved to London, he had pleaded with Henry to abandon the boarding-school idea. After many arguments, the old man gave in. He couldn't bear to see his darling girl upset. Aurora, decked out in her new blazer and skirt, followed Laura through the school gates and had never looked back. Sitting in a classroom was a new experience for her, so it took a while before she got used to the rules and regulations. Within months, she began to shine in languages and music, but her real love was English literature.

Her teacher, Mr. Crowley, was of Irish descent and so introduced his students to literary giants like Heaney, Yeats and Kavanagh. She used to love watching him recite poetry, his glasses held between his index and middle finger, his eyes closed as he softly spoke of love and loss and life. There was something about the words – the beautifully crafted words – that touched her heart, despite her young age. When she heard of Kavanagh's isolation: a poet amongst a rural farming community who felt different to everyone else, she related to him immediately. He didn't fit in and nor did she. No matter how hard she tried, her classmates still saw her as strange.

Not that they were mean about it. On the contrary. She made new friends easily and quickly. One girl in particular became her best friend almost straight away: her name was Theresa Carter and she was a keen literature fan too. Together they would sing and write small madcap plays to perform during break time. They sat together in most classes and auditioned for the school musical. When Aurora got the part of Artful Dodger in the Christmas play, Theresa displayed no jealousy or animosity. In fact, she was delighted for her friend.

One summer day they were lazing on the grass in the back garden. Aurora was making daisy chains. Theresa sat up straight and looked serious for a moment.

'Aurora,' she began.

'*Hmmm?*'

'I've decided to change my name.' Her blue eyes shone and her red curls bounced around her freckled face. 'I'm never going to be famous with a name like Theresa, so I've decided to change it to Ophelia.'

Aurora started. 'Are you serious?' she exclaimed. 'Wow, that's some change. Why choose Ophelia?'

'Well, it's a cool name for a start and she had some great lines in *Hamlet*.'

'I suppose.'

'I'll definitely get noticed with a name like that. I mean, look at you! You have a brilliant name for show business. Aurora Sinclair! It's perfect.'

Aurora had never really thought about it. Her name was her name. However, when Theresa pointed it out, she could see how wonderful it would be to have it in lights above a theatre on Broadway.

'Right, Ophelia it is,' she said, shaking her friend's hand. 'Daddy is slow to change, so don't get insulted if he continues to call you Theresa when you come over next weekend.'

'Oh, that's fine,' she said breezily. 'My parents laughed when I told them, so I don't think they'll be calling me Ophelia quite yet.'

Now, years later, Aurora and 'Ophelia' were sharing a flat together. They had both taken French, English and Music for their A-Levels, been accepted into RADA and left with glowing reports. Justin Debussy had cast Aurora right away when he saw her perform a scene from *Cat on a Hot Tin Roof*, enchanted by this beautiful girl with the cloudy brown hair. His first play was about the American Civil War and so Aurora was the perfect choice for the Southern Belle heroine, as she could speak in any accent required.

Two plays later and she was still his leading lady. She never complained and put up with his demands. She stayed late and allowed him to criticise her interpretations, change them and then revert back to her original take on a particular scene. She trusted him completely and although he had been tempted to ask her out for a drink, something had stopped him. Mixing business with pleasure had never worked in the past and he had a gut feeling that she was going to make them both very famous.

Ophelia picked up work quite easily too. She had a natural presence on stage and directors loved her long red curls and bright-blue eyes. 'I was always Annie in school productions,' she would quip. 'Stereotyped or what?' She and Aurora still got on like a house on fire. They took turns at cooking dinner; Ophelia stuck to basics like penne and tomato sauce, whereas Aurora tried more exotic dishes like ramen and tagine. Gloria, although not a proficient cook, had tons of recipe books lying unused on the shelf near the kitchen window. As a teenager, Aurora would read anything, from the back of cereal boxes to the instructions on a packet of Uncle Ben's – so she read the recipes. She had grown up with Maggie making bread and dinners from scratch – how hard could it be?

So, Aurora the Chef emerged. She had started with basics like white sauce and spaghetti bolognese. Then, as she became more confident, she tried to emulate Maggie's cherry pudding. James had three helpings and praised her to the sky, scraping his bowl clean. She had glowed with pleasure, delighted that her baking had been a success.

Laura had taken one taste and spat it out. 'Ugh, did you add any sugar?' she gasped, wiping her mouth clean in disgust. 'That's just vile.'

Aurora's hand flew to her mouth in horror. 'Oh no! I forgot. Oh, it must taste awful.' She gazed at the pie in dismay. She had been concentrating so hard on the batter mixture that she had forgotten to add sugar to the sour cherries.

James glared at Laura and then turned to smile at Aurora. 'Well, I thought it was amazing,' he lied, winking at her and patting his belly.

Aurora smiled at him gratefully. He always looked out for her; he had eaten three helpings of the bitter fruit pudding and had been so encouraging. The next time she made it, she got it right. A quick phone call to Maggie had worked wonders as the old lady gave her tips and quantities. Aurora, who had a red notebook for recipes, wrote '*Maggie's Cherry Pudding*' in her blue scrawl at the top of the page. It made her feel close to her as it was her link to her old life.

The next Sunday morning, she made drop scones for the whole family. William wolfed down three and held his plate out for more.

'You're not bad for a first-timer,' he concluded as she slipped a freshly made pancake onto his plate.

Now, Aurora tried her best to make healthy meals each evening. Her funds were low as rent was high in that part of London. She made it her business to go to the market each week and stock up on fresh produce. The traders grew to recognise the beautiful young girl who religiously bought fruit, vegetables and fish. She was a lovely sight to behold on a frosty morning.

Now she wrapped her shivering body in a fluffy robe and placed her towels on the radiator. Turning on the water, she waited until it was hot enough and then hopped in. Immersed in the cascade of heat, she massaged her scalp with whatever shampoo came to hand. She wasn't fussy when it came to beauty products; in fact, she rarely wore make-up and always let her hair dry naturally. Ophelia, on the other hand, was constantly trying to find a way to conceal her freckles. Her dressing table in her room was overflowing with little tubes of foundation and pallets of eye shadow. Aurora couldn't understand her friend's aversion to her natural beauty.

'Freckles are lovely,' she told her honestly. 'I had a friend once and his freckles were a part of him. They complemented him.' Freddie's smiling face flashed through her mind.

Ophelia laughed scornfully. 'Are you mad? Anyone who's afflicted with these stupid stains understands my struggle. Now, pass me the Maybelline.'

The shower water grew cold towards the end, just like it always did. She squeezed the droplets from her hair, grabbed one of the waiting towels and wrapped her hair in it. After drying her skin vigorously, she pulled on her robe and padded back into her bedroom.

Suddenly, her phone buzzed in her bag. Rummaging around, she eventually located it and unlocked the home screen. It was a message from Laura, asking her to meet for drinks down town.

Aurora beamed. Her older sister wasn't due back from New York until later in the week so it was a lovely surprise. Laura had a high-flying job at a PR firm which required her to travel quite a bit. She was naturally good at convincing clients and had climbed the ranks of the company quite rapidly. She now had regular companies who used her skills and her boss adored her.

She texted back eagerly and suggested a wine bar in Soho. Laura replied instantly, saying that she'd see her there in an hour.

*An hour?* That didn't give her much time. She released her mane from its towel. She rubbed some Estée Lauder cream on her face and pulled open her wardrobe. It was packed full of dresses, skirts and jumpsuits. All her jeans and trousers were neatly stacked on a shelf, along with her tops and T-shirts. She liked to keep things tidy; Maggie had taught her that.

Ten minutes later, she was ready. Her long legs were clad in black tights and long black boots; her short woollen dress was scarlet and added a Christmassy feel to the outfit. Her mother's silver pendant glinted in the light. As promised, she rarely took it off. Her hair was slightly damp, the tendrils wavy as they flowed down her back. A smidgen of mascara and a touch of lip gloss and she was ready.

Ophelia arrived home just as she was buttoning up her coat. Her red curls were contained by a purple beanie hat and her cheeks were rosy from the cold.

'Hey, you,' she greeted, hanging her green coat on the rack. 'Where are you off to? Out on the town?'

Aurora nodded, winding a black scarf around her slender neck. 'Laura texted and asked to meet for drinks.'

'Laura? I thought she wasn't due back for a few days?'

'Well, so did I.' Aurora shrugged. 'She's never been predictable.' She slung her bag over her shoulder. 'There's leftover quinoa salad in the fridge if you fancy it. See you later.'

Ophelia hugged her gratefully. 'You are an absolute star, you know. I was just about to ring up for a pizza and add at least five million calories to my already questionable diet. Now, I'll be all virtuous with my healthy grains.'

Aurora made a face. 'You'll thank me when we're middle-aged and you still look like a twenty-year-old.'

'Botox will help me with that, darling,' Ophelia answered. 'Botox and face lifts. Ophelia Carter will still be box office gold when she's fifty!'

'If you say so.' Aurora laughed and blew her a kiss. 'Talk later.'

# Chapter Fifteen

Leicester Square was teeming with people. The Odeon's lights sparkled in the rain and crowds moved in packs, chattering loudly. Christmas music blared from shops as Aurora passed and children squealed in delight as a man dressed as Santa walked around ringing a bell and booming '*Ho, ho, ho!*'

There was a pungent smell of roasted nuts as she walked up into Chinatown.

Laura was sitting by the main window of the small wine bar just off Old Compton Street. Her blonde hair was sleek and cut into a bob and she was dressed in a sharp dress coupled with black stilettos. A diamond bracelet dangled from her wrist and she was tapping furiously on the screen of her iPhone.

Aurora walked up behind her and said, '*Boo!*'

Laura jumped and dropped her phone with a clatter. 'Aurora!' she chided. 'You almost gave me a heart attack.' She reached out and hugged her stepsister tightly. 'Good to see you though.'

Aurora smiled and took a seat, draping her coat and scarf on the back of the chair. She shook out her long hair and picked up the cocktail menu. 'What are you drinking?' she enquired, eyeing Laura's large glass of white wine.

'Picpoul de Pinet,' she replied. 'It's a lovely wine from Languedoc. I recommend it.' She sipped it elegantly and put her phone to the side. 'So, how's the theatre? Is Justin still exploiting you?'

'Oh, stop it!' laughed Aurora. 'He's wonderful. I've learned so much from him.'

'Still though, he gets some bang for his buck.'

Aurora smiled at the waiter as he approached the table. 'I'll have a glass of that,' she said, pointing to Laura's drink.

'The Picpoul,' said Laura briskly, 'and bring me another.' She fiddled with the beermat on the table and took another gulp of wine.

Aurora could tell that she was on edge, but she knew better than to ask.

'Have you been home?' she enquired instead.

'Not yet,' Laura answered, blushing slightly. 'Well, I've been in London for the past few days but I've been staying at –'

'Two white wines,' interrupted the waiter, smiling broadly.

'Thank you,' said Aurora. 'Happy Christmas!'

She raised her glass, took a sip of the cool liquid and sighed. 'Wow, this is nice. Good choice.'

Laura took another large sip of wine and coughed. 'What I want to say is, I've been in London for the past few days and I've been staying at Claridge's.'

Aurora's eyes widened. 'You have? Why? With whom?'

'My boyfriend.'

'Your *what*?'

'I've been seeing this man for about six months and he's perfect and I think I really like him and –'

'Why have you not mentioned it?' Aurora regarded her shrewdly.

'Well, it wasn't that I didn't want to but –'

'Is he married?'

Laura choked on her wine. 'Well, not exactly. I mean, he's in the process of getting divorced ...'

'*Divorced?*' Aurora squeaked. 'How old is he?'

'Um, around fifty-three?'

'What?' Aurora stared at her incredulously. 'You're only twenty-six, Laura. He's twice your age. What will Gloria say?'

There was a pause. 'Well, I was going to invite him for Christmas. Do you think she'd mind?'

Aurora didn't answer. She could imagine Gloria's reaction. Laura's love life, or lack thereof, had been a sore subject for years. She'd had countless one-night stands and short relationships, but had no interest in getting married. Her mother often lamented how she would never have grandchildren as James was too busy staying alive, William was obsessed with the hospital and Laura had clearly stated that she would never tie herself down with a baby. 'You're my only hope, Aurora,' Gloria would say.

'So, where did you meet him?' she asked eventually. 'Why have we not heard about him before?'

Laura took a deep breath. 'Well, do you remember my friend Lydia? The girl that I worked with in Paris?'

Aurora nodded. Of course she remembered Lydia. Years before, just after Gloria's cancer diagnosis, Laura had flunked college, given up her law degree and taken off to Paris. There, she found a job as a waitress in a bistro on the left bank. Her excellent French and bubbly personality soon made her a favourite amongst the locals. Lydia, an Irish girl, who was of a similar age, had ended up as waitress there too. She too had dropped out of college and fled to the city of lights, desperate for a new beginning. The two girls had hit it off straight away.

'Well, she's getting married next year to an American guy called Luca. They had a baby together a few months ago.'

Aurora gasped in delight. 'A baby? Wow, that's amazing.' The Irish girl's image flashed through her mind. Pretty and slim with long brown hair and green eyes, Lydia had it all. She had been really kind and welcoming the few times Aurora had gone to Paris for the weekend, including the younger girl in their plans and chatting to her in her lilting voice. It didn't seem that long ago that the three of them were sitting in a bar near République, drinking carafes of wine and laughing long into the night.

'Oh, she's a natural,' Laura assured her. 'We were all shocked, to tell the truth. The baby, Sienna, is sweet. I mean, I'm not one for small people, but she's very cute.'

'But what has this got to do with your new man?' Aurora traced the rim of her glass with her forefinger.

Laura took a deep breath. 'My new man, as you call him, happens to be Luca's father. He's called Christian.'

'*What?*' Aurora nearly knocked over her glass.

Laura drained her wine and faced her. 'He's a lawyer, a partner in fact, at a big firm in New York. He's of French descent.'

'Rich?' asked Aurora innocently, remembering Laura's criteria for the perfect man.

'Well, yes. He's not badly off,' she admitted. 'We met at Sienna's christening.'

'And?'

'Well, we exchanged details and suddenly he turned up in London and then –'

'You started bonking,' finished Aurora with a giggle. 'My favourite word.'

Laura laughed out loud. 'Oh, yes, I remember you and your obsession with it. Well, we didn't bonk, as you call it, right away. I played hard to get.'

'Why?' Aurora's eyes were wide.

'Well, I knew that he was off the market – I mean, Lydia's likely to kill me for a start …'

'She doesn't know?'

Laura shook her head. 'Gosh, no. I'm pretty sure she wouldn't like it. He's Sienna's grandfather, for goodness' sake.'

Aurora bit her lip, trying to process the news. 'It's all a bit crazy, Laura – how will this Luca guy feel about it?'

Laura looked uncomfortable. 'He won't be too thrilled, I will admit. However, he knows that his parents have been miserable for years. The divorce is almost finalised so at least we can make things public then.' She tapped the table with her fingers. 'Please keep it quiet for the moment though. We plan to tell Luca and Lydia the news after Christmas.'

'The news? Are you getting married too?'

Laura's face reddened. 'Not at all,' she answered, flustered. 'You know that I'm not the marrying kind.'

'*Hmmm.*' Aurora didn't look convinced. 'So, do you have a photo of this Christian? Is he grey and wrinkled with a paunch?'

'Hardly,' Laura scoffed, activating the photo stream on her phone. She scrolled down until she found the picture she was looking for. '*Et voilà*, my boyfriend.'

Aurora took her iPhone and gasped. 'Wow, he's pretty fit for an old-timer!' She gazed at the picture in fascination. A tall, tanned man stared back at her, with hair slightly greying at the temples and chiselled cheekbones. He looked really fit and he had a haughty, superior look. 'Where was this photo taken?'

Laura smiled at the memory. 'Oh, that was in Mauritius. He took me there a couple of months ago. We hired a five-star complex and had our own waiting staff. It was just bliss.'

'Sounds amazing,' said Aurora enviously. 'I have to admit, Laura, he's really something. How do you do it?'

'It was so unexpected,' she reminisced with a soft look. 'He walked into a room and *bam*! I was hooked. I'd always laughed at that love-at-first-sight nonsense so I was pretty gobsmacked.' She chuckled. 'For the first time, I was like a little girl, tongue-tied and nervous. He held all the cards. He was the powerful one. It was just irresistible.'

'So, how did you end up together?' Aurora pressed on, enthralled.

'Well, he messaged me a couple of times and I responded politely. I didn't know what his game plan was, yeah? Then, he turned up at the office one Thursday afternoon out of the blue. He strode up to my desk, took my hand and we headed off to Cannes for the weekend.'

'What did your boss say?'

'She didn't say a word. I found out later that he had cleared the whole thing via email.' She sighed. 'Taking control like that? It's a real turn-on for me, I have to say.'

'Was Cannes nice?'

'Magical,' she replied dreamily. 'We stayed at the Eden-Roc in Antibes – it was just heavenly. We spoke French and drank champagne. So romantic.'

'Romantic?' Aurora shook her head. 'What has happened to you? It's extraordinary. I've never seen you like this.'

Laura blushed. 'I get what you mean. It's strange for me too.' She looked Aurora in the eye. 'I think I'm in love.'

'Have I entered the Twilight Zone?' Aurora mocked. 'Oh, how I wish that Will were here! He'd have a field day.' She regarded her stepsister in amusement. 'Gloria will be fine about this. To be honest, she'll probably be more worried about your personality transplant. Laura Dixon in love.' She laughed melodiously. 'I've seen it all now.'

Laura made a face. 'It happens to the best of us, missy. This will be you someday, just wait and see.'

'Maybe.' Aurora frowned. *Certainly not yet.* 'Another wine?' she prompted, signalling to the waiter.

'One more then,' said Laura, checking her watch. 'I'm to meet Chris at eight and he hates when I'm late.'

'Where?'

'Oh, The Ivy,' she replied breezily. 'Just for something small.'

Aurora giggled. 'Oh, *The Ivy*, 'she mimicked. 'That old place.'

Laura shrugged. 'What can I say? I enjoy life.'

Aurora turned restlessly and plumped up her pillow. Sleep was evading her despite the fact that she was exhausted.

Three glasses of wine later, she had arrived home to find Ophelia watching a dating programme on television. 'You just have to watch this,' her friend had insisted, gesturing for her to join her on the couch. Two hours later she had crawled into bed, vowing to fall asleep as quickly as possible. She still had a half-day shift at the florist's in the morning, followed by an afternoon rehearsal with Justin. Then she would finally be on holidays. She planned to go home to Oxshott straight away but she hadn't packed a thing. Her busy schedule afforded her little time to get organised. Closing her eyes, she made a mental list of things to throw into her suitcase. Maybe that would help her to fall asleep. She would need chilling-out clothes like her cosy pyjamas and woolly socks – it was Christmas after all. However, she would also need a few party dresses for Christmas Day and, of course, her birthday party on New Year's Eve. She always celebrated it with her father. All through the years she had made it her business to be with him for the event. It made him feel close to Grace and she liked the tradition of it all.

William was due home the next day also. He had saved up his annual leave and Gloria had ordered him to leave his pager at the hospital. She had a speech ready for her second son where she outlined the importance of relaxation and socialising. He was an eligible man with his promising career and handsome features. He needed to let loose once in a while. Ophelia had a huge crush on him and had already organised drinks on Christmas Eve down the local pub. 'Oh, let me sit next to him,' she pleaded to Aurora. 'If I get him drunk enough, he might just crack.'

In his last email, James had promised his mother that he

would be home by Christmas Eve. It had been a short paragraph, explaining that he was bunking with the crew from Médecins Sans Frontières, helping them to administer much-needed vaccines to the children of Aleppo. Aurora could just imagine it: James making silly faces and calming a terrified child while a doctor inserted a needle. He was so good with kids and he probably had nicknames for them all. She was happy for him; he was making a difference and was clearly suited to humanitarian work. It's just that she missed him terribly. His absence left a hole in her heart that no one else could fill.

Frowning, she drowned out the sound of traffic outside by reciting lines from the play, willing her tired brain to shut down and sleep. She had a lot to do the next day. Marianne, her boss at the florist's, was knee-deep in poinsettias and festive arrangements of pine and holly. Hundreds of people had ordered wreaths and, in the end, she had stopped taking orders.

Aurora had met Marianne at the market over a year ago. She had been selling flowers from a stall right next to the organic vegetables.

'Oh, what beautiful flowers!' Aurora had exclaimed, touching the velvety petals gently. 'My father sent a bunch of roses to my mother to convince her to marry him.'

Marianne, enchanted by the pretty girl with the soft voice, had offered her three for five pounds. 'You should put one in your hair,' she suggested. 'That's what the Spanish girls do.' Dressed in a multi-coloured poncho, her own dark curls were pinned up at one side with a bright pink carnation; gold bracelets jangled on her wrist as she moved. Slightly plump for her short frame, she tended to wear oversized clothes that flowed to the ground. Aurora guessed that she was of Mexican origin and was proved right later when Marianne informed her that her mother came from Cancun. What had started as a conversation about roses ended up with Aurora mentioning that she was looking for a part-time job and Marianne offering her a few hours at the shop while she manned the market stall.

Now, a year later, Aurora worked at the florist's three days a week. She liked the interaction with customers and learning about the different blooms on offer. Marianne's business was thriving now that the recession was waning. People were spending again. Houses that had ceased buying luxury items like bouquets for the mantelpiece were now slipping back into old habits. The economy was on the way up again and business was booming.

Justin had insisted that she come to the theatre in the afternoon for a couple of hours. He wasn't happy with Act One and wanted to run through her lines. His new play, a Roaring Twenties version of the legend of King Arthur, set in Chicago, was dramatic and dark. It was called *La Morte* – its title an Italian take on Malory's *Le Morte d'Arthur*. It was about a powerful mob boss called Joey Sloane and his much younger wife, Elise. Sticking to the traditional storyline, a young mobster called Jimmy Romano becomes his right-hand man and, in turn, falls in love with the beautiful wife. Aurora had been devouring DVDs of *Chicago* and *The Sopranos*, learning the accent and nuances of a gangster's moll. Her long mane of hair had to be pinned up meticulously so that it would fit under a short wig that framed her face. Her flapper dress fell to below the knee and her cigarette holder had a Gauloise jammed into it. Long beads trailed down over her breast and dark gloves covered her white arms, just up to above the elbow. Her love interest, Jimmy, was played by a young actor called Paul Lewis, who was also a graduate of RADA. Tall, tanned and blond, he was already being called the new Jude Law. They had become firm friends and often went for drinks after rehearsal. They were a beautiful couple to see: Paul with his handsome looks and Aurora with her cloudy hair and beautiful face. However, nothing ever happened between them. Paul was gay and had been in a happy relationship for three years.

A siren began to wail in the distance, its sound getting nearer and nearer. Aurora groaned in frustration. She had a nine o'clock start. Why was she still awake? Inevitably, she thought of Laura and her bombshell. It was hard to tell how Gloria would take it. Christian was closer in age to her than to her daughter. Laura had never been conventional. Would Gloria overlook it and be happy for them? She just didn't know.

Gloria had changed since her cancer diagnosis. Aurora remembered it like it was yesterday. She had come home from school with Ophelia in tow. They had been forced to participate in a school sports day and were complaining about how 'naff' the egg-and-spoon race was. She had been seventeen years old and the only child left at home. Laura was living in a flat near King's College where she was studying law and William was in his final year of medicine. James was in New York, completing his Master's in Moving Image.

However, when she and Ophelia walked into the kitchen that day, the whole family was seated around the kitchen table with grim expressions. Henry, ever the gentleman, got to his feet and politely asked Ophelia to go home.

Gloria had then related in a tight voice that she had found a small lump on her left breast a few weeks before. After a hurried biopsy, it had been discovered that it was malignant and she due to have a lumpectomy the next week. Laura started sobbing and a sombre William had pulled her into his arms. James had motioned for Aurora to join him at the table, where he hugged her close and clutched his mother's hand simultaneously.

Henry was speechless, starkly reminded of Marcella's diagnosis years before. He had aged that day. His face became even more lined and his cheerful exterior faded. Having gone through the deaths of two wives, he didn't know if he could handle a third. He loved Gloria so much he couldn't bear to think about it.

What had followed passed in a blur. Gloria had her surgery and recovered well. However, she had a round of chemotherapy and lost her hair in the process. With a stiff upper lip, she got on with it, pretending to the world that it didn't bother her in the slightest.

But it did. Very much so. She cried and cried over her new appearance when she thought that no one was looking. Henry had a top-of-the-range wig made which was almost identical to her old hair. It scratched her scalp and she hated it. She projected a calm exterior even though inside she was screaming. The notion of death terrified her. She didn't want to die and leave her kids. She still had lots to do: babysitting her future grandchildren, travelling around the world or maybe bungee-jumping off some bridge somewhere. She was not ready to die.

Her first husband's death had been a shock. He had collapsed at the surgery after a massive coronary and lost consciousness. He had died two days later at the hospital, having never woken up. The suddenness of it all had been difficult to deal with; she had found it mindboggling to contemplate that her husband had mowed the lawn and taken out the bins the day before he died. When he left the house that morning with *The Times* under his arm and a cup of coffee in his hand, she could never have imagined that she would never see him again. His death had been unheralded and cruel. It had robbed them of him without mercy and it had taken years for the pain to fade. However, she was rapidly realising that a sudden death was far better than a long, drawn-out equivalent. It took superhuman effort for her to get up every day and the constant shadow of mortality loomed over her every move.

Now, almost six years later, she was in a better place. She had responded well to the treatment and her old hair had grown back. She was slightly thinner now, but she put that down to anxiety. She had resumed her duties at the flower club and was an active member of the bridge club. Henry had been a rock throughout the whole ordeal; she couldn't have done it without his constant encouragement and support.

# Chapter Sixteen

'Good morning!' said Marianne cheerfully, inserting a painted silver branch into a giant glass vase. The arrangement she was working on was *Narnia*-themed: white roses with silver baubles and pine branches surrounding it all. 'You look tired, my love,' she tutted. 'Were you out late?'

Aurora shook her head and hung her coat on the rack by the back office. 'It took me hours to fall asleep,' she said, shrugging. 'You know how sometimes your brain just won't shut down?'

Marianne nodded. 'Lavender helps. I'll give you some dried leaves for your bedroom.'

Aurora checked the book. 'Gosh, you have a lot of wreaths to be collected.'

'I know,' said Marianne, rolling her eyes to heaven. 'I spent hours assembling them last night. I can't wait to close the doors this afternoon and begin my holidays.'

'I have rehearsal,' said Aurora. 'Justin is panicking as there are only a few weeks to opening night.'

'So, when are you going home?'

'Tomorrow. A quick shopping spree and then I'm off to Oxshott.'

Marianne regarded her thoughtfully. 'Would your mother like a wreath? I have a spare one.'

'Are you sure?' Aurora beamed at her. The entrance to Gloria's house was large with pillars, and the huge oak door would look very festive with one of Marianne's arrangements. 'And, by the way, you're very welcome to pop down to my birthday party on New Year's Eve.'

Marianne shook her head. 'You're an angel to invite me but I have a family do that night in Kilburn. Next year?'

The door of the shop pinged as a customer entered. It was an elderly lady in a fur-lined coat and large black shades.

'I'm here to pick up my bouquet,' she announced in her plummy accent.

Aurora smiled brightly. 'Of course. May I have your name?'

Justin Debussy was an only child. He had been a latecomer to the family, born when his mother was thirty-eight and cherished because of it. His father, Richard Debussy, was a retired army general. A tall forbidding-looking man, he had devoted his life to Queen and Country. His wife, Caroline, was related to Her Majesty herself and Justin grew up immersed in the world of the British upper-class. His decision to write plays and subsequently direct them was frowned upon by his ageing father who deemed 'show business' a flighty career for a young man. His mother, however, supported him completely. Her own brother was the famous actor Albert Wells, known as Bertie to his friends. He had given Justin a leg up in the industry when he was a fledgling unknown playwright. He had encouraged his famous friends to attend his début play *Georgia* and, as a result, media coverage had been huge. Bertie himself had missed his nephew's first two plays due to their short run and his busy schedule. 'I read the reviews, my boy,' he boomed down the telephone. 'Bloody good!' He had promised to attend the opening night of *La Morte*.

Justin adored Aurora. Not only was she the daughter of the renowned Henry Sinclair, she was also the daughter of the famous Grace Molloy. His mother Caroline had often told him of Grace's talent, having seen her on the West End stage. Then, to her fans' chagrin, Grace swapped the lights of London for her native country. At the peak of her career, she had left for Dublin. The theatre world had been shocked at this; no one quite understood why this talented young actress left a promising career in the one of the biggest cities in the world. People had said that she would return, bigger and better. However, fate's tragic twist put an end to that.

Aurora, like her mother, had great presence on stage and effortlessly morphed into whichever character she was playing. Her depiction of Clara-Mae in *Georgia* had wowed critics and her next role as the daughter of a French aristocrat, Antoinette Travere, was equally as good. She was Justin's muse, just as Grace Kelly was to Alfred Hitchcock and Maud Gonne was to W.B. Yeats. When he wrote a scene, he pictured her in it, with her long hair flowing down her back and her clear voice delivering the lines. He also admired her work ethic and her calmness in the midst of his melodrama. She never complained nor did she criticise. She was his dream woman.

Did he fancy her? Of course. Any man would. She was the epitome of beauty and elegance. His mother Caroline would be thrilled if he presented Aurora at home. She was the spitting image of her famous mother. He desired her, but something always held him back. He was old enough to realise that business and pleasure do not mix. If their relationship didn't work out, he would lose her forever. Something told him that she was the key to his success: she was his lucky charm.

The door of the theatre slammed shut and a breathless Aurora rushed onto the stage. 'So sorry I'm late,' she said, her cheeks flushed. 'The shop was so busy and Marianne couldn't manage and –'

Justin put his fingers to his lips. 'No more talk of the real world. You are now Elise Sloane. You are no longer Aurora Sinclair.' He walked towards her, not taking his eyes off her for a second. 'Forget the shop, forget who you are. Give me everything you've got.'

Aurora let him mesmerise her. His voice demanded obedience and she succumbed right away. His blue eyes were trained on her brown ones; his strong arms were now holding her shoulders. There were a few inches between them and the world stopped. He always got the best out of her. With his blond good looks and his tall athletic frame, any girl would kill to have him. However, he had never made a move. Not once.

Did this irk her? Slightly.

She never had a problem attracting the opposite sex, but she kept her distance. Having spent her life immersed in romantic novels and poetry, she had high expectations when it came to the opposite sex. She knew that men found her alluring, but she didn't exploit it. Justin's position of power in her life was definitely attractive, but she understood that a relationship could ruin everything they had worked for. Her career was her love interest; she dreamed of making it. That fuelled her ambition and encouraged her to work as hard as she could. Justin was her ticket – she didn't want to jeopardise anything with him.

The next day, William was lying on the couch when Aurora arrived home. She kicked open the living-room door with her foot as she was laden down with her suitcase and bags from an impromptu shopping trip to Oxford Street. She dumped everything near the Christmas tree and flopped down on an armchair.

'Where's Daddy and Gloria?' she enquired. The sitting room was festively decorated with tinsel draped on the picture frames, candles on the mantelpiece and a large tree in the corner with twinkling lights. A plate with a half-eaten beef sandwich lay discarded on the coffee table and Jamie Oliver was on the TV making gravy.

William yawned and stretched. 'I think they went to Waitrose. Mum wants to make the stuffing in the morning and she was all out of thyme.' He turned to face her. 'Any scandal?'

Aurora suppressed a giggle. 'You haven't seen Laura yet, I take it.'

'No,' he replied brightening. 'Have we news? Anything that I can blackmail her with?'

'Yep, it's pretty good, I have to admit.' She put up her hands. 'I'm sworn to secrecy, Will. You'll have to wait.'

'*Dish it,*' he commanded, swatting his blond hair away from his eyes. 'If Lolly has done anything remotely scandalous, I deserve to know. Remember how she shafted me that time I sneaked off to Glastonbury with Nigel? She told Gloria right away. Or that time I smoked weed at Ella's leaving party and vomited?' He scowled. 'She's always landed me in it. It's your duty to tell me.'

Aurora paused. *He would know in a few hours anyway ...*

'Right, I'll give you an inkling but you're not to tell Gloria.'

'Hand on heart,' he said solemnly, making a cross on his chest. 'I'll just take the piss out of my dear sister incessantly. Surely that's allowed?'

'Of course,' conceded Aurora. 'Well, it seems our sister has fallen in love ...'

'Bollocks,' he interrupted scornfully. 'Are you making this up?'

'No, I swear to you. I met her last night at a wine bar in Soho and she told me all about it.'

William sighed. 'This so-called scandal is lame, Aurora. Honestly, you're wasting my time. Gloria will relish the fact that her glacial daughter has finally found some poor bloke to boss around.'

'That's not all,' she continued, her eyes gleaming. 'He's not your average guy.'

William perked up again. 'What are you saying? Is he unsuitable?'

'Well ...'

'How bad are we talking?' he pressed on.

'He's fifty-three and soon to be her best friend's father-in-law.'

'Are you having a laugh?' He snorted. 'There's no way Lolly would date a geriatric.' He took a bite of his abandoned sandwich and chewed loudly. 'Unless ...'

'He's rich?' she finished helpfully. 'Well, I can confirm that he's not short of a few pounds.'

'Bloody brilliant!' He whooped. 'Revenge is mine. Gloria will have a canary when she hears about this.'

'Wait for the best part,' she went on in her soft voice. 'She's bringing him home for Christmas.'

William almost choked. When he had recovered, he sat back, a broad smile on his face.

'This is shaping up to be a right laugh. Bet you ten quid Gloria flips.'

'Maybe not,' she mused. 'Laura is an adult. She can choose whom she dates.'

William rubbed his hands together gleefully. 'One hundred per cent, she'll flip. Let's make sure that we have front-row seats.'

Gloria plonked the big casserole in the middle of the table. 'Help yourselves,' she ordered, walking back to the kitchen to get the bowl of buttery mashed potatoes.

Henry was seated at the head of the table with his half-moon glasses perched on his nose. William and Aurora were on either side of him and Gloria sat in her usual spot at the other end.

It was seven o'clock and there was still no sign of Laura. William kept looking at the door, willing it to open. He couldn't wait to see his mother's face.

'How's the new play coming along?' he asked Henry conversationally.

The old man shrugged. 'Slow, to be honest. I just find it hard to concentrate these days.' He sprinkled some salt on his dinner and smiled as Gloria filled his glass with red wine. He was almost seventy-three and had begun to slow down. Aurora would often find him asleep on the sofa in the afternoon, dozing by the fire with a book on his lap.

His last three plays had been huge successes. One had even been snapped up by a film company which was eager to adapt it. His agent was in talks with Hollywood and a deal was on the horizon. The film company wanted complete control of the script but Henry wouldn't allow it. He didn't want a sub-standard film released associated with his name. Cinema spoke to the masses whereas plays reached a smaller number of fans. If Henry Sinclair was to go global, then he would supervise it.

The front door banged and Aurora's eye met William's in excitement. The time had come. She could imagine Laura in the hall, taking deep breaths and smoothing down her hair. How would she introduce her older lover? The word boyfriend seemed too juvenile for a man like him.

William sat back and crossed his arms. 'Showtime,' he whispered loudly.

They could hear some scuffling outside before the kitchen door swung open. Aurora inhaled sharply, waiting for her first glimpse of the mysterious Christian. However, instead of Laura and her new beau, James stood in the doorframe with a small woman by his side.

'James!' gasped Gloria, dropping her fork with a clatter and jumping to her feet. 'My darling! I didn't expect you until tomorrow!' She rushed over to her eldest son and smothered him in kisses. 'Oh, James, I'm so happy you're here and safe.'

William saluted his brother and winked.

Henry got to his feet and shook his hand. 'Good to have you home, son,' he said warmly. 'What has it been? Six months?'

Aurora's eyes sparkled as she regarded her stepbrother. It had been so long since she had last seen him and even then it was fleeting. She sidled up shyly and hugged him close. 'Merry Christmas,' she whispered in his ear. 'Long time no see.'

'Merry Christmas,' he said. 'Good to see you, Borealis.'

He rubbed her cheek fondly and she beamed up at him. He looked the same with his warm brown eyes and hint of stubble. The world always seemed calmer when he was around. It stemmed from her childhood: he had looked after her and spoiled her. She counted on him more than anyone else.

Stepping backwards, he pulled the girl by his side into view. 'Everyone, I want you to meet somebody.' He paused. 'This is my fiancée, Claire.'

The small girl smiled and waved, clearly uncomfortable at being introduced so bluntly. She had short brown hair and large brown eyes. Her petite frame was clad in jeans and a check shirt and she wore hiking boots with laces. Blushing, she lifted her left hand upwards to reveal a small gold ring with a tiny diamond in the middle.

No one reacted for a few moments.

Gloria opened her mouth and shut it again. Her James, her darling baby boy, was engaged to be married? Who was this girl? Where did they meet? Was she a suitable match? She felt her chest tighten. James was always so sensible. It just wasn't like him to behave this way.

William took a gulp of wine and stared at his older brother. He had been so looking forward to Laura's bombshell and now Jiminy Cricket had ruined it all by stealing the limelight completely.

Henry clapped his hands in joy and was the first to congratulate the happy couple. 'Wonderful news,' he enthused, 'just wonderful!' He patted James on the back and kissed Claire on the cheek.

Aurora was another story. The world had slowed down as the words came out of his mouth.

*Fiancée? What?*

She shrank back, unable to believe her ears. James was getting married? To this girl? He had never mentioned her before. He had always claimed that he had no time for love. Yet now he was standing in front of her proudly, holding this girl's hand tightly. She didn't know why, but something knifed her heart. Was she being selfish? He had always given her his full attention. Now, she would have to share him with someone else.

She had never been good at hiding her emotions and she could see James looking at her in concern.

Pulling herself together, she walked up to him purposefully and gave him a brief hug. 'That's great, James, I hope you'll be very happy.' Then she turned to the girl. 'Congratulations,' she said softly, kissing Claire's cheek. 'You're a very lucky girl.'

'Oh, I know,' agreed Claire. 'This guy is the best.' She smiled at her warmly and moved closer to him, nuzzling her face in his arm.

Aurora smiled and retreated to the table.

James pulled out a chair and motioned for Claire to sit down. Then he took a seat next to her, opposite Aurora.

'So, where did you two meet?' asked William, voicing everyone's thoughts.

'Claire has been in Aleppo for the past few months. She's a doctor with MSF ...'

'MSF?' repeated Gloria. 'Whatever's that?'

'Médecins Sans Frontières,' explained Claire in a soft voice. 'I've been with them for two years now.'

'Wow,' said William in admiration. 'You're very brave to face out there.'

'Not really,' she blushed. 'I was working for the NHS and suddenly I realised that I could give so much more. My talents could be used to help those in dire need.' She took James' hand. 'We both feel this way. I guess that's what brought us together.'

'Well, there's that and the bomb,' said James with a laugh, accepting a glass of wine from Henry.

'The bomb?' squeaked Gloria, fanning her face. 'Oh, James.'

'We were bunking in the same hotel the night of the air raid.' He looked grim for a moment. 'Everyone was told to go downstairs to the basement as it was a makeshift shelter. That's where we met: huddled under the ground floor of a dingy hotel.'

Claire smiled and it lit up her whole face. 'Not the most romantic of encounters but here we are.'

'I suppose, the circumstances were so extreme and our lives were hanging in the balance.' James looked stricken for a moment. 'The most natural thing to do was to be together. Now, I'm the happiest man alive.'

Aurora had stopped eating, her appetite gone. She couldn't identify the emotions flooding her very being, but she felt uneasy and out of control. It was similar to the day Henry had announced that they would live in London. A huge change was coming and she didn't want it. She liked things just the way they were.

'Would you like some casserole?' asked William politely, helping himself to a second plate. 'Gloria, you outdid yourself this time.'

James shook his head. 'This is a flying visit, I'm afraid. We're going to Claire's place tonight. I have yet to meet her parents.'

'Claire's place?' echoed Gloria. 'And where's that?' She plastered a smile on her face.

Claire smiled. 'We live in Richmond. Not too far from here, in fact.'

'Will you be there for Christmas?' Aurora blurted out.

James shook his head and winked at her. 'No, Borealis. I'll be back tomorrow. I'm afraid you're stuck with me for the big day.'

Aurora visibly relaxed and sat back. She could see that Gloria felt the same way. This was all so new: James had a fiancée and new allegiances. It was unnerving to think that he was slipping away even further. She watched Claire smile at Henry. She was pretty in an under-stated kind of way. She guessed her age to be about thirty, only a couple of years younger than James. Like Gloria, she was anxious to know more about this girl. What was her background and how had she bewitched her stepbrother?

'Claire, do you have a big family?' Aurora asked in her clear voice.

Claire turned around and shook her head. 'Just my parents and one sister: Melanie. She's an accountant with Deloitte.' She looked at James lovingly. 'They'll be as shocked as you are, trust me on that. I guess, I want you all to understand that we are happy. It may be unconventional and spontaneous, but why wait?' She leaned over and kissed James tenderly on the lips. 'He's everything I want.'

Aurora's phone buzzed on the table and she jumped. Glancing at the screen, she could see Laura's name. Nudging William, she accessed the message.

It read: **FIVE MINUTES. GET GLORIA DRUNK!!!**

William guffawed out loud. 'Could this evening get any better?' he whispered.

Aurora nodded numbly, trying to engage with William's banter. She found herself looking at James with a strange feeling in her heart. She should be delighted for her brother but instead she felt like she had been punched in the gut.

Laura paused outside the front door. She had her key in her hand but it was shaking so much she couldn't insert it into the lock. What the hell was wrong with her? She had always been so self-assured and confident. Her mother would come around, she always did. The bottom line was that she was blissfully happy. Christian Jacob, Attorney-at-Law, was everything she wanted in a man.

It all began when her close friend Lydia had invited her to Ireland for her baby Sienna's christening. She and Lydia were close since the Paris days. Together they had worked in the same restaurant and had often sipped wine late into the night. Both had tried to escape reality for a while, but that brief interlude had run its course after a few years. Laura had returned to London and started working for a PR company. Lydia had returned to Cork and resumed her love affair with Luca: Christian's only son.

Luca, however, was married and so much drama ensued. He and Lydia had had a rocky start to say the least. Missed opportunities and lies had kept them apart, but after the birth of their child and the finalisation of his divorce, things seemed to be back on track. Laura knew that her friend needed support at the christening so she had dutifully flown to Cork, unaware that it would change her life forever.

It was there, at a hotel in a small West Cork town called Skibbereen, that she had encountered Christian for the first time. He had flown in for his granddaughter's day, along with his wife, the famous artist Tara Jacob. The attraction had been instantaneous and, horrified, Laura had tried to ignore it. He was off limits; there was no way she could go there. The devil on her shoulder whispered in her ear, pointing out that his marriage was on the rocks. That was all very well, but she didn't want to be the catalyst. After two months of texts and flowers, she succumbed to his advances and had never looked back. Despite being in the throes of a messy divorce with Luca's mother, he still made time to be with her. He had changed her life completely.

Christian walked up behind her and kissed her neck softly. His iPhone was in his hand – he had just finished talking to

Josephine, his secretary in New York, about an important ongoing case.

He had no interest in the family thing. When she had suggested calling to Oxshott, he had refused point blank. All he wanted was Laura; why then should he have to small-talk with people he didn't know? Christian Jacob didn't do small talk. Then, after a huge argument, he had relented. He could see that her family meant a lot to her. What was a couple of days, right? She mattered to him. Hell, he wanted to make her happy. For the first time in years, he felt alive again. She was the reason for that.

'Right, let's do it.' Laura pushed open the door and walked into the hall. The familiar smell hit her immediately and she was strangely comforted by that. This was her home and everything would be okay. For a moment, she was transported back to the time she had been given detention at school. Her heart thumping, she had entered the house with the same feeling of trepidation, waiting for the inevitable showdown.

'*Is that you, Laura?*' called William innocently from the dining room. '*We're all in here!*'

Laura cursed Aurora – clearly she had told him. Oh, she could just imagine him lounging at the table with a giant smirk on his face. Taking a deep breath, she opened the cream door.

'Merry Christmas!' she declared, a bright smile plastered on her face. The table was full and the image swam in front of her eyes. The whole family were in situ, even James. Talk about getting it all over with in one go!

'Hello, darling. Dinner's on the table. Just grab a plate.' Gloria, deep in conversation with James, barely looked up.

Henry waved and resumed typing a message to his agent. Aurora didn't react – she was staring at James.

It was only William who got to his feet and loped over. Opening his arms wide, he pulled her into a massive bear hug. 'So, where's lover boy?' he whispered in her ear. 'Or should I say lover man?'

'Shut up,' she hissed. 'He's just in the hall.'

Christian walked in at that very moment. His tanned, handsome face was impassive and he didn't look remotely nervous. Did he care what these people thought? Not at all. Laura was what he wanted. If they had a problem with that, then they could go jump.

'Hello,' he announced curtly. 'Happy Holidays.' His brown eyes drank in the occupants of the table, figuring out who was who and analysing the situation. Being in a courtroom taught him that. He was adept at reading faces and deciphering reactions.

At the sound of his voice, Gloria tore her eyes away from James. Laura hadn't mentioned bringing a guest. She stared at the handsome man standing in the doorframe with his expensive cashmere overcoat and his haughty demeanour. Irrationally, she wondered if her chicken casserole would stretch to feed the newcomers.

'Laura?' she asked.

'This is my boyfriend, Christian,' announced Laura breezily. 'Christian, this is my family: my stepfather Henry, my mother Gloria, my brothers James and William, and, of course, my stepsister Aurora.' She paused in confusion when she saw Claire. 'Oh, I'm sorry, and you are?'

Claire waved. 'I'm Claire.'

James stood up and came over to hug his sister. 'Claire is my fiancée,' he whispered in her ear. 'We met in Syria.'

'What?' It was Laura's turn to do a double take. 'What did you say?' She looked wildly at her brother.

'We're engaged.'

'What the hell?' she mouthed.

His eyes crinkled in amusement and he whispered, 'We fell in love, is that so crazy?'

He helped her off with her coat and stepped out into the hall with it, Laura following.

'It's pretty quick, don't you think?' she whispered, narrowing her eyes. 'What's with the outfit? She's like a lumberjack.'

'Hey, stop that right now.' He looked stern. 'We just got off a flight from hell. Give her a break.'

They went back inside and sat down at the table side by side.

Henry had taken Christian's coat from him and offered him a chair, his good manners masking his surprise.

'May I get you a drink?' he asked now.

'A scotch would be good,' Christian replied. 'Have you guys got a Wi-Fi code I could use?'

'The modem is over there,' said William helpfully. 'The password is long and complicated so you'd better type it in directly from that.'

'I got it.' Christian strode over to the small white box on the bookcase. Taking out his half-moon glasses, he punched in the long code to activate the internet on his phone.

'He's American?' mouthed William to Aurora, noticing his twang. 'Even better.'

James nudged Laura and whispered, 'So, why are *you* seeing a sugar daddy?'

'He's not a sugar daddy,' she retorted. 'He's amazing.'

'Still though, he's on the wrong side of fifty. Gloria looks like a fish. Her mouth is opening and closing so much.'

They both regarded their mother, who was desperately trying to process the news. Her son was getting married to a girl she'd never met and now her only daughter was dating a man old enough to be her father.

William scraped his second plate merrily and refilled his wineglass. It felt good to be the son who caused no trouble. He knew that his mother had been planning to lecture him on his lack of social life and now that had all been forgotten. He blessed his siblings silently. Gloria would have too much to think about now.

It was Aurora who had given him the heads-up regarding his mother's concerns. 'She's worried about you, Will. You're a catch yet you never seem to meet anyone.' He had waved her away dismissively. What he did or didn't do was none of their bloody business. He did meet women. He just didn't broadcast it to the world. In fact, he had just split from an intensive-care nurse last week. They had been seeing each other for two months. Yet, for some reason, it had fizzled out. His crazy workload afforded little time for wooing and she had grown fed up of coming second-best.

Was he upset about it? Not really. Penny had been fun and someone to cuddle up to at night, but she wasn't the one. He had known that from the start. The only girl who had ever had a major effect on him was Ella, Laura's friend from years ago. He had admired her from afar and had never even tried to make a move, despite dreaming of her constantly. She had always fancied someone else and they had been firm friends: nothing more. Then she had moved away when she was fourteen. Her father was involved in foreign affairs and had been offered a job in Canada. So, Ella Taylor had emigrated, leaving a heartbroken Laura behind. Unbeknownst to everyone, she had broken his heart too. He never had the chance to tell her.

'James?' said Gloria, getting to her feet. 'Would you join me in the kitchen? I want to show you something.'

Claire's eyes met his and they smiled. It was only natural that Gloria wanted details. This was a huge bombshell and she was having difficulty processing it.

He sauntered into the kitchen and closed the door behind him. 'Mum?'

She had her back to him and her shoulders were slightly slumped. 'Please explain.'

He took a seat and drummed his fingers on the table. 'Can you face me at least?'

Gloria turned around and lifted her head. 'You must understand my concerns, James. This is so sudden.'

He smiled. 'I know. It caught us by surprise too.'

'Are you sure it's the right thing? Are you rushing into something?'

'No.' His tone was firm. 'I'm nearly thirty-three years old, Mum. The time is right. She's perfect for me – surely you can see that.'

She shook her honey-blonde hair. 'I don't know her from Adam, darling. She seems pleasant enough but I just can't tell. Why marriage? Isn't it a bit extreme?'

James took her hands in his and urged her to look at him. 'We met in a world where nothing mattered. Human life, children, homes, families – nothing was held sacred any more. It was living hell. Then, in the midst of all the pain and chaos, she was real. She held me and talked me through it. She symbolised everything that was good and hopeful about this crazy world.' He paused, his brown eyes sad. 'I don't think I'd have survived if it had not been for Claire. She kept me going.'

'In extreme circumstances,' Gloria argued. 'Now that you're back to reality, will your love survive?'

He nodded. 'It will. I've never been so positive about anything. She's my world.'

His mother stared at him speculatively for a moment. 'You're my son. I want what's best for you. Please don't make a mistake.'

'I won't.'

'So, I'm a partner at a law office in New York,' said Christian, sipping his scotch. 'I work sixteen-hour days. I've got to say that I love it.'

Henry nodded. 'I never understood the appeal of the legal profession myself. Frightfully boring, one would imagine.'

'Boring?' Christian raised an eyebrow.

Henry sipped his cognac. 'Maybe in America it's more exciting . . .'

'You got that right.'

James appeared in the doorway and winked at Aurora. She half-smiled but her mind was racing. Laura's and Christian's arrival had been a blur. All she could think about was James and that girl and that ring. It had knocked her for six. She watched him lift his jacket from the back of his chair and put it on. His handsome face looked tired and his eye was twitching slightly. It always did that when he was tired. She knew that.

James cleared his throat and nodded at Claire. 'We're off,' he announced, taking her hand in his. 'I apologise for the short visit, but we want to get to her house relatively early.'

Claire beamed at everyone. 'Thank you for the wine. I'm so sorry that we shocked you all.'

Henry waved and, getting to her feet, Gloria hugged her meaningfully. 'Not at all, my darling. We're delighted that you two are so happy.'

'Rather you than me,' quipped William, winking at her. 'Jiminy is hard work.'

James made a face at his brother. 'Well, see you all tomorrow then,' he said, waving.

'Have a good evening,' drawled Christian, sipping his scotch. 'What with you guys gone, I guess I'll take centre stage.'

Laura glared at him. 'Don't be rude,' she mouthed.

Aurora followed them out to the hall. 'Happy Christmas,' she whispered as James opened the door.

Claire kissed her cheek. 'I hope that we'll be great friends,' she said with a conspiratorial wink. 'James has told me so much about you. In fact, I feel like I know you already.'

Aurora hugged her back awkwardly. 'Of course we'll be friends. We're going to be sisters.'

'Night, Borealis,' said James, giving her a quick hug. 'See you tomorrow for our annual chess tournament.'

'Yeah – night, Borealis,' echoed Claire, with a small wave.

The door closed and Aurora rested her head against it.

No one was allowed to call her Borealis.

No one, except James.

The family had retired to the sitting room when she rejoined them. Christian, having refused a plate of dinner, had accepted a refill of scotch and was chatting to Henry about American politics. Sitting with her back to them, Gloria was speaking in hushed tones with her daughter. Laura looked menacing. Aurora could almost predict the conversation. Not only was Christian much older, he was still technically married. She could see how Gloria would be worried.

William patted the sofa next to him and signalled for her to sit down. In a daze, she sidled in next to him, clutching a crimson pillow close to her chest.

'Mum is close to a complete meltdown,' he muttered. 'Look how red her face is. Laura looks like she's about to pop.' He chuckled softly to himself. 'Am I a terrible person that I find this amusing?'

'Yes.' Aurora said. 'You're awful.' She regarded her stepmother berating Laura. Getting angry served no purpose at all. She sighed. 'Hopefully it will all settle down in a while. Christian seems nice and you know Laura – she's so independent.'

'Why are you so depressed?' asked William, noticing her gloomy exterior.

'No reason,' she replied, plucking a stray thread from the cushion. 'I'm just tired.'

Henry's laugh resonated through the room. 'Gloria!' he called, 'Christian knows Arthur Mackenzie, my old golfing pal. Can you believe it? He acted as his lawyer during his divorce with that American.'

Gloria reluctantly turned around. She had only begun with Laura and she didn't want to be interrupted. 'That's nice, darling,' she said, smiling tightly before resuming her muffled conversation with her daughter.

'He was difficult to say the least,' Christian went on. 'I earned every buck with that guy.'

'That's Arthur all right,' agreed Henry. 'Super chap, but hard work nonetheless.'

'Oh, just back off, Mother!' shouted Laura suddenly, jumping to her feet. 'Let's talk about this openly. I'm not twelve any more!'

William sat up in excitement. Aurora, alerted by Laura's outburst, tuned back into her surroundings. Christian regarded Gloria calmly, swirling the amber liquid around his glass.

'Christian,' beseeched Laura, her chest heaving. 'Please tell Gloria here that we're serious about each other.'

'*We're serious about each other*,' he repeated slowly, enunciating every word.

Gloria bristled. His arrogance and self-assuredness annoyed her. 'You must understand our concerns,' she began in a brisk tone. 'You're much older and married –'

'*Married?*' shouted Henry. 'Is that true?'

Christian nodded. 'Sure, but not for long more,' he said calmly. 'The divorce is almost final. Tara didn't put up much of a fight which was desirable. Tara Jacob – she's an artist. Have you guys heard of her? She's pretty popular over here. She has a gallery on Canary Wharf.'

Henry clapped his hands together. 'She sculpts as well,' he declared. 'I saw an exhibition of hers years ago in the Tate Modern. She's your wife?'

'Ex-wife,' he corrected. 'We have a son – Luca. He runs her European empire and lives in Ireland with his fiancée, Lydia.'

'Lydia?' repeated Gloria dangerously, comprehension dawning. 'Not Lydia from Paris?' she asked her daughter directly.

Laura shrugged helplessly.

'Not Lydia who had a baby a few months ago?'

'Why, sure,' nodded Christian, crossing his legs. 'Sienna, my grandkid, is incredible. Easily the cutest kid I've ever seen. I'm flying over in a couple of days to see her.'

'So, you're a grandad,' stated William helpfully and got a furious glare from Laura.

'I sure am.'

Aurora stood up. It was time to curb the animosity. Everyone needed to move forward. She'd had quite enough of drama for one night.

'Well, I'm very happy for you,' she announced genuinely. 'Love knows nothing of age or circumstance. I believe that we should be happy regardless. Best of luck to you both.' She raised her glass.

Laura shot her a grateful look and Henry smiled at her proudly.

'*Hear, hear!*' he shouted in agreement. 'Well said, my darling!'

Gloria sat back, defeated. There was no point even fighting it. With any luck, it would fizzle out on its own. She had always known that Laura would be troublesome. She had never been conventional. Sure, Christian was in good shape for his age and looked handsome now, but what about in ten years? Her daughter would only be in her mid-thirties and her boyfriend would be well into his sixties. Time was cruel and she wasn't sure if Laura understood that.

# Chapter Seventeen

Ophelia texted the next morning to remind Aurora of their plans.

**Pub later? Bring your hunky brother XX**

She texted back, saying that she would meet her at five, but only for a couple of drinks. Gloria liked to have the family around her on Christmas Eve. They would watch a film and drink mulled wine by the fire. She and James would have their annual chess competition which she suspected he allowed her to win. This irked her as she was a good player and it took from the glory when she shouted '*Checkmate!*' He would hold his hands up in defeat and toast her alleged superior strategy. However, she watched him make stupid mistakes throughout the game: mistakes she knew were on purpose. She could see why he did it as he always tried to make her feel good about herself. It's just sometimes she wished that he would stop treating her like a child. She had grown up but he didn't seem to realise it.

She sighed loudly and glanced at the time on her phone. It was almost noon. She never stayed in bed that long. It was just that today she had no desire to face the world. All she wanted to do was sleep.

James was getting married.

It had come from out of left field and she couldn't get her head around it.

She realised now that it was naïve to think that he would stay single forever. He was handsome and intelligent, funny and kind. Claire didn't know how lucky she was. Oh, why couldn't she be happy for him? Was she being selfish, wanting him in the background at her beck and call all the time? He always gave her his full attention, ever since she was a little girl. Now, she was losing him and it hurt like hell.

James arrived home at lunchtime, cleanly shaven and dressed in a smart navy hoodie. He dumped his rucksack in the hall and joined William in the conservatory. Gloria loved her 'sun room', as she called it. It was a place where the family used to relax on a Sunday morning.

'Hey, Will,' he said amiably. 'Where's the rest of the family?'

William, still in his sweatpants from his run early that morning, didn't look up from the newspaper. His blond hair kept falling into his eyes and he kept swatting it away. A quick coffee and a flick through the paper had turned into an hour-long session of refills and in-depth analysis of events around the world.

'Laura's gone into the city for some last-minute shopping. Her man wanted to go to Harrods and she needed chocolates for Mum from Fortnum and Mason.'

'Henry?'

'Meeting Dumb and Dumber for lunch at the Ritz.' William made a face. 'Thank God they don't ever call here.'

James nodded in agreement. 'How did a man as nice as Henry produce such utter reprobates as sons?' He entered the kitchen and switched on the kettle. Popping a teabag in a mug, he asked, 'Where's Mum?'

'Annual bridge lunch at the Savoy.' William leaned closer to read a small piece on the new *Fifty Shades of Grey* movie. It was coming soon and anticipation was reaching fever pitch. All he heard about was Christian Grey and Anastasia Steele during coffee break at the hospital. It had taken over the world. Christian, huh, he thought. A sexy name, it seemed . . .

James appeared at the sliding door of the conservatory, mug of tea in hand. 'Where's Borealis?'

'She's upstairs in her room. Avoid her, Jiminy. I put on my Ed Sheeran playlist a while ago and she lost the plot, screaming at me to turn it down.' He sat back and jabbed the paper with his finger. 'The nurses at work are going wild for this film, James. It's being released on Valentine's Day.'

'Which film?'

'You know: that raunchy one with the billionaire businessman called Christian and sadism.'

James raised an eyebrow. 'I'm glad to say that I've never heard of it.' Taking a seat, he sipped his tea gingerly as it was hot. 'Are you planning on going to see it?'

William scoffed. 'Hardly. I have some standards, you know.' He popped a mince pie into his mouth and chewed loudly. 'Aurora's planning to go,' he said with his mouth full. 'It's Ophelia's favourite book apparently. Can you imagine her watching sex swings and whips in action?' He laughed loudly.

'Aurora?' said James sharply, nearly dropping his tea. 'Surely not. It doesn't sound like her thing.'

'She thinks the actor who plays Grey is fit. Plus, it's what one would call a phenomenon.' He regarded his brother's disapproving face shrewdly. 'Jeez, Jiminy, she's not nine years old any more.'

James said nothing. He just frowned and drummed his fingers on the table.

Aurora, alerted by the sound of deep voices, padded into the kitchen wearing her favourite cosy pyjamas and woollen socks. Her long hair was wound up into a messy bun and her eyes looked tired.

'Borealis!' exclaimed James, brightening. 'We were just talking about you.'

She half-waved and switched on the coffee machine. She couldn't face the world without coffee. Her tummy rumbled as she yanked open the bread bin and pulled out its contents. A half loaf of granary bread and some pitta breads were her only options. She shoved two slices of granary into the toaster with force.

William jabbed a finger in her direction and mouthed, 'Like a bear.'

James was watching Aurora. It wasn't like her to be sullen.

'Borealis,' he said, 'what's eating you?'

She ignored him and continued with making her breakfast. Opening the jar of Nutella, she noticed that it was almost gone. *William!* She slammed the jar onto the countertop in annoyance. The jar had been half full the day before. It was like living with a wolf.

James tapped her shoulder. She turned to face him and he smiled as he placed his hands on her shoulders. She was quite tall, measuring five foot seven. Her big brown eyes met his and they gazed at each other for a moment.

Suddenly he let go of her and, stepping back, said, 'Wow, you look exhausted. Did you stay up late practising for our chess tournament later?'

'Of course,' she replied tonelessly. 'Just in case you don't *let* me win again.'

Turning away, she opened the fridge and took out a carton of juice. James didn't need to know that her lack of sleep was caused by his revelation. She just couldn't get her head around it.

'Will, did you eat all the smoked salmon?' she asked in annoyance, scanning the top shelf of the fridge. 'I wanted some with my eggs.'

'Oops!' he apologised, putting his hand over his mouth. 'I put some on toast earlier.'

She glared at him. First the Nutella, now the smoked salmon. He was a bona-fide pig. All he ever did was eat his own body weight in food. Now what would she do?

'It was very nice,' he added unhelpfully.

James calmly pushed Aurora to the side. 'Let's see what else is there,' he suggested, rummaging around the fridge. 'How about some tomatoes? Or some sliced pepper?'

She shook her head mutinously. 'I wanted salmon.'

'Well, get over it,' said William with a laugh. 'You're behaving like a spoilt princess.'

James gave him a pointed look. 'Well, she *is* a princess, Will. Have you forgotten?' He nudged her playfully. 'Come on, Borealis. Cheer up. It can't be that bad.'

She stared at him for a moment. Here he was, defending her again. She knew that she was behaving abominably, yet he allowed it. William had it in a nutshell: James spoiled her rotten. Now, she was upset because he wouldn't have time to lavish attention on her any more. He would be too busy with Claire and possibly his own children.

With a huge effort, she smiled. 'Tomatoes sound wonderful,' she said. 'Thanks, James.'

He visibly relaxed and resumed his seat at the table, grabbing the newspaper that William had just discarded. There were the usual stories on the front page: the immigrant crisis and the American presidential race.

Aurora cracked two eggs into a bowl and whisked them briskly. She poured the mixture into a pan on the hob and stirred. Then she added chopped tomatoes and a sprinkle of salt and pepper.

'Ophelia texted earlier about drinks this evening,' she announced. 'She made a special request that you be there, Will.'

He made a face. 'I don't like redheads.'

Aurora wagged her finger at him. 'It's what's inside that counts. I think that she's really pretty.' She tipped her omelette onto a white ceramic plate. 'So, will you come? Laura can't make it as she won't be back from the city.'

'Why not?' he answered, shrugging. 'It beats watching *Strictly* with Gloria.'

James cleared his throat purposely and tried to look affronted. 'Am I invited?' he asked. 'Or am I too old?'

Aurora blushed. 'Of course you are. I just didn't think that it'd be your thing.'

'As long as we have our chess competition when we get back.'

'Nerds,' mocked William, stealing a slice of Aurora's toast.

Ophelia, tipsy after six vodkas, pressed up against William. 'So, doctor,' she purred, 'I could do with a whole-body check-up.' Her red curls were tied up to one side and novelty tinsel earrings hung from her lobes.

William pushed her away gently. 'I work in Paeds,' he stated matter-of-factly.

'Ah, go on!' She winked at him and blew a kiss.

James caught Aurora's eye and they smiled. Ophelia was a hoot, especially when she'd had a few drinks.

The pub was packed with people young and old, drinking mulled wine and hot port. Christmas music played in the background and a fire burned merrily in the grate.

'Oh, Aurora!' Ophelia called over the din of the pub. 'I found our old poetry anthology today! Remember Mr. Crowley and his penchant for Irish poets?'

Aurora nodded. 'He was an amazing teacher. I really looked forward to his classes.'

'*Aurora had a crush on Mr. Crowley*,' said William in a silly voice. 'No wonder you're such a poetry buff.'

Aurora made a face. 'Yeah, yeah, at least I have taste. Unlike you, William. We all knew that you succumbed to Mary Jane Andersen's charms all those years ago.'

William held up his hands in protest. 'Out of order, Aurora.'

'Liar.'

'You can never prove it.'

Ophelia put her hand on her heart. 'All jokes aside, Mr. Crowley was pretty gorgeous. Remember that poem he taught us about the posh girl?'

Aurora put her head to one side. 'Not really.'

'You do! It was about a planter's daughter or something. He explained how she was the daughter of the local gentry and everyone admired her. It was such a lovely poem.'

'What's a planter?' queried William, sipping his beer.

'An English person who got land when Ireland was colonised,' said James. 'They were the landlords.'

'Oh, yes,' breathed Aurora as a realisation dawned. 'I do remember it. It was by Austin Clarke.'

'I have to admit, it always reminded me of you, Aurora,' said Ophelia, hiccupping slightly. 'You know, the posh girl that everyone admired but never approached.'

Aurora blushed. 'Don't be daft, Lia.'

William nodded in agreement. 'Yeah, don't be daft. We all know the reason Aurora didn't score at school was because she was horrendously ugly.'

Aurora stuck out her tongue at her stepbrother and mouthed 'Mary Jane Andersen'.

'Who?' he replied innocently.

'I loved the line where the poet compares the girl to a Sunday,' sighed Ophelia dreamily. 'How wonderful!'

'What a silly metaphor,' scorned William, breaking the spell. 'I mean, Sunday is the most depressing day. It signifies the end of the weekend and work the next day.'

'On the contrary, Sunday was the highlight of the week for many,' said James, sipping his pint. 'It was a day when they would dress up and look their best. Clarke is saying that this girl was the high point.'

'And it reminds you of Aurora?' said William to Ophelia. 'You've lost the plot, my girl.'

'But look at her,' crooned Ophelia, getting emotional. 'She's just so lovely.' She put her hand on her heart. 'Everyone at the theatre fancies her.'

James' face was impassive; only a muscle flickered in his cheek.

Aurora blushed furiously. 'Would you all stop right now! Let's get another round and move on.' She flicked her long hair to the side.

'Hear, hear!' agreed William. 'Maybe some water for Lia this time.'

'What?' she protested.

'Doctor's orders,' he smiled and she beamed at him.

'Well, okay then,' she preened. 'Let's all go to the hydration station. Anything for you, William.'

James took a deep sip of his beer and smiled. He suspected that Ophelia was right. Aurora's beauty would stop you in your tracks. He could see how pubescent boys would be intimidated. She never seemed to mention boyfriends or dates and, idly, he wondered if she had any experience with men at all. Being away so much, he had missed huge chunks of her life. Maybe she was waiting for her Prince Charming to drive her away in his Barbie Ferrari, like in her favourite childhood game. He chuckled. She could be waiting a long time for that.

She always made him feel protective and even though he knew it was selfish, he didn't want her throwing herself away on a no-hoper. Those actors she worked with were totally unsuitable, flitting from one relationship to the next. Thankfully there was no mention of any love interest at the theatre. That Justin Debussy was another problem. He had only met him once – after Aurora's first performance in his début play *Georgia*. He could instantly tell that he had feelings for his stepsister. The way he looked at her and slung his arm possessively around her shoulders. His upper-class twang booming over everyone else, talking about how his 'protégée' was the next big thing. Aurora had smiled and dutifully talked to the press, telling them in her sweet voice how playing the main character, Clara-Mae, had been a dream come true. Justin, tipsy after a few glasses of champagne, had kissed her full on the lips as cameras flashed.

*Oh how he wanted to kill him.*

Only because he could tell that his mauling made her uncomfortable.

New Year's Eve dawned. Aurora woke and stretched, snug under her soft duvet. For a moment she remembered her old bedroom in Cornwall: the damp walls and freezing floor. How she could never heat up, despite having two duvets and a fire blazing in the grate. Her new room was painted lilac and was the complete opposite. She had posters on the walls, framed pictures of her family and Maggie, a laptop and a flat-screen TV mounted in the corner. Even though she rarely came home any more, her bedroom was left untouched. Gloria insisted that all her children had a space to come back to if needed.

Swinging her legs over the side, she contemplated what to do for the day. Henry had planned his usual soirée, inviting Gordon and Helena, now both in their seventies, and anyone else Aurora would like to come along. He extended an invitation to George and Seb each year, but they never turned up. Still, he felt that it was his duty to be civil, despite feeling like a huge gulf had grown between them. He often relayed his guilt and frustration about this *froideur* to Gloria and she listened quietly. Not once did she bitch about them or try to turn him against them, despite having ample reason. Instead she encouraged him to bridge the gap and attempt some sort of rapprochement, always around Christmastime.

Ophelia was coming, as were a few friends from work. Marianne, her boss at the flower shop, couldn't make it due to family commitments. William, who was nearing the end of his annual leave, said he would attend, to make her look 'popular'. Laura, who had been in Cork since Boxing Day, was due to fly in that afternoon. Christian had gone back to New York and she planned to join him in a week. Aurora was dying to know how the big reveal went: telling Luca and Lydia about their relationship. All she had received were sporadic WhatsApp messages with anxious-looking emojis. 'I'll tell you when I see you…' was the last update.

James had stayed with the family until Boxing Day. Claire had arrived in her Prius and picked him up, much to Gloria's dismay. She had been hoping that he would stick around for the week. 'I'll be back for New Year,' he promised, kissing his mother fondly. 'We've got some friends to visit and I've got to get to know my new family.'

Aurora watched with a heavy heart as he waved and hopped into the car. She and Gloria looked at each other and they both knew that they had lost him. His loyalty would be to his fiancée from now on and they would have to accept it. However, he had promised to return for the party so at least they would all be together for that.

Grabbing a towel, Aurora headed towards the bathroom and closed the door. Unlike the unpredictable plumbing in her Notting Hill flat, her shower at home pumped out piping-hot water for as long as she liked. Aurora adored long hot showers so she stayed under the powerful jet for ages.

Henry was pinning some bunting to the wall when she arrived downstairs. His gold wedding ring glinted in the winter sun steaming through the window.

'Morning, my darling,' he greeted fondly. 'Enjoy your last day of being twenty-two.'

'I'm ancient,' she sighed.

He smiled and pressed a pin forcibly into the architrave. 'Now, do you like your décor?'

She stared at the coloured strands hanging from every available hook and picture. There was text printed on a pink sparkly background that read: *Happy Birthday, Princess Aurora!* Next to that were little pictures of the iconic Disney princess. Henry always got the same decorations from the party shop down the road. Aurora was pretty sure it was for a young child, but he got it nonetheless.

'I adore it, Daddy,' she enthused. 'I just love it.'

'Gloria's in the kitchen, attempting to make you some drop scones.' He raised an eyebrow. 'She's trying her best,' he whispered loudly.

She giggled and joined her stepmother at the stove. An impressive pile of pancakes lay on a plate next to the hob and Gloria was whistling the new Beyoncé tune.

'Morning, sweetheart,' she said, offering her cheek for Aurora to kiss. 'Take a seat. I'm almost ready.'

On the kitchen table was a gift, neatly wrapped and tied with ribbon, and a card with her name handwritten on the envelope. Judging by the shape of the parcel, she could tell that it was a book. That was the tradition: each year Henry would give her a priceless book from his collection.

'Gifts already?' she said in surprise. 'But it's not my birthday yet.'

'Henry and I wanted to give it to you before the madness descends.'

She was suddenly accosted by a strong feeling of *déjà vu*.

On her sixteenth birthday, Henry had given her a poetry anthology by Seamus Heaney. He and Gloria had presented it to her in the very same spot. To this day it was her favourite gift.

'Seamus signed that book for me just before he died,' Henry

said wistfully. 'He was an amazing chap – a great loss to the literary world.'

Aurora had opened the first page and there, in blue ink, lay an inscription saying:

*To Aurora,*

*Etiam in morte, superest amor*

*(Even in death, love survives),*

*S.*

She gasped in delight. 'Oh, Daddy. This is the most wonderful thing I've ever received. I adored his poetry at school. Mr. Crowley taught us all about him.'

'He was a gentleman and a scholar,' agreed Henry, 'a credit to academia and literature.' He smiled sadly. 'He knew Grace also, from her Dublin theatre days. When I showed him your picture, he couldn't quite believe it.'

'You showed him *my* picture?' she echoed in disbelief.

'Why, yes. We met at the launch of *Arachne* – do you remember my play from about seven years ago? He knew of the circumstances of your birth and he felt that this inscription would offer you solace.'

'Oh, it does,' she said, her eyes filling with tears. 'It really does.' Grace flashed through her mind: her ill-fated mother who had been denied the chance to hold her close.

'Even in death, love survives,' she murmured softly.

Gloria dropped the frying pan loudly into the sink, bringing her abruptly back to the present.

Aurora called for her father. '*Daddy! Come here! I want to open my gift with you!*'

Henry appeared and put his arm around Gloria's waist.

'On you go, my darling,' he said to Aurora.

She removed the ribbon and tore open the paper. Inside was a book: a first edition of *Salomé* by Oscar Wilde. It was dusty and old with *Salomé* written in gold lettering on the front.

'Oh, Daddy! You met Mummy when she played Salomé!'

'Yes,' he confirmed. 'The first time I saw her perform was in the title role.' He smiled at the memory and turned to Gloria. 'It was in Dublin and it caused a stir, I can tell you. Irish society was quite conservative until recently. The sexuality of Salomé caused outrage and the production almost didn't happen. It was like the riots regarding Synge's *Playboy of the Western World* in 1907. It was publicity gold, of course, and only served to make Grace even more famous.'

Aurora opened the book carefully, aware of its age and fragility. Its pages were yellowing slightly and, with the lightest touch, she opened *Act One*.

'Oh, Daddy, it's perfect,' she sighed. 'I just love it. Thank you so much!' She hugged Henry fiercely and then Gloria, almost crushing her glasses in the process.

'Right!' said Gloria with a laugh. 'Now, where is that delivery from Waitrose? If they don't arrive, we'll have no canapés tonight.' She deposited a plate of drop scones on the table, along with a squeezy bottle of honey. 'Dig in.'

# Chapter Eighteen

James kissed Claire's shoulder and hugged her close. He knew it was almost noon but he had no inclination whatsoever to face the world. Sleeping in was such a luxury, he wanted to relish it before they went back to the war.

Claire threaded her fingers through his and pulled him even closer, sighing in contentment. Her bed was warm and cosy, and the duvet clung to them both like a glove. She could hear her parents pottering round downstairs but, like James, she had no intention of getting up.

'Did you sleep well?' she murmured with her eyes closed.

'Like a log,' he replied.

Her room was sizeable enough, dominated by a large bed and a tall bookcase filled with medical books and journals. Posters of Oasis and Pulp still hung on the walls and old hockey trophies still stood on the shelf. As it was just Claire and Melanie, her parents had left their bedrooms as they were. They had two spare rooms for guests so there was no need to box anything away.

James' iPhone buzzed on the bedside locker. 'Ignore it,' he mumbled, his eyes fastened shut, hovering between awake and asleep.

Claire squeezed his hand gently and nodded.

The phone buzzed again. Still he didn't move. It was only when it vibrated for the third time that he sat up and yawned.

'I should've put it on silent,' he said, stretching. 'What does a guy have to do for some peace?'

He unlocked the home screen and Aurora's name popped up. Accessing the messages, he smiled. The first one read:

**Daddy gave me a first edition of Salomé! Delighted. What are you up to?**

James raised an eyebrow. He clicked on the following message.

**What time are you coming home? Don't forget my party!!**

He typed back straight away saying that he would be over in the afternoon, finishing the text with a smiley emoji.

'Who is it?' asked Claire sleepily.

'Borealis,' he replied, replacing the phone on the locker. 'She's wondering about her party tonight.'

Claire's eyes opened and she turned to face him. 'What party?' she asked.

'Her birthday party. I thought I mentioned it.'

'No, you didn't.' She sat up straight. 'You do remember that we have a brunch date with Melanie and Charles tomorrow?' Her little sister and her fiancé had booked a table at Coya, a posh Peruvian eatery in Mayfair.

He shrugged. 'Not really, but that's no problem. We can just get the tube from Mum's place.'

'You want to stay over?' She looked doubtful. 'Remember how hungover you were after Christmas? The same thing might happen if Henry produces his Calvados.'

He grinned. 'That was some night. God, I was so sick on Boxing Day.'

'Yes, I remember.' She frowned. 'You arrived here like death warmed up. My poor parents didn't know what to say.' She forced a smile. 'Let's go tonight for a couple of hours and make our excuses. Melanie booked this brunch especially and I've been really looking forward to the four of us getting to know one another. Charles is a top guy.'

'A couple of hours?' he repeated. 'I just texted her and said that I'd be over this afternoon.'

'But we're supposed to meet my friend Molly down town. Do you remember anything? She's dying to meet you.' She crossed her arms. 'Aurora will have lots of people around her. She won't even notice if you're not there.'

James got out of bed and pulled on his jeans. 'She'll definitely notice, Claire.' He pulled a T-shirt over his head. 'I've never missed her birthday.'

'You won't miss it,' she argued. 'How about we show our faces at around ten, have a glass of wine and then leave?'

'Her birthday is at midnight,' he argued. 'She was born on the stroke of the New Year.'

'She's not a child, James.' Claire's eyes flashed. 'As I said, she'll have plenty of people around her to sing and clap. You'll not be missed.'

He stared at her speculatively. 'I've barely seen my family since we got back. It's been your friends and your relations. Now, you don't want me to attend my sister's birthday party.'

'I wasn't saying that . . .'

'Well, I'm going over this afternoon as promised. You can join me later if you want.'

He stalked out and banged the door. Claire punched the pillow in frustration. She didn't want to go to some kid's party on New Year's Eve. There were a million other things they could do. Now, she would have to smile and be polite and endure small-talk with strangers. He needed to realise that Aurora was a big girl.

When they had first met, she had been eager to hear about his family: Gloria the matriarch, Henry the playwright, William the joker, and Laura the spoilt brat with a heart of gold. He talked about Aurora the most and from his stories she had imagined her to be a small girl. The adult version she had met before Christmas had been a shock. She hadn't expected such a beauty or someone with such a bond with James. She obviously meant a lot to him.

She flopped down the pillow and sighed. He was always so easy-going so this was definitely a side to him she had never seen. Melanie always teased her about her tendency to be a control-freak. Maybe he had a point: their week off had been predominantly about her family. She curled up into a foetal position. Should she compromise and go to the party? With any luck, they could sneak off at a decent hour. She just wanted the brunch to go well. What was the problem with that?

Aurora zipped up her new dress and straightened the hemline. It was a short sparkly figure-hugging ensemble with a scooped neckline and short sleeves. Ophelia had convinced her to buy it the week before, claiming that it was 'made for her' and that she would 'regret it forever' if she didn't take it.

She had to admit that her friend was right. It looked really well with her long hair cascading down her back and her black heels giving her extra height. Laura had promised to do her make-up after a quick sandwich. She had just arrived back from Ireland, her arms laden down with duty-free bags filled with black pudding, cheese, whiskey and Guinness merchandise. Aurora couldn't wait to hear about her trip – how had Lydia reacted to the news that her friend was going out with her future father-in-law?

The door swung open and Laura arrived into the room, her Louis Vuitton overnight bag on her arm. Throwing off her heels, she sat on the bed and sighed. 'I'm knackered!'

'How did it go?'

She reddened slightly. 'Well, it was more positive than negative . . . in the end.'

'Oh?'

'Christian was already there when I arrived. He had flown in the day before. Lydia opened the door of her flat and nearly collapsed!' Laura smiled. 'She couldn't figure out why I was paying a visit out of nowhere.'

'Where does she live?'

'Oh, she and Luca live in the centre of Cork city. Quite a plush place, I've got to say. Her cousin Colin lives in the same building. Did you meet Colin when you visited us in Paris? He was always flying over on mini-breaks so you may have crossed paths.'

Aurora shook her head. 'I don't think so.'

'Colin is one of a kind: very good-looking, ridiculously spoilt by his rich parents, incredibly kind and as gay as Christmas.'

'He sounds like fun.'

'Oh, he is,' Laura agreed. 'He absolutely adores Lydia and is almost like a father to Sienna. He keeps buying her Baby Dior and fur jackets.'

'Anyway, tell me about Lydia and Luca. How did they react?'

Laura inhaled sharply. 'As I said, I rang the doorbell and Lydia answered. She was so shocked . . .'

'You said that already.'

'Okay, okay, give a girl a bloody chance. Anyway, the flat was full, needless to say. Colin and his boyfriend Val had called over with wine and Thai take-away, Christian was on the couch with Sienna on his lap and Luca was watching a baseball game. I was slightly taken aback, to be honest. Chris had promised me that it would be low-key.'

'So what happened then?'

'Well, Colin poured me a glass of wine and offered me some leftover Pad Thai –'

'Laura!' said Aurora in exasperation. 'Did you tell them or not?'

'Well, I couldn't, could I? Not then,' she protested. 'There was no opportunity. Sienna started crying as she was overtired and then Lydia pulled out a game called *Cards Against Humanity* and insisted that we all play.'

Aurora giggled. 'So, you ended up drinking wine and playing a board game. Oh, Laura, Mission Accomplished!'

'Then it got worse. Lydia asked me if I wanted to sleep on the couch as Christian was using the guest room. I waited for him to interject, but he ignored the conversation. He just smirked infuriatingly and gave Sienna her bottle. I mean, I thought that I'd be sleeping with him.'

'So, did you sleep on the couch?' asked Aurora, wide-eyed. She couldn't imagine her sister slumming it.

'No, thank God. Colin offered me his spare room, so off I went.' She shook her head. 'I mean, don't get me wrong, I was grateful and Colin is the best host in the world. The guest room in his place was like something out of the Ritz with an amazing bed, a flat-screen TV and Netflix. I felt like I was in a hotel. He even made me pancakes with berries and syrup the next day.' She got up and picked up a kohl pencil. 'We might as well work as we talk. Now, look up at the ceiling and don't move.'

Aurora obeyed and her eye flickered as Laura expertly drew a line along the base of her lid.

'So, I presume you broke the news at some stage?'

Laura nodded. 'The next day actually. Lydia invited me over for coffee. Christian had been texting all night apologising but saying that it was not the right time *blah blah*. When I arrived over, Luca and he were out so it was just Lydia and Sienna.' She brushed some eyeshadow onto her lid and blended it slightly. 'So I told Lydia.'

'How did she react?'

'Not too badly, I must say. She knows me for a long time and she also knows that Christian's marriage is on the rocks. I tried to explain to her that I didn't mean for it to happen and all of that.'

'When did you tell Luca?'

'I didn't.' Laura looked relieved. 'I don't know him as well, so I was pretty apprehensive. Chris told him over drinks downtown.'

'So, you've been accepted.'

'Gosh, no. Not yet.' She shook her head vigorously. 'That evening, Christian got up to go to bed and gestured for me to follow. Luca looked like he wanted to vomit.'

Aurora giggled. 'How did Colin react? Was he shocked too?'

'Oh, it would take a lot more than that to shock Colin. His only qualm was the possibility that I might get married before him!'

'Married?'

'He has been trying to convince his boyfriend Val to propose ever since same-sex marriage was voted in by the Irish public last May. He hints all the time and gets weekly manicures 'just in case', but Val won't budge. When Luca proposed to Lydia, it nearly sent him over the edge as she had always been such a commitment-phobe. He couldn't believe that she would be hitched before him.'

'So, he's paranoid that you'll pip him to the post.' Aurora laughed. 'Fat chance of that, right?'

Laura said nothing. She just continued to dab eyeshadow onto her skin. 'Who's coming later?' she asked, changing the subject.

'I'm not sure. Ophelia, of course. Some old friends from school. Some of the RADA crew and maybe Paul.'

'Paul?'

'My co-star.' She smiled. 'He plays my lover in the new play.'

'How about your director?' Laura looked at her slyly. 'Will he make an appearance for his favourite leading lady?'

Aurora blushed furiously. 'Gosh, I don't know. Probably not. He has plans: some exclusive party in Chelsea.'

'Any news there?' Laura dabbed some blusher on her cheek innocently.

'No way! He's off limits. I mean, a director can never get involved with his actors. Everyone knows that.' She sighed. 'He's so handsome though. I mean, there are times when I wish he would just kiss me.'

'So you fancy him then?'

'Of course. Everyone does. He's very fit.'

Laura nodded in agreement. 'He's all that. Now, look up at the ceiling so I can apply the mascara. Don't blink.'

Aurora obeyed and focused on a cobweb dangling from curtain rail. Her eyes blinked involuntarily which earned her a frown from her stepsister.

'Right, you're all done.' Laura sat back in satisfaction. 'Not bad if I do say so myself.'

Aurora looked in the mirror and her hand flew to her mouth. Looking back at her was a different girl. Her large brown eyes were bigger than usual, circled with black kohl and enhanced with long lashes. Her lids were smoky and her lips were painted a glossy nude colour, making them look full and sensual. Her cheekbones were accentuated with a soft blusher and her skin was like porcelain.

'Wow, Laura. Thank you.' She shook out her hair and arranged it so it framed her face. 'I look my age for once. Although Daddy will have a heart attack when he sees me done up like this,' she added laughing. 'You know he still thinks of me as ten years old.'

'Well, *Daddy* needs to lighten up.' Laura flicked her blonde hair out of her eyes. 'This is the twenty-first century. I think you look fab.' She pulled a bottle of Prosecco out of her bag. 'Let's have a tipple before the party,' she suggested. 'It's not as chilled as I'd like but *c'est la vie*.' She popped the cork and glanced around the room. 'Have you got any mugs or glasses up here?'

Aurora shook her head. 'Just espresso cups that I got from Maggie to complement my new Nespresso machine.' She pulled a box out from under a pile of clothes. Opening it, she extracted two small white cups and placed them on the dressing table.

'They're small but functional.' Laura handed her a small cup filled with bubbles. 'Happy birthday, little sis. *Santé!*'

They sipped their drinks and almost immediately Laura had to refill the cups as they were so tiny.

'Shall we just swig from the bottle?' suggested Aurora, laughing.

Laura smiled. 'There's uncivilised and there's totally uncivilised. Espresso cups aren't ideal but far better than necking from a bottle like tramps.' She handed the replenished cup to Aurora. 'Speaking of Maggie, can she make it tonight?'

Aurora shook her head sadly. 'It's too far for her to travel. I understand completely. I mean, her back is very troublesome.' She looked wistful for a moment. 'It feels like centuries since I've been back there, you know? It's funny how memories fade. I mean, do you remember Freddie Thompson? He just graduated from university and is now a horticulturalist.'

'Freddie the pig farmer?'

'Yes!' She laughed. 'I haven't seen him in years. Whenever Daddy and I went to visit, we never crossed paths. He was always off somewhere.'

'You two were close, yeah?'

'Oh, yes. We were best friends. He wrote to me for two years after I left. I still have the letters. Then, the letters stopped. I guess he moved on.' She sighed. 'He doesn't use social media so the only news I get is from Maggie.'

'Perhaps you should go back,' said Laura thoughtfully. 'It was a huge part of your life.'

'Perhaps.'

Thinking of Cornwall and her old life made her feel so guilty. There was a variety of reasons for her absence: Henry's advancing years and his reluctance to drive such a long distance, George and Seb taking over the maintenance and supervision of the big house and, of course, the memories it evoked. When she was a little girl, she had seen nothing wrong with her upbringing. Her lonely life and her isolation had seemed normal and she had accepted them. Now she could see how disadvantaged she had been. Her teenage years in London had shown her that.

Maggie kept in touch but she never came to the city. She hated London and made no bones about it. Being separated from the old lady had been hard at first. There was many a night that James had calmed her down as she screamed in her sleep, calling for Maggie and sobbing. That all faded as time went on and Gloria became a replacement. She was kind and motherly. Albeit not as good a cook, a worthy substitute nonetheless.

She imagined her mother's grave for a moment: the white pillars standing steadfast against the howling wind and crashing waves. It had been three years since she had last visited. She and Henry had travelled down for the twentieth anniversary of her death and he had placed roses near the headstone as always. Time healed everything and memories inevitably faded away. When she was a child, Grace's memory remained fresh in her head as she saw her portrait every day. Now, that same painting was covered to protect it from sunlight and she only had an image of it on her wall.

# Chapter Nineteen

James crept up behind his mother and said '*Boo!*' in her ear.

Gloria jumped sky high and yelped. 'James!' she chided. 'You frightened me.'

'Do you need any help?'

'No, darling, I've just unpacked my last box of canapés.' She shoved the packaging into the recycling bin. 'There! We're ready.'

On the countertop were plates of various snacks such as sausage rolls, mini-hamburgers, duck wontons, mini-quiches, bruschetta and goats'-cheese filo parcels.

'You outdid yourself,' said James smiling. 'You must have been up all night preparing this feast.'

'Don't be cheeky!' His mother regarded him thoughtfully. 'You look nice today, darling,' she said, straightening his collar. 'Navy is your colour.'

James shrugged. 'I just threw this on. It's the only decent shirt I own.' He ambled over to the table and took an apple from the bowl in the centre. 'Claire will call over later.'

'I didn't like to pry . . .'

'She has to meet friends for drinks.' His face tightened. 'I'm sure she'll turn up at some stage.'

'Everything okay?'

'Fine.'

William pushed open the door with his foot and barged into the room, a large case of wine in his arms. 'I think I've broken my back,' he said through gritted teeth, laying the box gently down on the table. 'Please tell me that's all.'

Gloria peered in at the contents. 'Looks like the red, Will. There's a case of white and champagne too.'

'Up you get, Jiminy. The boxes are in the garage. Many hands make light work.'

Henry ambled into the kitchen with his glasses perched on his nose. 'Did anyone see the charger for my laptop?' he asked, scratching his head. 'I'm getting quite forgetful in my old age.'

'Try next to our bed,' said Gloria briskly. 'Then get dressed, my darling. Gordon and Helena are due any minute.'

Henry disappeared again, mumbling under his breath. He was in the middle of a new play and when he was working nothing else mattered. Gloria was a patient woman but Aurora didn't know that it had taken hours of nagging for him to erect the bunting that morning. She would often wake up to find the other side of the bed empty and the light on in his study. Inspired by the refugee crisis dominating the news each day, he had started to pen a two-act play on their plight. Hence, lots of research and debate. There were mumblings in the House of Lords that Britain might leave the European Union. Nothing seemed stable any more and he had become obsessed.

Gloria frowned. James also played on her mind. She was convinced that this proposal was a knee-jerk reaction to living in extreme circumstances: an attempt to grasp normality in a chaotic world. What better than marriage? An ancient custom that had shaped society for eons. She could see that he liked this girl but she suspected that he liked the idea of stability more.

Laura and Aurora arrived into the kitchen, both stumbling

slightly in their heels. The Prosecco had gone to their heads. Laura had opted for her usual attire: a short dress and Louboutins. Her blonde bob was sleek and her eyes were painted various shades of brown.

'Grab a drink, girls, and let's retire to the lounge,' said Gloria.

Laura poured a glass of white wine and handed it to Aurora. Then she filled a glass for herself and they followed Gloria.

'Oh, the place looks wonderful,' gasped Aurora in delight.

The dining-room table was covered with a vermillion cloth that flowed elegantly to the ground. The surface was cluttered with silver plates filled with various nibbles and a large cake stood on a stand in the middle. It was a chocolate sponge: Aurora's favourite. William and James had successfully stacked the sideboard with bottles of red wine and had struggled to shove as many bottles of white into the already packed fridge. The bunting Henry had pinned up earlier gave colour to the walls and soft music played in the background.

Gloria focused in on her stepdaughter. 'Oh, you look nice, darling. Very pretty.'

'Laura did my make-up.'

'Beautiful.' Gloria stared at her for a moment, a faraway look on her face. Aurora's uncanny resemblance to Grace knocked her for six regularly and tonight was no different. Sometimes, she wished Grace was alive as her death had been so needless and tragic. She felt no jealousy whatsoever when she thought of her dead predecessor – quite the contrary in fact. She lamented the loss and made it her business to fill the void as best she could.

'James is outside on the phone to the missus,' whispered William conspiratorially. 'Trouble in paradise.'

Aurora raised an eyebrow. 'Really?'

'Oh, he was giving her hell for trying to stop him from coming here tonight.' He paused. 'It's not very often that Jiminy gets mad, right, Laura?'

Aurora felt her throat constrict. Claire didn't want him to come to her party? What was that all about? He was her brother, her best friend. Why would she deny him a night with his family?

'I reckon she's an able lady,' reflected Laura, sipping her wine. 'I've only met her once, but I get the impression that she's a tough cookie.'

William laughed. 'Like you should talk. Blimey, you're pretty "able" yourself, Lolly.'

Aurora zoned out and headed towards the garden. She didn't want James to be upset over her birthday. Of course, it was hurtful to think that Claire had tried to prevent him from attending. They had barely seen him all week. The only quality time she had spent with him was when they played their annual chess tournament on Christmas Eve.

He was sitting on a bench under the willow tree with a sombre expression when she appeared.

'James,' she said in her clear voice.

He looked up and, for a moment, she couldn't read his expression. Blushing, she pulled down the hem of her dress and hung her head to hide her embarrassment.

'Did Laura give you a makeover?' he asked, a slow smile forming on his lips. 'You certainly look different.'

'Good different or bad different?'

He said nothing for a moment. 'I'm not sure.' He turned away and kicked a pebble with his shoe. His phone lay discarded on the grass.

Aurora took a seat on the bench beside him and nudged him playfully. 'Thanks for coming tonight.'

'William told you about Claire,' he said matter-of-factly.

'Well, yes.' She reddened slightly. 'All I wanted to say was that you are free to go now. I don't mind at all.' She bit her lip, waiting for his response.

'You don't mind, Borealis?' He put on an insulted face. 'Wow, thanks a lot.'

'No, no, I mean, of course I mind. It's just I want you to be happy, that's all.'

He tapped his foot for a moment and remained silent. She could hear sirens in the distance, wailing incessantly. The noise polluted the night air and got louder and louder.

'That sound reminds me of Aleppo,' he said softly. 'All you hear are sirens, explosions, gunshots and screams.' He hung his head. 'We're pulling out of there in a few weeks. We're coming home.'

Aurora started. 'You're coming back to England?' Her heart soared. 'Oh, James, that's wonderful news!' Her face shone in the twilight.

He shrugged. 'Claire wants to get back into the NHS as she wants to be eligible for maternity leave when the time comes.'

'Maternity leave?' she repeated stupidly.

'Well, yes.' He gave her a sideways glance. 'I'm an old-timer now, Borealis. I have to start thinking about kids and things.'

She felt her skin grow cold. James actually saying it made it all too real.

'I'll apply for work at the Beeb,' he continued, seemingly oblivious to her shock. 'I mean, I gave them six years of my life, spending months on a clifftop waiting for a bird to appear.'

She nodded numbly. Of course the BBC would want him. He was so talented. He would probably have to travel but at least he would be based in London.

*Based in London.*

Living in his two-up two-down house with his wife and children.

*James: the married man.*

She closed her eyes. He was slipping away from her. The irony was that geographically he would be close, but so far away in other ways. If Claire was that possessive now, what would she be like after the wedding?

'Borealis?' he whispered softly.

She came back to earth and found him looking at her in the dusky light. Her brown eyes locked with his and, for a moment, she felt like everything made sense. Nothing could harm her when he was close. She savoured the moment.

'Aurora?' he said more loudly.

She jumped. He rarely called her by her real name.

'Earth to Aurora!'

'Sorry, I was just thinking about my new play,' she lied.

He understood immediately. She was always apprehensive before her début as a new character. He barely knew what this play was about as communication between them had been slack for months now. It was so different to her first performance in *Georgia* as he had been based in London at the time. On her opening night, he had been seated in the front row, clapping like a mad man, overtly demonstrating his support. Now, he barely knew the title.

'When's opening night?' he asked gently.

'A few weeks.' She put her head in her hands. 'I'm so nervous, James. It's always the same before the first performance. Everything depends on opening night. Then, if it's a success, I forget all about the nerves.'

'If? It *will* be a success,' he said. 'With you as leading lady, how could it fail?'

'Oh, it could most certainly fail,' she argued. 'Critics are fickle. Sure, they loved me as Clara-Mae but maybe this time they'll turn against me.'

He shook his head. 'Not a chance. You're the ultimate professional. I'm quite sure that it will be a huge success.'

'Will you be back in time to see it?' She tried to sound cool.

He shook his head. 'Probably not for opening night, I'm afraid.'

She masked her disappointment. 'Just let me know if you need tickets. I can get you and Claire complimentary seats up the front.'

'Oh, you can.' He grinned. 'Well, I'll certainly let you know.'

'Justin is so nervous too, although he hides it quite well.' Her director's face flashed through her mind.

'How is my favourite guy?' James made a face.

'He's very well actually.' She gave him a look. 'I don't know why you don't like him. He's so good to me.'

'He's good to you? Well, we all know why.'

'What do you mean?'

'Oh wake up, Borealis. He's been trying to get you into bed for years. Anyone can see it. Although, how anyone could fit in a bed with him and his ego is beyond me.'

'James!' She raised herself up on the bench. 'You're totally out of order! He likes me for my talent, not for any other reason.'

'I don't disagree that he thinks you're talented. He also fancies you though. A blind man could see it.' He regarded her thoughtfully. 'Given your reaction, maybe you fancy him too?'

'He's handsome and talented, of course I fancy him.' She shrugged. 'What girl wouldn't? However, I'm not foolish enough to think that I can mess around with him without consequences. If I have to choose between a tryst with Justin Debussy and my career, then the latter will always win.'

'Thank God for that.' James nudged her playfully. 'I wouldn't approve if you brought him home for Gloria's Sunday pot roast from the slow cooker.'

'Oh please!' She threw her eyes to heaven. 'You never approve of my boyfriends. Remember how vile you were to Tristan, the French exchange student?'

James guffawed loudly. '*Visage Poisson!* How could I forget?'

'You see? Calling him Fish Face was so mean.'

'He looked like a fish,' protested James. 'A monkfish or

something equally as hideous. *Visage Poisson* was a justified title.'

'And poor Graham . . .'

'That chess geek? With the acne and the glasses? I mean, he was punching far above his weight.'

'He was very nice. He knew more about *Harry Potter* than anyone.' She smiled at the memory. 'He taught me how to play chess like a master. He knew every strategy in the book.'

'Hence your annual victory.' He smiled.

'I *know* that you let me win.' Her cheeks grew red. 'I know you do, so don't deny it.'

'Me?' He put on an innocent face. 'How could you say that?'

The branches of the willow moved gently in the breeze, the leaves trailing on the ground gracefully. There were shouts from inside, signalling the arrival of guests. Aurora stole a glance at James whose face had resumed its sombre look. Whatever had happened earlier with Claire had clearly upset him.

'You and Claire will be fine, you know,' she said softly. 'Remember when Henry and Gloria were newly married? They fought constantly over silly things.' She grasped his hand in hers. It felt cool to the touch. 'Arguing is normal, James. I'm sure it will be all forgotten tomorrow.'

'Well, aren't you a real Dr. Phil?' he quipped. 'Relationship advice from a girl so young.'

'Hey! I'm not that young.'

'You're young enough.' He reached out and brushed a tendril of hair off her cheek. 'I remember you running along that beach in Cornwall, your hair blowing in the wind. It's hard to think that you're turning twenty-three tonight.'

She said nothing. Their eyes locked again and for a moment they didn't speak.

Pulling herself together, she plastered a smile on her face. 'Come inside,' she said, getting to her feet. 'Laura is probably on her third glass of wine by now.'

'I'll follow you in.' He pulled out his phone. 'I just have to make a call.'

Laura sipped her wine and watched her mother air-kiss her friends from the bridge club. Henry was laughing loudly at something Gordon had said. Marcella's brother hadn't changed a bit. He was still as jolly as ever. Helena, his reserved wife, sat regally on an armchair, sipping her sherry demurely. She had aged over the years and weight loss had rendered her face even more lined than before.

'Would you like a refill?' William appeared with a bottle of Chablis.

Laura nodded and held out her glass. 'Might as well get tanked up, yeah? I can't see this little soirée getting too wild.'

'You probably need some down-time after your dramatic week of revelations.' He took a seat beside her at the dining-room table. 'I was thinking, does this make you Lydia's mother-in-law?'

'Good Lord, I'm not married.' Laura took a gulp of wine. 'And even if I were, I would never assume a maternal role. Do you know me at all?'

William held up his hands. 'I was joking, Lolly. Calm down.'

She scowled. 'Why is life so complicated? This whole situation is quite simple to me. Christian is locked in an unhappy marriage, Christian gets divorced, Christian is happy again with me. Why all the objections?'

'Well, Christian has a son and a granddaughter. Plus, an estranged wife. He's not a free agent, Laura. You can't simplify this, little sis.' He rubbed her arm. 'I'm sure it will all work out. Just have faith.' He flicked his blond hair out of his eyes and pointed discreetly at a tall pale girl in the corner of the sitting room. Her hair was scraped back into a bun and her teeth protruded noticeably. 'Is that Marjorie King?' he whispered.

Laura nodded. 'Who else could it be, Will? I mean, she hasn't changed at all.'

He stared at her in wonder. 'Why didn't she ever get braces? Her parents neglected her.'

Laura giggled. 'She's reading English at Oxford now. Turned out to be a right brainbox.' She paused. 'You're so bloody critical. I mean, you're no Adonis yourself.'

'I'm not that bad,' he argued. 'If I suck in my breath really hard I have a two-pack.'

Laura laughed. 'By the way, I got a Facebook message from Ella Taylor last week. We haven't been in touch since she left for Canada.'

William's head swung around. 'Ella from years ago? Your friend?'

'Yeah. She found me through a mutual friend and sent me a request. I accepted, of course. I mean, we were very close back in the day.'

'Where is she based?'

'Well, she has some big job in Toronto: an advertising executive or something like that. She said in her message that she got a promotion and that she's moving to London for a few months. She wants to meet up.'

William peeled the label off his beer bottle with an impassive face. 'Soon?'

'Oh, in a couple of weeks. I suggested lunch in town.' She sighed. 'Life is funny sometimes, isn't it? I mean, we were best friends. We were together every single day. I smoked my first cigarette with her on the basketball courts at school. Then, her dad gets a big promotion and that's it.' She placed her glass carefully on the table. 'That was a long time ago. 2005, 2004, maybe?'

'2003,' said William without hesitation.

'Oh, right.' Laura shrugged. 'Before Facebook anyway. I can't believe it's taken so long for us to connect.'

'Let me know when you're meeting her,' said William casually. 'I might tag along.'

'Of course.' Laura masked her surprise. 'If you like.' She tapped the screen of her phone and accessed Ella's profile. 'Look at her! I think she hasn't changed a bit.'

William took the iPhone and focused in on Ella Taylor's profile picture. Her blonde hair was shoulder-length and slightly wavy, her pretty face was smiling and her skin was tanned. She looked like she was on holiday somewhere. He gazed at her face. Laura was right: she looked the same. Just an adult version.

'Let me know when you're meeting her,' he repeated, giving her back the phone.

'I said so, didn't I?' Laura gave him a look. 'It'll be a couple of weeks.'

Aurora appeared with Ophelia in tow. 'Has everyone got a drink?' she asked.

Laura held up her glass. 'Will just replenished my glass. Any sign of lover boy?'

'Who?'

'Justin.'

'Oh, no.' She blushed. 'As I've said a million times, he has a party in Chelsea tonight. I hardly think that he'll come all the way down here.'

Laura smiled and said nothing. She had seen the way Justin looked at Aurora. Anyone could see that he was smitten. Sure, he might have the best intentions at work: no romantic involvement. However, men in social situations tended to forget. Throw lots of alcohol into the mix and she could see Justin making a move quite easily.

'*Crack open the Calvados, Henry old boy!*' boomed Gordon, who'd had far too much brandy already. 'That stuff should warm the gullet.'

James, who had just arrived into the room, waved his hands in protest. 'God, Henry, don't. That stuff nearly killed me at Christmas.' He winked at Aurora. 'It made me lose that chess game.'

She made a face.

Henry smiled. 'It's extremely strong. I have a farmer near Deauville who has been supplying me for forty years. It comes in a barrel and should be consumed with caution.'

'What is it?' asked Ophelia, confused.

'An apple brandy,' explained Aurora. 'When I was a child, Maggie would mix it with cream and serve it with her apple pie at dinner parties.'

Gordon clapped his hands together loudly. 'Righty-oh. No more procrastination. Let's find that barrel.'

The evening flew by. In no time at all, it was quarter to twelve.

Ophelia nudged Aurora in excitement. 'You're almost twenty-three! Are you excited?'

She shrugged. 'I don't pay much heed to birthdays, Lia. They're always a bittersweet affair, with my mother and all.'

'Oh, sorry.' Her friend's hand flew to her mouth. 'I didn't think.'

Aurora laughed. 'Don't be sorry at all. That was all so long ago. Come on, let's position ourselves near the champagne before Gordon drinks the lot.'

Her uncle was practising 'Auld Lang Syne' in the corner with William. It had become an annual duet, much to the family's chagrin. Neither was blessed with much musical talent. Despite this, they got the crowd going and after a few minutes the combined melody of voices drowned out their slightly off-key offering.

Aurora didn't notice him come in. She was too busy talking to Betsy Smith, a girl she played hockey with at school.

'Happy birthday, Mrs. Sloane,' he said in his deep voice.

She swung around and gasped. There, standing in front of her, was Justin Debussy. He looked gorgeous in a duck-egg-blue shirt, slightly open at the neck, and navy pants that clung to his narrow hips. His blond hair was slightly tousled and his eyes stared at her intensely.

'Justin!' She threw her arms around his neck and hugged him close. Not accustomed to drinking wine, she was extremely tipsy. The sight of him made her excited and happy, so hugging him was the natural thing to do.

He reciprocated and kissed her hair. 'You smell so good,' he murmured, pulling away.

'Why did you forsake your A-list party to come here?' she asked, wide-eyed. 'I thought your uncle had invited Elton John?'

'It was cool,' he said shrugging, 'but Bertie started playing piano and soon it turned into a singsong from the seventies.' He grimaced. 'I made my excuses and left.'

'You're so good to come,' she said shyly. 'I'm really flattered.'

He stared at her for a moment. 'Well, I had to make an effort for my favourite, didn't I?'

She blushed again, her pale skin turning red.

'Drink?' offered Ophelia, handing him an empty glass. 'There's a makeshift bar in the corner so help yourself.' She attempted to hide her dislike. She and Justin had met years before at an audition and he had been scathing in his critique. Now, she avoided him whenever possible, delighted that Aurora didn't mix with him socially. In her opinion, he was an overindulged spoilt brat who had an ego the size of Africa.

Justin nodded. 'How are you, Cordelia? Any luck with roles?'

'It's *Ophelia*,' she corrected coldly. 'Not at the moment, no.' She backed away. 'As I said, help yourself.'

Justin already had had lots to drink and headed straight for the whiskey.

Henry appeared as he was filling his glass and thumped him on the back, congratulating him on his success. Aurora watched them together: two playwrights at different stages of their careers. She knew that Henry would approve if she brought Justin home.

He had hinted at it often enough. In her tipsy state, she couldn't really remember why she thought it was a bad idea. He was young, fit and good-looking. Sure, he was her director but couples worked together all the time. She was just tired of being on her own. She wanted love: someone to come along and sweep her off her feet. Her gaze wandered over to James. He was texting someone on his phone, his brows furrowed in concentration. He was getting married and was even talking about kids. Everyone was moving on. Her own mother was nearly married at her age. Not quite, but almost.

Laura sidled up beside her and poked her in the ribs. 'I saw lover boy making a beeline for you the minute he arrived.'

'Oh stop it. I'm one of the few people he knows here.' She gulped her wine and coughed. 'Anyway, as I've said a thousand times before, we're work colleagues.'

'Yeah, right.' Laura cut her off. 'He wants you, anyone can see it. I bet you ten pounds he'll make a move when the clock strikes twelve.'

'I'm not bloody Cinderella.'

'Ten pounds, little sis.' She ambled away. 'Only a few minutes to go . . .'

Aurora sighed. What if Laura was right? What if Justin made a move? Maybe denying their attraction because of professional ties was futile. Maybe, just maybe, he could be the one.

She had little or no experience with men, mainly because she had high standards and was also terribly shy. Despite being pursued by the rugby jocks in school, she had always opted for the quiet, nerdy types. They didn't put pressure on her to have sex or drink vodka and they loved to talk about Comic Con and literature which suited her just fine. Then there had been a guy called Harry at RADA who had broken her heart. Used to relationships that moved at a faster rate, he was reluctant to play the honourable boyfriend, deeming her 'no sex' rule old-fashioned and conservative. So, after two months of walks and dinners, he had called time on their love affair, preferring the company of a blonde girl in their class who had a similar outlook to his own. Had she been hurt? Of course. For a wild moment, she had considered giving in to his demands. What was the big deal about sex anyway? Just because it wasn't true love. Ophelia had often laughed at her romantic ideals and urged her to join the party, as it were, but she had refused. The right man would come along and then it would be so much more special.

James walked towards her purposefully. 'So, Borealis, are you all set?'

She nodded. 'It's all downhill from here.'

'You said it. I can see your wrinkles already.' He examined her face gravely, tilting it upwards into the light. 'What does Gloria use again? Oil of Olay?'

She smiled. 'Something like that.'

Justin appeared, a full glass of whiskey in his hand. 'Your father is just an inspiration,' he said loudly. 'I insisted that he come to opening night and give me feedback on my direction.'

'I think he had planned to anyway.'

'Well, I want him to review this one. No holds barred. Although, I think it's damn near perfect.'

James regarded him coolly. 'I think Henry will be there for Aurora, first and foremost. There was no need at all to *insist* on anything.'

'And you are?' Justin said in surprise.

'Her brother.' James stood up straight. 'We've met before.'

'Can't say that I remember.' Justin looked bored. 'Say, Aurora, how about we take off? I know a great wine bar near Mayfair.'

'Oh, I'd love to but I can't,' she said reddening. 'This is my party, Justin. Everyone's here to see me.'

'I'm sure they won't notice,' he pressed. 'Come on, the city will be buzzing.'

James pulled Aurora close. 'She said no.'

Justin drained his drink. 'Let her speak for herself.'

The two men glared at each other.

Aurora reached out and grasped Justin's arm. 'Justin, I can't. It would be rude,' she explained kindly. 'I'm always with Daddy as the clock strikes twelve. It's a tradition.' She bit her lip, waiting for a response. James' grip tightened around her waist. She could tell that he was angry. She knew he didn't like Justin but he didn't know him well enough to judge. Nor did Ophelia for that matter. Yes, he was spoilt and forceful, but underneath all that he was vulnerable too. She had seen that side to him many times.

'Oh, suit yourself,' said Justin eventually. Taking her hand, he pulled her out of James' grasp. 'Let's go over here and discuss the revelation scene. I think Paul needs to work on his accent.'

James watched them walk away with a dark expression. He could see that Aurora was taken by this guy, but surely she could see that he was a pompous arrogant upstart? She never spoke badly of him and worked crazy hours to please him. Maybe he should have a talk with her in the morning. There were a million guys out there. Justin Debussy was certainly not her Prince in a Barbie Ferrari.

'Hey, you,' came a voice in his ear.

He turned around to find a sheepish-looking Claire behind him. Her eyes were warm as she waited for a response.

All thoughts of Justin melted away and his heart soared. 'I didn't think you'd come,' he said, pulling her close. 'I hate when we fight.'

'Me, too.' She kissed him softly. 'Let's never fight again. Especially over something so stupid.'

He cupped her face in his hands and kissed her thoroughly.

She arched towards him, delighted to be forgiven. It was only after her mother forced her to look at things from James' point of view that she realised how selfish she was being. Of course he should be at his sister's birthday party. She had monopolised his time for long enough over the holidays. So, she had hopped on a train and turned up just in time for midnight. They were due to move home to the UK in little under a month and she didn't want to have any bad blood between the families.

Aurora listened as Justin went through Paul's interpretation of Jimmy, nodding at appropriate times and smiling. It was just like when they were at the theatre: he always became completely immersed in his train of thought and could talk for hours. Her gaze travelled around the room. Laura and William were laughing at something. Probably Gordon with the feather boa around his neck. Henry was sitting in his favourite chair, sipping his cognac and smiling benignly. Gloria was head to head with Helena, her bracelets jangling as her hands moved during their conversation. Ophelia was staring at William longingly and her old friends from school were in a group together by the plant.

Then her gaze rested on James. He was holding Claire and staring into her eyes.

She didn't notice Henry shouting '*Ten, nine, eight, seven –*'

Justin pulled at her arm. 'It's almost time,' he whispered.

'*Five ... four . . . three . . . two . . . ONE*!'

'*Happy New Year!*'

The room erupted. Champagne corks popped and there was shouting and singing. William crossed his hands and started singing 'Auld Lang Syne', signalling for the rest of the room to join in.

Aurora waited for James to come over and hug her, just like he always did. All she could see was his dark head bent down towards Claire. Still, she waited. He always hugged her and said, 'Happy Birthday, Borealis'.

Instead, he picked Claire up and twirled her around and around.

'*Stop it!*' she squealed in delight, her face radiant.

Then he bent his head and kissed her like before: deeply and passionately.

'Do I get a kiss?' Justin's voice seemed miles away.

*He didn't come to hug me.*

'Aurora?'

She turned around in a daze and he swooped in to kiss her hard on the lips. Her initial reaction was to resist, but then she let it happen. Why not? Justin was handsome and they were both a bit drunk. It felt good to be touched. It felt nice to be desired.

'Let's go upstairs,' he breathed, his eyes cloudy. His breath smelt of whiskey.

She looked at him incredulously and shook her head firmly. 'In Daddy's house? Are you insane?'

'How exciting!' he pressed on, a blond lock of hair falling over his eye. 'Think about it – they're all down here and we'll be up there . . .'

'No.' She pushed him away gently. 'I'm not that kind of girl.'

He regarded her thoughtfully. 'No, I guess you're not.'

He let it drop. Alcohol had dulled his senses and made him careless. He had vowed not to jeopardise their extremely successful working relationship. Not yet anyway.

# Chapter Twenty

Two weeks later, William got a message from Laura as promised.

**Ella in town! Lunch today at Roux. Sorry for late notice! Hope you can make it.**

He paused for a moment. He had a busy morning and had planned to eat at the canteen for lunch. Typical Laura to text him at the last minute. Accessing his phone, he checked his schedule. The restaurant was in Westminster so he would need at least half an hour to get there. He had rounds and then a meeting with a renal consultant at eleven.

He texted Laura back, asking for a time. She replied immediately, saying around one. He glanced at his schedule once more. If he postponed his private appointment until late afternoon, he might just swing it.

*Ella Taylor.*

Her image was as plain as day in his head. She had never once acted coquettishly around him, flirting badly and trying to be cool. Being a few years older and blond, he had been a hormonal teenage girl's dream. Deflecting unwanted attention had been second nature to him throughout his sister's adolescence. Ella, however, had been different. She had talked to him like a person.

He smiled when he remembered her unrequited love for Simon. If only she could see him now. The years had not been kind. Gone was the brawny rugby player with the limited vocabulary. He was now an electrician with a paunch, three kids and a balding head.

William emerged into the sunshine with a spring in his step.

Laura was waiting at the table when he finally arrived. Her blonde head was bent downwards as she typed furiously on her phone. The maître d' smiled amiably at him as he led him to the table. The white walls in the small dining room gave it a fresh feel and the accompanying white linen on the tables was spotless. A chair was pulled out for him and he took a seat.

'My God, Lolly, thanks for the notice,' he said with a pointed look. 'You do realise that I have a job and can't just flit off when I please?'

She finished her email and placed the phone on the table. 'Sorry, Will. It was last minute on my end too. She messaged me this morning.' She regarded her brother. 'You look nice. New shirt?'

William reddened slightly. 'Hardly. Gloria gave me this for Christmas.'

'*Hmmm.*'

The waiter arrived and offered them a drinks menu.

'Just a Pellegrino for me,' said William.

'I'll have a white wine, please,' said Laura.

'We have many varieties to choose from, madam,' he said, expertly opening the desired page of the wine list. 'They vary in price but I would recommend the Bel Air.'

Laura scanned the list with a frown. 'That sounds fine,' she said eventually. 'Please bring some Evian as well.'

'Of course, madam.' He scurried away.

'Wine at lunchtime?' William gave her a disapproving look.

'Are you finished work for the day?'

'No, smarty,' she retorted. 'In my defence, my job entails a lot of wining and dining. Drinking wine at one o'clock is deemed normal.' She examined her nails. 'I recruit clients and that sometimes requires some alcoholic persuasion.'

William raised an eyebrow but said nothing.

Laura had a talent for convincing clients and had risen up the ranks quite rapidly. She had regular companies who used her skills and her boss adored her. She was a valuable asset to the firm and her needs were catered for.

'She's late,' she observed, glancing at her watch.

'Just five minutes.' William poured his sparkling water. 'Where's the loo?'

Laura shrugged. 'Ask the waiter.'

William walked away and Laura immediately picked up her phone. There was no reply from Christian regarding his planned trip to London the following weekend. Did that mean that she would have to fly over to New York again? This long-distance thing was hard work.

The maître d' arrived with a pretty slim girl in tow. Her face sparkled and her red coat was a vibrant splash of colour against the white walls.

'Laura?' she said in her plummy accent.

Laura's head shot up, alerted by the familiar voice. 'Ella! Wow, look at you! You're the same.'

She stood and they embraced fondly.

'Shall I take your coat, madam?' said the maître d'.

Ella hesitated. 'Well, yes, I suppose.' She unbuttoned the heavy overcoat and handed it to him.

Laura sat down and took a frantic sip of wine to mask her surprise. Ella was painfully thin. It was obvious when her slight frame was no longer concealed by the big coat. Her collarbones were jutting out and when she had turned to hand her coat over

Laura could see her shoulder blades through the thin fabric of her blouse. On closer inspection, she could see that her face was uncharacteristically caked in foundation, giving artificial colour to her pallid cheeks.

'Would you like a drink?' said Laura, trying to mask her horror.

'Just some water, please.' She took a seat and smiled. 'So, how's life with you? I'm so glad we got to meet. I have so much that I want to ask you.'

Laura pulled herself together. 'Well, I'm in fine fettle actually. I'm in love and he's great and work is busy –'

'In love? *You?*'

'Yes, in love.' Laura sighed. 'Everyone has that same reaction.'

Ella giggled. 'Well, you were never one for roses and chocolates.'

'Quite.'

'So, do I know him? Is it one of the boys from school?'

Laura took another sip of wine. 'Well, no . . .'

Someone cleared their throat behind them and Ella swung around. 'Will?' she gasped. 'You're here too?'

He wasn't sure but he thought he saw a brief look of dismay. He smiled. 'Well, hello to you too.'

A multitude of emotions passed over her face. Sadness, trepidation, panic. Finally, she smiled and got to her feet. 'It's just a surprise, that's all. Good to see you.'

She pulled him close briefly and kissed his cheek. William could feel her ribs through her shirt and pulled back. She was practically emaciated. Her clothing, though chic, was hanging off her. His eyes met Laura's and she sent him a silent message to stay quiet.

He took a seat.

'So, how have you been?' Laura asked, buttering a sesame seed roll. 'How's Canada? How are your parents?'

Ella smiled brightly. 'Oh, Toronto is a fabulous city. Have you been? I had such a happy time there. Father is still working at the embassy so he travels a lot and Mother is a permanent figure at charity functions.' She laughed nervously. 'Life is so good there.'

'What about your brother Mark?' asked William. 'He was a brilliant rugby player.'

'Oh, the rugby dried up when we moved,' she said. 'It's not so big over there. He ended up doing law and is an attorney now.'

'Married?'

'Divorced.' She shrugged. 'She was a socialite. Totally unsuitable. Father warned him but he was mesmerised by her bottled-blonde hair and massive cleavage. There were no children, thank God. At least we were spared a custody battle.'

The waiter arrived. 'Shall I bring you some menus?' he asked politely.

'Yes,' said William. 'I'm under a bit of time pressure so I'd like to order as quickly as possible.'

'Time pressure?' repeated Ella, wide-eyed. 'You were always the most laid-back guy ever. What on earth do you do for a living?'

Laura laughed out loud. 'Oh, Ella, this is hilarious. Listen to this.' She pointed at William.

William glared at her. 'I'm a paediatrician at Great Ormond Street.'

Ella stared at him for a moment. 'Are you pulling my leg? William Dixon? A doctor?'

'Yes, I'm afraid so.' He grinned. 'I'm not so bad at it either.'

'Well, I'm very impressed. Well done, you.'

Their eyes met for a moment and he felt his stomach somersault. She really was so pretty and he could listen to her speak all day.

Ella accepted the menu from the waiter's hand and barely looked at it.

Laura pored over the main courses and after a minute's deliberation snapped it shut. 'I'll have the monkfish.'

'I'll have the beef.' William handed the leather-bound menu back to the waiter. 'Rare.'

Ella smiled up at him. 'I'll have the monkfish too.'

'Wine, Ella?' Laura asked. 'I think I'll have another.'

'No. No wine. Just water.'

'Water for me too,' said William.

The waiter disappeared and within moments Laura's glass of wine had been replaced and a new bottle of Evian was placed on the table.

'So, what brings you back to London?' asked Laura.

'Well, I got a chance to work here for a few months so I took it.'

'What do you do?' asked William, tearing a bread roll in half.

'I'm in advertising,' she answered vaguely. 'Huge pressure as there's always a deadline, but I love it.'

'Where are you staying?' he continued airily.

'Um, Chelsea?'

'You don't sound too sure,' laughed Laura.

Ella smiled. 'No, I'm quite sure. I live in Chelsea. In a huge flat. It's just fabulous.' She sipped her water slowly. 'So, tell me all about your lives. I've missed so much.'

Laura brightened. 'Do you remember James? Well, he's engaged . . .'

When it came time to pay, William took out his card.

'Oh, Will, let me get this,' said Ella. 'It's too much.'

He waved her away. 'You can get it next time.'

Ella beckoned to the waiter to come to the table.

'May I have my coat, please?' she asked politely.

'Of course, madam.'

'And the bill too,' added William.

'Of course, sir.' He scurried off and returned in record time with Ella's red coat and the bill on a silver plate.

'I'm sorry that I have to dash,' said Ella, standing and slipping on her coat. 'I have an important meeting with my boss at three.'

'Not at all,' said Laura. 'We must do this again. I'll message you on Facebook.'

Ella shook her head. 'My Wi-Fi isn't the best. I had to go to a cyber café this morning to message you.' She rummaged in her bag. 'Here, this is my number. Let's keep it old school.' She wrote it out twice on a paper napkin and tore off the pieces. Then she handed one to Laura and one to William. 'It was wonderful to see you both,' she said warmly. 'Let's do this again.'

Then she was gone.

Laura looked at William and waited for him to speak.

'She seems well,' he began lamely.

'Give me a break! She's a mess. Did you see her hide her monkfish under the samphire?'

He shrugged. 'I'm not sure . . .'

'She didn't eat a bite. She's anorexic. I've no doubt about it.'

'Do you really think so?'

'I know so. I could feel her bones jutting out when I hugged her.'

'Yes, I noticed.' He got to his feet. 'We should keep in touch with her, Lolly. She won't know many people any more.'

'I don't know about that. Ella was always very sociable so I can't see her being too lonely.'

'I still think that we should keep in touch.' His tone was firm.

'Well, it looks like I'm off to the States again this weekend, so you're on your own.' She drained her wine. 'Thanks for lunch, Will. Much appreciated.'

'Maybe she'd like to go to Aurora's new play or something,' he said, thinking out loud.

'When is that again?' Laura frowned. 'Please say it's not this weekend! She'll murder me if I miss opening night.'

He patted her back. 'It's fine. It's the weekend after next. I met her yesterday. Talk about stressed! Justin changed something at the last minute and she's panicking.'

'Are they a couple yet or what?'

He shook his head. 'She didn't mention anything anyway. The play has taken over so I guess they don't have much time for anything else.'

'Thank you, sir,' said the maître d' as they left. 'Have a great day, madam.'

They walked out into the cold air. 'Jiminy's due back at the end of the month with wifey,' said Laura. 'It'll be great having him around again but I'd say he'll be under this.' She held up her thumb. 'I've said it before: Claire is a tough cookie.'

'It takes one to know one,' laughed William, kissing her cheek. 'Enjoy the Big Apple.' He walked off in the direction of the Tube station.

# Chapter Twenty-one

Paul and Aurora were backstage in the dressing room, taking off their costumes after a successful dress rehearsal. Justin had left, claiming that he had to meet his uncle, the famous actor Albert Wells. He was on a break from filming and had promised his nephew that he would attend the upcoming opening night. He had missed his other two plays due to filming abroad. Justin wanted him and his A-list pals to add the celebrity factor. If Albert Wells turned up, it would be in the papers. Publicity was welcome from any angle.

'One week to go!' announced Paul, fixing his hair in the mirror. 'I don't want to sound cocky but I think this is the one.'

Aurora knew what Paul meant. She could feel it too. The accents that they had struggled with for so long had finally clicked. Paul had cracked the moody demeanour of Jimmy Romano. The chemistry between them was almost palpable. They sizzled on stage and they knew it.

Paul took off his shirt and hung it on a rail. His muscles rippled as he moved.

'It's such a pity you're gay,' she said, gazing at his tanned torso. 'You're very pretty.'

'Are you still waiting for Debussy to pounce?' Paul's eyes crinkled. 'You know he won't think of anything else but the play for the next week or so.'

'Not pounce, exactly.' She blushed. 'It's just he came all the way down to my birthday party and kissed me once.' She took off her wig and shook out her long tresses of hair. 'Then nothing and he's practically ignored me since.'

'What do you expect?' said Paul. 'You rejected his offer of sex.'

'Sex upstairs in my family home with my parents downstairs,' she corrected. 'I don't know about you, but the thought of Henry barging in while we are *in flagrante* doesn't do it for me.' She wound her hair up into a messy bun. 'I want it to be special, if it ever happens. Although given his mood the last few weeks, I think he's gone off me.'

Paul ambled over and grasped her shoulders. His dark-blue eyes regarded her honestly. 'You're a goddess, Sinclair. I'm gay and even I can appreciate it. Justin is crazy about you but, as I said, he's not going to jeopardise anything this week. Not until the critics have written their piece on *La Morte*. Be patient. True love will conquer all.'

'True love?' she echoed scornfully. 'I wouldn't get carried away.'

'You know what I mean.' He pulled on a dark-green hoodie. 'Now, I'm off to get some sushi. Want to join me?'

She shook her head. 'I have to meet Lia later. She's holding a candlelight ceremony to remember David Bowie.'

'Oh.'

'She adored him,' she continued. 'I've spent the last week consoling her. Although, Alan Rickman broke my heart. What a loss.' She sighed. 'Snape was one of my favourite characters in *Harry Potter.*'

'Oh, for sure.' Paul pecked her cheek. 'Right then, see you in the morning. *Ciao*, my lover!'

He disappeared out the back door. The only people left at the theatre were the sound engineers and a girl sorting out props. Ray Rossi, the older actor playing the role of her mob-boss husband Joey Sloane, had left almost straight away after rehearsal. Justin always became very demanding before opening night and the actors would often be obliged to work twelve-hour days. As a result, the minute the curtain went down, they disappeared like wildfire.

She picked up her Mac and draped it over her shoulders. Every part of her body ached. It always felt like a comedown after a day of playing someone else. For hours she had transformed into Elise Sloane. Her mannerisms and accent were a world away from Aurora Sinclair. Now, she was back to herself and it felt strange. The transition always took time.

A quick pit stop at 'Remembering Bowie' and then a long hot shower. Her bed beckoned. There was only one week to go and she needed her sleep.

William waited three days. Three days before he texted Ella. He typed the message four times before he sent it. He wanted to sound cool and nonchalant.

**Hey! It's Will. Want to meet for a drink? I'm off tomorrow. Text me.**

He sent it at eight in the morning. Everyone checked their phones first thing over a coffee. Even busy popular girls like Ella.

At ten thirty, he checked his phone. No reply. *Maybe she hasn't seen it.*

At two thirty, the same.

He ran his fingers through his hair. The least she could do was reply. Even if her answer was no. Surely no one was that busy.

He grabbed a stained porcelain mug from the cupboard in the break room. Denise, the sister on the ward, had just boiled the kettle. A cup of tea was just what he needed. Work had been tough over the past week. A child under his care had passed away. It never got easier.

He pushed it out of his mind and thought of Ella once more. She had given him her number. She had even gone to the trouble of writing it out twice: once for Laura and once for him. She had laughed at his jokes and had seemed friendly enough.

He picked up his phone and unlocked the home screen, willing a message to appear.

*Nothing.*

He threw the phone onto the table, just as Denise appeared.

'Are you making tea?' she asked in her soft Irish accent. She was a sturdy woman in her fifties who ran the ward like clockwork.

'I was just about to.'

'Then I'll make a pot for us all. Brenda is on the way with a packet of biscuits.'

William smiled. 'What would I do without you?'

That evening William's phone buzzed, signalling a new message. With a beating heart, he pressed the green icon but it was a text from Laura who had just arrived at Christian's apartment in New York.

**Do you need anything from duty-free? Flying back on Sunday.**

He answered straight away saying that he was fine and to enjoy her weekend.

She sent back a smiley emoji. Throwing his phone on the bed, he deliberated what to do. The most obvious explanation was that she didn't see the message. Ella was well brought up and would never deliberately ignore him. Should he text her again? To jolt her memory or alert her to the existence of the original message?

**Hey, Ella. Can you let me know about tomorrow? Thanks. Will.**

He pressed 'send' before he could change his mind. Switching on the TV, he was gratified to see a repeat of a David Attenborough nature documentary was on. It was the perfect way to wind down after a long day. He put Ella out of his mind. If she didn't reply this time, he would leave it go. He had wasted his day worrying about it.

A funny-looking green insect filled the screen and a familiar voice began to narrate. He felt his body relax and within minutes he had fallen asleep.

Laura opened her eyes and sighed. She just loved Christian's bed. It was a giant mahogany structure with expensive cotton sheets and plump pillows. He was gone since seven that morning. Josephine his secretary had called about an impromptu meeting with a client. Laura had pouted. I mean, who had meetings on a Saturday morning? Christian explained that he could charge double for an out-of-hours consultation. That mitigated things. There was time for a shower before he got back. She needed to sort out her hair.

Christian's French mother, Marcheline, had died a couple of years back and he had inherited her plush apartment on the Upper East Side. It boasted three bedrooms, antique furniture and a Monet on the wall. His mother's bedroom remained closed off as he wasn't ready to clear out her things just yet. Then, down the corridor was his son Luca's room. It too remained closed up, only to be used when he visited.

Luca had spent the most of his childhood in this place, being cared for by his doting grandmother. When he was little, Christian had been busy trying to make partner at the law firm and his mother, Tara, worked unpredictable hours as an artist. As a result, Marcheline, or Mimi as he had called her, practically raised him as her own. She adored her *petit* Luca and they had been really close. Her unexpected death had been a huge blow.

When Sienna was born, Lydia and Luca named her Sienna Marcheline, after the Jacob family matriarch.

Lazily, Laura draped her leg over the blanket. She could see by the gold clock on the mantelpiece that it was close to ten. He had mentioned being back for eleven. Maybe she should wait and they could make love before she wet her hair. She closed her eyes and sighed in contentment. The bed was just heaven. Framed photographs stood next to the clock, all filled with various family members. One was of a ten-year-old Luca, holding a Little League trophy with his front tooth missing. Another was of Marcheline and Henri, Christian's father, on their wedding day. Henri was the spitting image of his son. They shared the same impressive height, tanned skin and chiselled cheekbones. Finally there was a new addition to the gallery: a family photo of Luca, Lydia and Sienna outside the church where the baby had been christened. Both mother and child were in white and Luca looked like a model in a sharp suit. He resembled the Jacob men in all ways but one: he had his mother's blue eyes.

The front door slammed and she heard a clatter as someone dropped keys on the granite countertop in the kitchen.

*He's early!*

Scrambling up, she debated whether to cover her naked body with one of his shirts. At the last moment, she decided not to. He would be delighted if she sauntered out in the nude. She slipped on her black four-inch Louboutin heels and walked out the door into the corridor. She could hear noise from Luca's room.

*Odd. He never goes in there.*

The door was slightly ajar, so she stretched out her long leg suggestively around the door-frame. There was no reaction so she pushed open the door fully to reveal a small woman with vibrant red hair holding a baseball jersey. She was eye-catching in a multi-coloured dress that flowed to her ankles. Bracelets jangled on her wrist and a silver Celtic torc necklace sat around her neck. Only the fine wrinkles around her blue eyes revealed her age.

'Hello,' she drawled, unperturbed by the sight in front of her.

'*Fuck!*' screamed Laura, falling backwards in shock. Painfully aware of her lack of clothing, she covered her breasts with her arms and crossed her legs.

The woman in front of her was Tara Jacob, Christian's ex-wife. She had only met her once before at Sienna's christening.

'Sorry to disappoint, but my husband isn't back yet.' Tara swept past her. 'I needed to get this for our son, Luca. I didn't realise that there was someone here.'

She had an Irish accent with the addition of an American twang. Lydia had mentioned once that she was originally from Cork and had met Christian while working as a waitress in the eighties.

'How did you get in?'

'I have a key, darling. All family members do.' She picked up her Mulberry bag, her blue eyes glittering. 'I'd put on something fast. It's sub-zero outside. Heels aren't sufficient attire during a New York winter.'

Laura backed away in mortification. Of all the times to come face to face with her predecessor. She felt exposed and vulnerable. Oh, why didn't she put on Christian's shirt?

'He should be back any minute,' she said lamely.

'He told you that, did he?' She laughed bitterly. 'Oh sweetheart, you've got a lot to learn. You won't see him until late tonight if you're lucky. He's married to the job. At least, it's the only marriage he stays faithful to.' She regarded her for a moment. 'I always wondered what he saw in you. I mean, I can see how blonde hair would appeal and, of course, the youth. However, seeing you naked has really knocked me for six. Let's just say, I wouldn't walk around in the nude if I were you.'

The door slammed shut. Laura dashed back to the bedroom, tears stinging her lids. How dare she speak to her that way? How dare she just barge in here without warning? She crawled under the covers with a pain in her heart. Oh, why didn't she stay in the bedroom?

*What if she's right? What if he doesn't come home?*

She picked up her phone and dialled his number. He answered on the fifth ring.

'Yes?' His tone was abrupt.

'Will you be long?' she asked in a small voice.

'Where am I usually when you call?'

She brightened. 'You mean, you're outside?'

'Just paying the cab driver.'

'Oh thank God!' She rubbed her nose. 'Please hurry.'

'You still in bed?'

'Yes! Yes, I am. I can't wait to see you.' She really meant it.

'Be there in five.'

He found her huddled under the covers, her face set in a taut line. He almost tripped over the discarded heels as he rushed to her side.

'Laura! What the hell's wrong, baby?'

She sniffed. 'I just made a right arsehole of myself.'

'Oh?' He rubbed her shoulder.

'Your wife called over.'

'What?' He looked startled. 'Tara was here?'

'Yeah. She came in unexpectedly to get something from Luca's room.' She felt the tears well up in her eyes once more. 'I thought it was you as she had a key. Why does she have a key, Christian?'

He kissed her forehead. 'The divorce hasn't gone through yet so technically she's still my wife. If I ask her for her key of this place, she could contest the settlement. She's entitled to half. I guess, I want things to go as smoothly as possible.'

'But you're giving her millions,' said Laura angrily. 'Why would she try to take your mother's apartment off you?'

'Divorce is a bitter business,' he said simply. 'She's pretty pissed that I've moved on.'

Laura curled into a ball. 'She said only family members have a key to this place. Then she implied I look awful naked.'

'She said what?' He shook his head in bewilderment. 'Why the hell would she say that?'

Laura reddened and buried her face in the pillow. 'I heard a noise and I thought it was you. I put on my heels and nothing else and walked out to surprise you.' She moaned in embarrassment. 'I met her head on, wearing nothing but my Louboutins.' She didn't dare look at him.

'You're kidding, right?'

'No.'

Christian started to laugh, a deep throaty sound.

Laura sprang up and started to pummel him. 'Shut up, you pig,' she shouted. 'It was singularly the most mortifying moment of my life. Thank God I had that Brazilian wax before I jetted out here.'

He continued to laugh, his eyes creased in mirth. 'What a sight for my ex-wife. Oh, Laura. You're awesome.'

'Chris!' She pushed him away in exasperation. 'You're so out of order. Get out and laugh somewhere else.'

He pulled her into his strong arms and ignored her squeals of protest. 'Can we do it again? You in the heels, I mean?'

'What?'

'If I go out there, will you put on your heels and try again?' He gave her a hot look. 'You know how I love heels.'

She felt her breath quicken. 'I suppose I could do.'

'Great. Don't take long.' He strode out of the room without looking back.

She jumped up and rubbed her tear-stained face. Her hair was tousled but that didn't matter.

'Righty-oh, boys. Here we go again.' She slipped her feet into the offending heels once more and followed Christian out into the hall.

# Chapter Twenty-two

William handed the woman twenty pounds and smiled when she gave him his change. He hated shopping after work but there wasn't a morsel of food in the house. The hospital had been busy all day and he hadn't even had time for a cup of tea. Now, he had the bare essentials for a crude pasta dish. Lots of carbs sounded great. Carbs, a beer and then bed.

His flat was cold when he finally got home. Checking the thermostat, he realised that the heating was only timed to come on in the morning. Twiddling the dial, he amended it. It was freezing outside and, being tired, he felt it even more.

His phone buzzed in his pocket but he hadn't the heart to look at it. Despite his two messages the week before, Ella hadn't replied. Nothing. He was sick of checking his phone, willing a message to appear. The disappointment grew every time and now he was fed up of it. Laura rang after he had wolfed down a plate of cheesy fusilli.

'William! You'll never guess!'

'Never guess what?'

'Things have moved up a notch with Christian. I think it's really serious.'

'Did he propose?'

'Crikey, no. But he did give me a key to his apartment. A key reserved for *family*.' She emphasised the last word.

'Whoa, Lolly, that's pretty heavy.'

'I know, yeah. I'm delighted. I mean, I'm rarely in New York, but now I have my own place.'

'Wicked.' He flicked the channel on the TV. 'So, any other news?'

'No, nothing from my side. He's flying over for Aurora's play next Saturday. Are you going? Did you invite Ella?'

His heart plummeted. 'No.'

'Why ever not?'

'I texted her twice but she never answered.' He sighed. 'I mean, I remember her in the old days. Her phone was like another limb. She must have seen the messages.'

'Will! Are you sure you have the right number?'

He paused. 'I think so. I mean, I hope so.'

'Well, that's the obvious reason, Will.'

His heart lifted. 'You know, you have a point. I threw away that piece of napkin that she wrote it on. Maybe I typed it into my phone wrong.'

'I'll send on the one I have and you can check.'

'Thanks, Lolly.'

'Make sure you ring her, okay? No more dilly-dallying.'

'Right, boss!'

'Then you'll know for sure. Speaking to someone is far better anyway.'

'Okay, okay.'

'Do it, William. Ask her to the play. She'd enjoy it.'

The line went dead.

William grasped his phone tightly in his hand. Laura was right. Ringing her was the mature thing to do.

He waited for Laura's text to come through. True to her word, she sent on Ella's number immediately. He was surprised to find that it was identical to the number he had.

For a moment, he lost his nerve. What if she didn't answer?

*Then you'll know the truth!*

With a beating heart, he pressed call. She answered on the third ring.

'Will!' she said breathlessly. 'Oh, it's so good to hear from you.'

He hadn't expected that. 'Hi, Ella, are you well?' Closing he eyes, he winced. What a conversation-opener.

'Oh, wonderful. So busy at work and all that.' She paused. 'Are you well?'

'Oh, great. Busy at work too.' He bit his lip. Why was it so awkward? He decided to bite the bullet. 'So, I was just wondering if you would like to meet me for lunch? Say tomorrow?'

'I'd love to,' she answered without hesitation. 'Where do you have in mind?'

'The Swan? It's a pub near the hospital.'

'Great – around one?'

'Yeah, one is perfect.'

He pressed 'end call' and let out a deep breath. He had not expected such enthusiasm. Why then had she not answered his texts? He had the correct number. Women were such a mystery. Still, she had agreed to meet him which was positive.

Whistling, he washed his plate and left it on the rack to dry.

The January air was crisp and cold. Pushing open the door of the pub, he was gratified to see a blazing fire in the corner. Right next to the giant mantelpiece was a cosy booth: the perfect spot for a cosy lunch *à deux*. He took off his coat and hung it on a hook. Glancing around, he could see that she had not arrived. There were the usual lunchtime punters having beer at the bar and a few of the nurses were eating pie and chips in the corner. He waved amiably over at them and received lots of smiles in return.

A waitress approached him with a menu and he accepted. 'Drink?' she asked.

'Just an orange juice, please,' he replied.

The front door of the pub opened and his heart leapt. However, it was just a woman with a buggy. Idly, he started to shred a beermat, his thoughts filled with her.

Then the door opened again and he steeled himself. It was Mary from the hospital.

'Hi, Will!' she called, waving madly.

He smiled and blew her a kiss.

The next time the door opened, he didn't bother to look up.

'Hi, Will,' came a soft voice.

Looking up, he was confronted with Ella. She was soaked to the skin, her blonde hair plastered to her head. He could see that she was shivering uncontrollably.

'Good God, take off your coat,' he said, jumping up. 'Here, take mine.' She allowed him to peel off her flimsy anorak and wrap his warm woollen coat around her shoulders. Again, he was struck at how thin she was, her bones jutting out and her face pale. 'Sit down and I'll get you a hot drink.' He beckoned to the waitress. 'May I have a pot of tea?' He looked at Ella. 'Unless you'd prefer coffee? Or something stronger?'

She shook her head, her teeth chattering. 'Tea is fine.'

The waitress nodded.

'Did you walk here?' he asked, glancing at the weather conditions outside.

Ella nodded. 'I tried to get a taxi but for some reason not one would stop.'

'What about the Tube? Or a bus?'

'Oh, you know me and public transport, Will. We just don't mix.' She didn't quite meet his eyes. 'I just kept hoping that a cab would take pity on me and stop.'

'So you walked all the way from Chelsea?' he went on incredulously. 'In this weather? You're a lunatic.'

She smiled at that. 'Yes, I suppose I am.'

The waitress placed the steaming teapot on the table, next to a cup and saucer.

'Would you like menus?' she asked pleasantly.

William nodded.

Ella poured her tea and held her cold hands over the ensuing steam.

He regarded her thoughtfully. She looked pensive and her blue eyes had a faraway look.

'So, how's your new job? Are you working late?' He sipped his orange juice.

'Oh, it's wonderful! So busy and full on. I don't get home until past midnight most evenings.' She smiled brightly. 'They're thinking of extending my contract so I may be here for longer. Although with all the partying, I'm not sure I'm able for it.' She laughed.

'So you're staying in London?' He smiled broadly. 'That's just great.' He scanned the menu. 'The food is nice here. It's all pie-and-chips sort of stuff. Will that suit?'

She shrugged. 'I'll just have a soup or something like that.'

'Are you sure? Steak and kidney pie doesn't tempt you?' he teased.

A shadow passed over her face only to be replaced by a smile almost immediately. 'Tempting, but I'll give it a miss. Just order me the soup. I'm just going to pop out for a cigarette.' She rummaged through her bag and pulled out a box of Marlboro.

'You still smoke?'

'Yes.' She got to her feet. 'I blame you entirely, William Dixon. You were the one who bought them for me all those years ago and now I'm hooked.'

'Ella!' He held up his hands. 'Please say that's not true.'

'Well, I did steal them from my father's study as well,' she reflected. 'However, your contribution definitely sealed the deal.'

She placed a cigarette between her painted lips and for a moment he could see the sassy young Ella of old. The one who loved Simon unconditionally and was effortlessly cool.

Her eyes met his for a moment. They stared at each other.

'Why didn't we, you know, when we were kids?' she asked softly.

He reddened slightly. 'Didn't we what?'

'Kiss. Have a relationship.'

'You were obsessed with Simon.'

'We were great friends.' She looked wistful for a moment. 'You always looked out for me. Remember that time Henry found that empty bottle of vodka in my bag and you took the blame?'

'Well, you were already grounded for sneaking out to that disco,' he said, smiling. 'It was the right thing to do.'

'Or that time you handed in an essay you wrote to Mr. Crowley, claiming that it was mine, all because I was on my last warning.'

'It was an old piece on Milton. Nothing special.' He shifted uncomfortably in his seat.

'You were always so kind, Will.' Her eyes shone. 'I'm so glad we got to meet again.'

She walked away, her cigarette and lighter in her hand. He watched her push open the heavy stained-glass front door at the entrance to the pub and disappear.

The waitress arrived with an electronic pad.

'So, have you decided?'

William nodded. 'A soup and a steak and kidney pie.'

'Coming right up.'

An hour later, the table was cleared. Ella's soup went back almost untouched. William pretended not to notice, but his face was troubled. Instead of food, she had smoked three cigarettes and had two cups of tea. Her face was gaunt and wan. Her wrists were so thin they looked like they could break.

'So, Aurora's new play is opening next Saturday,' he said. 'I have a spare VIP ticket if you'd like to come. No pressure, it's just, there's an after-party and it's supposed to be really good . . .' He trailed off.

'I'd love to come.' She smiled warmly. 'Where shall I meet you?'

'I can come to pick you up.'

'*No!*' she said sharply. 'I mean, no, it's fine. I'll get a taxi and meet you at the theatre.'

'I'll send you the address later then.' He gave her a guarded look. 'It starts at seven thirty but it would be better to arrive around fifteen minutes early as it's the first night.'

'Is she nervous?'

'Yes and no. She's worried about the critics of course, but the actual performance doesn't knock a feather out of her. She's so different when she's on stage. Baby Aurora disappears and this professional emerges.'

'Baby Aurora?'

'Yeah, because at home James treats her like a ten-year-old.'

Ella laughed. 'I'll probably do the same as my only memory of her is when she was that age.'

William got up and checked his watch. 'I have to make a move,' he said apologetically. 'I'm on wards this afternoon.' He took out his wallet. 'I'm also paying so don't even argue. You can get it next time.'

'That's what you said last time!'

'Well, I mean it. Obviously it'll be the Ritz when you're paying.'

She made a face. 'Oh, funny.'

She picked up her anorak which was still sodden. William noticed and took it from her grasp.

'You're not wearing that,' he said firmly. 'Take mine. The hospital is only two minutes away so I don't need it.'

'Oh, I couldn't,' she protested. 'You'll freeze.'

'Give it back to me next time we meet.'

She relented. 'I'll give it you on Saturday then.'

He brightened. 'Yes, on Saturday. I'm looking forward to it.'

# Chapter Twenty-three

Aurora secured her wig and stared at her reflection. The stage make-up looked heavy in the bright lights of the dressing room, but she knew that it would look great on stage. They had practised the last scene up to an hour before and they were ready. There was nothing more to be done. *La Morte* was about to be unleashed onto the world.

Paul poked his head in the door. 'Five minutes,' he said in his deep voice. He was wearing a pinstripe suit and a trilby hat on his blond head. He looked every inch the Jimmy Romano in the script. Now, she was Elise Sloane. The mobster's wife: the Queen of Chicago. She inserted her hands into the long black gloves and pulled them up over her elbows. Her stomach kept flipping over and over but she ignored it. It would go well. She knew her lines inside out. Justin was pleased with her delivery and she and Paul were as tight as they could be. She took a deep breath. Only fifteen minutes to the curtain. Only fifteen minutes . . .

Her phone beeped, distracting her. She glanced down at the screen and saw James' name. Her glove came off immediately so that she could activate the touch screen. It was a simple message that read:

**Break a leg, Borealis. Not literally of course. Send me pictures. J x**

She typed back furiously saying that she didn't plan on breaking any bones and that she wished he were there. He replied saying that he wished he were there too.

She sighed. He had never missed an opening night. It felt weird not to have him around. She put on her glove once more and threw the phone into her bag. It was time to leave Aurora Sinclair behind and enter the world of 1920s America.

It was time.

Ella was waiting outside the theatre when William arrived. She had his coat on her arm and looked stunning in a short green dress, black tights and boots. Instead of her anorak, she had her red coat on, which was far better suited to the cold weather.

She smiled and kissed his cheek. 'You're late.'

He held up his hands. 'The bloody train was delayed. Not my fault.' He gazed at her for a moment. 'You look so beautiful.'

'Beautiful?' she scoffed. 'Oh, Will, you need glasses.' She handed him his coat, then linked arms with him and pulled him towards the entrance. 'Let's go in and get a programme. I hope you got us good seats.'

'Oh, it'll be front row. They're complimentary.'

The theatre was small and old-fashioned with ornate balconies on the side and deep-red velvet curtains on stage. It was over a hundred years old and the seats were in disrepair with threadbare upholstery and worn arms. However, it had an undeniable charm and was already quite full.

Gloria and Henry were sitting in the front row along with Ophelia, Laura and Christian. There were four free seats: two for William and two for Maggie. Aurora always sent tickets to Cornwall, but to date her old nanny had never turned up.

'Good evening, all,' said William, leading Ella to their seats.

'Is that Ella Taylor?' said Gloria standing up. 'My word, it is too. Hello, my darling!'

Ella fell into her embrace and squeezed her tightly. Having spent the majority of her childhood in the Dixon household, she knew Gloria very well.

'It's so good to see you,' she said. 'You look just the same.'

Gloria laughed. 'Hardly. It's been a long time.'

Henry waved amiably but he had no idea who Ella was. She had moved to Toronto quite soon after his arrival and Laura had had many friends throughout the years. It was all very confusing. On his left was Theresa, except she wasn't Theresa any more, she was Ophelia. He settled back into his chair and opened the programme. There was a brief synopsis of the story and pictures of the cast. Aurora's face stared out at him. An array of emotions passed over his face. Sadness, pride, regret, love . . . She was her mother's daughter and it soothed him to think that her memory remained safe and alive in her only child.

Laura yanked Ella's sleeve. 'So glad my dumb brother convinced you to come,' she said, smiling. 'I'd like you to meet my boyfriend Christian.'

Ella focused in on the older distinguished man on Laura's right, who was typing an email at breakneck speed on his Blackberry.

'Your boyfriend?' she mouthed, wide-eyed.

Laura nodded. 'Isn't he fabulous?' she mouthed back. She touched Christian's arm. 'Christian, this is my friend Ella Taylor – we've known each other since nursery school.'

'Hey, honey, good to meet you.' Christian held out his hand and Ella shook it.

'Delighted,' she said politely.

He turned back to the Blackberry, his brow furrowed.

'Work,' explained Laura, ushering her along the row. 'He's frightfully busy.'

William gestured for her to sit down. 'It's about to start,' he whispered loudly. 'I hope Aurora is holding it together backstage. She was quite nervous when we spoke on the phone earlier.'

The red curtains on the stage moved slightly. There was no sign of Justin Debussy. He was notoriously elusive on a first night, preferring to stay out of the limelight. Most people wouldn't believe it if they were told that he was nervous. Only Aurora knew how vulnerable he was; she understood the terror he was feeling.

A tall sandy-haired man sat down on the last available seat by Ophelia. She glanced sideways and nodded in salutation. He had taken one of the seats reserved for Maggie. He had an impressive profile, skin dotted with freckles, a long straight nose and a strong jaw. She flicked her hair and straightened her dress. He was quite cute, even though he was clearly in the wrong seat.

'Would you like to look at my programme?' she whispered, fluttering her eyelids.

'You're all right,' he answered in a deep voice. 'Thank you kindly.'

He had an accent she couldn't quite place. It reminded her of a pirate. The lights dimmed in the theatre and the curtains began to open. The crowd quietened down immediately and darkness descended on the small auditorium. A spotlight appeared and focused on a round table at the centre of the stage. At the table sat Joey Sloane, the mobster boss with his troop of men. Next to him, like Brutus, was his right-hand man Jimmy Romano. The audience settled back in their chairs and watched the story unfold.

'*Bravo!*' shouted Henry, clapping madly. '*Bravo, my darling!*'

Aurora bowed again, Paul and Ray by her side. When the curtain had gone down, there had been silence for ten agonising seconds. Then the crowd had erupted, yelling and clapping. The curtains had opened again to reveal the audience on their feet.

Justin appeared from stage left and joined his actors. The crowd clapped loudly again, applauding the writer and director. As a play, it had ticked all the boxes. Joey Sloane, the kind-hearted king of the Chicago Mafia, betrayed by his protégé Jimmy. Elise, his faithful wife, succumbing to Jimmy's charms and breaking hearts in the process.

'*Speech! Speech!*' called no one in particular.

Justin held up his hands for silence and the noise gradually faded away. His handsome face was triumphant as he viewed the enraptured faces below him.

'Thank you, thank you,' he said in his commanding voice. 'We're overwhelmed by this response. Thank you all for coming here this evening.'

More cheers.

'This play would not have been possible without this wonderful set of actors up here with me.' He held up Paul and Ray's hands. 'My King Arthur and his Launcelot! Ray Rossi and Paul Lewis!' He pulled both men forward and the crowd went wild, cheering and clapping. 'And of course, my Guinevere: *Aurora Sinclair!*' He wrapped his arm around her waist and stepped forward. She stared at the faces below her, all beaming and smiling.

'*Wonderful!*' called Henry. '*You were wonderful!*' He raised his hands over his head, clapping madly.

She blew him a kiss. It had gone well, she could feel it. Joey's death scene hadn't left a dry eye in the house. The noise was deafening and she bowed gracefully. People were stamping their feet and shouting.

'Thank you!' said Justin, backing away. 'Thank you.' He nodded at the stagehand to bring down the curtains once more. The old red drapes closed slowly and the applauding crowd disappeared.

Aurora took a deep breath. It had been a success. All the hard work had paid off.

'You were incredible,' said Justin in her ear. 'Incredible.'

He kissed her neck lightly and she shivered. She didn't know if it was the adrenaline, but she wanted him to pull her into his arms. She pressed closer to him and he stiffened. Squeezing her waist, he walked off in the direction of the stage door.

Paul took off his hat and slapped Ray's back. 'Great show, old man.'

Ray Rossi grinned. 'I should punch you in the jaw for sleeping with my wife.'

Aurora felt like she was floating. There was a sense of real accomplishment after all the hard work. If there were critics in the audience, and she was pretty sure that there were, surely they would be impressed. Her performance had been flawless, she was sure. Everything had turned out exactly as she had planned. Maybe she would never reproduce acting like that again but, if she was going to get it right, then opening night was the time to do it.

Her dressing room was filled with flowers. She gasped in delight. A huge bunch of red roses took centre stage; she knew immediately that Henry had sent them. Marianne had delivered a colourful bouquet with lilies and irises and there were dozens of other arrangements from family and friends. She took a seat in front of her mirror and sighed. The make-up she had caked on earlier had served its purpose. There were just slight blemishes from the glaring lights.

She released her hair from its wig and let it fall down her back. Taking a wipe, she started to remove the heavy foundation on her face. Wipe after wipe was discarded as her skin slowly regained its natural glow. Next to come off were her gloves and then her beads. She slipped the beaded flapper dress over her head and stared at herself in the mirror. The white silk slip she had on under the dress clung to her curves and her eyes looked huge with smudges of black underneath. She felt like Elise Sloane: the sultry temptress who had bewitched Jimmy Romano.

Her thoughts drifted to Justin. Maybe this would be the night. She had never felt closer to him. The only thing that niggled her was that he blew hot and cold. He made the effort to come to her birthday and had propositioned her to go upstairs. Yes, he had been drunk, but *in vino veritas*, right? Since then, they'd had the odd embrace or moment, but nothing else. He had been a saint around her. Maybe it was because of the play. He was under pressure and probably didn't want to run the risk of any drama.

There was a knock at the door. She grabbed her violet robe and wrapped it around her body. Opening the door, she was confronted with a tall man in a suit. His sandy-coloured hair was falling over his eye and his ruddy complexion was flushed.

'Sinclair?'

She stared at him in confusion. Then she focused in on his eyes. She knew those eyes.

'Freddie?' she whispered. 'Freddie Thompson?'

He held out his arms and she fell into them.

'Oh Freddie!' she cried, holding him close. 'Why are you here?'

He pulled back and gazed at her. 'Maggie gave me 'er ticket, she did. Told me I should come up 'ere and see you. It's been so long.'

'It's so good to see you!' She held his hand in hers. 'How is Maggie?'

Freddie smiled. 'She's in great form,' he said genuinely. 'She 'as a little garden now and she grows 'er own vegetables. She sends 'er love.'

Aurora gestured for him to come in and take a seat.

He stared at all the flowers around the room. '*Wowee*, you're a popular lady!'

She laughed. 'It's always the same on opening night. After that, not one bloom.'

Blushing, he pulled a battered-looking rose from inside his jacket. 'I brought you this from the rose garden at the big house.' He put it in her hand. 'Mr 'Enry always plucked a rose from the same bush for your mother.'

'Oh, Freddie, I love it.' She clutched it to her chest. 'A real gift from home.'

'You still call it 'ome?' He looked dubious. 'We never see you no more, Sinclair. You must come down.'

She frowned slightly, manifesting the guilt she felt deep inside. Like anything unpleasant, if you didn't think about it, it faded into the background. However, Freddie was now calling her on it and she felt uncomfortable. He was right of course. It was disgraceful how she had left her old life behind.

He squeezed her hand tightly. 'Look, I didn't come 'ere to make you feel bad.' His eyes were kind. 'I've been so busy with college and all that, I've barely been back myself.'

'How are your parents?'

'Dad is slowin' down and 'ee wants me to take over the runnin' of the farm. I got ideas for that place. I think we should go organic but 'ee laughs when I say it.' He grinned. 'Not very progressive, old Conny Thompson.'

'How's Susie?'

'She got married to some Chemistry professor and she's almost finished her PHD. She lives in Bath all the time now. I visit when I can.'

Aurora smiled. 'Remember all those tapes she gave me? I would listen to them over and over, singing all the songs.'

'Why didn't you sing tonight? I kept expecting it.'

She shrugged. 'I've only been acting so far. Singing has never been required. I don't think Justin likes musicals anyway.'

'Justin?'

'My director.' She reddened at the sound of his name.

'Are you two –?' He nudged her playfully.

'God, no.' She shook her head furiously. 'Not at all.'

Freddie gave her a sly look. 'What is it you theatre folk say – "The lady doth protest too much?" Or somethin' like that?'

Aurora laughed: a sweet melodious sound. 'You're funny.' She took his hand in hers once more. 'Are you staying nearby? Would you like to come for a drink?'

'I booked into a 'otel but I gotta go soon. I 'ave to leave early so I'm back in time to feed the pigs.'

'Oh.' She tried to mask her disappointment. 'That's a shame.'

'Visit me when you come back 'ome,' he said softly. 'You were so good tonight, Sinclair. I cried a little.'

'You did?' She laughed. 'Oh Freddie, you softie.'

'Come and see us,' he said again. 'We miss you.' He stood up. 'Until we meet again.'

At the door he turned on his heel and she watched his broad back disappear into the darkness.

Closing the door, her face broke into a smile. Freddie Thompson. All grown up. He looked fit and healthy, just like a man who spent his life outdoors. She couldn't believe how tall he had become. Especially as Conny, his father, was so small. The rose he had brought was lying on her dressing table: a flower from her old life. She opened a bottle of Evian and emptied half its contents down the sink. Then she inserted the rose into the neck of the bottle. She would preserve it as long as possible.

Her phone beeped over and over but she didn't check it. She knew it was message after message, congratulating her on her success. The outfit she had chosen for the after-party was a black chiffon knee-length dress. It had a scooped neckline and layers of floaty material creating a full skirt that fell to below the knee. She slithered into it and tied the zip. Her heels were waiting in the corner but she delayed putting them on. Instead, she walked barefoot around the room, mentally going through her performance and breathing a sigh of relief. She had been nervous and it took a while for that to dissipate.

Suddenly the door opened and Justin strode in. 'Aurora! Look who's here to meet you!' Coming in behind him was the famous actor Albert Wells, Justin's uncle. He was dressed in a blue suit with a purple cravat and his grey hair was tousled. The famous blue eyes crinkled when he smiled and his booming voice resonated around the room.

'Aurora Sinclair! A pleasure.' He took her hand and kissed it lightly. 'You, my dear, are a revelation. Are you married?'

'What?' She glanced at Justin in bewilderment. 'Married? No, I'm not.'

'Then marry me,' he said playfully, kissing her hand again. 'You're just exquisite.'

Aurora blushed a deep red. She didn't know what to say. Here, in front of her, was a famous actor of the silver screen. He had been in countless box-office hits and he even had two Oscars. He looked smaller in real life, but then all actors did. He took her hand in his and she noticed a gold signet ring on his pinkie.

'You're the image of your mother, my dear,' he said, gazing at her. 'I knew Grace in the old days. She was a lady.'

'You knew my mother?' She was drawn to him immediately. She loved to hear about Grace. Henry didn't reveal much about her personality, so her memory was like the portrait that hung in the main drawing room: cold and inanimate.

'Well, we were both struggling actors in the eighties. She was such a star, my dear. Not only could she act but she had a voice like an angel. Andrew had great plans for her.'

'Andrew?'

'Lloyd Webber, of course.' He smiled. 'She was so versatile, you see. Then, she disappeared. At the peak of her career, she moved back to Ireland, leaving it all behind.' His face fell. 'I admire her in one sense. You know, for staying true to her craft and not selling out. One could argue that I did the opposite.' Then he brightened again. 'Then again, standing on the podium with an Academy Award is pretty damn great as well.' He kissed her hand again. 'You are just delectable, Ms. Sinclair. Let's have a passionate affair!'

'Back off, Bertie,' said Justin, pulling him back. 'Give her a chance to come down. We all need to get back to reality.'

'I know exactly what you mean, old boy,' said Bertie, nodding. 'All one wants to do is retire to a quiet room and mull over one's performance.' He winked at her. 'You have made it tonight, my dear. I saw at least two of the harshest critics in London wiping away tears when you had Joey dying in your arms.'

Aurora blushed again. 'I wouldn't dream . . .'

'No need to dream any longer. It's up and up from now on. For you and my nephew.'

Justin grabbed his arm. 'We should leave Aurora to it.' He kissed her cheek lightly.

'I will see you later, won't I?' she said, suddenly vulnerable.

Justin paused for a moment, then grasped her shoulders and stared into her eyes.

She felt the ground give away.

'You're guaranteed that. We need to talk about every moment.'

She relaxed slightly. He understood. She didn't want to see anyone but him. Only he could talk about her performance in the detail that she desired.

'Will there be a party?'

He shrugged. 'I'm not too enthused about a noisy get-together but we'll see.'

Bertie clapped his hands. 'Then you must come to my place! We can drink champagne and relax without crowds and pressure.'

Justin looked at Aurora. 'Would you like that?'

She nodded in delight. Champagne at Albert Wells' house? It was like a movie in itself. A quiet get-together was exactly what she needed.

He left and the door opened again almost immediately. Ophelia's head appeared, her red curls bouncing.

'Can I come in?' she asked. 'I just saw lover boy walking off with Bertie Wells. Handy to have an A-list uncle, isn't it?'

Aurora nodded. 'Bertie seems really nice.'

'You look pretty,' said Ophelia fingering the light material of her dress. 'Is there a party later?'

'Bertie has invited us over for champagne. Pretty low-key, I think. I just want some peace and quiet.' She could feel the tiredness invading her body. She had been gearing up for this all week and now that it was over everything just seemed to crash.

Ophelia made a face. 'I'll give it a miss then, no offense. I can't imagine a close-knit soirée with Mr. Debussy.'

'He's not so bad . . .'

'Maybe to you.' She scowled. 'He treats me like an annoying insect he wants to step on.'

'Oh, Lia, don't be like that. Think of the champagne!'

She shook her head vehemently. 'Not a chance. Anyway, there's more of a chance of something happening if it's just you there.' She bent her head to look out the small window in the corner. 'I think that I see a moon. Maybe a few stars. It's looking romantic out there. High chance of getting lucky.'

Aurora giggled. 'I doubt it.'

Suddenly, there was a knock on the door. Three loud raps.

'I'll get it,' said Ophelia, bounding over. She yanked open the old oak door to find no one there. Poking her head out, she glanced up and down the corridor. It was empty. 'Hello?' she called. A dark shadow moved to her right and she whipped around. Peering into the gloom, she called again. 'Hello?'

No answer.

'Just close the door,' said Aurora, putting on her black heels.

Ophelia was about to do as instructed when something caught her eye on the ground. She bent down and picked it up. 'Someone left some flowers on the threshold,' she announced, holding a small bunch of red flowers wrapped in purple tissue paper.

'More flowers? Just put them with the others.'

'There's a card.' She handed it to Aurora. 'Open it.'

Aurora took the small card out of its envelope. Someone had written '*For Aurora Grace*' in black pen. She felt her pulse quicken. Very few knew her second name. She turned it over but the back was blank.

'They don't look very expensive,' Ophelia went on, pointing to the crude string holding the tissue in place. 'Maybe that's why someone dropped them and ran.'

Aurora tore the paper away. The flowers in her hand were like little bells, with rose-red and purple petals and multiple deep-pink stamen hanging down. She touched one gently. It was identical to the flower she wore almost every day. Rushing over to her handbag, she pulled out her belongings. She had stashed her jewellery in a small pocket before the show. She pulled out the necklace: the one her mother wore.

'Look,' she gasped, 'look, Ophelia!'

She held out the pendant and the flowers. The necklace was a uniform silver colour, but the real flowers were bright and exotic. She looked at the card again. *For Aurora Grace.* Someone had left them there and run away. Someone had knocked so that she would find them.

'Did you see anyone outside?' she asked, running over to the door and opening it wide. The corridor was empty. 'Lia! Did you see anyone?' Her tone was desperate.

Ophelia shook her head, shocked by her friend's reaction. 'They were on the ground and I almost stood on them. What's going on?'

'I don't know! I don't know what's going on. All I know is that this means something.'

Ophelia rubbed her arm. 'Hey, you're overreacting. Come on, you're just tired from the performance. It's just a crappy little bunch of flowers.'

'There's a link!'

'It's certainly strange . . . but, look, forget about it for now – you need to calm down. Come on, Bertie will be waiting.' She handed Aurora her coat. 'Let's get out of here and get a stiff drink.'

Aurora closed the door after them in disappointment. Whoever had left the flowers was long gone.

Ella walked out of the theatre into the cold night. The stars were visible in the sky which was rare for the city. William followed her and pulled his coat tightly around him.

'Would you like to get a drink somewhere?' he said casually.

Ella shook her head. 'Not really, Will. I'm exhausted.'

His face fell for a moment. 'Oh . . .'

She reached out and rubbed his sleeve. 'Thank you so much for bringing me here tonight. I loved the play. Your little sister is a star.'

William could feel her slipping away from him. She leaned up and kissed his cheek.

'So, call me and we'll do lunch again someday.' She waved and turned around.

'*Ella!*' he called and she stopped. 'Can I walk you home?'

She paused for a moment and then turned to face him. 'No, Will. I'll be fine.'

'It's no problem. I can go home via Chelsea.'

She shook her head firmly. 'I'm fine. You stay with your family.' She blew him a kiss. 'Stay in touch.'

Then she was gone.

William kicked a can on the street and ran his fingers through his hair in frustration. He thought it was going well and then she had pulled back.

With a heavy heart, he started to walk home, his thoughts filled with her.

# Chapter Twenty-four

Bertie's house was an old Georgian mansion near Belgravia. He had instructed his butler to chill some Cristal and to prepare some sushi for his guests. They took his private car from the theatre: Justin and Aurora were the only guests in the end. Laura had cried off saying that Christian was tired and had to catch the red-eye to New York the next day, William had gone home, Henry and Gloria had never planned to socialise and Justin's parents, Richard and Caroline, had said their goodbyes as well. Aurora was secretly relieved; she didn't want crowds or noise. Her brain was whirring and her thoughts filled with the little red flower. When she had mentioned it to Justin, he had switched off, changing the subject mid-conversation. He had no interest in jewellery or wildflowers. Terrified of boring him, she decided to keep her mouth shut. Justin liked when they talked about him or his plays.

*James would understand . . . James would listen . . ..*

Bertie filled three flutes of champagne and handed two of them to the others. Aurora gazed at the expensive art on the walls and the white furniture. The floors were marble and there was a stained-glass door leading out to a large garden with a heated pool. In the corner of the room was a Steinway complete with a velvet-covered stool. Above that, there were dozens of framed photos: Bertie with Bill Clinton, Bertie with Nelson Mandela, Bertie holding his Oscar, Bertie kissing Princess Anne. It was like a Who's Who of the celebrity world.

Justin flopped down on the white couch and sipped his drink. 'So, what did you really think?' he asked Bertie directly.

His uncle put his hand on his heart. 'I loved it, my boy. I swear to you. I think this one will catapult you into the bigtime. Especially with this goddess at your side.' He blew a kiss at Aurora. 'I'll tell everyone I know to book tickets. You should sell out for months. Then, with any luck, you should get a run on Broadway.'

Aurora gasped. 'New York! I've always wanted to go there.'

'Oh, you'll love it,' said Bertie. 'It truly is the city that never sleeps. I'm always popping over for this and that. If you're there, we must meet, my darling. For cocktails and what not."

Justin held out his glass for a refill. 'Will you stop flirting with my leading lady? That's my job.'

Aurora glowed with pleasure.

'Well, you'd better improve your wooing skills. I haven't seen much evidence tonight.'

Privately, Aurora agreed. She had expected far more attention than this. Justin had barely spoken to her, let alone flirted with her. He seemed to be in a daze, deep in thought and withdrawn. She walked over to the couch and sat down next to him.

'Did I do a good job?' she asked with huge eyes.

He turned to look at her and they stared at each other.

'You were sensational,' he said softly. 'As I've said a million times, you are my true muse.'

She smiled and settled in beside him. The champagne started to take effect and she felt relaxed and at peace.

'You're so like your mother, you know,' said Bertie, draining his glass. 'I remember Grace Molloy and her wonderful voice. We all trucked around together in the old days.'

'Did you know her well?' Aurora asked.

'Oh, quite well. She was so witty, your mother: the life and soul of any party. She and Michael would duet together.'

'Michael?'

'Oh, Michael Ball, back in his Marius days. He was so dishy then.'

'Anything else?' she asked pleadingly. 'I know so little about her.'

'Well, one time I took her to see *Swan Lake*,' said Bertie wistfully.

'You took my mother to the ballet?'

'Of course. She was the most beautiful woman in London. I just had to make a play for her.'

'Did you succeed?' she asked, fascinated.

'Not at all. She shot me down in her charming way, saying that her heart belonged to another.'

'Daddy,' said Aurora logically.

Bertie raised an eyebrow. 'It would seem not.'

'What do you mean?'

'This was before she met Henry, before she moved back to Ireland.'

'So she was in love before Daddy?' She sat up straight. 'With whom?'

Bertie sipped his champagne, debating what to say. 'No one I know,' he said eventually.

'You do know! Tell me.'

'Well, there was this one chap. He wrote poetry and plays. He was a director back then and we were all in the same circle.'

'So why do you think Mummy was interested in this man?'

'There were rumours and gossip. He was married, you see.' Bertie reddened. 'I shouldn't speak of such things, forgive me.'

'I'm sure you're mistaken,' she said firmly. 'Mummy was so in love with Daddy that she gave up the theatre and moved to Cornwall.'

'Yes, of course. I must be thinking of someone else.' Bertie got up and took a seat at the grand piano. 'Let's see if you inherited her talent. It will only add to your charm.' He played couple of scales and straightened his shoulders. 'What shall we perform together? Something challenging. Let's see . . .' He played the intro to *The Phantom of the Opera.* 'I saw your mother play Christine on stage,' he said over the music. 'With her dark hair and that white dress, she was incredible. How she hit those high notes, I'll never know.'

Justin took out his phone and checked the twenty messages. 'You go ahead, Aurora,' he said, typing some replies. 'Sing a few ditties to keep him happy. You know how I feel about musicals.'

Aurora got to her feet and took off her heels. Barefoot, she ambled over to the Steinway and waited for her cue. 'Will you sing the Phantom's part?' she asked and Bertie nodded.

Thank God Susie Thompson had given her those tapes all those years ago. She had devoured them, pretending to be Fantine one day and Eva Peron the next. Over and over she had practised, her voice resonating around the old house.

Bertie nodded at her to begin. Taking a deep breath, she closed her eyes. Her voice wobbled slightly at the beginning, but then gained in power.

Bertie felt shivers go down his spine. Aurora's voice soared over his thundering piano and climbed higher and higher. He sang his part to the best of his ability but he was an actor not a singer. After two verses, he realised that he was seriously outclassed. On and on she sang, her soprano reaching the top notes effortlessly. She seemed lost in the music, her body swaying slightly as she performed.

'*Justin!*' he whispered loudly, trying to get his nephew's attention. '*Justin!*'

Justin looked up from his phone and Bertie yanked his head in her direction. They were nearly at the end where the Phantom urges Christine to sing. Taking a deep breath, she tackled the aria, the key climbing all the time.

Justin started to take notice, watching Aurora's enraptured face. How did he not know that she could sing? She had never mentioned it in her auditions. Bertie was right, she was off the scale.

The song ended. Aurora came back to earth and opened her eyes.

Bertie clapped slowly and then his clapping got faster and louder. 'Bravo, my girl! You're wonderful, just wonderful!'

Justin walked up behind her and put his arms around her waist. 'You never said that you could sing.'

'You never asked,' she replied simply.

'May we do another?' Bertie clapped his hands in excitement. 'This is like having a doll to play with. Let's try some opera.'

'May I use the bathroom first?' Aurora asked.

'Of course. Down the hall, second on the left.'

She walked away.

Bertie refilled his glass. 'My word, Justin! She's an excellent actress, but I think that she's a better singer. That was stupendous.'

Justin nodded. 'I'm not really into musicals but I can see that she's special.' His expression darkened. 'I don't know what to do, Bertie. Things are complicated.'

His uncle nodded knowingly. 'I can see exactly what you mean. She's like a young teenager around you. You know that if you make a move, she will be yours in a moment. However, you don't want to risk losing her if things don't work out.'

'I'm practical,' agreed Justin. 'If things go sour, which inevitably they will, she might leave me. I'm not sure it's worth it.'

'Oh, I think she's worth it.' Bertie's face softened. 'She's absolutely beautiful. I know what I'd do.'

'You're an old goat,' said Justin drily. 'Don't think I don't realise that you would seduce her in a moment.'

'But of course!' He laughed. 'She ticks all the boxes. Hell, I'd marry her if she sang to me every day.'

Justin frowned. 'What should I do?'

'Follow your heart, my boy. Enjoy yourself. No one knows how things will work out.' He patted his back. 'Just hurry or I'll do it for you.'

# Chapter Twenty-five

The following Tuesday, Aurora went to work at the flower shop as usual. The performances were from Thursday to Sunday night, so she only worked Tuesday and Wednesday at the moment. She was still on a high from the weekend. Bertie's house had been so much fun, what with the singing and the champagne. Then, after her tenth song, she had felt lightheaded and Justin had ordered a cab to take her home. One kiss at the front door and that was it. She couldn't understand it. He seemed to fancy her yet something was always holding him back. On New Year's Eve, he had been drinking heavily. That was why he had suggested sex upstairs. Since then, he had oscillated from attentive to introverted and she was finding it hard to figure out.

Bertie, on the other hand, had been very attentive. He gave her his private number, insisting that they meet again very soon. She liked him, despite his inappropriate flirting. He made her laugh and was very complimentary. When she listened to him talk about her future like fame was a given, she almost believed it. She had never felt so close. This was what she had dreamed of; she had yearned for this since she was a little girl.

'Hello, beautiful,' said Marianne with a huge smile on her

face. 'I have my tickets booked for Friday night. Make it your best performance yet!'

Aurora smiled warmly. 'I'll give it my all,' she promised. 'Do you have good seats? I can upgrade you if not.'

'I'm about five rows back, I think. That should be fine.'

She inserted some white lilies into a stainless-steel container and added some greenery. Aurora took off her jacket and looked at the order book.

'Shall I get started on Mrs. Granger's centrepiece?' she asked.

Marianne nodded. 'Please do. I have a couple of funeral wreaths to finish.'

They worked in silence for a while, both concentrating on the job at hand. A customer arrived and left again without buying anything. The main street was quiet for a Tuesday, probably because of the rain teeming down outside. London had a reputation for being grey, especially in winter.

'Marianne?'

'Yes, lovey?'

'May I show you something?'

'Sure.'

Aurora opened her bag and pulled out the bunch of flowers Ophelia had found at her door. They were crumpled now from being in her bag, their petals wilting and drooping.

'Do you recognise this flower?' she asked, laying them on the table.

Marianne picked up the bunch. 'Vibrant little things, aren't they?' she mused carefully lifting the petals and examining the stamen. 'They're fuchsias.'

She walked over to her computer and typed 'fuchsia' into the search engine. Pictures with identical flowers popped up immediately.

'There,' she said in satisfaction. 'It says fuchsias were so called as a tribute to the botanist, Leonhart Fuchs. They come from South America.'

'Oh,' said Aurora, puzzled. 'I thought they were native to here.'

'Wait!' Marianne scrolled down. 'The fuchsia grows wild along the hedges of Cornwall and also Ireland, particularly in West Cork where it has now become the symbol of the region.'

Aurora brightened. 'In Ireland? Really?'

'Yes, look!' She tilted the screen towards her and pointed to the emblem. 'Why are you so interested?'

Aurora put her hand down her blouse and pulled out her necklace. 'This belonged to my mother. She wore it all the time.'

Marianne peered closely at it. 'Oh, it's a fuchsia!'

Aurora nodded. 'Then, on opening night someone knocked on my dressing-room door and then ran off, leaving that bunch of fuchsias on the ground.' She bit her lip. 'I think that there's a link.'

'A link to what exactly?'

'To my mother.'

Marianne scratched her head. 'It's a coincidence, I'll give you that – and it's an odd choice of flower for a bouquet . . .'

'But that's not all.' Aurora sat down on a chair. 'There was a card with the flowers. It had *For Aurora Grace* on it. No one knows my second name.'

'No one?'

'Well, not anyone here. I've never mentioned it.' She twirled her necklace around. 'Now there's a link to Ireland. My mother was Irish. What if someone is trying to tell me something?'

Marianne shook her head. 'I think you should put it out of your head, honey. It's just a coincidence. Someone probably just left a bunch of flowers to say congratulations. Maybe they were too intimidated by the big star, Aurora Sinclair, to face you.' She rubbed her arm. 'Forget it, sweetie. You look troubled.'

Aurora nodded. 'You're quite right.' She got to her feet. 'Now, back to Mrs. Granger's arrangement.'

William groaned when his alarm went off. He was sick of this

*Groundhog Day* scenario. He got up, went for a run, showered, ate some muesli and went to work. It had been five days since the play: five days since he had seen or heard from Ella. He kept willing his phone to buzz, signalling a message. He just wished that she would make a move. He was tired of being the one who chased her.

She had said to keep in touch. She had suggested meeting for lunch again someday. Maybe he should just ring her up and ask her out. Again.

He turned over and closed his eyes. He was no fool. She just wasn't interested.

The second alarm programmed on his phone rang and he pulled the pillow over his head. He wasn't in the mood today.

Half an hour later he was dressed for the hospital. Grabbing his woollen coat, he buttoned it up. It still had a faint trace of her perfume since the day she had worn it.

Blimey, he was turning into a sap. Laura would scoff at him. Enough was enough.

The streets were empty as it was plummeting with rain. His large umbrella protected his top half from the incessant downpour but by the time he got to the hospital, his pants were soaked.

Bugger, he thought as he entered the foyer. Maybe he had a spare pair in the break room. It was unlikely but he could check. Otherwise he would have to wear blue scrubs and endure the jokes from his colleagues.

'Morning, Adrienne,' he called at the receptionist on the main desk. 'Dreadful outside.'

'Morning,' she called back, smiling warmly. 'Got tickets for your sister's play. Can't wait to see it!'

He gave her a thumbs-up and kept walking.

Mary, the ward nurse, was waiting for him. 'We had two admissions last night. One leukaemia and one febrile. Here are the notes.'

He took the clipboard from her outstretched hand and forgot about his wet knees. The hospital was busy and there were children to be cared for.

'Coming for lunch, Dr. Dixon?' called Myra, a nurse on the same floor. 'We're heading to the pub.'

'I'll follow you,' he answered, filling in details of a patient he had just seen. 'Get a seat by the fire.'

He frowned and checked his watch. All the stats and results had been accounted for so all he had left to do was sign off. He scribbled his name and the time. Now he could take a well-deserved break. He had no appointments in the afternoon and was toying with taking a half day. Gloria had mentioned that she wanted help moving a bed in the guest room. Henry simply wasn't up to it.

The main foyer was quiet when he got there. It could be either way: one minute it was full of parents and grandparents visiting their loved ones. Other times it was empty, just like today.

'Enjoy!' called Adrienne, waving madly. She adored William. Such a nice boy. He always brought her a cake from the French pastry shop on the corner.

He walked out into the dreary weather to find Ella Taylor outside, smoking a cigarette. She was soaked to the skin and shivering.

'Hey, Will,' she said, blowing a large cloud of smoke into the air. 'You free for lunch?'

He rushed to her side and wrapped his coat around her shoulders. 'Why do you wear that stupid anorak?' he asked. 'It's bloody useless in the rain.'

She smiled wanly. 'I keep my red coat for special occasions.'

'Why do women suffer for fashion?' He led her away down the street, his heart thumping in his chest

'God knows.'

'Where would you like to go?' He paused at the traffic lights.

'I don't mind.'

'There's nice Italian on the corner.'

'Perfect.'

The owner was Sicilian and ushered them inside out of the rain with large hand gestures and rapid Italian. Soon they were seated in a secluded corner with a small table and a candle stuffed into a wine bottle. Andrea Bocelli sang in the background and the small room was warm and cosy.

'Wine?' William asked.

She shook her head. 'Not for me.' She nibbled on some grissini and took small sips of water. He noticed that her hands were bright red from the cold so he took them in his and started to caress them gently. She closed her eyes and let him massage the pain away. Within minutes, they had regained their normal colour and didn't sting any more.

'The play was fantastic – thank you for taking me.'

He shrugged. 'I got two free tickets so –'

'Oh, charming.' She laughed.

'What I mean is, I could think of no one better to go with,' he said seriously.

She shrank back at the intensity of his gaze. 'Will?' she said slowly.

'*Hmmm?*'

'Do you fancy me, Will?'

He reddened and took a frantic sip of water. 'What do you mean?'

Ella gave him a pointed look.

'What would you say if I did?' His blue eyes met hers steadily.

For a moment, she said nothing, her hand still in his. He felt his hopes rise as she stroked his finger. Then she spoke.

'I would be flattered,' she began. 'You're a great guy and any woman would be lucky to have you . . .'

He pulled back. This was not what he wanted to hear. There was an enormous 'but' on the way.

'But,' she went on, 'I'm not in a good place at the moment. You would be miserable with me, Will. There are far better girls out there for you.'

'You don't get to decide that,' he protested hotly.

'I know. It's just I'm not the one.'

'How do you know that?'

'Oh, I know.' Her tone was bitter. 'I know.'

The waiter arrived with his pen poised.

'Just give us a minute,' said William abruptly.

The waiter backed away immediately.

'Ella, I don't want to pressurise you in any way.' He took her hand once more. 'But please give us a chance. Give *me* a chance. I think we'd be great together.'

She looked at him wistfully before answering. 'Let's be friends,' she said genuinely. 'I love having you in my life. Friendship is all I can offer.' Her eyes shone with tears.

He frowned, weighing up his options. If he made a big deal of it, she might bolt forever. If they were friends, he could work on convincing her otherwise.

'Fine. Friends it is.' He smiled and beckoned to the waiter to come back over. Best to be normal. 'Now, you should try the gnocchi. I love it here.'

She insisted on paying, despite his protests. 'You always get the bill,' she argued. 'It's my turn.'

He insisted that she take his coat. 'It's a five-minute walk to the tube,' he said. 'You'll get soaked.'

'Oh, I'll get a taxi on the main street,' she said airily as she got up. 'I've told you before, I hate public transport.' She bent down and kissed his cheek. 'See you soon, Will.'

Then she left.

The waiter came to clear the plates. 'She no like?' he asked, pointing to Ella's untouched plate.

William shook his head. 'She's not feeling the best,' he lied. 'Here, just a small tip.' He handed him a five-pound note.

'*Grazie,*' said the man, smiling broadly.

William took his wallet and walked towards the main door of the restaurant. Suddenly the waiter yelled at him to stop. '*Signor! The lady, she forget her telephone.*' He had Ella's iPhone in his hand.

William took it and thanked him for his honesty. He ran out onto the street. She had mentioned getting a taxi on the main street so he started to run in that direction. Just in time, he saw her small frame turn the corner.

'*Ella!*' he called. '*Ella! Wait!*'

She didn't hear him so he ran on. Turning onto the main street, he could see a line of taxis parked at a rank. However, Ella had walked past them all and was scurrying down the street. She paused to cross the road and then took off again in the direction of the city centre.

Something told him to follow her. He knew how attached she was to her phone. He crossed the road.

'*Ella!*' he called but she kept walking. It was only when she passed another taxi rank that something didn't feel right. She had specifically said that she was going home to Chelsea by taxi yet she was walking in the opposite direction entirely. He slowed down and kept a safe distance behind.

On and on they walked until they were in the East End, passing market traders and rundown buildings. He had given Adrienne a ring, telling her that he wouldn't be back in until tomorrow.

Suddenly, Ella stopped outside a tall dilapidated block of flats. She raised her head and walked towards the main entrance. There was graffiti on the walls and two windows were smashed in. William hid behind a van and watched as a large woman with bright-red hair emerged and started shaking her fist at Ella, screaming about rent. Then she spat on the ground and stalked back inside, leaving Ella visibly upset.

Then Ella disappeared into the building and closed the door.

Without a second thought, he strode up to the door and knocked. The woman with the red hair popped her head out and barked, 'Wot you want, sunshine?'

William straightened his shoulders. 'I would like to see Ella Taylor, please,' he said in his clipped accent.

'And wot you want 'er for?' She put her hands on her hips. 'If that little whore is turning tricks then she's got to get out.' Her face reddened with rage. 'I run a respectable building 'ere. I don't want no prostitute tarnishing my name.'

William felt his hackles rise and he glared at her contemptuously. 'I can assure you that my intentions are entirely honourable,' he said coldly. 'Now, where is she?'

'I asked wot you want,' she retorted nastily. 'You ain't goin' in wivout tellin' me wot you want wiv 'er.'

'It's none of your business,' he said angrily. 'Now let me in!'

'Get out of my sight,' she sneered. 'You ain't going nowhere.' She slammed the door.

William didn't wait. Using all his strength, he kicked the door again and again until it opened and he fell into a long dark corridor.

The woman reappeared, shouting in anger. '*What the bloody 'ell you doin'?*' she screamed. '*Look at my door! I'm calling a bobby right now!*'

William ignored her and started banging on doors. '*Ella!*' he called. '*Ella, where are you?*'

A little girl opened the third door he knocked on. 'The blonde lady? She's upstairs.' She smiled brightly. 'She gives me sweets sometimes.'

He didn't wait. Taking two steps at a time, he bounded up to the first storey and started banging on doors once more, calling her name.

An old man, dressed in a white vest, appeared. 'You lookin' for the posh girl?'

William nodded.

'She's in 14.' He pointed down the hall.

William ran down and banged on the door. No one answered so he banged again. Still nothing. He had seen her come in, right? She had to be inside.

Using all his weight, he kicked in the door. Mercifully, it buckled quite easily and he stumbled into the room. There was a narrow bed with a brass frame, an ancient old dresser and a wooden chair. In horror, he stared at the damp walls and the holes in the carpet. The air smelt musty and the windows were grimy.

A toilet flushed behind a wooden door in the corner. It opened and a white-faced Ella walked out, wiping her mouth. She gasped when she saw him. 'Will?' she said in horror. 'Why are you here?' She fell backwards against the wall, hitting her head with a crack.

He was by her side in an instant. 'I should ask you why you're here,' he answered grimly. 'What the fuck is going on, Ella? Why are you living in this hellhole?'

He picked her up easily and carried her to the bed.

Tears rolled down her cheeks. 'How did you find me?' she asked in a hoarse whisper.

'You forgot your phone.' He placed it on the dresser. 'I followed you back here.'

She closed her eyes. 'Oh, Will. I'm in such a mess.'

He rubbed her back. 'Tell me what's wrong and I'll help you.'

'You can't. No one can.'

'Tell me,' he said gently.

She inhaled sharply. 'I left Toronto before Christmas.'

'What? Laura said you only arrived a few weeks ago.'

She shook her head. 'I didn't tell her. I lied and pretended that everything was okay.'

'Why?' he stroked her cheek. 'Why did you leave?'

'I had a great job with a cutting-edge advertising company. I was so good at it, you know? I loved the pressure and the unpredictable hours. My boss was so good to me. He was gorgeous and so attentive. We started messaging each other and so on. Soon we were sleeping together. I thought I was in love. He was the whole package: rich, successful and handsome. I was on cloud nine.'

'So what happened?'

She sighed. 'He was also married. I knew it but I did it anyway. He told me all the usual crap: how he was miserable with her and was planning to leave. I fell for it like a fool. Then, my period was late. I did a test and discovered that I was pregnant.'

William rubbed her back compassionately. 'Go on,' he urged.

'Oh, I was so happy. Josh loved me and now we had the perfect excuse to be together. I ran to his office with the news.' She started to sob. 'He was so calm, Will. He told me that this had happened before and that he knew a great clinic downtown. He had sent girls there before and they were so efficient.' She rubbed her nose. 'He wrote me a cheque for ten thousand dollars and said to keep the change.'

'Oh, Ella.'

'That's not all. He fired me too. Oh, it was no longer appropriate for us to work together apparently. He sent me an email advising me to leave without a fuss.'

'What did you do?'

'I went to the clinic. I met a nurse who explained everything. I was about to make an appointment when I freaked out. When it came to it, I couldn't do it. I just couldn't do it.'

'Did you tell anyone?'

'No.' She shook her head. 'My father would disown me for a

start. I was a difficult teenager to put it mildly. He has it up to here with my antics. Father is quite old-fashioned and an illegitimate grandchild might drive him over the edge.'

'Your mother?'

'Even worse.' She laughed bitterly.

'So why did you come here?'

'I had nowhere to go. I cashed the ten thousand and decided to come back home. I foolishly thought that I would pick up a job in a few days. So, I booked a ticket to London and stayed in a hotel. Two weeks went by and no work. My money started to run out. I moved to a smaller hotel but that only lasted a few days. Then, I ended up here.' She coughed and her small frame hunched over. 'I've been so sick, Will. I'm so sorry about all that food you paid for. It was such a waste.'

'Don't even worry about that,' he said kindly. 'I feel terrible for letting you pay today.'

'I pawned my gold necklace,' she said simply. 'I wanted to see you but I had to appear normal.'

'You did what? Where?' He ran his fingers through his hair. 'That's just awful.'

'Doesn't matter,' she said. 'It was worth it.' She coughed again. 'I don't need to buy food at the moment as I can't keep it down. I know I look emaciated, but I can't help it. The vomiting is incessant.'

'Does Laura know?'

'Gosh, no. I arranged to meet her that day in order to ask for help regarding work. Maybe I would've told her the truth but then you turned up. I couldn't say anything so I kept the façade going.'

'You should have told me,' he said. 'I could have helped you.'

'No one can help me,' she said miserably. 'My money is almost gone and that witch downstairs is threatening to kick me out. I'll have to ring up my father.' She laughed sardonically. 'The only problem is that my phone has had no credit for weeks. I can only receive calls.'

'Is that why you didn't respond to my texts?'

She nodded. 'I was so glad when you rang, Will. I'm so sorry if I seemed rude.'

With a shaking hand, she took out a cigarette and fumbled with a lighter. William whipped it from her mouth and frowned. 'No more of this, Ella.'

'But I need –'

'Don't smoke.' He stroked her cheek. 'Please.' He threw the lighter onto the floor.

'I can't afford them anyway,' she said bitterly.

He got to his feet, his face set in a determined line. 'Right, get your bag. You're coming with me.'

'What? Where?'

'You're coming home with me.'

'Are you crazy? I'm not your problem.'

'Don't argue. Just pack your belongings and we'll leave.'

Her blues eyes stared at him for a moment and she exhaled slowly. He wanted to look after her. It had been so hard for so long, and maybe he would save her. Maybe this all happened for a reason.

She obeyed his command. Pulling out her bag, she stuffed it with clothes and books, some make-up and her toothbrush. Anything she could find at short notice.

He helped her put on her red coat. 'Right, off we go.' He held out his hand and she inserted her small one into his grasp.

The little girl who had answered the door earlier waved as they walked past. When they got to the front door, the red-haired owner was waiting, blocking their exit.

'Wot's goin' on 'ere, then? You off wivout payment?'

Ella shrank back and William pulled out three twenty-pound notes, which was all the cash he had on him.

'*Take that and get out of my way!*' he roared. '*Charging people for sub-standard accommodation like this? I'll report you!*'

He barged past her, Ella by his side and walked to the nearest main street. A black cab screeched to a halt and they got in.

'Bloomsbury,' he said, helping her into the back seat. He kissed her cheek. 'You're going to be fine. Just leave it to me.'

His flat was dark and cold when they arrived. He strode straight over to the heating and cursed. 'I fixed this the other day,' he said in annoyance. 'I timed it to come on at six.'

Ella stood there, unsure of what to do. He had deposited her bag on the floor and was now twiddling the heating thermostat.

'Finally!' he said triumphantly. 'It should work now. I want hot water so that you can have a bath.'

She walked over to the sitting-room area. It was sparsely decorated with a painting on the wall, a couch and a flat-screen TV. A bookshelf in the corner gave the room some character but it was essentially a bachelor pad: functional and minimalist.

'I only have one bedroom so you can have it.' He pointed to a door on the right. 'I'll take the couch for the moment until we sort things out.'

'Oh no, Will,' she protested. 'I can't take your bed.'

'Don't even argue,' he said firmly. 'I'll just run you a bath and then you can relax.' He set to work, taking towels from the airing cupboard and a robe from his room.

She took off her red coat and hung it on the hook by the front door. The heating began to work and soon the flat was cosy with warmth.

'*Ella?*' he called. 'The bath is ready.'

She walked into a small bathroom to find a tub filled with lavender-scented bubbles. William was beaming at her with his sleeves up around his elbows.

'I've never filled this thing before,' he admitted. 'I'm a shower kind of guy.'

She smiled. 'It looks like bliss. Thank you.'

'Just enjoy it. I'll find something for us to eat.'

Her face fell. 'Please don't . . .'

'You have to eat something,' he insisted. 'Even if it's just dry toast. I'll see you in a while.' He closed the door and left her to it.

Pulling his phone out of his pocket, he accessed his contacts. Noelle Hilton, a girl from his class at university, was now a GP nearby. Ella needed to be checked out as soon as possible. She looked malnourished and dehydrated. Noelle answered and they arranged that she call over in an hour.

Satisfied, he opened the fridge, looking for bland food. Her vomiting was exacerbated by more vomiting. She was trapped in a cycle that needed to be broken. Maybe she'd like some eggs? He took out two and cracked them into a bowl. Something was better than nothing.

Noelle emerged from his bedroom after a thorough examination of Ella.

William jumped up from the couch. 'All okay?' he asked.

She shook her head. 'She's resting now but I would recommend that you take her to hospital as soon as you can.'

'Hospital?'

'She's dehydrated, Will. The sickness has robbed her of all her back-up. She's underweight and I suspect she'll need a drip.' She put her plastic gloves in the bin. 'That baby needs to be scanned also. Everything needs to be checked out properly.'

He nodded. 'I'll take her right away. Christ, Noelle, I should have gone straight to A&E.'

'Don't beat yourself up. Just get her sorted as soon as you can.' She wrote a prescription for anti-nausea tablets. 'Try her with these. We prescribe them for vertigo but they might just stave off that incessant vomiting.'

William walked her out. 'Thank you for coming over at such short notice.'

'Oh, it was a blessing. The in-laws were round for dinner and

I was dying of boredom.' She laughed. 'You saved my evening.' She grasped his arm. 'I don't know what your situation is, Will.' Her eyes were kind. 'If this baby is yours, well and good – I'm not prying. However, she needs to look after herself. There's a long road to go before she'll be back on her feet.'

He opened the door. 'I've got it from here, Noelle. Trust me on that. She's my number-one priority.'

# Chapter Twenty-six

Aurora put on her wig for what seemed like the millionth time. The Saturday night performance was always the big one. The show had been running for almost three weeks and she was getting better and better. As promised, Bertie had spread the word and each night there were familiar faces in the crowd. The knock-on effect of this was lots of media coverage and paparazzi, which already added publicity to excellent reviews. The play was sold out for the next month and *Hello!* magazine was due to do a small piece on Aurora herself. The beautiful daughter of Henry Sinclair and Grace Molloy was a perfect candidate for an interview; the public wanted to know more about this young rising star.

A knock on the door interrupted her prep so she left the gloves on the dressing table. 'Coming!' she called, her flapper dress swinging as she walked.

Opening the door, she screamed in delight. Standing there, in his favourite navy hoodie, was James.

'*Borealis!*' he cried with his arms wide open. '*Look who's back!*'

She felt her heart fill to the brim. It seemed like months since they had met. This meant that he was home safely. Home in London: back where he belonged. She catapulted herself into his arms and hugged him close.

'*Whoa, whoa!*' he said, pushing her back. 'You're covered in make-up. Just look at my hoodie.'

'*Lipstick on your collar, told a tale on you!*' she sang softly. 'Remember Gloria and that Connie Francis tape in the car?'

'I only recall Doris Day.' He walked into the room. 'Nice digs,' he said, laughing at the small dark area where she put on her costume. 'No chance of you becoming a diva in here.'

'It suits me fine,' she said firmly. 'What more do I need? I have a mirror, a clothes rail and my make-up.'

'I just thought that now you were such a huge star you'd have a palatial dressing room with marble floors and a flat screen TV.'

'Not yet,' she laughed. 'However, did Gloria tell you my news? *Hello!* magazine want to interview me!'

'She mentioned it once or twice,' he said, grinning. 'I don't think I've ever seen such excitement.'

'Are you alone?' she asked casually.

'No, Claire is outside. She's reading the programme and guarding our seats like a Rottweiler.' He smiled. 'She's never seen you in action.'

'I hope I don't disappoint.'

He regarded her thoughtfully. 'You know, you don't look half bad with short hair.'

'Should I get a haircut then? It would be far easier to fit into this wig.'

He shook his head. 'No. Never cut your hair.' He kissed her cheek. 'Good luck! Don't mess up your lines as I'll be watching you and judging you.'

'*Blah, blah!*' She stuck out her tongue at him. 'You'll probably fall asleep anyway. It's a love story.'

'Hey now, I'm not against love stories. Remember all those

Disney Princess films I sat through for you?'

She laughed. 'Oh, you loved them really.'

Elise backed away from Jimmy, her eyes wide and her chest heaving.

'You gotta leave, Jimmy,' she breathed, her leg exposed through the beads of her dress. 'Joey can't find you here. You gotta leave.'

'I can't,' he answered, taking off his hat and shaking out his blond hair. His white shirt clung to his tall athletic frame as he moved. He was the antithesis to small rotund Joey Sloane.

She eyed him in fear and excitement, her breathing shallow. Her dark smoky eyes were huge as he moved closer.

'This can never be, do you hear? I'm a married woman. He'd kill us both.' She hung her head. 'Please get out.' The tone of her voice said otherwise.

Jimmy traced his finger up her thigh and she threw her head back.

'What we got is special, Elise. I know you feel it too.' He grabbed her arms and forced her to look at him.

'I love Joey,' she protested, 'Goddammit, I love him but I can't stop thinking about you. I can't stop wanting you.'

'Let it happen, Elise.'

'Don't touch me . . . please .. .'

'I can't stop myself.'

'Oh, Jimmy . . .'

James clapped madly, whooping as Aurora bowed again and again. '*Fantastic!*' he yelled over and over.

Claire pulled at his sleeve. 'Good Lord, calm down! You're easily the loudest person here.'

James ignored her and kept shouting '*Fantastic!*' as loudly as he could.

The noise died down and the curtain fell.

'Right, shall we go back to Richmond?' said Claire, putting on her coat. 'I have to meet Melanie in the morning for a run.'

'Running on a Sunday?' James gave her a look. 'We're just back, Claire. Can't we just relax and enjoy ourselves for a few weeks?'

'I have a job interview on Monday,' she said primly. 'Which is more than you have. Will you please ring up the BBC and organise a meeting? I really want to make an offer on that house near my parents' place. You know what property is like here, James. We'll miss the boat.'

Her small face was set in a frown as she spoke so he kissed her nose. 'You need to calm down,' he said truthfully. 'This is not the place to discuss all this. I want to see Aurora to congratulate her before we go.'

'Really?' Claire looked peeved. 'I'm exhausted.'

'Just go and get the car,' he suggested. 'I'll be out in a sec.'

He walked through the stage door and down the dark corridor once more. He knocked on her door and she opened it right away. Her wig had been removed and her face was back to its normal colour. She looked like the girl he knew, not that sultry temptress on stage.

'Well?' She waited for a reaction.

'You were,' he paused, 'fantastic! Just fantastic!'

'So that was you yelling in the crowd.' She giggled. 'All I could hear was "Fantastic!" over and over.'

'Well, it's an apt word tonight.' He slapped her on the back. 'Remember me when you're famous, Borealis. Don't forget the guy you beat at chess every Christmas.'

'The guy who *lets* me win at chess every Christmas,' she corrected. 'No, I could never forget you.'

They stared at each other for a moment.

Eventually James spoke. 'Are you and that Paul, you know...?'

'Paul Lewis? As in Jimmy Romano?' She burst out laughing. 'He's gay, James.'

'Really?' He looked dubious. 'He looked pretty hetero up on that stage. I thought he'd tear your dress off.'

'So you think we had chemistry?'

'I was hot around the collar.' He crossed his chest. 'Hand on heart, I believed that you were made for each other.'

'Forbidden love is always more exciting and alluring,' she said matter-of-factly. 'They knew it was wrong, so that added to the frisson.'

'Forbidden love? Whatever's that?'

'You know, like Launcelot and Guinevere . . . or Heathcliff and Cathy.'

'Heathcliff and Cathy? What was forbidden about them?'

'The fact that they were brother and sister,' she explained. 'That made it even more exciting.'

James said nothing for a moment. 'Except they weren't really brother and sister, were they? Not biologically.'

Her heart started to pound. 'No. They weren't.'

'So, it was quite acceptable.'

'Maybe . . .'

Justin burst into the room. 'Dare I say it, but you were even better tonight!'

Aurora smiled. 'It was because my darling brother was in the audience judging me.'

James made a face at her and then turned to Justin. 'Well done,' he said, shaking Justin's hand. 'It's excellent.'

Justin nodded curtly. He hadn't forgotten James' animosity at the party at Oxshott. Still, he had complimented his work and looked amicable enough.

'So, Borealis, I have to go,' said James. 'The ball and chain is waiting outside.'

'Oh.' She tried to mask her disappointment. 'Will I see you soon?'

'Gloria is preparing a welcome home feast next weekend. I think the whole family is invited. Laura is bringing her sugar daddy, I'm bringing Claire, and Will is bringing Ella Taylor.'

'So, they're official then?'

'Well, no one knows exactly. He's being all cagey. Mum's thrilled as she thought he had commitment issues. So, there should be a huge crowd.'

'The poor slow cooker will explode,' she said.

'Are you bringing someone?' he asked innocently. 'A boyfriend or someone like that?'

Aurora's eyes widened as Justin reddened.

'Right, I'll see you later,' he said hurriedly. 'Ray needs to discuss something with me.'

The door slammed shut.

'James!' she hissed. 'How could you?'

'What's his problem?' he said. 'I mean, you're not that ugly.'

'He's a professional.'

'If you say so.' He blew her a kiss. 'See you next week, Mrs. Sloane. Remember, you were . . .'

'Fantastic?'

'You said it.'

# Chapter Twenty-seven

Ella opened her eyes. The waves of nausea began, but she stayed lying down. William had left a flask of ginger tea and some dry crackers on the bedside locker. Steeling herself, she took a bite and a sip, praying that it would balance her sugar levels.

Five minutes passed. Maybe she could sit up? She levered her body upwards and rested her head against the headboard. She was definitely feeling better – there was no comparison to before. William worked most days but he made it his business to come home for lunch to check on her. He googled foods that wouldn't trigger the nausea and he wiped her brow if she vomited.

That night in A&E had passed in a blur. The doctor had been right. They had inserted an IV right away and kept her in for three days. During that time, an obstetrician came and examined her. She had a dating scan, they took her bloods and she was given medication to help with the sickness.

William had stayed by her side, making her laugh and holding her hand. She didn't quite understand why he would bother with a thin, pale, pregnant wretch like her, but she thanked God that he was looking after her. The scan had shown that she was just over nine weeks. The doctor had assured her that with any luck the nausea should abate soon. Despite the malnourishment and dehydration, the baby was perfect. The first time she saw it on the screen, her heart did a little jump. It had a huge head and the makings of limbs, but you could already sense its personality. It was zipping around like a boss and it reminded her of her childhood self.

Now she was almost twelve weeks: just on the cusp of the famous second trimester. Oh, how she yearned to feel normal again. She was sick of being cooped up all the time, too weak to go out alone. She started to resent the crackers and the dry toast. The last two months had been the closest to absolute suffering that she had ever experienced. Her life was in limbo: trapped between reality and a dreamlike world where she slept all day and had no concept of time. She was no fool; soon it would impossible to conceal her protruding belly. Being thin, it showed even more. She also couldn't live off William's charity for ever. She needed to sort out her life. Maybe she should go back to Toronto and face her parents. She sure as hell wasn't fit to get a job at the moment.

Swinging her legs over the side, she decided to have a shower. Her hair felt lank and greasy. Maybe if she felt somewhat well, she could meet William for lunch at the pub.

Her stomach heaved.

The reality was that the shower would zap her energy levels. Her bed would beckon once more. She felt a wave of depression wash over her and she sighed. She felt like a prisoner in her own body – nothing was worth this misery. Maybe she was being punished for sleeping with a married man. Each day rolled into one: days of sickness, sadness and despair.

William arrived home at six with two bags full of groceries. She was watching some quiz show on TV, propped up by cushions on the couch.

*'Honey, I'm home!'* yelled William playfully. 'Did you have a good day?'

Ella shrugged. 'It was no different to any other,' she said with a sigh. 'Just dry crackers, naps and more dry crackers.'

He stopped filling the fridge and was by her side in a moment. 'What's up?'

'This isn't working.' She looked him straight in the eye. 'I can't hide away forever.'

'Meaning?'

'I need to get well and find a job. I need to stop relying on your kindness.'

'Ella, be reasonable,' he said. 'You're in no state to work. I don't mind sleeping on the couch. In fact, I'm quite fond of it.'

'No, Will, I have to do something. Maybe I should go home. Maybe I should face my parents. They don't have to know who the father is. I can just imply that it was a one-night stand.'

William started to pace the room. 'You're being crazy here, Ella. If you go home, you will have to deal with legalities and all that.'

'Legalities? How do you mean?'

'Well, if you go back to Toronto and have the baby, that Josh bloke will hear about it. What if he wants custody?'

'Are you joking? He paid me to have it eliminated from his life!'

William grimaced. 'Well, I think you should stay in London, that's all. You're safer here.'

'I'm a nobody here,' she said angrily. 'I know I sound ungrateful, but I'm not.' Her eyes filled with tears.

He sat down on the edge of the couch and pulled her close. 'Don't cry, Ella,' he soothed. 'I understand what you mean. *Shhhhh . . .*'

She sobbed silently on his chest, breathing in his familiar smell.

'Stay here,' he said, stroking her hair. 'Temporarily. You can tell your parents if you wish . . . they may take it better if they know I'm taking care of you . . . however they may interpret that. Then, once the baby is born and you're back on your feet, all should settle. You can get a job again and be independent.' He paused. 'If that's what you want.'

She said nothing as her brain was in overdrive. William was right. Her father would be far more amenable if he knew that a young doctor was on the scene. He had been great friends with Andrew Dixon when they lived in London so that was another plus. He and William's father had played golf together every Saturday. Plus she truly had nowhere else to go. William's kind face was waiting for an answer. She took a deep breath.

'Okay.'

'It will buy you time.'

'I know. I just feel so guilty about taking your bed.'

'I'll pick up a foldaway one at IKEA. Problem solved.'

She smiled and took his hand. 'Thank you,' she whispered, 'thank you from the bottom of my heart.'

# Chapter Twenty-eight

'So, Justin scarpered when James mentioned the family dinner?' said Ophelia, buttering some toast. 'What a loon.' She and Aurora were having a late breakfast in the kitchen of their flat.

'He has been so strange lately. I mean, I catch him looking at me, you know, in a hot way, and then he closes off straight away.' Aurora sipped her tea.

'There's something behind it,' her friend said. 'By all accounts, he's not shy around the ladies.'

Aurora gasped. 'Are you saying that he's a womaniser?'

'Not exactly, but he's had his fair share of one-night stands.' Ophelia bit her lip. 'Maybe he's scared of commitment. Maybe he's restraining himself with you because you might be the one.'

'Hardly,' scoffed Aurora.

'Don't be so sure. He could be in love and totally overwhelmed.' She took a big bite of her toast. 'I reckon you should feed him with whiskey. That'll do the trick.'

'Whiskey?'

'He was drinking it neat the night he asked you to go upstairs. I think it might be the trigger.'

Aurora laughed. 'Right, I'll produce a bottle on Saturday

night after the performance and he'll crack.'

'Something like that.' Ophelia grinned. 'What are your plans for today?'

'Bertie rang me last night,' she began.

'*Oooh*, Bertie! Hobnobbing with the rich and famous now, are we?'

Aurora stuck out her tongue. 'Anyway, he was asking about my agent and I told him that I didn't have one and –'

'Agent? *Wowee*, that's bigtime stuff.'

'Anyway, he's setting up a meeting with his agent, Harry Finkelman. He's the best, so he says.'

Ophelia looked impressed. 'You are going to be such a star, Sinclair. I can see your name in lights. Wait until that interview goes to print in *Hello!* Everyone will know your name.'

'It will be a small, one-page spread,' said Aurora dismissively. 'Hardly top billing.'

'When is that interview anyway?'

'Next week. Gloria is dying for me to do it at her house. She has done a huge spring clean in preparation.'

'Will you go there?'

'I might. The sunroom is nice. The willow tree might be a good background for a photo too.'

'Harry Finkelman! Look at you go.' Ophelia winked. 'Don't forget me when you're bathing in Dom Perignon.'

'You'll be right there with me,' she promised.

'Henry! We need another table. This one simply won't do.' Gloria clutched her hair. Everyone was due to arrive in fifteen minutes and there was no space around the table for nine adults.

'Calm down, my darling,' he said smiling. 'They'll squeeze in.'

'We can't have that Christian sitting on top of William, now can we?'

'I'm sure that won't happen. Now, have a drink. There's

nothing more to do.'

Cooking was not Gloria's forte and she habitually used her faithful slow cooker for family get-togethers. This time, with all the partners, there was no way she could fit enough in her trusty old machine. So, she bought ready-made Thai green curry and tipped it all into a giant Le Creuset pot her aunt had given her as a wedding present.

Laura arrived first with two overnight bags and a bottle of Nuit St. Georges. 'Any chance Chris and I can bunk here tonight?' she asked. 'He has to be up very early and by the time we get back to my flat . . .'

'Of course,' said Gloria stiffly. 'You're more than welcome.' It was no secret that she didn't approve of her daughter's partner. She deemed him too old and arrogant to make her happy. Every week she waited to hear that everything had gone sour. However, their relationship seemed to be getting stronger and stronger.

James and Claire arrived next.

'We brought some pud,' said Claire, depositing an apple tart on the table. 'James forgot the cream.'

'I'm sure we have some in the fridge.' Gloria pecked her cheek.

'Help yourselves to some wine,' said Henry. 'There's a bottle open on the table.'

James picked up Laura's bottle. 'Ooh, fancy! Who brought this?'

'I did, Jiminy,' said Laura, appearing into the room. 'I'm so classy, don't you know.' She poured a glass of white wine for herself and a scotch for Christian. 'So, have you heard from Will lately?'

James shook his head. 'He's off the radar completely. Why is he bringing Ella Taylor? Are they an item?'

'I don't know,' she said honestly. 'They acted like strangers around each other when we met a while back. It's all very odd.'

'He always fancied her though, didn't he?'

'Really?'

'Oh, one hundred per cent. I could tell. But she was always banging on about some bloke called –'

'Simon!' Laura laughed. 'God, she adored him.'

'So James says that you've been offered a job,' Henry said to Claire. 'Congratulations, my dear.' His lined old face smiled warmly.

'Yes, I'm so delighted. Especially in this climate.' She jabbed her finger at James. 'I wish he would make more of an effort. He won't ring up the BBC and make an appointment. I'm anxious that we won't be eligible for a mortgage.'

'Don't push him,' advised Henry. 'All in good time. If they take him on, he'll have to travel, I expect. I imagine that he wants to stay around for a while longer.'

'Yes, but I want this house by my parents' place,' argued Claire. 'We're adults, Henry. Life goes on. We've been forced to rent this tiny flat down the road and it's dead money. That's the reality.'

Aurora arrived in her black fur-lined jacket and a black hat. Her cheeks were rosy from the cold and she was beaming. 'Hello, all,' she said, taking off her gloves.

'Borealis!' James was the first to hug her. 'God, you're frozen. Go and stand by the fire.'

'Any sign of Will?' she asked in a whisper.

James shook his head. 'Are he and Ella, you know?'

'I can't say.'

Claire patted his shoulder. 'Can I have a word?' she asked sweetly, pulling him away.

Aurora smiled tightly at her. She didn't know why, but there was a definite *froideur* between them. She could sense it when Claire looked at her.

'Where *is* Will?' said Gloria in exasperation. 'My rice has plumped right up. Soon, it will be mush.'

As if in answer to her prayers, the door opened and William walked in. His blond hair was concealed under a beanie hat and his bomber jacket was ample protection from the freezing temperatures outside. Then, clad in her red coat, Ella trailed in behind him. She eyed the family warily.

'Finally!' said Gloria, disappearing into the kitchen. 'Everyone squeeze in.'

'Hey, Ella!' called Laura waving. 'Wine?'

Ella shook her head. 'Not for me, thanks.'

'But it's Nuit St Georges!'

'I'm okay, Laura.'

James laughed out loud. 'Pretentious much?'

Laura made a face and refilled her own glass.

Henry patted the seat next to him. 'Sit here, my darling girl,' he said to Aurora.

'Of course, Daddy.' She sidled in beside him. 'It's good to see you.' She kissed his soft cheek. 'How's the new play coming along?'

'Oh, very well.' He sipped his wine. 'I'm almost there, in fact. Gloria will be pleased. I'm working such unpredictable hours. She often finds me in my study at three in the morning.'

'It will be worth it, I'm sure.'

'Quite.'

Christian refused wine and had another scotch instead. 'I'm just back from Cork,' he told Claire. 'My grandkid, Sienna? She was one last week. There was a party.'

'Oh, how sweet. Was it a big event?'

'Hell, no. Just my son and his fiancée, Lydia, the grandparents and a few aunts and uncles. Oh, and Colin of course.'

'Who's Colin?'

'Sienna's godfather. He's a funny guy. He got her about thirty presents and he made an awesome cake.'

'So, you had a nice time.' Claire smiled.

'It was okay. My ex-wife kinda ruined it, but everything else was good.'

'I wasn't there,' added Laura. 'He does the grandad thing on his own.'

'Proper order,' said James. 'No place for you, Lolly.'

She sighed. 'I can't argue with you there.'

Christian took Laura's hand in his. 'My divorce was finalised a few days ago so all's good.'

She beamed back at him. 'So, I've decided to take a year sabbatical,' she said, 'and move to New York.'

Gloria's head swung around. 'You've decided to do what?'

'Move to New York,' said Laura happily. 'Now that he's a free man, we can live together. Up to now, it would have interfered with proceedings. Isn't that right, Chris?'

He was busy emailing again. 'Sure, sure. We couldn't technically co-inhabit,' he said distractedly.

'Then it struck me! Why not take a year off and experience American culture?'

'And live off a rich boyfriend,' whispered James to Aurora. 'She's something else.'

Gloria put her head in her hands. This was not the news she was expecting at all. She had hoped things would fizzle out. Now her daughter was giving up her fine job to move in with her newly divorced boyfriend.

Henry patted her back. 'Don't fret, my darling,' he whispered. 'What will be, will be.'

Laura, oblivious to her mother's shock, turned to Aurora. 'By the way, Lydia and Colin are coming over next weekend to find a wedding dress. I got them tickets to your play. Do you want to meet for drinks afterwards?'

'Oh, yes please!' Aurora beamed. 'I'd love to see Lydia again. Shall I upgrade the tickets? We always have two or three to play around with.'

'There will be four of them. She's bringing her younger sister and best friend too.'

'Look, I'll see what I can do.'

'Great. You'll adore Colin. He's a hoot.'

Ella said nothing. William had her hand in his under the table, stroking her wrist rhythmically. He had read that the acupuncture pressure points for nausea were in that area so he pressed her skin every so often.

His mother arrived with a giant pot of rice and a ladle.

'Will?' she called. 'Can you bring in the curry? It's quite heavy.'

'Sure.' He got up and followed her back to the kitchen.

As soon as they were out of sight, she pulled him close. 'Are you in love?' she said in excitement. 'I never thought I'd see the day!'

He eyed her warily. 'Stay calm, for God's sake – it's not what it looks like.'

'Oh?'

'We're just friends.'

'Friends?' said Gloria in disappointment. 'Why?'

'She's been ill lately.' He sighed. 'I'm helping her out.'

'Ill?' repeated his mother in alarm. 'How do you mean, ill? Is something wrong? She's looking very thin.' Her brow furrowed. 'Oh darling, is it serious?'

'No, Mother, it's not. Now, open the door for me while I carry this in.' He kissed the top of her head. 'I'll explain another time.'

Everyone had helped themselves to rice when they reached the table.

'Dig in,' said Gloria. 'Thank M&S for your lovely curry this evening.'

James laughed. 'I admire your honesty,' he said, taking a huge spoon.

Silence reigned at the table while everyone ate.

Ella had taken some rice and nothing else.

Laura nudged James to look at her plate and he nodded in comprehension. 'She's anorexic,' she whispered in his ear. 'No doubt.'

'So, Bertie made an appointment for me to see his agent, Harry Finkelman,' announced Aurora.

Henry clapped his hands. 'Wonderful news!' he enthused. 'He's quite right, you should have representation.'

'I'm due to meet him tomorrow,' she continued. 'He's quite abrasive, apparently. Bertie says to stand up to him.'

'Are you going alone?' asked Laura. 'Maybe you should take someone with you? You know, for back-up.'

Aurora bit her lip. 'Ophelia is working . . .'

'I'd take you, my darling, but I've an appointment with my cardiologist,' said Henry regretfully.

'I'm working too,' said William, forking up his curry. 'Can this Bertie bloke go with you?'

'He's filming in Seville,' she said with a sigh. 'Look, I'll be fine. How bad can he be? I won't let him railroad me into anything.'

'I'll take you, Borealis,' said James.

'What?' said Claire. 'You can't! You have to start looking for a job.'

'What time?' asked James, ignoring her. 'Do I look beefy enough to be a security guard?'

'Are you serious?' Aurora gasped. 'Oh, James, that would be wonderful!' The she noticed Claire's thunderous face. 'Although, if you have plans . . .'

'Yes, he does have plans,' said Claire. 'James! You promised!'

'Look,' he said calmly, 'one more day won't make a huge difference. I'll ring Bob on Tuesday and arrange a meeting.' He held up his glass. 'Bravo, Borealis! This is the beginning!'

She glowed with pleasure. A whole day with James sounded heavenly. They could go for lunch and hang out, just like the old days. If that Harry Finkelman person tried to hoodwink her,

James would be there. She glanced at Claire who was picking at her curry mutinously. She was obviously smarting from being disobeyed. Something told Aurora to keep quiet.

Laura was waiting outside the toilet door when William emerged.

'Sorry, Lolly,' he said, 'I didn't realise that there was a queue.'

'What the hell is going on?'

'What?' He looked around frantically. 'Keep your bloody voice down.'

'Are you and Ella going out?'

'Not exactly.' He ran his fingers through his hair.

'*Bollocks!*' She jabbed his chest with her finger. 'You're a couple. Don't deny it!'

'We're not . . . she's . . .'

'What?'

'Just leave it.' He started to walk away.

'William! Don't walk away from me. There's more to this, I know it.'

He stopped and hung his head for a moment. 'She's pregnant,' he said eventually.

'Pregnant? How the hell did you manage that?'

'I'm not the father.'

'*What?*' Her blue eyes widened. 'She's pregnant, it's not yours – then why is she living with you?'

'Laura!' He put his fingers to his lips. 'Keep your voice down!'

'What is going on? I demand to know. Why are you taking on something that has nothing to do with you? Is she in trouble? Tell me, Will!'

He sighed and hung his head, debating what to say. 'She's all alone – abandoned in fact. I'm just helping her out.'

'Helping her out?' she repeated incredulously. 'Where's the father?'

'Canada. He doesn't know she's still pregnant – paid her to have an abortion and disappear.'

'Will . . .'

'She needs me,' he insisted. 'She's very ill, as you can see. Was hospitalised in fact for dehydration and vomiting. So, I've offered to look after her. She has nowhere else to go.'

'But *are* you a couple?'

William shook his head. 'No. I guess, we'll see how it goes. Our priority now is the baby.'

Laura eyed him speculatively. 'You know, James mentioned that you fancied her but I rubbished it. I mean, I never noticed it, not once. Now, I'm not so sure.'

'I don't,' he protested hotly. 'I'm just doing the right thing.'

'*Hmmm . . .*'

'Just bugger off, Laura. Don't say a word to Mum for a while, okay? We'll announce the pregnancy soon but not tonight.'

'Soon? I'd do it as soon as possible, Will. Mum should know. She's worried about how thin Ella is.'

'I'll talk to her.' He walked away.

'Will?' she called after his retreating back.

'Yeah?' He stopped dead, without turning around.

'Be careful. Don't get hurt.'

He closed his eyes. 'I won't.'

# Chapter Twenty-nine

Harry Finkelman's offices were on the third floor of an impressive stone building near Shaftsbury Avenue. The chic receptionist smiled at Aurora and told her to take a seat. Then she disappeared behind her huge Mac once more. The waiting area was plush and modern with white couches, glass tables and pictures of Harry with famous clients all over the wall.

'He represents everyone,' observed James. 'Look, is that him with Prince Harry? I didn't know that he was in show business.'

Aurora giggled. 'It was probably at the BAFTAs or something. As far as I know, the prince isn't a thespian.'

She had chosen a pretty green dress with black boots. Her hair fell loose down her back and her eyes were ever so slightly defined with kohl. James, in his habitual attire of jeans and a hoodie, picked up a magazine and started to flick through it.

'It won't be long until you're on the front cover,' he said, nudging her.

Rather than brushing it off like she always did with others, she turned to him with big eyes. 'Do you really think so? Really?' She could always be honest around James. He told her the truth and never judged.

'Yes, really. You're a star, Borealis. Literally.' He winked.

'Aurora Sinclair?' called the receptionist. 'Harry will see you now.'

They got up and walked towards his office. Harry Finkelman was written in gold lettering on the glass door. She pushed it open and entered a large room dominated by a mahogany desk and a giant fern plant in the corner. A small man was sitting on a swivel leather chair, barking down the phone. He had dark features, a large nose and was dressed in a white shirt and grey suit. Hs hair was balding and on one finger he wore a giant gold ring.

'Like I said, get the frickin' ball rollin', you hear? I'm a busy man.' He replaced the receiver with a clatter. 'I hate dealing with schmucks. You know what a schmuck is, lady?'

Aurora shrugged. 'A silly person?'

He laughed, showing two gold teeth. 'You got that right.' His New York accent was strong and his voice was deep.

She stared at him in fascination.

'So, you're an actress-slash-singer, am I right?'

She nodded.

'Okay, this is how it works. You sign a contract, my people find you jobs that will increase exposure, every goddamn dime you make you keep, except for my ten percent.' He held up his hands. 'Yes, it's steep, but with an unknown like you, I gotta make sure it pays. Then, if after twelve months things ain't workin' out, we part ways.' He smiled. 'Sound good to you?'

James spoke first. 'What kind of jobs will *your people* find exactly? I mean, I don't want her starring in a reality TV show about the Playboy Mansion.'

'Are you the boyfriend or something?' Harry asked in annoyance.

'No, he's not,' said Aurora, flushed. 'He's just asking a question.'

'The jobs? I guess we look at what's big right now. I'm talking

*Game of Thrones*, I'm talking *Homeland*, I'm talking Disney –'

'I always thought she was made to play Lyanna Stark,' interjected James enthusiastically.

'Too late,' said Harry immediately. 'That was cast months ago.' He tapped on his computer screen. 'Bertie says you sing like an angel. It's a goddamn shame we didn't meet a year ago. You would be perfect for the remake of *Beauty and the Beast*. That Harry Potter girl got the part.' He frowned. 'You know, they're planning to remake all the classics. Maybe with a bit of fake tan, we could make a Pocahontas out of you.'

'I understand that reference,' said James solemnly to Aurora. 'Thank you for my education regarding the princesses.'

'Anytime,' she said back with a smile.

'The thing is, you're a nobody. Sure, Bertie thinks you're the next best thing, but I gotta be convinced.' He rubbed his chin. 'Just sign today and we'll get the ball rolling. The word on the street is that you'll be on Broadway soon. I wanna limit that as I don't want you trapped on a stage for two years. Theatre is not like film. In fact, TV is the way forward now. That's what everyone wants: to be immortalised in a box set.' He picked up the phone once more. 'I'll just tell Tasmina to bring in the documents. You can sign and that's it for now. I'm a busy man. Maybe there's a commercial you could do to start.'

'Mr. Newman,' said Aurora in her clear voice.

He stopped and looked at her. 'Yes?'

'I'm not signing today.'

He dropped the phone with a clatter. 'You're not signing today.' He shook his head. 'Say again?'

'Thank you for your time, but I'm not sure that your agency will take me where I want to go. You see, I don't see myself in advertisements, or commercials as you call them, and I don't want to rush things.'

James squeezed her hand in support.

'I understand that it's a gamble taking me on. I really appreciate your seeing us today. Perhaps if you give me a few days to mull over your offer, we might move forward.' She smiled warmly. 'My daddy says never to rush a big decision. He recommends taking one's time.'

'The way you talk – holy shit, you could've been Lady Mary in *Downton Abbey*!' He stared at her in fascination. 'So, you're telling me that you're not signing today?'

She nodded.

'Do you realise how goddamn lucky you are to even get an appointment with me? I got people trying to see me for months. I know actors who would kill to be in your place right now.'

'I know,' she said, 'and don't for a moment think that I'm ungrateful. I shall ring you by the end of the week with my answer.'

'Oh, you will.'

'Yes.' She stood up and held out her hand. 'It was a pleasure, Mr. Newman. I hope we meet again very soon.'

He shook her hand. 'Have fun mulling or whatever the hell you called it.'

'Goodbye.' She walked away with James in tow.

Harry stared after them. Crazy broad. Did she not realise what she missed today? He felt like throwing her file in the trash.

*I'm not signing today.*

What the hell was she thinking?

James initiated a high five outside the building. 'I'm so impressed, Borealis,' he said, laughing. 'You played hardball.'

She shrugged. 'I don't want to end up in a washing-powder ad or something.'

'Commercial,' he corrected grinning. 'It's all about the lingo.'

'You know what I mean.'

They paused to cross the street. The neon signs of Piccadilly were luminescent in the grey winter day.

'Right, let me take you for lunch,' he said. 'Anywhere you like.'

She hugged herself in delight. He was all hers for a few hours. It had been so long.

'Let's go to Covent Garden,' she said. 'I know a nice little café there.'

'Right, off we go.' He linked arms with her and they walked through the crowds of people on the footpath. 'Remember when you called it Convent Garden? I couldn't convince you otherwise.'

She giggled. 'I thought lots of nuns lived there.'

'Green-fingered nuns,' he added, winking.

'Ha, bloody, ha.'

After toasted cheese sandwiches and mugs of tea, they sat together in the corner of the café, talking incessantly. Janes filled her in on his life in Syria and she told him about Marianne and her theatre work. The waitress interrupted them, wanting to know if they'd like a refill of tea. Aurora waited for James to shake his head and say that he had to go, but he didn't. Instead, he nodded cheerfully and held out his empty mug.

'So, do you think you'll get a job?' she asked, tracing the rim of her mug with her finger.

'I'll pick up something,' he answered. 'I'll have to freelance which will drive Claire mad, but what can I do?'

'Why will she be mad?'

'I'll be self-employed and it's harder to get a mortgage without a steady income.'

'Oh.' She frowned. 'Do you want a mortgage?'

He started. 'What do you mean?'

'You're so young and you'll have to live so close to her parents. I never imagined you in that situation.'

'Oh? How did you imagine me then?'

'In a cool studio apartment in New York, taking photos of the skyline.' She smiled. 'You're so talented, you could go anywhere with your skills.'

He said nothing, but she knew she'd hit a nerve. His brown eyes, those eyes she knew so well, looked dark for a moment.

'Jiminy?' she said softly.

'Yep?'

'Just be happy, okay?'

'I will.' He smiled brightly, back to his cheerful self.

'Put yourself first for a change.'

His eyes met hers. 'I do.'

She shook her head. 'No, you don't. You're the most selfless person I know. You saved me for a start. And made things difficult for me – it's going to be very hard to find a boyfriend as good and as kind as you.'

'Debussy might measure up.'

She scowled. 'Don't mention him. He's driving me crazy. He sent me a dozen red roses on Valentine's Day and nothing since. Bertie thinks he's trying to be honourable but life's too short.'

'I have to disagree,' said James. 'I'm all for him being honourable. You should be treated with respect.'

'At this rate, I'll be an old lady before he pounces.'

'Don't!' He held up his hands defensively.

'Don't what?'

'That mental image makes me want to vomit.'

She threw a sachet of sugar at him. 'I'm not a little girl any more! Stop babying me!'

His expression changed. 'I'm starting to realise that,' he said quietly. 'I suppose, I don't want you to get hurt.'

'No matter what happens, I'll get hurt. That's life. I was hurt the moment I was born.' She flicked her long hair away from her face. 'However, I want to be kissed and held and loved. I want to *fall* in love. Is there anything wrong with that?'

'No, there's nothing wrong with that at all.' He smiled. 'Whoever you love will be one lucky man.' He drained his tea. 'I'll probably hate him though. Just so you know.'

'We won't be invited over to your little semi-detached house for dinner then?'

He laughed. 'Probably not.'

William arranged to meet Gloria for coffee a couple of days later. They met at the Swan pub near the hospital as he only had a short lunch break. She was seated by the window when he arrived.

'Over here, darling!' she called, waving madly.

He smiled and undid the buttons of his coat.

'Lovely to see you, Mum,' he said, kissing her cheek. 'Thank you for coming all the way up here.'

She waved him away. 'Not at all. I had to come to the city any way.'

'Oh?'

'Why, yes, I'm all out of that hand cream I like from Harrods.' She smiled. 'Vitally important for my daily life, of course. So, what's so important?'

He took a seat and inhaled sharply. 'It's about Ella.'

'Hmmm, I expected as much.'

'Well, she and I … we're not … I mean …'

'Spit it out,' she said kindly.

'She's pregnant but it's not mine.'

Gloria's eyes widened. 'Pregnant?' she echoed. 'Oh no!'

'She has terrible morning sickness – that's why she looks so thin.'

Gloria put her hand over her son's. 'Where's the father of the baby?'

William sighed. 'In Canada. He's married and she doesn't want anything to do with him. Or he with her.'

'Why is she living with you?'

He shrugged. 'She has nowhere to go. This guy, the father? He was also her boss so she lost her job.'

'Good lord!'

'So, I found her living in a squalid flat in the East End with barely enough money for food. She couldn't eat anyway and then was hospitalised with dehydration.' He looked up. 'I have to look after her, Mum. She has no one else.'

'What about Arthur and Maureen? She's their daughter, for God's sake!'

'She hasn't told them. She's afraid to.'

Gloria raised an eyebrow. 'I can see why, to be fair. Arthur was always quite stuffy.'

A waitress appeared and held up her pen. 'Are you ready to order?' she asked.

Gloria shook her head. 'Not quite yet, thank you.'

The waitress walked away, shoving her notepad into her apron pocket.

'Look, Mum. I want you to support me, us. I'm going to look after her until the baby comes. Until she's back on her feet.'

Gloria said nothing. Instead she looked at her son compassionately.

'Then, when she's back to normal,' he said, 'she can get her life back together.'

'Don't get hurt, my love.'

William's head shot up. 'What? You sound just like Laura!'

Gloria stroked his cheek with her finger. 'You're a lovely man, William. You remind me of your father. Just make sure you don't end up with a broken heart.'

He met her gaze steadily. 'I'm not a fool, Mum. I know that Ella doesn't like me like that. I just want to help her, that's all.'

'Then I'll support her too,' said Gloria with conviction. 'Bring her down someday for lunch and we'll celebrate the baby news.'

William exhaled slowly and sat back. 'You are so great, Mum. Thank you.'

Bertie rang the next day during a break from filming.

'Aurora! Greetings from Andalusia!'

'Hello, Bertie,' she said warmly. 'How's Seville?' She curled up on the armchair in the sitting-room area of her flat.

'Oh, dreadfully hot. I'm currently availing of the wonderful air con in my villa.' He laughed. 'I'm ringing you, my dear, to congratulate you on your performance with Harry Finkelman. He rang me in a frightful tizz about this uppity girl who had refused his offer of a contract.'

'Oh, Bertie, I hope you don't think that I'm ungrateful.' She bit her lip. It was he who had organised the meeting after all. 'It's just, I don't want to rush something like this. Daddy told me not to take the first offer on the table.'

'He's spot on,' agreed Bertie. 'What makes me laugh is the fact that Harry has been at the top for so long, he's forgotten what it's like not to have people fawning all over him. Genius move, my darling. He'll want you even more now.'

She wasn't so sure. He could just as easily tell her the deal was off.

'I'm also ringing to ask you out for dinner when I return next week.'

'Oh?'

'Yes, I'd love to wine and dine you. Are you available?'

'Well, I'm busy at weekends as you know.'

'Then I'll book us something for midweek. I'm pining for you, Ms. Sinclair. Your beautiful image fills my mind constantly. In spite of all the señoritas I meet every night here, I'd give it all up for you."

'Bertie,' she warned, 'you know we're just friends.'

He chuckled. 'I had an inkling. You've relegated me into that place all men fear: the friend zone.'

It was her turn to laugh. 'Yes, yes, I have.'

'Still,' he continued, 'you won't deny me your company, will you? Give an old man something to look forward to. Who knows? After a few glasses of obscenely expensive wine, you might reconsider. We'd have the wedding of the century! '

'Of course I'll have dinner with you,' she said, ignoring his flirting. 'I'd love to hear all about your stint in Spain.'

'Magnificent. Now, I'll ring off. The director is waving at me from outside. Bloody upstart. He insists on shooting each scene twenty times. I'm overworked.'

'Bye, Bertie. Thank you again for your help.'

'*Ciao, bella*. Until we meet again.'

# Chapter Thirty

William and Ella went to Oxshott a week later. Gloria had organised a lunch as promised and insisted they travel down for her famous chicken cacciatore.

Ella baulked when they arrived at the house. 'Oh Will, I feel so nervous.'

He took her small hand in his. 'No need. Mum is delighted with your news.'

Ella wasn't so sure. William inserted his key and held the door open. 'After you.'

Gloria met them in the hall. 'Will! Ella! Lunch is just ready.' She embraced them fondly and bid them follow her into the dining room.

Henry was sitting at the head of the table, reading a worn book of poetry with his glasses perched on his nose.

'Hello, you two.' He smiled warmly. 'Good to see you again so soon.'

Ella took off her jacket and felt her stomach somersault. Her loose black top fell becomingly over her belly, which was protruding noticeably now.

William relieved her of the jacket and hung it with his own

coat on the rack in the hall. 'Is it just us?' he asked.

Gloria nodded. 'James is at Claire's and Aurora is busy at the theatre. Wine?'

Ella shook her head. 'Not for me, thanks.'

'Oh, of course.' Gloria blushed. 'Although, I wasn't as abstemious as you when I was pregnant. I suppose we didn't know as much in those days.'

'So that's what happened to Lolly,' quipped William, taking a seat near Henry.

Henry smiled at Ella. 'You look much better today, my dear. Has the nausea abated?'

Ella was at a loss at what to say. She had concealed the pregnancy news for so long, it felt strange to talk about it so openly.

'I am feeling better,' she admitted. 'I'm not confined to my bed all day at least.'

'Hey, you mean *my* bed!' interrupted William with a grin.

Gloria disappeared into the kitchen and reappeared a few moments later with a large pot of aromatic chicken stew. 'Get the bread for me, Henry,' she said, placing the hot casserole on a ceramic tile in the centre of the table. 'I hope this won't make you sick, Ella.'

'I'll just have a little,' she answered. 'It looks lovely.'

Gloria laughed. 'Well, I wouldn't go that far. My talents do not lie in the kitchen, I'm afraid.'

She doled out a small helping of the stew on a plate and handed it to William. 'Give this to Ella,' she said and he passed it along.

Henry arrived back with a basket of sliced baguette and resumed his seat.

'Have you thought of any names?' he asked conversationally.

Ella started. 'Names? Gosh, no. Not yet.'

William accepted a plate piled high with stew from his

mother. 'Of course it'll be William if it's a boy,' he said, winking, and Ella smiled.

Gloria served Henry and finally herself. 'Right, dig in,' she said, picking up her fork.

Ella nibbled on some chicken and tried a piece of red pepper. To her surprise, she enjoyed it. Things were definitely on the up. Tension seeped out of her body and she relaxed back in her chair.

Gloria caught her eye and smiled warmly. 'Is it edible?' she asked.

Ella nodded. 'It's lovely, thank you.'

Henry sipped his wine. 'Jolly good result in the rugby, right, Will?'

They started to discuss the last English game at Twickenham.

'Sport!' said Gloria to Ella. 'How I loathe these conversations. Frightfully boring, aren't they?'

'I must admit I like rugby,' said Ella apologetically.

William's and Henry's voices grew louder as they argued over the referee's decision.

Gloria put down her fork and leaned closer to Ella. 'Don't you worry about a thing, my darling,' she said in a low voice. 'We're all here and we're going to look after you and your little one.'

Ella felt tears well up in her eyes. 'You're so kind.'

'Think nothing of it,' said Gloria briskly. 'I practically raised you myself.'

'No, I'm serious,' said Ella. 'I'm so grateful.'

William stood up and imitated a move the fly half made in the rugby game. 'I mean, he was bound to miss that kick.'

'I have to agree,' said Henry.

Gloria raised her eyes to heaven. 'Sport!'

Laura knocked on Aurora's dressing-room door after the performance the following Saturday evening. '*Yoohoo!* Are you ready? I hope you remember our date?'

The door swung open and Aurora appeared, wearing tight black pants, a black lacy top and black heels. Her hair shone from brushing and her eyes sparkled. 'Will I do?'

'Holy Moly! You look like Sandy from *Grease*.' Laura shook her head. 'I got chills, they're multiplying. You know that Colin's gay, yeah? The rest of the party are female and straight as far as I know.'

'I know,' said Aurora, closing the door behind her. 'I just felt like wearing something minxy.'

'Good for you. Come on, they're waiting outside. You know Lydia, of course. Her sister Molly is here, plus her best friend Samantha.'

'Bridesmaids?'

'Yes. They're very nice.'

They walked down the corridor.

'When's the wedding?'

'August.' Laura descended the steps gingerly as her heels were quite high. 'In Venice no less. Everyone is flying out for a long weekend.'

'How romantic!' said Aurora dreamily. 'I'd love to get married there.'

'Not so romantic for me,' said Laura grimly. 'Christian and Tara are the groom's parents. He'll be tied up in that. I'm Lydia's close friend so I have to go. Therein lies the problem. If I so much as dance with Chris, I'll be shot.'

'Hardly shot.'

'You know what I mean. It's going to be awkward.'

They reached the stage door. 'Colin loved your performance by the way. His boyfriend Val is an actor so he has seen his fair share of plays. He was inconsolable when Joey died.'

'That's so lovely,' said Aurora, blushing.

They emerged into the darkness. Standing in front of them was a small group, rubbing their hands together for warmth. Aurora recognised Lydia straight away.

'We're here!' announced Laura.

'Finally,' said a good-looking young man with bouncy brown curls and dark-brown eyes. 'I'm about to freeze.' He held out his manicured hand. 'I'm Colin. You must be Aurora.'

'Hi!'

'Loved you as Elise Sloane. Like, *loved*.' He put his hand on his chest. 'That death scene was just so emotional.'

'Hi, Aurora,' said Lydia, hugging her. 'Long time no see.' She looked the same: small and slim with long brown hair and green eyes.

'Congratulations on your wedding,' Aurora said shyly. 'You must be so excited.'

'Not as excited as me,' interjected Colin. 'I mean, at the rate my boyfriend Val's going, I'm never going to walk down the aisle. I'm forced to live my dreams through my darling cousin here.'

Laura raised her eyes to heaven. 'I'm not surprised he hasn't proposed. You're too pushy.'

A girl with blonde curls and twinkly blue eyes approached Aurora next. 'Hi, I'm Molly. Lydia's younger sister. Fair play on your performance! You look way different with long hair.'

Aurora smiled. 'The wig is very effective.' She guessed Molly was of a similar age to her. She had an air of mischief about her and she liked her immediately.

Finally, a girl with dark features came forward. 'I'm Sam, the best friend. Really nice to meet you.'

'Hello!' Aurora memorised the names.

Laura checked her watch. 'Right, let's hit the pub. I could murder a gin and tonic.'

'Let me just call Val and check on Britney,' said Colin, pulling out his iPhone. 'You walk on and I'll catch up.'

'Britney?' echoed Laura. 'Who is that?'

'His dog,' explained Lydia. 'She's a Pom, you know, the small cute hairy dogs.'

'An overindulged, spoilt brat is what she is,' interrupted Molly.

'My 4G isn't working,' complained Colin, ignoring her. 'I'll just have to wait until I have Wi-Fi.' He put his phone into the pocket of his long cashmere coat.

'How old is Britney?' asked Aurora politely as they walked along.

'Oh, eight months,' said Colin. 'Easily the most beautiful dog I've ever met.' He sighed. 'The day we brought her home was just . . .' He choked and fanned his face.

'The greatest?' said Lydia helpfully, patting his back.

'The greatest,' he agreed. 'She has made our life complete. Lydia has Sienna, so now I have Britney. Although, I'm a lot stricter than my dear cousin here.' He gave Lydia a pointed look. 'No offense, but Sienna is spoilt rotten.'

Molly laughed out loud. 'Are you serious? Since you've become a Doggy Daddy, that Pom has been treated like a princess.' She turned to Laura. 'He buys clothes for her and jewellery. She has a four-poster dog basket and only eats freshly prepared chicken fillets.'

'*Free range* chicken fillets,' corrected Colin haughtily.

'Thank God Val is rational,' Samantha said. 'There are no diamond collars when he's around.'

'Val is Colin's reverse,' explained Molly. 'The complete opposite to my cuz here.'

'That's why I need to FaceTime as soon as I can,' said Colin grimly. 'I need to check if he's following the schedule.'

'Schedule?' scoffed Laura. 'For the bloody dog?'

Colin looked affronted. 'Lydia left a list for Luca to follow. You know, all about Sienna's feeds and nap times. Well, I did the same for Val.' He accessed his phone. 'According to this, she should be in bed by now if she's to get her full eight hours.'

'Oh, Colin, you're a pity,' said Molly, shaking her head.

The local pub was buzzing so they decided to go for drinks there.

Music emanated from the front door as they approached.

'Town is too far and expensive,' said Laura. 'This place will do nicely.'

'Right, gin and tonics for everyone,' said Colin. 'My round.' He walked up to the bar with Laura in tow, chattering incessantly.

'So, I hear you have an agent,' said Lydia to Aurora when they were seated. 'How exciting!'

She nodded. 'I rang him yesterday and accepted his offer of representation.'

'Laura says that you sing too,' said Samantha, draping her jacket over her chair. 'That has to be a bonus with all the musical opportunities there.'

'I haven't utilised my singing to date,' admitted Aurora, 'I've just been acting with Justin, my director, really.'

Colin arrived with three large glasses of gin. 'They have much fancier tonic over here,' he said in excitement. 'Far bigger bottles too.' He placed three large goblets on the table filled with ice cubes, gin and lemon slices.

Laura followed with the remaining drinks. 'Right, let's toast! *To Lydia and Luca! Wishing you all the best!*'

They all raised their glasses. '*To Lydia and Luca!*'

'Fitting toast from her future mother-in-law,' whispered Molly to Colin and they giggled.

'I heard that!' shrieked Laura. 'No jokes about Christian, please.' She turned to her friend. 'Any luck finding a dress, Lyd?'

'Well, we did make progress.'

'Progress? We have it sorted,' interrupted Colin. 'We're getting it made! It will be an original gown by this new up-and-coming designer.'

'A friend of Luca's from New York,' explained Lydia. 'She's based in London.'

'She could be the next Chanel,' continued Colin. 'Just saying.'

Samantha agreed. 'The sketches she showed us? The dress

suited you down to the ground, Lyd.'

Lydia shrugged. 'It's just a dress. A one-day wonder.'

Colin snorted. 'It's an original design, darling. Not just any old dress.'

'Speaking of Luca, has he told his mother that I'll be there?' asked Laura, reddening slightly.

Lydia bit her lip. 'Not exactly,' she said uncomfortably, 'but soon. He's waiting for the right moment.'

'Well, Chris and I are moving in together, surely that counts for something,' said Laura defensively. 'I'm not just some consort he picked up at a bar.'

'She doesn't know that yet,' said Lydia diplomatically. 'The only reason she didn't take Christian to the cleaners was because Luca asked her not to. You two weren't very discreet throughout the whole thing. She could've made things very difficult.'

'Oh,' said Laura, blushing an ugly red. 'I didn't realise.'

Lydia looked away. She didn't want Laura to know the fights she and Luca had had over the issue of her coming to their wedding. Tara had made it quite clear that she didn't want her day marred by Laura's presence but, as Lydia argued over and over, it was *her* day, not Tara's. She and Laura were close and there was no question of her friend being excluded.

'How about you, Lyd?' Laura pressed on, twiddling the lemon in her glass.

'Hey, you know how I feel.' Lydia smiled warmly. 'You're my friend and I know more than anyone how complicated relationships can be. Remember, Luca was married when we got together. Now look at us. It's worth it in the end.'

Aurora nodded in agreement. 'Love knows nothing of race or rank or age. When it happens, it happens. You must fight to protect it.'

Molly whistled. 'You could be in *Downton Abbey.* Honest to God.'

Aurora laughed. 'You're not the first to say that.'

'Or a Jane Austen movie. Get your new fancy agent to start looking for parts like that. You were born to play a princess or a duchess.'

'So, what do you do?' Aurora asked Samantha and Molly.

'Well, I'm in my final year of nursing,' said Molly happily. 'I'm working crazy hours, but I love it.'

'I'm a teacher,' said Samantha, 'of Spanish and History.'

'Are you married, Molly?'

Molly snorted. 'Gosh, no. I'm only twenty-two. My whole life is ahead of me. I'm no Colin – hankering to walk down the aisle.'

'Well, I *am* married – my husband Craig is a solicitor,' said Samantha. 'He's Luca's cousin actually. So, we're all connected.'

'I work at a magazine now,' said Lydia. 'I write articles every week. Colin works there too. It's called *Papped!*.'

'What kind of articles?' enquired Aurora. 'Editorials? Political?'

Molly guffawed. 'Try, '*How to get the most out of your fake tan*' or '*Is cellulite a myth?*''

Lydia glared at her sister. 'You back off,' she said dismissively. 'I admit our articles aren't heavy-hitting investigatory journalism, but I make a difference.'

'Of course you do,' said Molly with a serious face. 'I mean, I now know the difference between a Hollywood and a Brazilian wax.'

Colin drew himself up to his full height. 'You need not patronise us, Molly Kelly. At least we don't clean arses for a living.' He picked up his phone. 'Silence for a moment. I'm FaceTiming home.'

The call connected and Val's face appeared. He looked older than Colin, with dark features and merry eyes. He was wearing a plaid shirt and had a can of beer in his hand.

'Hi, Col,' came his deep voice.

'Hi, honey. Is our baby asleep?'

Val nodded. 'Sienna's been asleep since nine.'

'You know I mean Britney,' said Colin sternly. 'Where is she?'

A volley of high-pitched barks could be heard over the phone and a small white dog appeared, licking Val's face.

'*She's still awake?*' shouted Colin. '*Val!* It's way past her bedtime. Honestly.'

'Oh, don't get your knickers in a twist. I'm watching some rugby. I'll put her to bed later.'

Colin got to his feet with an indignant expression on his face. 'I'll take this call outside,' he said, stalking off.

'Can the dog even tell the time?' asked Molly.

Lydia turned to Aurora. 'Colin likes to be in control. He's obsessively tidy and has an schedule for everything.'

'If you go to his place and forget to use a coaster?' Molly trailed her finger along her throat.

'Or leave your dirty ware in the sink?' added Samantha, making a Sign of the Cross.

Lydia laughed. 'Well, he's not quite as bad as that, but almost.'

The gin and tonic was cool and refreshing and soon they were all empty again.

'My round,' said Samantha waving her purse. 'Same again?'

Everyone nodded.

Colin arrived back to the table and exhaled dramatically. 'Parenting is so hard. You read all the books and think you're doing a great job and then *bam*! Wake-up call.' He poured the tonic into the giant glass. 'Right, let's get drinking. I need to relax.'

'*Hear! Hear!*' whooped Molly. 'So what if Britney is up past her bedtime? We're in London, baby. No more talk of schedules or dogs.'

'Do you have a picture of Sienna?' said Aurora to Lydia. 'I've heard so much about her.'

Lydia nodded and accessed her photo stream on her phone. 'There, that's my baby.'

Aurora took the phone and saw one of the cutest little girls she'd ever seen. Sienna had blonde curls, big green eyes and was laughing in the photo. A gold bracelet dangled on her chubby wrist and she had a tiara on her head.

'That was taken at her first birthday party,' said Lydia, her face softening. 'Colin had just given her a giant Elsa doll as she's obsessed with *Frozen*. To date, she has about four words: Baba, Dada, Mummy and Elsa.'

'Oh, don't talk to me,' said Molly, throwing her eyes to heaven. 'I know every word of every song from that bloody film. Every time I baby-sit, we watch it about ten times.'

'Scroll across,' said Lydia. 'There are some nice ones of her at the park.'

Aurora swiped the screen to reveal pictures of Sienna in a swing, on a slide and in the arms of a blond man. She inhaled sharply. His face was identical to the little girl's. On closer inspection, she noticed his chiselled bone structure was similar to Christian's. He was probably one of the most handsome men she had ever seen. 'Is this Luca?' she asked, reluctant to swipe.

Lydia peered at the screen. 'Yep. That's him.'

Aurora's eyes widened. 'Is he a model?'

Molly burst out laughing. 'A model? What a laugh!'

Colin glared at her. 'He a fine thing, Mol. We're just used to him. I mean, we don't appreciate his beauty any more.'

'Beauty?' she repeated incredulously. 'My dear brother-in-law-to-be is far from beautiful.'

Lydia held up her hands. 'Would you all just stop? Luca is Luca. Try living with him, that'll demystify him in no time.'

'I can't argue there,' agreed Colin. 'Luca and Lydia lived with me for a few months, Aurora, and I'm still finding mess. It was a happy day when they got their own place down the hall.'

Samantha snorted. 'A happy day? You bawled your eyes out when they moved out.'

'Well, it was emotional,' he admitted, 'but then I got Britney and it filled the void.'

'*What did I say?*' Molly looked threatening. '*No more Britney!*'

'So, what colour are the bridesmaid dresses?' asked Laura who was on her fifth gin.

'Fuchsia red,' said Lydia, sipping some water. 'You should all hydrate,' she warned. 'You'll die in the morning.'

Aurora's muddled brain struggled to focus. 'Did you say fuchsia?'

'Yes. They grow near my home in West Cork. I love that colour.'

Aurora pulled her necklace from its resting place between her breasts. 'Like this, you mean?'

Lydia peered at the silver pendant. 'Yes! That's exactly it. Where did you get that?'

Aurora fingered the flower. 'It belonged to my mother. I've had it for years.'

Molly got up and glanced around. 'Toilets?'

Laura pointed to the back of the pub. 'That way.'

As soon as she was out of sight, Colin accessed his photos on his phone. 'Aurora, I just have to show you this photo shoot I did last week with Britney.' He looked over his shoulder to make sure that Molly was indeed in the toilets.

'Oh?' She glanced at the screen. There were hundreds of pictures, all categorised into folders: Britney's First Bath, Britney's First Day at the Kennels, Britney at the Beach . . .

'Are you a fan of Britney Spears?' asked Aurora, gazing in astonishment at the photos.

'Yes. I adore her. Even after her meltdown and head-shaving.

I always sing her stuff at karaoke.'

'Colin is the Karaoke King,' explained Samantha. 'He can't help himself.'

'Speaking of karaoke,' he began, jabbing his thumb in the direction of a noisy group of women in the corner, 'I just met a girl at the bar called Chanelle. She's with that hen party over there. She said that there'll be some karaoke soon. I'm so excited.'

Samantha groaned. 'Oh please God, no! Save us!'

Lydia put her face in her hands. 'Are you serious?'

Colin looked insulted. 'I'd have something to say if I couldn't sing. I mean, I'm fab.'

Laura patted his back in encouragement. 'You *are* fab,' she agreed. 'Just get a round in before you perform. We're almost out.'

Colin held up the microphone and tapped the nozzle for attention. 'It's been a long time, people. I'm a bit rusty.'

The hen party cheered.

'I'm going to start with some ABBA.' He nodded at the DJ and the opening bars of 'Gimme! Gimme! Gimme!' began to play.

'That's Colin sorted for the rest of the night,' said Molly. 'He'll sing at least twenty songs. God help anyone else who wants a go.'

Aurora started to move in time with the music. 'He's pretty good,' she said, clapping her hands. 'Those women seem to love him.'

'I just watched them have two Jägerbombs in a row. They can't even see him properly at this stage.' Molly turned to Lydia. 'Is he still putting pressure on you about singing at the church?'

Lydia nodded. 'He says it at least ten times a day. It's exhausting.'

'Singing? At the wedding?' Laura looked aghast.

Lydia sighed. 'I still haven't found a soprano. You know,

someone to sing the "Ave Maria" and stuff. He's been practising for weeks, learning the Latin and reaching the high notes.'

'Good Lord! How on earth will you tell him? I mean, he can hold a tune but he's no Maria Callas.' Laura drained her drink. 'What a pickle.

'I know,' agreed Lydia glumly. 'I mean, he's a good singer and all, but he'll want to belt out "Purple Rain" at the offertory, complete with air guitar and gyrating hips.'

'Give him another role at the ceremony,' suggested Samantha, 'like a reading or a prayer.'

Colin finished the song and took a deep bow. 'Thank you, thank you all!'

The women screamed for more.

'Oh well, I suppose I could do another.' He winked at the bride-to-be. 'Right, in the words of Robbie Williams: let me entertain you!'

The DJ nodded and selected the song.

'Look at him go,' said Samantha laughing. 'You know, his church gig could be entertaining.'

Lydia shook her head. 'I love him dearly, but that's not happening. I'll make him a bridesmaid or something.'

'I don't think fuchsia red is his colour,' said Molly seriously. 'Plus, he'll find it hard to hold up a strapless gown.'

'Ha, ha.' Her older sister made a face.

'Last orders!' shouted the barman. 'Last orders, get 'em now!' He rang a bell loudly.

Colin arrived back to the table breathlessly. 'Right, the DJ reckons we only have time for two more tunes. I want to do "Empire State of Mind" by Jay Z and Alicia Keys. Mol? Will you do the honours?'

Molly looked pensive for a moment and then said, 'No.'

'Sam?'

'You know I can't sing.'

'Lyd?'

'Same.'

'Laura?'

'Bugger off, Colin.'

'Aurora?'

'Why not?' She got up. 'That's the one about New York, am I right?'

He held out his hand. 'It sure is. Now, try your best. I'm so used to performing that I tend to drown out other singers. If I notice that you're off key or anything, I'll improvise.'

'Thank you.'

'So, as my part is mainly rapping, I might sing the second chorus? You know, to give them the benefit of my voice.'

'Of course.'

He tapped the microphone once more. 'I'm nearing the end of the night, ladies,' he said to the hen party. 'So, this will be my swan song.'

They booed and stamped their feet. '*Keep singin', darlin'. You're bloomin' brilliant!*' called one.

Colin smiled modestly. 'It's been a pleasure. Now, I have a special guest. Everyone welcome Aurora!'

The women screamed in response.

'I wanted to thank you for your support.' He paused and closed his eyes. 'My *raison d'être* is singing on stage. I'm incredibly fortunate that I'm so good at it.'

'*Get off the stage, you plonker!*' called an old man at the bar.

'So, without further ado . . .'

The intro began to play. Colin started to strut around and then began to rap. Aurora watched him in fascination. He bent down and tickled one girl under the chin, then whipped around and did the splits in front of another woman. She squealed and put a pink feather boa around his neck.

Then came Aurora's cue to sing.

Her voice, loosened by all the gin, resonated through the room. The barman stopped polishing glasses and stared at her open-mouthed. The old man at the bar turned around and peered at the young girl singing on the makeshift stage. The women screamed in delight.

Lydia, deep in conversation with Samantha, stopped dead. 'Laura,' she hissed, 'why didn't you tell me she could sing like that?'

'*Shhhh!*' said Molly and they all fell silent.

Colin had stopped in his tracks and his mouth fell open. Within seconds, it was his cue to rap again, but he fumbled his words.

The time came for the second chorus. Aurora nodded at him to continue but he bowed his head. 'Please,' he said, gesturing for her to sing instead.

So, she did.

The song ended and the crowd erupted. Even the DJ clapped, unused to such talent.

'*More! More!*' screamed the hen party.

Aurora blushed. 'I couldn't possibly – it's far too late . . .'

The barman held up his thumb. '*We 'ave time for one more!*' he called over the din.

Colin bowed out gracefully, fully aware that he had been outclassed. 'I suggest something by Adele or Barbra Streisand.'

'Please sing "Let it Go" from *Frozen,*' pleaded the bride-to-be. 'It's my daughter's favourite song. I'll record it for her.'

'Of course,' said Aurora kindly. 'Would you tell me her name so I can dedicate it to her?'

'Michelle.'

Aurora cleared her throat. '*This last song is for Michelle!*'

The crowd cheered. The DJ pressed 'play' and the piano intro began.

Aurora closed her eyes and began to sing. The women moved in sync, waving their arms above their head. When she reached the chorus, everyone joined in. Lydia turned to Colin. 'Sienna would adore this,' she said.

The barman watched the young girl as she sang. This was no ordinary drunken punter, belting out a tune at the end of the night. This girl was special – she had a voice like an angel. He debated whether to video her on his phone. She could well be famous.

The crescendo began to build at the end of the song. Aurora's voice climbed the scale easily, never faltering. She threw her head back and sang with all her might.

The crowd erupted, singing at the top of their voices.

The song ended. The remaining people in the bar got to their feet and clapped.

Aurora walked back to the table, her face flushed. 'That was such fun,' she said, sipping her drink. 'I can see why you love it so much,' she added to Colin.

'You're amazing,' he said honestly. 'I'm super-impressed.'

'Amazing,' echoed Samantha. 'How did you hit those notes?'

Lydia, feeling a bit tipsy, had an epiphany. 'You must come to Venice,' she declared suddenly. 'If I pay for your flights and hotel, will you sing at my wedding in August? Only if you're free. I mean, I'll pay you, of course.'

'At your wedding?'

'Yes! It makes perfect sense. You're Laura's sister and you're better than most professionals I've heard.'

Aurora's face broke into a huge smile. 'I'd love to, Lydia. What an honour. Would Luca mind? I mean, should you ask him?'

'Not at all. He lets me do what I want.'

An alarmed Molly stole a glance in Colin's direction and found Samantha doing the same. Everyone knew that he had his heart set on singing at the church.

To their relief, he looked delighted. 'Fantastic,' he enthused. 'I thought that I'd have to do the honours. You've just taken the pressure off.' If he was disappointed, he didn't show it.

'Splendid!' said Laura. 'Now I'll have another ally.'

'Knowing Tara Jacob, that's a good thing,' said Colin, patting her arm.

'I'll have to check with Harry my agent, but I'm sure it will be fine.' Aurora beamed at them all. 'Just send me the dates and I'll book that weekend.'

'All's well that ends well,' said Samantha. 'I usually hate all that "Panis Angelicus" stuff, but now I'm looking forward to it.'

'Maybe you could sing "Let It Go" again for Sienna – not actually in the church of course!' said Lydia. 'She would hero-worship you forever.

'Of course,' said Aurora. 'Venice! How wonderful! I've never been.'

'That's settled then,' said Lydia, delighted. 'Colin – you can be Chief Bridesmaid.'

'Seriously?' he gasped. 'Like, I'll get to walk up the aisle?'

'Yup.'

'Oh, *thank* you! It may be my only chance ever, you know!'

'Oh, don't be so pathetic,' said Molly.

# Chapter Thirty-one

William paced the room. Ella was sitting on the sofa, barely moving. The clock on the wall ticked incessantly, each tick bringing them closer to the time: the time her parents were due to arrive.

Bang on one o'clock, the doorbell rang.

'Right,' said William, straightening his shirt. 'Let's do this.'

Ella, now almost twenty-four weeks pregnant, had decided to tell her parents. They would inevitably find out and she didn't want them to hear it from anyone else but her. A few weeks before, she had messaged her mother to come and visit, describing how happy she was and how she'd love to show them her new life. She suggested a long weekend break where they could meet and go for afternoon tea. Perhaps take in a show. Her mother, who still had close friends in London, was easy to convince. Her father initially resisted. Why would he want to go back there? Flights were expensive and he didn't like this Brexit business at all. However, after a while, he had relented and they were due any minute.

Arthur Taylor had worked for the British Foreign Office for years. A conservative man in his late sixties, he valued two things:

hard work and respectability. His wife, Maureen, was a perfect companion. Quiet and demure, she had hosted dinners and luncheons with grace and style, and had never caused trouble or fracas during their thirty-five-year marriage. Their first-born child, Mark, was a successful attorney in Toronto who made a point of visiting them once a week and was the perfect addition to any soirée.

Ella was a different story. She had rebelled from day one. The week before they had left for Canada, Maureen had found an empty bottle of vodka, a ten-pack of Marlboros and a bong in her daughter's room. They sent her to a strict school in Toronto but she didn't excel. Instead, she became involved with a boy from Moss Park and began to use drugs. Years afterwards, her parents gave her an ultimatum: shape up or shape out. They couldn't handle her wayward behaviour any more.

Ella, realising that she was on her last chance, pulled things together. She went to night school and got a job as a copywriter at an advertising agency. It was there that she met Josh. The rest was history.

Her father held out his arms. 'Come and give your old dad a hug,' he said in his clipped voice. She fell into his arms, breathing in his familiar smell. Her mother watched this exchange and waited her turn.

William hung back, waiting to offer drinks and snacks.

'So, William, you're a doctor at Great Ormond Street I hear. Jolly fine profession.' Arthur took a seat on the armchair.

'Yes, Mr. Taylor.'

'Arthur, please.'

'Yes, Arthur. I enjoy it immensely. It's so rewarding.'

Maureen beamed at him. 'It's so lovely that you two have met up after all this time.'

Ella glanced at William. She had a cushion in front of her tummy and was finding it hard to look inconspicuous.

'Would you like some tea?' he asked politely.

Maureen shook her head. 'No, my darling. We've just come from a late brunch.'

Arthur shook his head. 'We're quite all right, old chap. Now, what's this great news?'

Ella stared at her parents for a moment. It was quite obvious that they were expecting an engagement announcement. It seemed like the obvious thing to happen. They looked delighted at the prospect. Their little Ella: a doctor's wife. It was far better than her previous relationships which included a guitarist in a heavy metal band and an artist.

Well,' said William, 'we do have some news –'

Ella cut him off. 'I'm pregnant.'

There was silence. Arthur's face darkened to a deep shade of magenta. Maureen's hand flew to her mouth.

William took a seat beside Ella and took her hand in his.

'We're having a baby,' he said.

Ella threw a startled glance at him.

'Are you married?' spluttered Arthur, getting to his feet.

'No.' Ella met his angry gaze full on.

'How far along are you?' asked Maureen.

'Six months or so. I'm almost in my third trimester.'

'What do they say at the agency?' went on her mother. 'I thought you came here on a temporary contract. Surely they won't be too pleased if you take off on maternity leave.'

'They're fine about it,' said William smoothly. 'All's well.'

'Please be happy for me,' Ella pleaded. 'This is a positive thing.'

'*Positive?*' her father roared. 'You're unmarried and pregnant. I thought your generation were more savvy than this. That child will be illegitimate, Ella. Is that what you want?' He turned to William. 'And as for you! Are you a man? You two should've made it official right away instead of floundering for months.'

'No, Daddy, it's not like that,' Ella interrupted. 'William's not responsible. It's not his.'

'*What?*'

Maureen began to fan her face with a newspaper from the coffee table.

'If it's not William, then who on earth is it?'

'It doesn't matter,' she said quietly. 'He won't be on the scene.'

Maureen wiped a tear from her eye with a white handkerchief. 'Well, it's a dreadful shock, Ella. We certainly didn't expect you to let us down like this.'

'Yes, I understand that,' she said. 'But I want your blessing. This baby will be your first grandchild and I want you to be part of its life.'

Arthur's mind was racing. He felt torn two ways. His sense of betrayal made him want to explode in anger again and order his daughter from the house. But then there was this young doctor . . . it might be wiser to keep him on board and not offend him.

Maureen waited for her husband to speak, just as she had been conditioned to do throughout their marriage.

At last Arthur spoke. 'We're not going to lie and say we're thrilled,' he began. 'I can't understand how feckless the youth are today. However, what's done is done. At least you're not alone.' He gestured to William.

'Exactly.' William smiled. 'Right, Ella?'

Ella jumped. 'Yes, yes, of course.' She smiled too.

Maureen focused on her belly. 'My word, you're quite large, darling.'

William pulled her close. 'She's beautiful,' he said, kissing her head.

Ella smiled at him gratefully.

'Right, I'll ask again,' said William jovially. 'Would you like some tea or perhaps something stronger?' He clapped his hands together. 'Arthur, I've some nice Midleton in the cupboard. Shall we wet the baby's head?'

They left an hour later. Ella watched them from the window, her face troubled. William gathered the empty glasses and cups and placed them in the kitchen sink.

'Hey, are you okay?' he asked softly.

She nodded. 'I'm fine.' Suddenly she burst into tears. 'Oh Will, we can't go on like this.'

'Like what?'

'Living a lie,' she continued, 'My sleeping in your bed and you on the foldaway one. Your life has been put on hold and it's all my fault.' She put her head in her hands. 'I should leave, Will. You've gone far beyond the call of duty on this one. I'm not your responsibility. I'm not your problem.'

'Do you want to leave?' he asked.

Her eyes met his. 'I don't know. I'm beholden to you. You have your job and your life. All I have is Netflix and my daily conversation with that Indian guy at the corner shop. I have nothing to offer in this situation. Not even money. I feel so guilty. I can't bear to take advantage any longer.'

'That's my choice. That's my decision.'

He walked over to her and grasped her shoulders.

'Look at me,' he commanded.

Her head remained hanging.

'Look at me!' he said again, more forcibly.

She raised her head reluctantly.

'Do you want to leave?' he asked.

Her eyes filled with tears.

'*Do you?*'

She shook her head.

'Then don't mention it again.' He released her. 'Let's take this one day at a time, Ella. I'm quite happy to see this through. Once your baby is born, you'll be back to normal and more equipped to make decisions. You've seen my life. I work, eat, watch mindless TV and sleep. You being here is not an imposition. In fact, it's nice to have someone to watch David Attenborough with, to be honest.'

She half-smiled.

'Now, no more talk of leaving. I'd miss you.' He flicked his blond hair out of his eyes. 'I'd miss both of you.'

Ella's eyes locked with his. 'I'd miss you too.'

# Chapter Thirty-two

A few weeks later, Aurora was rushing home to get ready for the wrap party for *La Morte*. She had just had her hair done. The night before had been the final performance and the cast were meeting that evening to celebrate. She was bringing Ophelia as a date; her friend wanted to network and meet as many influential people as she could.

Her phone started to ring as she turned the corner of her street. She didn't recognise the number.

'Hello?'

'It's Harry Finkelman's office. You available to take this call?'

'Sure.'

There was silence for a moment and then she heard Harry's American twang.

'Aurora, I got an idea.'

'Hi, Harry. How are you? I hope you're well.'

'Cut the crap, princess. I'm a busy guy. Look, there's an audition coming up that's perfect for you. They're thinking of doing a remake of *Gone With the Wind*. I could see you as Scarlett. You interested?'

She stopped dead. Was she interested? It would be the

opportunity of a lifetime. She loved that film and had always admired Vivian Leigh.

'Do you think I have a chance?' she asked breathlessly.

'Probably not, but hey, we gotta try. I'm reading your resumé here. It says you played a Southern Belle before. Clara-Mae or something like that? Well, that's all good.'

'Oh, Harry! It would be a dream role. Scarlett O'Hara is everything I could hope for. She's spoilt and selfish, but what strength she has! What passion! I would just adore to play her.'

'Hey, calm down, Lady Mary. You gotta take things slow. I'll get my people to talk to their people and we'll try and organise a meeting. This is only at the talking stage. It'll be later this year before they start shooting.'

'Where will the audition be?'

'Probably L.A. You gotta come over Stateside and base yourself here. You gotta get that pretty face known.'

'Well, there was talk of the play moving to Broadway for a spell. That could coincide quite nicely.'

'Forget the theatre, you won't get enough exposure on stage. You need to get on the screen. There's no way we're signing any contracts that keep you on a crappy stage for six months. The time is now, doll. You gotta move now.'

'What do you suggest?'

'You should do a few auditions. I'll find some to practise with. Then, when it comes to *Gone With The Wind,* you should be ready.'

'I wonder who will play Rhett,' she said dreamily.

'Oh, probably Ryan Gosling or that Irish guy, Fassbender. He's hot right now. That's why they might take a chance on you. Now don't cut your hair or anything crazy like that. And practise your drawl. This could be the bigtime.'

The phone went dead.

Aurora stared at it in shock. It was simply the most amazing news she'd ever heard. She didn't for a moment think it would happen, but it was so wonderful to be considered. Scarlett, with her Irish heritage and dark beauty, reminded her of Grace. She felt as though she was born to play her.

Ophelia was curling her hair when she arrived in the door.

Aurora jumped up and down, clapping her hands. 'You'll never guess!'

'Please tell me that no more of my idols have passed away. I'm still in mourning over Prince.'

'No, Harry rang and said I might have a chance of playing Scarlett O'Hara in a remake.'

'*Wowee!*' Ophelia looked impressed. 'Come to think of it, you'd look the part.'

'Oh, Lia! It would be a dream come true.' She flopped onto the couch. 'It would be nice to have something lined up now that the play is over.' She looked glum for a moment. 'All I have in my diary is that wedding in Venice. Maybe I'll be forced to do commercials after all.'

'You'll be snapped up. Critics are raving about you. That article in *Hello!* was a huge success. You're Henry Sinclair's daughter. You'll have no problems.' She sprayed some lacquer on her hair to secure the curls in place. 'I, however, may be forced to get a job at Burger King. What did Mr. Crowley say again? *My woodland paths are dry.* Like poor W.B. Yeats, I'm at a standstill creatively.'

Aurora smiled compassionately. 'God, I'm such a narcissist. Here I am bleating on about myself and you're down in the dumps.' She squeezed Ophelia's hand. 'Let's have a glass of wine tonight and forget all about it. We have to cling to the fact that we're superstars.'

'I can always be your personal assistant.'

'But of course.'

They decided to hold the party in the theatre. Caterers had

delivered an impressive buffet and there were crates of champagne. A DJ played music in the corner and the lighting technician had organised some coloured bulbs to create an ambience.

Paul whistled when the two girls entered the room. 'Is that Ophelia I see? My word, with those curls you look more like Annie every day.'

'How original,' she sighed.

'And you, Ms. Sinclair.' He gazed at her short black dress and sparkly heels. 'You look like a goddess.'

'Oh charming,' snorted Ophelia. 'I look like a ten-year-old orphan and she looks like Aphrodite!'

Aurora kissed his cheek. 'I'm going to miss you, Jimmy Romano,' she said genuinely. 'I've seduced you more times than any man I know.'

Paul's long-term partner sidled up beside them. 'Hi, Aurora,' he said, shaking her hand.

'Hi, Dave,' she said, smiling. 'I was just telling your boyfriend here how I'll miss seducing him.'

'Maybe now we'll have time to go to Mykonos,' said Dave, giving Paul a pointed look. 'It's been all work and no play, darling. I'm oppressed.'

'Any work lined up?' she asked.

Paul shook his head. 'Nothing yet. Still, I could do with a break.'

Ophelia handed her a glass of champagne. 'There's a huge crowd here. At least forty people. How were they all involved?'

'Well, some of them are partners,' explained Aurora. 'But running a play takes a lot of man power.'

'Where's lover boy?'

Aurora scowled. 'He's no longer known as that, Lia. He has been positively asexual these past few months. That ship has definitely sailed.'

Her friend's face softened. 'Are you okay?'

'Of course. You don't miss what you never had.'

As if on cue, Justin burst through the swinging doors of the auditorium, his face blazing.

'*We did it!*' he shouted, pumping the air. '*We bloody did it!*'

'Did what, mate?' asked Ray Rossi, stuffing a canapé in his mouth.

'*New York!*' said Justin in triumph. '*We're going to New York!*'

Everyone gasped.

'New York?' repeated Paul stupidly. 'As in Broadway?'

'What about Mykonos?' said Dave.

'New York?' said Aurora in shock. 'How did that happen?'

Someone thrust a glass of champagne into Justin's hand. 'Well, I knew it was on the cards but I didn't want to say,' he said. 'Then I got a call this afternoon. They want it to run for two months in a small theatre off 44th Street. Starting in October.'

'*Yippee!*' yelled Ray, 'I've always fancied a trip to the Big Apple.'

Ophelia glanced at Aurora and frowned. She might not be available if the Scarlett O'Hara thing took off. By the look on her friend's face, she could see that she had realised the same thing. Such was Justin's arrogance that it didn't even occur to him that his cast could have other plans.

The DJ started to play the new Justin Bieber tune.

'*My idol!*' shouted Ophelia. 'Come on, Sinclair, let's dance!'

'Not now – later maybe.'

'Suit yourself.' Ophelia grabbed Paul's hand and dragged him out onto the dance floor. Aurora watched in amusement as she swung him around and around, singing 'What Do You Mean?' at the top of her voice.

'Hey, you,' said a voice in her ear. It was Justin, his handsome face smiling. He had abandoned his champagne and was now drinking whiskey instead. 'Great news about New York, eh?'

'Wonderful,' she agreed. 'I'm so happy for you.'

'Be happy for yourself too. This will catapult you into the big time.' He drained his glass. 'You can thank me later,' he added with a grin.

She said nothing. It was on the tip of her tongue to mention Harry's plans, but something told her not to say anything. Justin looked tipsy and she didn't want to ruin his good mood.

'This is a lovely party,' she said lamely, unsure of what to talk about.

'Oh, Aurora,' he said closing his eyes. 'Don't small-talk, it's so tedious. What a battle I've fought these past few months! Do you know how hard it was to watch you seduce Paul each night?'

Aurora blushed and took a sip of her champagne. Ophelia was right: whiskey did the trick. She pretended not to notice as his finger began to stroke her arm.

'Bertie told me to follow my heart but I didn't listen. I convinced myself that sleeping with you would be detrimental to our working relationship. Well, I may have been right . . . at the time . . .'

She stared at him with huge eyes. 'But what now?'

'Screw being sensible.' He took her face in his hands. 'I want you, Aurora Sinclair. I want to make love to you and wake up with you in the morning.'

She gasped in delight. His words, his beautiful words, were like music to her ears. This was the scenario she had dreamed of. This was the declaration of love she had craved. All her life she had yearned for a man to speak to her in this way.

'Let's go back to mine,' he said urgently in her ear. 'I'll meet you outside in three minutes.'

He turned and left, with a last lingering look over his shoulder.

Ophelia rushed over. 'Has he made a move?' she asked in excitement.

'Yes, very much so.' Aurora's chest was heaving. 'We're going back to his place. Oh, Lia, I think this is the night.'

'For God's sake, use protection and text me later!' She kissed her cheek. 'Enjoy yourself! I'll get a cab home with Paul and Dave.'

With a beating heart, Aurora followed Justin out the main doors. He was standing by the lamppost outside, smoking a cigarette. A black cab was waiting. He held out his hand and she allowed him to guide her into the car.

His apartment was large, but minimalist. Everything was black, from the sofa to the lamp in the corner. Press cuttings from his plays were framed on the wall and her picture featured in most of them.

'Drink?' he offered, brandishing a bottle of Jameson.

'I don't like whiskey,' she said awkwardly.

'There's white wine in the fridge,' he said, sitting down. 'Glasses are in the cupboard above the toaster.' He pulled a small white bag from his pocket and opened his wallet.

She took a crystal goblet and filled it with some wine. She'd had three glasses of champagne already and was feeling quite light-headed.

Turning around, she stopped dead. He had made three lines on the shiny glass table: three lines of cocaine. Licking the edge of his bank card, he rolled up a five-pound note. Bending down, he snorted the biggest line and sat back wiping his nose.

'Bliss,' he said, throwing his head back. 'I've been craving this all night.'

Aurora's eyes widened. She had seen people take drugs before, mainly at college parties, but she had not expected Justin to do so. Especially during their romantic night.

'Line?' he offered, holding out the rolled-up note. She shook her head and he laughed. 'Of course not. How stupid of me.

You're too innocent for all of that.' He bent down and took another snort, hoovering it all up in one go.

Aurora perched herself on the edge of the armchair, unsure of what to do.

Justin poured another glass of whiskey and regarded her.

'My father has an apartment on the Upper East Side,' he said. 'I'm sure he wouldn't mind if you stayed there.'

'With you?'

'Yes, of course with me.' He crossed his legs. 'He's *my* father, you know.'

'Of course.' She blushed. 'I didn't mean . . .'

'Come and sit over here,' he commanded, patting the sofa next to him. 'You're too far away.'

She got up nervously and walked slowly towards him. Something didn't feel right. There was a change in atmosphere and she felt uneasy. She sat next to him, her body rigid.

'You're quite the beauty,' he said, pushing her hair away from her face. 'I don't usually go for brunettes, but you have something.'

His breath smelt of smoke. Leaning closer, he kissed her lips softly. It felt quite nice so she closed her eyes and moved closer. Grabbing her head, he deepened his kiss, letting his tongue explore her mouth. She surrendered herself and let him take control. His hands began to move down, around her waist and lower again.

'You taste so sweet,' he murmured into her jaw. 'Take off your clothes.'

She jumped backwards. 'What did you say?' she asked, her cheeks flushed.

'Take off your clothes,' he repeated slowly. 'Kissing like teenagers is all very well, but I want a bit more. I'm not sixteen any more.'

She shrank backwards. 'I'm not sure that I want . . .'

He grabbed her arms. 'Take off your clothes, Aurora. Right

now.' He yanked at her dress and pulled the strap down her right shoulder.

'Stop it,' she said, struggling. 'You'll tear it.'

He ignored her and yanked it harder. The fabric split and he pulled the bodice wide open to reveal a black lacy bra. 'Nice,' he said approvingly. 'I like this.'

'*Stop!*' she shouted, pushing him backwards. '*I said no!*'

'Oh, so that's your game, is it?' he sneered. 'You like to play it that way, do you?' He flipped her onto the couch and held her arms down. 'I like it when women scream so knock yourself out.' He kissed her roughly, his teeth biting her lips. He ripped her dress even further, yanking her bra to release her breasts.

'Stop, Justin,' she said. 'Let me go.'

But he was too strong for her. Yanking her skirt upwards, he fumbled with his belt. 'You're going to take it like Elise Sloane,' he jeered, pushing her legs open. 'I saw how you oozed sex on that stage. Stop playing the innocent with me.'

She started to hit his chest, but he laughed.

'Is that the best you can do?'

'*Let me go!*' she shouted, frantically trying to break free. '*Let me go!*' Tears started to roll down her cheeks. 'I don't like this, Justin, please stop. Please!'

'Oh shut up,' he said dismissively. 'No woman has ever complained before. Just relax and enjoy it.' He pulled a condom out of the pocket of his pants and ripped the packet open.

'*No!*' she screamed, flailing wildly. '*Don't touch me!*'

He paused for a moment and stared at her red face. 'You really don't like it, do you?'

She started to sob. 'Let me go,' she repeated, shuddering.

He released her arms and sat back. 'You had better be careful, Aurora. Teasing men like that will only get you into trouble.' He picked up his glass and took a swig.

'Teasing?' she said in outrage. 'I did nothing wrong.' She

pulled her torn dress over her breasts. 'How dare you do that? How dare you frighten me like that?'

'Oh grow up,' he said in a bored tone. 'You asked for it. Coming back here in that short dress. What did you expect, darling?'

She gasped in horror. 'You're a pig,' she said, getting to her feet. 'A disgusting pig.'

'Oh get over it. Stop making a big thing about it.' He snorted the final line of coke. 'Now, fill up your glass and relax. We can try again in a while.'

She made a bolt for the door and struggled with the lock. '*Don't ever ring me again*,' she said angrily. '*Ever.*'

'Calm down. We have to go to New York.'

'*Never!* You can find another Elise. I never want to see you again.'

'Stop behaving like a child.' He drained his whiskey.

'*Goodbye!*'

The door opened and she rushed out, slamming it behind her. All she could hear was his drunken laughter as she ran down the stairs.

Once outside, she realised that she had left her bag on the coffee table.

'*Bugger!*' she said loudly. Now she had no money or no phone. Her dress was in ribbons and she shivered. They were in Chelsea – he had said that to the taxi driver. Maybe she could borrow someone's phone? Who could she call?

Laura was in New York so she was no use. William had some sort of flu and Gloria would kill her. She especially didn't want to disturb her father. His health had been poor in recent weeks and he needed his sleep. Ophelia had a new number that she didn't know by heart.

The only person left was James.

She spotted a group of girls at a bus stop. 'Excuse me!' she called.

They eyed her warily.

'Yes?' asked one.

'I've lost my bag and my phone. May I borrow yours to ring someone?'

The girl paused and stared at Aurora, whose dress was barely together and whose eyes were red from crying. She looked like she was in trouble, anyone could see that.

'All right,' she conceded, handing her a pink iPhone. 'Just be quick.'

Aurora accepted the phone gratefully and punched in his number. He had forced her to memorise it when she was teenager, just in case she needed him. Well, she needed him now. Surely that would count?

He answered on the fourth ring. His voice sounded sleepy. 'Hello?' he said, yawning.

'James? It's me, Aurora.'

'Borealis? What the hell?' He sat up.

'James, I'm in trouble. I'm so sorry to call, but I'm stranded in Chelsea and I've no money or phone and . . .' To her horror she started to cry. 'I need you. Please come and get me.'

'Of course, of course. Where are you exactly?'

'By a bus stop? There's a Starbucks across the road.' She sniffed. 'I'm so sorry to disturb you . . .'

'Stay right where you are. I'm coming.'

She handed the phone back to the girl. 'Thank you.'

The girl nodded and walked back to her friends. Aurora wrapped her arms around her waist and melted into the darkness.

*Please hurry, James. Please.*

James' Golf screeched to a halt and he jumped out of the car. Aurora emerged into the light, her head hanging and her arms firmly crossed to conceal her ripped dress. He was by her side in a flash.

'What on earth happened you?' he asked, pulling her close. 'You nearly gave me a heart attack. Were you robbed?'

'Not exactly,' she mumbled into his shoulder. 'Thank God you're here.'

He stepped backwards and looked at her properly. 'Where's your coat? We need to cancel your bank cards right away. I presume that they were in your purse.'

'No, it's okay,' she said in a small voice. 'My purse wasn't stolen.'

'Then where is it?'

'I left it at Justin's place. My phone is there too.' She didn't dare look at him.

'Borealis?' He shook her gently. 'Why are you out here without your things? Did something happen?' He pulled her arms down and then stared in horror at her dress. 'What the fuck happened?' he said slowly, fingering the torn material. 'Aurora?'

She started to sob. 'Please don't be angry. I should never have gone back to his place. I didn't realise.'

'What happened?' he said in a dangerously low voice.

'Justin invited me back after the party. He was drunk and high and then he kissed me.'

'Go on.'

'But he was rough and I asked him to stop and then he did this.' She gestured to her dress. 'I was so frightened, James. It seemed like ages before he listened.'

'And then?' He was rigid with rage.

'I bolted.' She looked him in the eye. 'I ran out of there as fast as I could.'

He was holding her arms so tightly she winced. Judging by his face, he was absolutely furious. Was he angry with her for going back to Justin's flat? She couldn't tell. Maybe she deserved it all. Maybe Justin was right: maybe she had asked for it.

'Where does Debussy live?' he asked, leading her to his car. 'Is it nearby?'

She pointed down the street. 'In that building down there. Why?'

'We should get your things.' He slammed the passenger door shut.

'No!' she said in panic. 'There's no way I'm going back there. I'll just text him in a few days to leave them at the theatre.'

'That building, you say?' he said, ignoring her. 'Right, let's go.'

The engine roared to life and they took off down the now deserted street.

Aurora shivered. Why did she say anything? She didn't want to go back there nor did she want to see Justin again. The car pulled up outside the building.

'Please, James. Please keep driving.'

'Let's go,' he ordered grimly. 'Can you remember which apartment it is?'

'You'll never get in the main door,' she protested. 'He won't buzz us in. Not now.'

He got out and approached the building. She followed fearfully.

Sure enough, you needed a code to get in. He banged his fist on the wall. 'Call him,' he said, pointing to the buzzer. 'Tell him you want your stuff. Call him, Aurora.'

Just as she was reaching up to press the button, the door opened and two men walked out. James took advantage of the open door and barged through. Aurora followed meekly.

'First floor,' she said as he called the elevator. 'Flat 1D.'

Minutes later, they paused outside the door.

'James, please,' she pleaded for the last time. 'We should go.'

A muscle flickered in his cheek and he rapped loudly on the wooden panel.

'*Debussy?*' he yelled. '*Open up!*'

'Stop!' she whispered urgently. 'He'll think it's the police. He has cocaine in there.'

'*Debussy!*' roared James, banging repeatedly. '*Open up!*'

Justin opened the door with a jerk.

'*What the fuck do you want?*' he shouted, raising his fist. '*Do you know what time it is?*' He glared at James and then noticed Aurora skulking in the background. 'Ah, Sinclair!' His tone softened. 'You've come to your senses. Get rid of your stupid brother and we can pick up where we left off.'

'I want my bag,' she said in her clear voice. 'It's on the table.'

'Well, get it yourself, my dear. No one's stopping you.' He opened the door widely and gestured her through. James attempted to follow but he put his foot in the way. 'Not you,' he said contemptuously. 'You can wait out here.'

James pushed him backwards and followed her inside. 'Are you okay?' he asked as she put on her jacket. 'Are all your things in the bag?'

She nodded.

'Right, let's get out of here.' He held out his hand and she grasped it gratefully.

Justin watched them. 'You know, we could've been great together,' he said to Aurora. 'You and me? We could've been the ultimate power couple.'

'*Never!*' she said passionately. 'I never want to see you again.'

'Oh, but you will,' he sneered. 'You need me, Sinclair. Without me, you're nothing.'

'*No!*' she shouted. 'I'm *everything* without you. I don't need your silly plays. I'm going to make it on my own.'

'Bravo, my darling,' he mocked, clapping slowly. 'Still doesn't take away from the fact that you're a frigid bitch.'

With a howl, James leapt forward and punched him square on the jaw.

'*James!*' she screamed. '*Don't! He's not worth it. Stop it!*' She pulled at his jacket but he shrugged her off.

'Don't you ever say that about her again,' he said, grabbing Justin and shaking him like a rat. 'You're scum, Debussy.'

Justin, momentarily dazed, gathered his wits and swung at James and punched him in the eye.

'*Stop it!*' Aurora started to scream. '*Stop fighting!*'

James pulled away, his eye bleeding. 'You're not worth it,' he said through gritted teeth. 'Crawl back into a hole where you belong.'

He allowed Aurora to drag him out onto the landing as Justin slammed the door.

Gloria and Henry were asleep when they crept up the stairs to Aurora's room. She sighed as she deposited her bag on her dressing table.

James looked in the mirror and cursed silently.

'Look at my eye,' he said, pointing to the dark bruise forming over his eyelid.

'Oh, James, I'm so sorry.' Her lower lip quivered. 'It's all my fault.'

He walked towards her and hugged her close. 'Of course it isn't your fault,' he said firmly. 'That guy's a creep and you were taken advantage of. If I had my chance again, I'd floor him.'

She clung to him, listening to his steady heartbeat. 'You're my hero,' she said softly. 'Like my Ken in the Barbie Ferrari. You saved the day.'

He laughed. 'My trusty old Golf isn't quite an Italian sports car, but it worked in a crisis.'

'Can you wait while I change my clothes?' Her eyes were huge. 'I'll be two minutes.'

'Of course.' He brushed a tendril of hair from her face.

She grabbed her pyjamas and disappeared into the bathroom. He sat on the bed and gazed at the pictures on the wall: one of her mother's portrait, one of Will's graduation and a nice one of her birthday party a few years ago. He remembered it well. He had turned up at the last minute and surprised her.

The door opened and she walked back into the room. Instead of the dishevelled girl in the torn black dress, she was now in over-sized tartan pyjamas and woolly slipper socks. Her hair was scraped back in a ponytail and her face was free from make-up.

'Thank you for waiting,' she said in a small voice. 'I'm just a bit shaken up.'

He got to his feet and pulled back the covers. 'Hop in,' he said.

She obeyed and he placed the duvet gently around her, tucking it right up as far as her chin. All that was visible was her big brown eyes staring up at him.

'Goodnight, Borealis,' he whispered, kissing her forehead gently. 'Sleep well.'

She closed her eyes and snuggled down deeper. 'Can you wait until I'm asleep?' she murmured. 'I like having you here.'

His heart melted. How could he refuse? He lay down next to her and rested his head on his arm. 'I'm here,' he soothed, stroking her hair. 'Don't be scared.'

# Chapter Thirty-three

Claire was sitting at the kitchen table when he got back to their flat. It was getting bright outside. Large streaks of red and pink dominated the skyline and the city was coming to life. Her hands were clutching a large mug of tea and her face was sullen.

'Hey, you.' James waved from the doorway as he took off his coat. 'I didn't realise that you were awake.'

'Where were you?' She was staring out the window.

'I had to pop out. Aurora lost her phone and was stuck in Chelsea. I picked her up and brought her back to Gloria's.'

'Oh, you did.'

'Yes. 'He switched on the coffee machine. 'She was really stuck, Claire. She rang me because I was the only number she knew off by heart.' He chuckled. 'I drilled it into her when she was a teenager so that she would always be able to call me if she was in trouble.'

Claire said nothing and continued to stare out of the window.

'Turns out that Debussy guy is a creep. I always knew it, but she couldn't see it. He attacked her by all accounts. Her dress was in bits.'

He took a seat opposite her, leaning his elbow on the table and keeping a hand over his eye.

'I was worried sick. I woke up two hours ago to find you gone. Then I waited for a text or a phone call, but obviously you were too busy with Aurora to extend me that curtesy.'

'*Whoa!*' He held up his hands. 'I was helping her out. She had no one else.'

Claire saw his black eye for the first time and gasped. 'What the hell happened to you?' she demanded, pointing to the large bruise. 'James?'

He touched it gingerly. 'Things got a bit heated. That Justin threw a punch.'

'Are you fucking serious?' she yelled with a red face. 'You have that job interview tomorrow or have you forgotten? How can you go now?'

'I'll put some make-up on it or something?'

'Jesus Christ, James, you have to get your life together! We're back two months and all you've earned is a couple of grand from that job in Norfolk. How are we going to get our mortgage?' She got up and started to pace the room. 'Meanwhile, I'm working every hour I can to make ends meet.'

'I pay my way –'

'Yeah, out of your savings,' she said dismissively. 'Soon to be *our* savings. It's just not good enough. Then, you have a great interview lined up and you mess up your face playing superhero with your kid sister!'

'What could I have done? Left her there abandoned on the street? She called me –'

'And you went running,' she finished sardonically. 'Big surprise.'

James got to his feet and slammed his mug on the table. 'I'm going for a shower. When I get back, I would like us to speak to each other like adults. I'm too tired to fight.'

The door slammed shut. Claire picked up a cushion and threw it at the wall. He was not the same man she had met all those months ago. Since their return, he had become complacent and relaxed, unperturbed about money or settling down. It wasn't cold feet. He loved her, anyone could see that. But he was being so immature. Her mother had warned her about men: how they sailed through life and left all the worrying to their wives. It was just so frustrating.

Her expression darkened.

James needed to shape up. They hadn't even set a date for the wedding yet. Things were all up in the air and she hated it.

# Chapter Thirty-four

Ella came home from her daily walk to find William's bag and coat in the hall. He had left for work as normal that morning. Why then would he be home early? All week he had been battling a head cold but he seemed to be better.

'Will?' she called.

A hand appeared over the back of the couch. 'I'm here,' he said feebly.

She rushed over to find him shivering on the couch, his face deathly pale and his hair wet with sweat.

'Will!' She felt his forehead. 'You're burning up. Have you taken anything? Should I call a doctor?'

'I am a doctor,' he said with a half-smile. 'No, I'll just have to wait it out.'

'Look at you!' she said in concern. 'You're far too tall for this bloody couch. I'm not having you suffering here.' She pulled at his sleeve. 'Come on, you're going to bed.'

'No, no. I'll drench the sheets.'

'Then I'll change them.' Her tone was firm. 'Get up and lean on me. Come on.'

He allowed her to lead him to the bedroom. 'I thought I had

come out the other side,' he said. 'Then I nearly collapsed at work.' He sat on the edge of the bed.

'Where will I find a clean T-shirt?' she asked.

'Top shelf.'

'Take off your clothes,' she ordered, grabbing a T-shirt and then pulling a pair of sweatpants from the wardrobe.

'Oh, how I've dreamed of you saying that,' he quipped and then groaned. 'Oh my head! It's throbbing.'

'Hurry now,' she said, helping him take off his shirt. 'You'll get cold.'

His shirt was wet from perspiration and his skin was clammy. She grabbed a towel from the bathroom and dried his skin. Then she motioned for him to raise his arms so that she could slip on the T-shirt. His chinos were harder to remove but she managed and soon he was tucked up in bed with a rug over him for extra warmth.

'Right, I'm off to make a honey and lemon hot drink.' She gathered up the clothes on the floor. 'You get some sleep. Have you taken some paracetamol?'

He nodded. 'An hour ago.'

'Fine. You'll be due another dose in five hours.'

He smiled. 'You're like a matron. I think I like it.'

'Well, it's karma, William. You looked after me when I was ill. Now it's my turn.' She smiled too. 'I'll be back in a sec.'

He closed his eyes, feeling zapped of all energy. Moments later, he was fast asleep.

The next morning he woke up to find the sheets drenched. His head was still pounding and the honey and lemon concoction she had made the night before lay untouched. He couldn't remember much about the night, just flashes of Ella's concerned face and doses of tablets.

*Ella!*

He clutched his hair. She must have slept on the couch. He immediately felt guilty. How uncomfortable for a woman in her condition!

As if on cue, she appeared at the door. 'Hey, sleepyhead,' she said fondly. 'I'm here to change the sheets.'

'Did you get any sleep at all?' he said, fretting. 'God, Ella, I'm so sorry. I passed out cold. I had fully intended to move back to the couch.'

'Don't be silly,' she said, pulling the pillows out of their cases. 'You were delirious. You kept calling my name and then laughing and then passing out.' She shook her head. 'You're a bit of a lunatic when you're sick to be honest.'

He eyed her warily. 'Delirious? What did I say?'

'Oh, this and that. I couldn't really follow it.' She laughed. 'You did mention Simon at one stage. I found that quite amusing.'

He said nothing.

'So, are you able to move for a moment? Hopefully the worst has passed with regard to the perspiration. I googled it.'

'Yes, I can move.' He swung his legs over the edge of the bed and immediately felt light-headed. '*Whoa!* No rapid movements.'

She helped him onto an armchair. 'Just give me two minutes.'

She whipped off the sheets and replaced them with fresh ones. Then she took more clean clothes from his wardrobe and waited while he stripped.

'Boxers too,' she said. 'I'll turn around.'

He laughed and threw his clothes in a pile on the ground. Minutes later he was dressed again.

'I'm decent,' he said.

'Right,' she said, propping up the pillows. 'Are you hungry? I can make you something.'

He shook his head. 'I'm fine.'

'Now, Will,' she warned, 'you'll vomit if you take tablets on an empty stomach.'

'Oh, okay then. Some toast.'

She smiled. 'Coming right up.'

Later that evening, she joined him on the bed to watch a movie on his laptop. He had improved immensely and when the closing credits appeared on the screen, he made a move to leave.

'Where are you off to?' she asked sleepily, her head on his shoulder.

'The couch,' he answered. 'There's no way you're sleeping there again tonight.'

'*No, Will,*' she said vehemently. 'You're too ill. I couldn't possibly allow it.'

He snapped the laptop shut. 'Well, out of us both, I'm the lesser candidate for the bed. You must have been very uncomfortable last night.'

'Unless,' she said softly.

'Unless?'

'We both sleep here.' She blushed and cast her eyes down. 'I mean, that way we could both get a good night's sleep and it's a pretty big bed.'

He regarded her speculatively. 'Are you serious?'

'Yes.' She looked him straight in the eye. 'It's crazy that one of us has to suffer.'

A broad smile spread across his face. 'Do you snore, Taylor? I might have to reconsider if you do.'

She pushed him playfully. 'Not that I'm aware. Nor do I talk in my sleep like other people.'

'I'm not delirious any more.'

'No.' She reached out and stroked his cheek. 'You're not.'

No one spoke for what seemed like the longest time. He took her hand in his and kissed her palm. Slowly, his lips moved upwards towards her elbow. Finally, he pulled her close and kissed her lips, gently and thoroughly. She relaxed totally and melted into his embrace, savouring the contact. It had been so long: so long since she'd been touched.

'Oh, Ella, are you sure?' he murmured into her neck. 'I don't want you to regret this.'

She pulled at his T-shirt. 'I could never regret this,' she said honestly. 'You saved me, Will. I don't want to be anywhere else.'

# Chapter Thirty-five

'Harry? It's Aurora.'

'Yeah? You got three minutes.'

'I'm coming to New York. I've decided to take the plunge.'

'That's awesome. Was there anything else?'

'Well, Daddy gives me an allowance but I will need to work . . .'

'I'll look into it. There's a new show goin' down about President Eisenhower. It's a period drama. You could be an extra or something.'

'That sounds lovely. I'll ring you when I arrive.'

'You do that.'

'Oh, and Harry?'

'Yeah?'

'Have a wonderful day.'

He paused for a moment and then laughed loudly. 'Why, you too, Lady Mary. You too.'

Aurora zipped up her suitcase and checked her gold watch. It was almost time to leave. Laura had texted saying that she would meet her at JFK so she needn't worry about taxis. She had offered her a room at Christian's apartment until she got sorted. 'It'll have to be Luca's old room,' she said. 'Hope that's okay.'

After a few weeks, the plan was to find her own place. Harry had secured an audition for the following Tuesday and if that went well, she could move forward.

Ophelia had cried when she told her that she was leaving as it meant that she would be moving out of their little flat. 'I'll find a replacement,' her friend sobbed, 'but it won't be the same.' Marianne had been equally sad. 'I'll miss you, my love,' she said, kissing her over and over. 'Go and shine! Be the star I know you are!'

Justin had called and called but she hadn't picked up. Not once. He was dead to her now. She had no intention of ever seeing him again. In the end, she blocked his number. It seemed to be her only option. However, she did read some of the texts he sent. They ranged from conciliatory to angry. Yes, he was sorry – yes, he was too drunk and acted out of character – yes, he was high on cocaine. Could she ever forgive him? Then the tone changed. How dare she ignore him? How dare she not pick up? He had made her and this was the thanks he got?

In the end, Bertie called from the Maldives and pleaded with her to make contact with his wayward nephew. 'He's dreadfully sorry, my darling. He should never drink whiskey.'

She wondered whether he really wasn't aware of the role cocaine had played in the debacle. She explained that it was too late to repair the relationship. It was ruined.

Bertie, sensing that he was getting nowhere, let it go. 'This won't affect *our* friendship, I hope,' he said.

She assured him that it wouldn't and told him to call her when he was in New York and they could do lunch.

Henry and Gloria had been delighted at her news. They agreed with Harry – America was the place to be if one wanted to be famous.

'Just don't stay away too long,' Gloria pleaded, kissing her forehead. 'We'll miss you.'

Aurora fingered the fuchsia necklace around her neck. What would her mother think of her flight to America? She had been successful in her day but had shunned the limelight at the peak of her career. No one understood why she left the West End and returned to Dublin. Googling Grace Molloy didn't give much information. There were just press releases and pictures from shows. There was a tabloid article on her wedding to Henry and a few reviews of her plays. In the past, she didn't know how many times she had typed her name into the search engine and gazed at the results. Now, she avoided it. It was an impersonal business as the whole world had access to that information. She was her daughter, not some random person surfing the net. She didn't want flimsy information from secondary sources. Henry remained as tight-lipped as ever and her maternal grandparents were dead. The information well was dry and she just had to accept that her mother would remain an enigma.

So, she was off on an adventure to the city that never sleeps. She had emailed Lydia, assuring her that she would fly back for the wedding, and asking her to let her know what songs she wanted at the church. She was really excited about going to Italy and she had already warned Harry that she needed that week off.

'Borealis?' came James' voice from downstairs. 'We have to go.'

He had offered to take her to the airport as everyone else was working. She smiled and at the last minute took the picture of the two of them from its place on the wall. It was her favourite: the picture at her birthday a few years back. She slipped it into her bag and activated the pulley handle.

'I'm coming!' she called as she closed the door behind her.

# Chapter Thirty-six

'Please tell me you're joking.' Laura stared at Christian in disbelief. 'No contact at all?' It was two months later and just a few days before Luca and Lydia's wedding. As father of the groom, he was expected to fly to Italy early to organise the French cousins and help Luca with some last-minute arrangements.

He nodded and picked up his suitcase. 'That was the brief. Just when we're in Venice, baby. Then, when it's over, we'll get out of there.' He opened a drawer of the bureau next to his bed and took out his passport. 'My flight is in a couple of hours so I've got to go.'

Her eyes filled with tears. 'It's so humiliating.'

He came and cupped her face with his hands. 'It means a lot to Luca. He doesn't want his mother upset. I've got to do what's best.'

'Christian, we're engaged! Have you forgotten that? Next month I'm going to be your wife. How can you let them treat me that way?' She pulled back, her face sulky.

'Keep that quiet for the moment,' he said in alarm. 'Don't do anything crazy, you hear me?'

'I can't even tell my own family,' she said petulantly. 'All because of your bloody ex-wife.'

'Laura!' he said, exasperated. 'The wedding is in a week. When it's over, we can do what we like. I owe this to my son. You got that?'

She turned away. 'Fine. Just go. Play happy families. I'll pretend we've never met.'

'That could be interesting,' he said, grabbing her waist. 'It'll be like the old days . . .'

'Just go.' She wriggled out of his grasp. 'Ring me when you land.'

'I love you.' His brown eyes were serious. 'Stay strong. Just one more week and we're free.'

'It's fine for you,' she said with tears shining in her eyes. 'You never have to explain or feel like an outsider. Blimey, Gloria isn't your biggest fan, but you never let it affect you.'

'What do I care?' he said with a shrug. 'Everyone else is incidental. Remember what I said that night I proposed?'

They had been on a long weekend at a hotel in Varadero, the famous Cuban resort. It was there, after a delicious dinner at an old mansion, that Christian had reached into his pocket and pulled out a small box.

'Laura, will you be my wife?' he said.

It had been a complete shock as marriage was not something they ever discussed.

'But why?' she asked confused. He was just divorced and she had never once insinuated that a long-term commitment was what she wanted.

'Hey, you know I don't do romantic,' he answered. 'Will you just put on the goddamn ring already?'

'But why?' she repeated.

'Because I love you. Because you're beautiful and sexy and I love your British accent. Because I want to grow old with you. Does that answer your question?'

'What about your family? What will they say?'

'They can say what they like. All I want is you.'

Now he brought her back to the present, demanding again, 'Do you remember what I said?'

'"All I want is you,"' she said softly.

'You got that right. Now stop being a diva. It's only one more week. Then we can tell the world.'

'We bloody have to, Chris. We only have a month to our big day. People need to book flights and get time off from work.'

'That's the advantage of a small wedding. No stress.' He kissed her nose. 'See you in Venice, baby.'

Laura met Aurora for dinner at Patricio's, Christian's favourite restaurant in Manhattan. They were flying out to Venice together the following day. The restaurant was packed to the brim with diners, and soft music played in the background. The island was quieter than usual in August; a lot of its residents went up to the Hamptons for the holidays to escape the stifling heat.

Laura beckoned at the waiter. 'Can you bring us some water, please? Evian.'

'Sure, lady. Coming right up.'

'So, the "brief" from Luca is that we can't interact at all.' Laura scowled.

Aurora sipped her wine slowly. 'Well, I can see both sides, Laura.'

'Yes, but I'll be his wife soon.'

'A fact that no one is aware of. Be fair about this.' She gave her a stern look. 'I'm the only person you've told, am I right?'

Laura nodded. 'Chris doesn't know that, of course. He made me swear to keep it quiet when he proposed.' She held up the sparkly solitaire on her left hand. 'I suppose I'll have to leave this behind too.'

Aurora nodded. 'It's pretty hard to miss it.' She pulled Laura's hand towards her for closer inspection. 'I mean, it's huge.'

'Yes – yes, it is,' she agreed in satisfaction. 'My dream ring.' She sighed. 'He's adamant that we have a tiny wedding: just immediate family. He doesn't want any fuss.'

'What do *you* want?' asked Aurora. 'I mean, he seems to be the one making the decisions all the time.'

'Look, small is fine with me. Just a couple of witnesses at the ceremony and then a dinner at the hotel.'

'So it's definitely Antibes then?'

'Definitely. I confirmed it last week. The rooms are booked and there's availability at the town hall.' She smiled dreamily. 'Remember, I told you – we stayed there on our first mini-break – when he took me to Cannes? It has a special place in my heart.'

'So the next hurdle will be telling the family.' Aurora giggled. 'What will Gloria say? She's hoping you two will spilt up.'

'Oh, I'm well aware of that.'

'Look, when all's said and done, I'm sure she'll be thrilled for you. We all will.'

'If it wasn't for Luca's bloody wedding,' said Laura grimly. 'I know I seem like a spoilt brat, but it's very hard to be relegated down to a nobody when I spend my days wearing this!' She flashed the ring again.

'Look, it won't be so bad. We'll only be in Venice for two nights. I'll be there and so will James, therefore lots of family support.' Aurora's eyes sparkled. 'I still can't believe he's going. It's just wonderful.'

Lydia had phoned Laura in a tizz two weeks before, saying that her photographer had broken his leg. She couldn't find anyone to fly to Venice at such short notice – was there anyone in London that she would recommend? Laura had suggested James. Within hours he was part of the wedding entourage. Laura was thrilled. She needed all the support she could get. Now, with Aurora and James by her side, she could face anything.

Aurora had screamed with delight when she heard the news. She hadn't seen James in months and missed him terribly. What added to her glee was when he emailed saying that he would be going solo as Claire had her sister's hen weekend in Brighton at the same time. James alone was far better than James with Claire. Even Laura agreed that his fiancée was on the domineering side. Plus, it was as clear as day that Claire didn't have much time for his family, especially Aurora.

'We'll have such a blast,' said Aurora joyfully. 'All we're missing is Will for a full family holiday.'

'He's superglued to Ella at the moment,' said Laura. 'I mean, honestly. She has another month to go. He has his pager on high alert all the time.'

'They're so cute though,' said Aurora her expression softening. 'The way he looks at her, Laura. It's so sweet.'

'Yes, they're quite the couple.'

The main courses arrived. Laura had opted for monkfish and Aurora had chosen risotto.

'More wine?' asked the waiter, staring at Aurora.

Laura shook her head reluctantly. 'We'd love to but we have to travel tomorrow.'

Aurora stared at her in surprise. 'I don't think I've ever seen you refuse wine.'

'I want to look amazing when we hit Italy,' she explained. 'Laura with a hangover and jet lag is not the image I want to present.'

They arrived at Marco Polo airport at 4 p.m. local time.

'It feels like we've been travelling for days,' grumbled Aurora, her hair sticking to her neck in the heat. 'Where's the hotel again?'

Laura checked her phone. 'We're at the Belmond,' she said. 'It's a five-star by Saint Mark's Square. Let's just get a taxi.'

'Right.' Aurora put on giant Bvlgari shades. 'It's a shame James couldn't get the same flight as us. I hope he'll be okay.'

'He's due in an hour,' said Laura, waving at a taxi. 'He's a big boy and has travelled the world. Why wouldn't he be okay?" She narrowed her eyes.

'I just meant, it would have been fun if we were all together, you know?'

Laura yelled as a taxi pulled to a halt in front of them.

'*Vaporetto*?' asked the driver, smiling at the two women.

'Good Lord, no,' said Laura in horror. 'I loathe that overcrowded floating bus. To a water-taxi rank, *grazie*.'

'*Prego*.'

Molly and Samantha were in the foyer of the hotel when they arrived.

'Hey, bridesmaids!' said Laura, pecking them both on the cheek. 'We're in dire need of a stiff drink.'

Molly laughed. 'Well, there's plenty of that here. We had a crazy night last night. The two families went out for a meal and then we hit the residents' bar and, well, here we are. Dehydrated.'

Samantha rubbed her temples. 'Bellinis. They'll plague you to have Bellinis. Be strong and say no. They could kill you.'

The receptionist had excellent English and within minutes they had their room key.

'We need to freshen up,' said Laura, hoisting her bag onto her shoulder. 'See you at the bar in an hour?'

Molly nodded. 'Hair of the dog is the best option,' she said.

Samantha groaned. 'I don't think I can, Mol. I've already thrown up twice.'

'Oh, get a grip, Sam,' said Molly in disgust. 'This is a wedding. It's your duty to go mad. Take some paracetamol and you'll be a new woman.'

Colin was sitting by the pool when they arrived back downstairs. He had a giant cocktail in front of him and was talking to a young man with glasses. On his right was another guy reading a newspaper who Aurora recognised as Val, Colin's boyfriend.

'*Laura! Aurora! Join us!*' Colin waved madly at a waiter who hurried over. 'Two more of these beauties,' he said, pointing to the cocktails on the table. Then, turning to the girls he said, 'You just have to try this drink. It's delish.'

'Hi, I'm Joe,' said the young man on Colin's left. He was dressed in a brown shirt, cream chinos and wore Buddy Holly style glasses. 'I work with Lydia and Colin at the magazine.'

'Hello,' said Aurora shyly. 'I'm Laura's sister.'

'How are things?' said Val to both girls before turning back to his paper.

'Val!' said Colin in exasperation. 'Would you put that stupid paper down?'

'No.'

Joe laughed. 'So, you're the singer,' he said conversationally. 'Colin has been raving about your talent.'

Aurora blushed. 'Gosh, I hope it goes well tomorrow. I won't have the added courage of gin like the last night.'

'Just get tanked up tonight and top it up in the morning,' drawled Joe. 'Problem solved.' He moved closer to the group. 'By the way, I have scandal.'

Laura laughed out loud. 'Oh, Aurora. Joe is the king of gossip. He's better than Facebook for news.'

'I am pretty good,' he admitted. 'Anyway, I was passing a bedroom on my way down here – the door was ajar and I heard raised voices. Naturally I stopped to tie my shoelace.'

'Naturally.'

'Anyway, who was it but the bride and groom!'

'Those two? They're always fighting,' said Colin dismissively. 'Then they make up and it's all hunky dory again. I've given up getting involved.'

'This sounded serious. He was shouting about his mother and

she was screaming back about some friend of hers.'

Laura gulped. 'And?'

'And then they closed the door. I was disgusted.' He picked a piece of pineapple from the cocktail stick in his glass. 'It was just getting to the good part.'

'As I said, nothing to worry about,' insisted Colin. 'Luca and Lydia have what I call a passionate relationship. Deep down, they are devoted to each other.'

'They'd bloody want to be. It cost me a fortune to get out here,' said Joe.

'It's the stress of the wedding,' said Val, folding his paper. 'Lyd was pretty pissed last night too which doesn't help. We all know what hungover Lydia is like.'

Joe made a face. 'Yikes.'

Aurora smiled at the waiter as he placed a cocktail in front of her. She squeezed Laura's leg and sent her a silent message not to worry. All would be well. The wedding was the last hurdle and then she could tell the world.

Three cocktails later and they were in great form. Molly joined them, as did Samantha and her husband Craig.

'Hi, I'm Craig, the best man,' he said, waving to the occupants of the table. His sallow skin had turned darker in the sun and he was casually dressed in a white shirt and navy shorts.

'He's Luca's cousin,' explained Laura. 'A solicitor. Very nice actually.'

Samantha still looked sick, her eyes disguised behind large shades. She refused a cocktail and opted for water instead.

'So, have you other brothers and sisters?' Aurora asked Molly.

'Yep, there are four of us.'

Colin coughed.

'Well, five if you add on my cousin there.'

'I'm an honorary child,' he said gravely.

'There's Sarah,' Molly went on. 'She's the eldest. Her son, Mini Seán – named after his grandfather – is the pageboy.'

'The most well-behaved child in the world,' said Colin. 'He's as disciplined as a North Korean.'

'Colin!' Molly shook her head. 'I have to admit, he's not allowed much leeway, but Sarah's not an *actual* dictator.'

'*Hmmm*,' said Colin.

'Then there's Ollie, my only brother –'

'Apart from me,' said Colin.

Molly rolled her eyes. 'Ollie – Mum's pride and joy. We call him the Son of God in our house.'

'The Messiah,' said Colin. 'He Who Walks on Water.'

'Then there's Lyd, who you know, and of course, *moi*.' She sat back. 'One big happy family. My parents, Helen and Big Seán are pretty funny too. You'll meet them later.'

'And of course, *my* parents: Oscar and Diana,' said Colin. 'You'll notice them right away as they're easily the most stylish people in the wedding party.'

'Sure they are,' said Molly.

'They *are*,' said Colin fiercely. 'I love Auntie Hel and all, but sometimes I can't believe she's my mum's younger sister.' He sighed. 'I'm so gutted that Britney couldn't come. I mean, all I wanted was a picture of her on a gondola.'

Samantha groaned. 'I feel awful!' she said, fanning her face with Val's discarded newspaper. 'I think I need to lie down.'

'Jesus, Sam, you'd better be okay for the church tomorrow,' said Molly in alarm. 'You look really pale.'

'Oh, I will,' she said definitely. 'I just need to sleep it off.'

Craig handed her the room key and, with a wave, Sam left.

'I wonder if James is here yet?' said Aurora.

Laura checked her phone. 'Any minute now. Although, knowing him, he probably opted for the *vaporetto*. Claire would murder him if he wasted their mortgage money on a water taxi.'

Oscar and Diana, Colin's parents, popped over to say hello en route back to their room. They were indeed as glamorous as Colin had said: Oscar was tall and distinguished and Diana was sophisticated in a white Chanel suit, with blonde streaks in her wavy hair.

'Did you get to the Guggenheim as I advised?' said Colin.

'No.' Oscar was busy checking his emails. 'Di wanted to go shopping instead. Look at the bags.'

Colin glanced down at his mother's feet to see Prada and Louis Vuitton bags. 'Oh, Mum! You're a woman after my own heart!'

'I wonder where Christian is?' whispered Laura to Aurora. 'I mean, I hope he's not avoiding me.' She glanced round the tables.

She'd been on constant high alert in case he appeared. Aurora noticed her surreptitiously checking her lipstick every five minutes and smoothing her hair. It was odd to see her confident sister so edgy.

'Oh, he's entertaining the French cousins,' said Colin, overhearing. 'They flew in from Paris last night.'

'You must have heard,' said Laura bitterly. 'There's to be *no* contact between us whatsoever. Luca insisted.'

'What now?' said Joe, alerted to gossip. 'No contact between whom?'

Molly filled him in.

'Oh!' His eyes sparkled. 'So there's a high chance of a showdown between the ex and the replacement?'

'Joe!' Molly wagged her finger at him. 'Poor Laura's upset.'

'If only you knew,' said Laura through gritted teeth. 'Replacement indeed.'

Aurora patted her arm. 'Don't rise. Think of next week.'

A loud laugh made them all turn around in the direction of the hotel. There, dressed in a Hawaiian shirt with a beer in his hand, was Tyler Trenton, Luca's best friend from New York. His red hair flopped over his eyes and his freckles were even more pronounced after a few days in the sun. '*Tyler in da house!*' he announced lifting his hands above his head. '*Let's PARTAY!*'

'Oh, Christ,' said Laura and got to her feet. 'See you later.'

Aurora watched her scamper off in confusion. 'What's the matter with her?' she asked Molly.

'I'm guessing it's because of Tyler, that loud American over there,' she explained. 'They had a bit of a thing a couple of years ago and he still holds a torch.'

'At my wedding as I recall,' said Craig, smiling.

Aurora looked flabbergasted. 'Laura and that redhead?' she said. 'I find that hard to believe. He's not her type at all.' She regarded the American burping loudly and then laughing his head off.

'Yeah, it was weird all right,' agreed Molly. 'I think she was pissed. Anyway, he's been obsessed with her since.'

Tyler took Laura's empty seat and winked at Aurora. 'Hey, you guys,' he said to the table. 'Venice rocks, right?'

'It's wonderful,' said Aurora amiably. 'Hello, I'm Aurora, Laura's sister.'

'Laura, you say?' He perked up immediately. 'Is she here?' He glanced around in excitement.

'She had to pop upstairs for a minute,' she lied.

'Now that's one hot girl,' he sighed.

Colin snorted. 'You need to give up there, Tyler. She's made it quite clear that she has no interest.'

Tyler smiled happily. 'Nothing a few vodkas won't fix.' He focused in on Aurora. 'Although, you're pretty cute.' He gave her a lopsided smile. 'Wanna dance at the wedding tomorrow?'

Aurora blushed. 'Perhaps.'

'*Perhaps*,' he said mimicking her accent. 'I frickin' love the British, man.'

'Is Lydia nervous about tomorrow?' asked Joe. 'She's barely

mentioned the wedding at work. No Bridezilla behaviour at all.'

Molly put her head to one side. 'You never know with Lyd, to be honest. She's pretty laid back.'

'Of course she's nervous,' said Colin briskly. 'You know how she hates attention. Everyone is going to be looking at her tomorrow.' He glared at Val. 'I, however, *love* attention. I'd be the perfect bride. Do you hear me, Val? *Do you*?'

Val whistled loudly, his eyes crinkling in amusement.

'Hello, all.' James appeared, dressed in a white shirt and beige pants. 'I'm James.' He had his Nikon on his shoulder and his sallow skin was already brown.

Colin looked him up and down. 'Who?'

'This is Laura's brother,' explained Aurora. 'The photographer.'

'Oh right!' Colin was instantly friendlier. 'God, sorry. I thought you were some sad case looking to join our group. No offence intended.'

'None taken,' said James, smiling. 'I do have a look of a sad case, I have to say.'

Colin looked him up and down. '*Au contraire*,' he said approvingly. 'I would say quite dishy.'

Aurora, unable to contain her excitement, pulled James down to sit beside her. 'I've been waiting all day for you to arrive,' she said, smiling beatifically.

'Well, I took that *vaporetto* thing. You know, the public transport boat? It took forever and it was so crowded and hot.'

'But you're here now,' said Aurora.

'I am, Borealis.' He smiled at her.

'Jeez, man, you're one lucky guy,' said Tyler. 'You got two gorgeous sisters. Although, I gotta say, you look more like Aurora. You both got that dark hair going down.'

'That's fascinating,' said James with a grin. 'Especially as I'm no blood relation to Aurora at all. She's my stepsister.'

'No shit!' Tyler laughed. 'I gotta keep my mouth shut.'

'Amen,' said Colin.

The sun blazed down, despite the late hour.

James picked up Aurora's bare arm for inspection. 'You're getting a great tan,' he said, observing the tawny colour of her skin. 'I'm so used to the pale look.'

'It's been so hot in New York,' she said. 'I can't avoid it. Harry keeps berating me about it as pale skin works better in period dramas. It was a sign of status, apparently.'

'How did your audition go last week?' he asked, referring to a new show about the American Civil War. Harry had insisted she try out for it, claiming it would look great on her resumé when it came to the Scarlett audition.'

'Quite well,' she answered. 'It's only a small part – the younger sister of an abolitionist – so fingers crossed.'

'Your emails make me laugh,' he admitted. 'I love hearing about the world of show business. It lifts my dull London life a bit.'

'Any luck with the Beeb?'

'Nothing permanent anyway. Just random jobs here and there. I've started taking portraits again so there's good revenue from that.'

'Will you take me?' she asked shyly. 'I could do with some pictures for my portfolio.'

'Oh, God, I don't know.' He looked horrified. 'I don't think I could do anything with that face.'

'Nice.'

'Right,' said Molly, standing up. 'See you all tomorrow. Mum is insisting that we all get an early night. We're going to order a bite in her room and call it a day.' She smiled at the group. 'See you at the church, peeps.'

Joe got up and stretched. '*Ciao*, all. I met a hot guy called Giacomo at the bar last night and he wants to have a drink. Keep me posted on any goss that may or may not occur while I'm gone.'

Molly crossed her heart solemnly. 'I will inform you of everything, Joseph.'

They walked off arm in arm.

'Okay,' said Tyler, 'who's on for a night on the town? Colin?'

Colin shook his head. 'I want to look fabulous tomorrow as I walk up the aisle and I still have a facial to apply.'

Tyler threw his hands up in the air. 'Are you serious? You don't want to party? That sucks!'

'You're welcome to join me and Luca,' suggested Craig, straight-faced. 'We're going to order room service and work on our speeches.'

Tyler made a face. 'That sucks even more. How about you British? Please tell me you're not calling it a night?'

Aurora bit her lip. 'Well, I'm the singer tomorrow, Tyler. I must rest my voice.'

'I have to be up early to take some shots of the canal at dawn.' James shrugged apologetically.

'Where's Laura? She might be up for a few drinks.' Tyler put his hands together in prayer.

Colin gave him a withering look. 'You think?'

Laura, James and Aurora decided to grab a quick bite. Colin had recommended a restaurant near Saint Mark's Square that he and Val had tried the night before. They dined on homemade pasta, lightly coated with a fresh tomato sauce. Their table overlooked the small winding canal beneath the restaurant and every so often a gondolier would pass, singing 'O Sole Mio'.

'I'd love to go on one of those,' said Aurora enviously. 'It must be so romantic.'

'I'll go with you if we have time,' said Laura, texting madly on her phone. 'I'm not exactly the love of your life but . . .'

'Anyone for a top-up?' asked James with the bottle of wine poised.

Aurora held out her glass. 'Yes, please.'

The air was balmy and there was a buzz of conversation. They were so close to the canal they could hear the water lapping gently against the stonework. Crowds of people of different nationalities and ages passed by on foot. A candle burned on their table, its light flickering slightly in the breeze.

'*Dolce*?' asked the waiter with a smile.

The girls shook their heads, but James nodded. '*Sì, gelato, per favore.*'

'I didn't know that you could speak Italian,' said Aurora in awe.

'I studied it at school,' he admitted. 'Before I met you.' His expression softened. 'Although, it's hard to remember life without you, Borealis.'

Laura, who was still texting furiously on her phone, whooped in delight. 'Look!' she said triumphantly, turning the screen around. There was a message from Christian which read: **234.**

'So?' said James.

'I'll see you later,' said Laura with a wink. 'Here's fifty euros – it should cover my part. *Ciao*, y'all!' She took off in the direction of the hotel, just as James' ice cream arrived.

'Two three four?' said James. 'His room number?'

'Obviously,' said Aurora. 'She'll sneak up there, spend the night and be back in time to straighten her hair in the morning.'

'You seem very worldly when it comes to these things. Sneaking into bedrooms indeed.'

'Oh, you have no idea,' she said, flicking her hair.

'Any love interest in New York?' he asked casually. 'Surely you've met someone.'

She traced the stem of her wineglass with her finger. 'Not really. I went on a few dates but they fizzled out. Actors are dreadful, egocentric bores so I tried a producer. Turns out they're even worse.' She laughed. 'Perhaps I'll just go for a fireman or a bus driver. Something completely different.'

He held out his spoon. 'You've just got to try this,' he said. 'I think it's hazelnut.'

She opened her mouth and let him feed her a spoon of creamy nutty ice cream. She closed her eyes. 'You're so right. It's heavenly.'

'More?'

'No! I have a very tight dress to fit into tomorrow. I've already had far too much pasta.'

He waggled the spoon in front of her. 'You know you want to,' he teased.

'Oh, okay.' She yanked the spoon out of his hand and licked it clean. 'Now, no more temptation. I need to be good.'

They strolled through the winding streets, walking up and down steps and over little bridges. The houses looked dreary and derelict from the outside, with shoddy décor and damp walls. Some had boats tied up outside the front door.

'I bet they're mansions inside,' said James. 'Never judge a book by its cover.'

'Pretty expensive real estate,' she agreed. 'I would love an apartment here.'

They approached a small bridge and waited for the crowd to dissipate so that they could cross. A gondolier with a striped shirt and a black hat called out, '*Gondola!*'

Aurora smiled and shook her head. 'No, thank you.'

'*Gondola!* Good price for *bella* lady.' He held out his hand. 'You come on my gondola and you see alla Venezia.'

She turned away and began to climb the steps when James pulled her back.

'Come on,' he said. 'I'll treat you.'

'Really? Oh, I'd love that!'

His brown eyes were warm. 'Then let's go!'

She stepped onto the long black boat and took a seat at the back. The cushions were dark-pink with a golden trim and the seat was shaped like a throne.

'You sit with the lady,' instructed the gondolier and James obeyed. Slowly he pushed the boat off and began to sing in Italian.

Aurora clapped her hands in delight. 'I can't believe that I'm here,' she said. 'This is so magical.'

Using his long oar, the gondolier angled the bow of the boat so that it turned the narrow corner.

'He's quite skilful,' said James, watching him expertly manoeuvre the boat past an approaching gondola.

'Just look!' she said joyfully. 'He's taking us out onto the Grand Canal!'

The water immediately became choppier when they emerged out onto the main waterway of the city. Speedboats passed, leaving a backwash that caused the gondola to sway from side to side.

'Oh! We'll capsize!' Aurora grabbed James' arm.

'Hopefully not,' he answered, looking in disgust at the murky water. 'I don't think we'd survive being submerged in that.'

She clung to him as they neared the Rialto. The night air was quite chilly and his body emitted heat. The old stone bridge was illuminated in the darkness.

'I take a photo?' asked the gondolier.

James handed him his phone.

The gondolier spread his legs to balance the boat. 'Look at me and say "*Amore!*"'

'*Amore!*' they chorused.

They turned back into the winding streets of Cannaregio, the old Jewish quarter of the city. Aurora kept expecting Shylock to appear and call for his ducats and his daughter. It was absurdly quiet compared to the bustle of the canal. The gondolier pointed out Casanova's house and then Marco Polo's. Finally, they came to a halt, right back where they started.

'You can let go of me now,' said James and she jumped. 'We're safe.'

'Oh, sorry,' she said, flushing. 'I must have stopped the circulation in your arm.'

'It will recover.' He regarded her fondly.

The gondolier blew kisses at them as they walked away. '*Amore*!' he called, winking.

# Chapter Thirty-seven

The day of the wedding dawned. The chapel Lydia had chosen was at the centre of a small piazza near the Rialto. It had a small doorway and stone walls. Crowds were gathering outside when Laura and Aurora arrived. Oscar and Diana were there looking stylish in a Hugo Boss suit and Roberto Cavalli dress respectively. Luca's French cousins were smoking cigarettes and talking rapidly with lots of hand movements.

'Any sign of Tara?' said Laura from the side of her mouth.

Aurora scanned the square for a red-haired woman. 'No.'

Laura relaxed and took out a gold fan she had purchased. 'The heat is shocking,' she complained, shielding her face from the sun. 'My clothes are sticking to me already.' She was wearing a dark-green dress which fell to just above the knee. She wore a light-green shawl and her heels were her trusty old four-inch Louboutins. She had a packet of cigarettes stashed in her clutch bag in case of emergency. Christian hated it when she smoked but she wouldn't be in contact with him so it didn't matter. She smiled to herself. The night before had been incredible. She had arrived at Room 234 to find him on the balcony in an open-necked grey shirt with a bottle of Cristal on ice. 'I missed you, baby,' he drawled, motioning for her to sit on his lap. Vacating his room at five thirty had been exciting, especially when she almost bumped into Sarah, Lydia's older sister, who was on her way for a run.

Aurora was watching the French guests. 'Strange to have such a large French contingent, isn't it? I mean, to an American-Irish wedding in Italy!'

'Yes – easy to forget the French connection – but it means a lot to Luca that they're here. He's still mourning his beloved grandmother's death. His greatest sadness is that the old lady died before Sienna was born, Chris tells me.' She fanned her face rapidly. 'Luca is fluent in French although you wouldn't think it.'

'Wouldn't think it?'

'Well, he's just so American, isn't he? It's all baseball and Hershey Bars and Jell-O.' She shaded her eyes from the sun. 'Of course, Christian speaks it like a native. It's so sexy. That time we were in Antibes, he kept being mistaken for a local.'

'Thank God you took French for A-level.'

'*Mais oui.*' Laura smiled. 'I'll have to brush up for when I meet the family officially.'

Aurora kissed her cheek lightly. 'I'm so sorry to abandon you, but I have to meet the organist inside the church. It's getting late.'

'It's fine,' she said, fanning her face. 'Tyler is about to make a beeline for me and even though he drives me bananas, he'll do quite nicely as a chaperone.'

The cool dark church was a welcome contrast to the blazing heat outside. She walked up to the altar and smiled at the priest.

'*Buon giorno,*' she said slowly. '*Sono Aurora – sono cantante.*' James had given her a few phrases to learn the night before.

The priest laughed. 'Jesus, I haven't a clue what you're saying. Wait till I get my iPhone and I'll Google Translate.'

'Oh, you're Irish!' she said in relief. 'Thank goodness.'

'Father Colum,' he said, shaking her hand. 'Lydia's cousin on her father's side. They flew me over to do the honours.'

'Aurora Sinclair, the singer.'

'Oh, great stuff,' he said. 'The fella playing the organ has been looking for you.'

'Is he Italian?' she asked. 'I'm afraid my vocabulary is limited.'

'Not at all, girl. He's from Bandon, a small town in County Cork. His name's Mike. I'll just call him there.'

He disappeared into the vestry.

Aurora gazed around the chapel. Statues of the Virgin Mary and Jesus stood in the corner with rows and rows of candles in front of them. The altar itself was simple: just a table with a white cloth and a bunch of flowers. The pews were mahogany and each one had a white rose pinned to the outside bench.

Father Colum arrived back with a small man in his fifties. 'This is Mike,' he said pleasantly. 'You two should have an old practice there before the groom arrives.'

'Hello,' said Mike. 'You ready to roll?'

Aurora smiled at him. 'I'll just warm up and then we're all set.'

The church started to fill up. The bride's family were on the left and the groom's on the right. Aurora decided to stand to the side of the altar so that she could see Mike on the organ nearby. That way he could nod as a cue for her to sing.

She scanned the faces in front of her. A woman with blonde curls and a large blue hat sat in the front pew. Focusing in on her face, Aurora could see that she was the image of Molly so she ascertained that it was Helen Kelly, Lydia's mother. Behind her was a young man who resembled Lydia. Molly had mentioned a brother who was adored, so it had to be him. An older couple sat by them – they had to be Nana Peggy and her husband Jack, Lydia's paternal grandparents.

Laura took a seat next to Joe a few rows behind the immediate family. He looked smart in a grey suit and shiny black shoes. 'Well, hello,' he said, squinting at her in his Buddy Holly glasses. 'I'm liking the dress.'

'Why, thank you,' she answered, pleased. 'You look very smart too.'

'Which is surprising,' he said drily. 'I was out with Giacomo until three this morning.'

'Are you in love?'

'Almost.' He sighed. 'To be fair, he doesn't have much English, but we don't need conversation. He's my dream guy.'

'Pack him away in your suitcase and bring him home.'

'That's a plan.'

The French contingent on Luca's side of the church were all talking loudly and incessantly. God, thought Laura, isn't it the Italians who are supposed to be voluble?

James appeared and took some photos of the guests, artfully catching impromptu shots of expressions and conversations. Then he turned and stared at Aurora. Her dress was gold and shimmery: a full-length figure-hugging gown with a cowl neckline and thin straps. Her long hair was piled up on her head and gold earrings dangled from her ears. Laura had painted her eyes with a blend of browns and golds and light gloss accentuated her full lips. Slowly he lifted the camera and took picture after picture.

'Stop!' she said, blushing. 'I'm only the singer.'

He lowered the camera and gazed at her. Eventually he spoke. 'Glad the ice cream and pasta didn't have an adverse effect on the dress.'

She laughed. 'Well, it was a tight squeeze, I have to say.'

'It's perfect.'

Craig and Luca marched up the aisle together, in dark-grey Armani suits, with fuchsia-red cravats, to applause from the congregation.

James took a couple of shots and then waited until they were standing at the top of the aisle to proceed. Craig looked relaxed and jovial, talking nonsense to Luca to distract him. James regarded the groom through the lens. He had tousled blond hair and sallow skin. His bone structure gave him a haughty look and he had a long straight nose and blue eyes. He looked lithe and toned. Only the muscle flickering in his cheek portrayed how nervous he was. Every now and then he would glance down the aisle and exhale loudly.

A small red-haired woman in a violet dress and a large black hat approached him. She smoothed his suit and picked a piece of fluff off his sleeve. He bent down and she whispered something in his ear.

Aurora regarded the woman curiously. *Tara Jacob: Luca's mother. Christian's ex-wife.*

Tara retreated and sat in the front pew. She took a tissue from her bag and dabbed her eyes. Aurora glanced down at Laura who seemed to shrink in her pew. She could sense how uncomfortable her stepsister felt. It was truly awkward. As if on cue, Christian arrived, looking a million dollars in a black suit. Laura shrank down even further. He went straight up to Luca.

'Good luck,' he said gruffly, patting him on the back.

Then he went back down to sit next to his ex-wife. 'Tara,' he said curtly.

She smiled tightly and turned away.

The crowd began to get restless. The women started fanning themselves in the heat and the men adjusted their long legs in the narrow pews. Mike the organist started to play some Beethoven in the background.

'Where is she?' muttered Luca to Craig. 'She's late.' He ran his fingers through his hair.

'She'll be here. Don't worry.'

'Oh, I'd say she's done a runner!' Lydia's brother proclaimed helpfully from his pew.

'Ollie!' said Helen warningly. 'It's no time for jokes. Your sister will arrive any minute.'

Val took out his phone. 'Will I ring Colin? He's with them.'

Ollie laughed. 'Knowing that crew, they're in the pub.'

'Ollie!' said Helen sharply as Luca's head swung around. 'They most certainly are not in the pub. Shur, Sienna is with them.'

Tyler sauntered over from the groom's side of the church. 'Whassup, ya'll?' he asked, his red hair flopping over his eyes. 'Have we got a no-show?'

'No,' said Val, hanging up the phone. 'It's as we suspected – they stopped for a quick Prosecco. Nothing to panic about.'

'*Ha!*' Ollie high-fived himself. 'I knew it.'

Helen looked uncomfortable. 'I'm sure they'll be here any minute . . .'

Tyler flopped down on the seat next to Laura. 'I guess I'll sit here,' he said, giving her a smouldering look. 'I can't talk French to that crew over there.'

'If you must,' said Laura stiffly.

The organ resonated through the church, startling the guests, as Mike launched into a thundering rendition of Handel's *Water Music* Suite Two.

Craig patted Luca's back and made silly faces but the groom didn't react. His handsome face was set and he kept checking his watch. A baby started crying down the back. The heat was making everyone cranky and restless. Helen Kelly prayed that her daughter would arrive.

Someone answered her prayers. Suddenly there they were: Sam and Molly in long fuchsia-red dresses, Colin holding Mini Seán and Sienna's hands and, behind them, Lydia and her father Seán silhouetted against the light.

'They're here!' announced Helen in relief.

Luca visibly relaxed. Aurora watched him smile as the organist changed to 'Pachelbel's Canon'. Samantha raised her head and put her shoulders back. At a nod from Colin, she went first, her long dress swishing as she walked by. James snapped madly as she approached and took her place at the top of the aisle.

'You're gorgeous, Sammy,' mouthed Craig in her direction.

Next came Molly, in her identical floor-length red dress. Her blonde curls were pinned to the top of her head and she laughed as she advanced, waving at random people.

'Looking a bit pink-cheeked there, Mol,' said Ollie with a smirk as she passed. 'Prosecco nice, was it?'

Next came Colin, dressed in a grey suit with a fuchsia-red cravat. Trailing along behind him was Lydia's nephew, Mini Seán, decked out in a miniature grey suit and a little fuchsia cravat. He carried a small silver cushion as if it were made of glass, his eyes riveted on the two gold rings pinned on top as if he was afraid they would jump off.

Colin climbed the altar steps to stand with the 'other bridesmaids' while Craig came to meet Mini Seán. Smiling, he relieved the little boy of the two rings. Mini Seán's sigh of relief was audible. He turned and his mother Sarah welcomed him with open arms and sat him next to her in the first pew.

'You were brilliant, Seánie,' she said, kissing him on the forehead. 'All that practice paid off.'

'Practice?' echoed Ollie. 'He's only three.'

'Oh, he has been weeks walking up and down the corridor at home,' said Sarah. 'You know how organised I like to be.'

Finally, a small blonde toddler danced up the aisle. Sienna, looking angelic in a white dress with a full skirt, a fuchsia-red sash around her waist and matching ballet slippers on her feet. Around her head, resting on her blonde curls, was a garland of little red-and-purple flowers.

Then, suddenly, she swung round and raced back down the aisle.

'*Sienna!*' called Helen. '*Come to Nana!*'

'*No!*' she yelled. '*No – Nana bold!*'

The congregation laughed as she pulled a white rose from its position at the end of a pew.

Suddenly she spotted Christian. '*Papi Istin!*' she shouted gleefully, running back up to the top of the aisle.

Stepping out of the pew, he swung her up in his arms and over his head. 'Hey, baby girl!'

'*Weeeeee!*' she screamed in delight. '*Weeeeee!*'

'Sienna, be quiet!' said Helen firmly. 'Mummy is on the way.'

'*No!*' she said vehemently. '*No, Nana!*'

Sarah raised her eyes to heaven. 'No discipline.'

Sienna then spotted Luca and held out her arms. 'Daddy! Sisi, Daddy!'

Luca walked down and took her from his father.

'You've got to be quiet, Sisi,' he said softly into her blonde curls. 'Mama's coming.'

'Okay, Daddy,' she said, stroking his hair.

Luca handed her over to Helen and went back to take up position on the altar.

Mike stopped playing the organ for a moment and silence reigned. Then, he began the 'Bridal March' and everyone got to their feet.

And there she was.

Aurora's breath caught in her throat. Coming towards her was a vision in white. Her gown has a fitted bodice and a full skirt, with layers of chiffon floating to the ground. Her lace veil was cathedral length. It covered her face as she walked towards Luca. Seán Kelly, her father, looked proud as punch, his grey morning suit matching his grey hair.

Then Aurora noticed Luca's face as Lydia approached. The intensity of his gaze sent shivers down her spine. How she would love to be looked at in that way!

Seán put Lydia's hand in Luca's and went down to join his wife in the front row.

'Mama princess!' said Sienna, struggling to get free from Helen's grasp. 'Mama Elsa!'

Luca lifted Lydia's veil and exposed her face. Then he cupped her face in his hands and kissed her thoroughly. On and on they kissed, and the priest jokingly checked his watch.

'I love you,' Luca whispered at last with his eyes closed.

Lydia smiled as James' camera flashed.

Father Colum greeted the congregation and welcomed the bride and groom. 'Better late than never, I suppose,' he quipped, winking at Lydia.

In no time at all, it was Aurora's turn to sing. Mike nodded and she launched into 'Ave Maria'. Helen felt shivers go down her spine as she sang. Her voice was pure and soared over the guests. James took photo after photo but Aurora didn't notice. She had her eyes closed and was lost in the music. Even Sienna was soothed by the song, her head resting on Helen's shoulder. At the end, there was stunned silence.

Father Colum, who had been lost in the music, pulled himself together. 'Sorry to digress, but that deserves a *bualadh bos.*' He began to clap loudly.

'A what?' said Christian.

'It's Gaelic for a clap,' said Tara stiffly.

Aurora blushed as the crowd erupted.

Lydia smiled at her and mouthed, 'Amazing.'

Father Colum stood between Lydia and Luca. 'Have you come here of your own accord?'

'We have.'

'Will you love and honour each other for as long as you both shall live?'

'We will.'

'Will you be prepared to accept children and bring them up according to the law of Christ?'

'We will.'

'*Too late for that!*' shouted Ollie.

'Now,' said Father Colum, taking both their hands and joining them together. 'Declare your consent before God and his Church.'

James took close-ups of Luca's face as his blue eyes locked with Lydia's.

'I, Luca, take you, Lydia, to be my wife. For better, for worse, for richer, for poorer . . .'

'Well, thanks to the massive inheritance he got from his dead granny, it'll be for richer,' said Joe to Laura.

'. . . in sickness and in health, till death do us part.' Luca smiled his heart-breaking smile.

James snapped and snapped, taking every angle he could.

'I, Lydia, take you, Luca, to be my husband . . .'

Helen wiped a tear from her eye. Tara dabbed hers with a tissue. Colin was openly crying. Even Christian looked moved as they exchanged vows.

'This is crazy shit,' said Tyler on Laura's right. 'To see The Jacob up there looking at her like that.'

'*The* Jacob?' Laura snorted. 'Why do you call him that?'

'Because he was the prom king in high school, every girl wanted to sleep with him and every guy wanted to be his bud. He was my hero, man.'

'Well, he is quite attractive,' admitted Laura.

Tyler swatted his red hair out of his eyes. 'It's so crazy to see him around Lydia. He was such a player and now he's like totally in love.'

'Yes, they're very sweet.'

'Warms my heart.'

They exchanged rings and Colin stared pointedly down at Val, mouthing, 'You see, easy peasy. Two minutes and it's over.'

Father Colum held up the chalice and gave communion to the happy couple. Mike launched into 'Panis Angelicus'.

The guests stood up to receive the host and Lydia called Sienna up to her. 'How's my baby?' she said, picking her up and kissing her soft cheek. 'I love you.'

'Mama,' she said, nuzzling her neck.

Luca stared at the gold ring on his hand. It fit perfectly and it felt like it had always been there. Everything made sense now. Everything seemed right in the world. He closed his eyes and thought of Mimi, his grandmother. He could sense her approval. He could almost see her wise old face smiling lovingly.

They reached the final verse of the hymn. Mike nodded at Aurora and she smiled. She started to sing, her voice angelic, and the small church resonated with sound.

*'Panis Angelicus, fit panis hominum . . .'*

Straight after the first line, Mike followed her with the organ, harmonising in the place of a choir.

'Jeez, you could listen to her all day,' said Molly dreamily. 'It makes me shiver.'

'How long is left?' asked Joe. 'I'm about to melt. Plus all that gin last night has made me dehydrated.'

'They sign something and then there'll be photos and that's it,' said Laura. 'I spotted a small bar across the road. We should slip over in a bit.'

'You're like my perfect woman,' said Tyler in admiration.

The reception was held in a hall with stone walls and a marble tiled floor. The ceiling had low wooden beams and the lack of windows gave it a dark medieval feel. On each round table was a tall candelabra with five long white candles, a starched white cloth and flowers strewn all over the silver cutlery.

Aurora checked the list of tables and found her name, right

next to Joe's, Tyler's and Laura's. Val's was there too as Colin was sitting with the wedding party at the main table. To her relief, James' name was right at the bottom. She was happy for Laura's sake. She knew her sister needed as many allies around her as possible. She had seen the glares from Tara throughout the day and how Christian pretended that Laura didn't exist. She understood the frustration her stepsister was feeling – in a few weeks she would be Christian's wife, yet she was a nobody at his son's wedding.

'Hey,' greeted Tyler as she took a seat. 'You were awesome at the church.'

'You were very good,' agreed Joe. 'The hairs stood up on my neck.'

Aurora blushed. 'It was a lovely ceremony.'

'Yeah, until Sienna screamed and said '*Shit!*' when Helen wouldn't let her go to the vestry.' Joe smirked. 'That kid has serious potential.'

Smiling waiters filled their glasses with ice-cold water. Tyler took some *grissini* from the basket on the table and chomped loudly.

Laura arrived and sat down. A whiff of cigarette smoke followed and Aurora wrinkled her nose. 'Are you smoking again?' she hissed.

Laura shrugged. 'Only when I'm stressed and, boy, am I stressed today.' She took a sip of water and made a face. 'Have we been served any alcohol yet?'

Tyler shook his head. 'I was thinking the same thing myself. Wow, we're totally made for each other.'

She scowled and turned back to Aurora. 'So, off I went for a pee and who did I meet coming out of the cubicle?'

'Oh, no.'

'Oh, no, is right. She just stared at me like I was a piece of poo on the ground and swept by.'

'Who now?' asked Joe innocently.

Laura sighed. 'Luca's mother. The worst thing was that the last the time we met face to face, all I was wearing was a pair of Louboutins.'

Joe moved closer. 'Go on,' he encouraged.

Laura related her tale and Joe clapped his hands. 'You were starkers? Wonderful.'

Tyler scratched his head. 'What's the deal with Tara? I don't get it. Why were you naked at Luca's place?'

Aurora filled him in and his eyes widened. 'You've got to be kidding me. Laura and Christian?'

'*Shhhh!*' Laura glared at him. 'It's the forbidden subject at this moment in time. Luca doesn't want it mentioned.'

'But he's so old,' said Tyler in disbelief. 'Are you crazy?'

James appeared and took the available seat next to Aurora. He winked and took a long sip of water.

'How did the photo shoot go?' she asked.

'Very well. Sienna tried to jump in the canal at one stage but otherwise it was fine.'

The waiters started to fill the wine goblets. Tyler took an enormous gulp and held out his glass for a refill straight away. He kept staring at Laura incredulously.

'I can't wait to dance,' said Aurora, sipping the ice-cold Sancerre. 'Now that my gig is over, I want to relax.'

'Has Harry heard you sing?' asked James, breaking a breadstick in two. 'You should audition for Broadway.'

'Oh stop it,' she said blushing. 'You're just biased.'

'I'm not,' he protested. 'You're world class, Borealis. Put yourself out there. I mean it.'

'Well, I thought that Disney song was awesome,' said Tyler. '"Let It Go"?'

Aurora smiled. 'Sienna seemed to enjoy it at least.'

Tyler laughed. 'I thought she'd lose it when you started to

sing. That kid's obsessed with *Frozen*.'

'I think we're all aware of that fact by now,' said Laura drily. 'She watches it on Luca's iPad a million times a day.'

The last remaining seat at the table was eventually filled by Val. He asked for a beer and waved at the other occupants of the table.

'Where were you?' asked Joe.

'Oh, FaceTiming Britney,' he replied. 'Colin wanted to make sure she saw our faces before bedtime to avoid abandonment issues.'

Laura snorted. 'Did she appreciate the gesture?'

Val shrugged. 'I barely got near the screen with Colin baby-talking and telling her about the ceremony.' He threw his eyes to heaven. 'Britney now knows about your lovely voice, Aurora. Oh, and Mike the organist, everyone's choice of style and, crucially, how Colin got to walk up an aisle.' He laughed. 'He emphasised how it was such a wonderful experience and at least he got to do it 'once' in his lifetime.'

'Oh, just marry him and be done with it,' said Laura.

'All in good time,' said Val.

The crowd quietened down as the wedding party arrived.

Craig took the microphone and tapped it for attention. 'Hello, everybody,' he said. 'If you would all raise your glasses for the bride and groom: Mr. and Mrs. Jacob!'

Lots of cheering ensued as Luca walked in with Lydia trailing behind. Her veil had been removed and her long hair flowed down her back. She waved at random people as she passed, her eyes sparkling. When they reached the head table, Luca took her in his arms and kissed her.

'Oh, get a room,' said Tyler, shielding his eyes.

'Judging by the state of Lydia's dress and hair, I'd say they have already,' said Joe.

Aurora gazed at the happy couple. You could see how much

they loved one another, it was as plain as day. It was like they couldn't get enough of each other.

'Hey, cheer up,' said James. 'You look all wistful.'

'Imagine being loved like that,' she said, without turning around. 'I'd love someone to look at me like Luca looks at Lydia.'

'No regrets about Debussy then?'

'*Ugh*, don't joke about that.'

A waiter placed a plate of roasted artichoke covered with parmesan in front of her.

'What the fuck is that?' asked Tyler in horror.

'It's an artichoke,' said Laura. 'Eat it. You'll enjoy it.'

'No way,' he said, shaking his head vehemently. 'I got standards. What's a guy gotta do for a goddamn hotdog in this place?'

Seán Kelly's speech was short but packed a punch. He talked about Lydia's childhood and made light of her flight to Paris all those years ago. Then he talked about Sienna and how she had changed their lives. Lydia's eyes were shining with tears by the end of it.

'I love you, Daddy,' she said, blowing him a kiss.

Colin stood up next. 'I know it's not traditional for a cousin to say a few words, but I'm no ordinary cousin.'

'You can say that again!' Molly laughed loudly.

Joe activated his camera app immediately. 'Judging by the amount of Prosecco he's had, this should be great material to mortify him with at the Christmas party.'

'You're bad,' said Laura.

Colin turned to Lydia and Luca. 'I've been there since the start: back when Lydia was practically married to Dominic. Remember him? The hunky doctor? The guy she cheated on with Luca?'

Lydia's eyes almost popped out of her head.

'Is he pissed?' whispered Helen in alarm to Seán.

Seán stared straight ahead, unable to respond.

'And, of course, there was Luca's first wife, Charlotte. She lied and stuff, but I don't blame her really. He did cheat on her and, let's face it, he should never have married her in the first place.'

The French cousins looked at each other, unsure if they quite understood what he was saying. Nana Peggy, Lydia's grandmother, looked thoroughly disapproving and shook her head at her husband Jack. 'Loose cannon,' she mouthed with pursed lips.

'Then, when she found out she was pregnant, it was me who helped her through it. The first scan, the vomiting in the first trimester, the constant bolstering up over the weight gain . . .' He fanned his face. 'When Luca was delayed in London that night she went into labour, it was me in the delivery suite when Sienna was being born. I've seen parts of Lydia no one else has.' He paused. 'Well, except Luca and her beautician. And Dominic.'

Ollie guffawed loudly while Lydia hid her face in her hands.

'I mean, I feel like I'm part of this marriage. It makes me so happy to be here today. It is the perfect *dénouement* to a crazy emotional roller-coaster ride. And so . . .' He raised his glass.

Molly clapped madly. '*Best speech ever!*'

'Thank you, Molly,' said Colin. 'So . . . if you could all raise your glasses. *To Luca and Lydia!*'

'*Luca and Lydia!*'

Luca got to his feet. 'Thanks, Colin,' he said, amused. 'It's pretty hard to follow that.'

Aurora gazed at him. 'Isn't he just gorgeous?' she whispered to the table.

Tyler nodded in agreement. 'He's *The* Jacob,' he said simply.

'I think Borealis has a crush on the groom,' said James in mock horror. 'What's he got that we don't?'

Laura laughed. 'Don't get us started, boys.'

'I guess all I want to say is this is the greatest day. Lydia is the woman I want to be with forever.'

Aurora watched him intently.

'As Colin said already, we've had a crazy journey but now everything's as it should be.' He stroked Lydia's cheek. 'She has given me so much: love, laughs and of course, my baby Sienna. I've never been happier.'

Tara wiped a tear away. Standing there, he reminded her of a young Christian. Back when they were in love and full of hope. Oh, how she hoped this marriage would be successful! She didn't want Luca to experience the pain she had felt along the way.

'The only thing that saddens me is the fact that my grandmother Mimi isn't here.' His face tightened. 'Marcheline was really special to me. When she died, I didn't think I'd ever get over it. Then Sienna was born and I realised that life goes on. *Tu me manques, Mimi. Je ne t'oublierai jamais.*' He raised his glass and the French cousins stood up as a mark of respect. Christian nodded in solidarity. He wished his mother was there too.

Nana Peggy groaned. 'That American speaks gobbledegook. What in the name of God did he just say?'

Ollie shrugged. 'My French consists of saying that I play tennis and asking where the tourist office is.'

'He said he misses her and will never forget her,' explained Molly. 'He was mad about her by all accounts.'

'So, thanks to the bridesmaids, you guys were awesome.' Luca held up his glass.

Colin stood up and bowed. 'We know,' he said smiling.

Samantha waved amiably. 'Thank you!' she called.

'So, to finish, I've got to say thanks to my parents, Christian and Tara. You guys have always been there for me and I appreciate it.'

Laura kept her eyes cast down.

'And to my wife . . .'

Everyone cheered.

'Lydia Jacob!'

More cheering.

'I love you.' He pulled her up and kissed her again, moulding her body to his. Sienna laughed and pointed from her high chair. 'Mama, Daddy!'

Craig took the microphone and cleared his throat. 'So, if you two are ready, the best man still has to speak.'

Luca smiled and tore himself away from Lydia. 'Knock yourself out, buddy.'

The DJ was an Italian man of around forty with gold jewellery and a purple silk shirt. The hotel had recommended him and he had promised to stick to the playlist Lydia had made.

'I wonder if his decks double up as a karaoke machine,' mused Colin.

'Please, God, no!' prayed Molly.

The DJ, who had limited English, gestured for Craig to announce the first dance. All the tables had been cleared and the dancefloor was empty except for Mini Seán and Sienna chasing each other. Sarah had tried in vain to stop her son from running around, but Nana Peggy had bought him a Coke on the sly, and he was as high as a kite.

'Right, can we have the Jacobs on the floor, please,' said Craig.

Luca took Lydia's hand and pulled her reluctantly into the centre of the room. She hated being the centre of attention and was dreading the first dance.

'What song did they pick?' asked Joe. 'Imagine if it was some hard-core techno.'

'Or some gangsta rap,' added Ollie with a smirk.

'It's neither of those,' said Molly who was in the know. 'Luca chose "She" by Charles Aznavour. Partly because it's a fab song and partly because his Frenchy accent will make the Parisian cousins feel at home.'

'Those Parisians look quite happy to me,' said Joe. 'Did you see all the empty wine bottles on the table after the meal?'

The opening bars of the song played and Luca pulled Lydia close.

'You can do this,' he whispered in her ear. 'Remember how we danced at Sam's and Craig's wedding?'

She relaxed in his strong arms and they whirled around. Sienna danced like a fairy around them and eventually Luca picked her up and they moved as a threesome.

'Now, more couples on the floor! Let's fill this place up with love!' said Craig.

Aurora looked around and her eyes locked with James. He got up slowly and walked towards her. For a moment, her breath caught in her throat. He held out his hand and she gravitated towards him. Then, just as he reached her, Laura stepped in and took his arm. 'You need to dance with me, brother mine. I have to save face.'

James laughed and followed her onto the dance floor. Aurora's face dropped and she turned around desperately. Joe was dancing with Molly and all the other couples were together.

'Want to dance?' Tyler appeared behind her, his shirt hanging out of his pants and a bottle of beer in his hand.

Aurora smiled gratefully. 'I would love to dance with you.'

He deposited the beer on a table and led her out onto the marble floor and placed his hand on her waist. Surprisingly, he had great rhythm and within seconds they were gliding around the room. Her long golden dress swished as she moved and tendrils of hair escaped from her chignon and trailed down her neck.

Over Tyler's shoulder, she could see the bride and groom. Sienna had been deposited on Nana Peggy's lap, who couldn't dance after her hip replacement. Luca was whispering something in Lydia's ear and they both laughed softly. Val and Colin were moving at an impressive pace, Colin holding his 'dance space' like his idol, Patrick Swayze.

Then she saw Tara, sitting in the corner drinking a glass of white wine. Her red hair shone in the disco lights. Christian had disappeared, just in case he was asked to dance with his ex-wife. Inevitably Aurora's gaze moved to Laura who was joking with James. Her loud laughter was forced. Aurora knew it, but others didn't. She could see her trying so hard to look unscathed and nonchalant. Every so often, she would glance around looking for Christian.

James looked over at Aurora. Tyler was talking and she was laughing. He whirled her around like a little doll, narrowly avoiding Colin and Val. Her cheeks were rosy and her body shimmered in the gold dress. Any minute now and the large chignon on her head would fall down, freeing her mane of hair from its constraints.

The song ended and Laura bolted. Aurora watched her retrieve a box of Marlboro Lights from her clutch as she exited the room.

'Thank you, Tyler,' she said, kissing his cheek lightly. 'You're a wonderful dancer.'

'You're so pretty,' he said blushing. 'You positive you don't wanna hook up later?'

She patted his arm. 'I'm quite all right. Thank you ever so much for the offer.'

'Well, if you change your mind . . .'

# Chapter Thirty-eight

Two hours later, Colin was sipping a Mai Tai and gushing about Britney to Nana Peggy. 'She's just special, you know? Her little bark is so melodious and her presence is all-encompassing.'

'She's a dog, Colin,' said the old lady briskly. 'It would more in your line to get married. Focus on getting that Valentine boy to propose.'

Colin put his head in his hands and wailed. 'Oh, Nana, it's all I do! I leave bridal magazines around the house, brochures for honeymoons with amazing special offers and I only buy ring doughnuts as a treat. *Ring* doughnuts.'

'He'd want a good kick up the backside. Will I have a word?'

Colin shook his head dolefully. 'Val will not be bullied. It's what I love most about him.' He started to wail again.

'Now, now. It will all work out. He's a lucky boy to have you.'

'Do you think I don't know that?'

Molly took the microphone and called for everyone's attention. '*Everyone on the dancefloor!*' she yelled.

The theme tune to *The Fresh Prince of Bel Air* began to play and she started to rap.

'*Awesome!*' shouted Tyler, jumping up and singing along.

Soon the dancefloor was full of people trying to rap and pretending they knew the words. At the end, the DJ went straight into 'It's Not Unusual' by Tom Jones and everyone started doing the Carlton dance. Even Mini Sean was trying to emulate the iconic dance from the hit TV show.

Craig appeared with his shirt out and his cravat around his head. 'This wedding is mental,' he said, wiping perspiration from his brow.

'Where's Sam?' asked Colin.

'Gone to bed. She's really sick with food poisoning.' Craig took a swig of his beer. 'Sandra, her mum, is up with her now. I offered to stay with her but she insisted that I party on for Luca's sake.'

'How noble of you,' said Nana Peggy with narrowed eyes.

The DJ changed the disc and 'Jump Around' by House of Pain came on.

'*Tune!*' shouted Craig, waving his hands over his head and heading back out onto the dancefloor.

'Tune? It's awful noise,' said Nana Peggy in disgust. 'I think I'll go to bed soon.'

'That DJ is incredible,' said Molly breathlessly. 'He's been playing for four hours straight.'

'Incredible,' echoed Craig.

Rihanna and Calvin Harris began to play, its heavy beat pulsating through the room. Aurora threw her hands up in delight. 'Oh, I adore this song,' she said, walking barefoot onto the dancefloor. Tyler followed and soon they were moving in sync.

'I've never seen her drink so much, 'said Laura speculatively. 'She's always such a good girl.'

James finished his mojito. 'I think we've all overdone it, Lolly.'

Christian strode into the room and went straight to the bar. Laura watched him order a scotch. He hadn't looked her way once. Throughout the day he had acted as if they were strangers. It seemed like days ago when she was lying in his arms with her leg draped over his thigh. There was no sign of Tara or the groom, so what was the problem? This was the man she was going to marry, for goodness' sake.

Getting to her feet, she kicked off her shoes and joined Tyler and Aurora on the dancefloor. Flipping her hair back, she started to move, closing her eyes and gyrating to the music. Tyler's eyes nearly fell out of his head. Encouraged, he grabbed her waist and pulled her to him. Glancing over his shoulder, she could see Christian watching them. Wrapping her arm around Tyler's neck, she let him swing her around, clinging to him tightly. Throwing her head back, she laughed loudly and allowed his hands to roam around her body.

'Jesus, look at that,' said Molly who was sitting with Colin, rubbing her sore feet. 'Will there be a sequel to Sam's wedding?'

'Luca's daddy doesn't look too pleased,' said Val, pointing to a dour Christian. 'He looks like he's going to pop.'

'She's making him jealous,' said Colin. 'Like, *duh*? There's no way she fancies Tyler.'

'Looks like it's working,' said Molly as Christian marched over and pulled Laura away. 'He's not a happy bunny.'

Laura tried and failed to free her arm from his grasp. 'Let me go,' she said angrily. 'You're not supposed to be seen with me, remember?'

'Don't speak,' was the reply and he hauled her after him out into the garden.

He strode on and then pulled her forcibly behind a large tree. Pushing her up against the trunk, he kissed her hard on the lips. She tried to resist, but weakened immediately.

'You've been smoking,' he said gruffly. 'You know I hate that.'

'You deserted me,' she retorted. 'What you hate is of no interest to me.'

He pulled the strap of her dress down and kissed her shoulder. 'Why did you dance with that boy?'

'Why not? It's been pretty boring so far.'

'You're going to be my wife,' he continued. 'You cannot behave like that.'

She pushed him back. 'I'll behave how I please. We're nothing here. You have no right at all to dictate.'

'Laura,' he said dangerously. 'Don't push it.'

'Oh, piss off,' she answered, pulling her strap back up. 'You've treated me so badly, Chris. I'm not sure I want to even talk to you.'

He grabbed her wrist. 'Then don't talk.'

'What?'

'Shut that beautiful mouth of yours.' He pressed up against her. 'If we stay quiet, no one will notice.'

Her breath quickened. 'What? Here?'

He yanked down her dress. 'I said, don't speak.'

Molly pulled Colin to his feet. 'Right, it's bedtime,' she said yawning. 'It's almost three.'

'Where's Val?' he asked sleepily.

'Oh, he headed off ages ago,' she answered, picking up her sandals. 'You kissed him goodbye and everything.'

'I did?' Colin's eyes were glazed.

'Joe headed off to meet that Giacomo guy and Tyler's chatting up the barmaid.'

'Where are James and Aurora?'

'They went outside a few minutes ago.' Molly squinted. 'They headed off arm in arm, laughing and singing.' She put her head to one side. 'I can't figure them out, to be honest.'

'Oh?'

'It's the way they look at each other. He knows everything about her and she's the same. They seem so in tune.'

'They're brother and sister, Mol,' said Colin. 'Of course they're close.'

'But they're not actually blood-related,' she argued. 'Not really.'

'I think you're imagining it. I mean, I'm sure he's engaged.'

'Maybe.' Molly didn't look convinced. 'Engaged or not, I bet you ten euros that most of the pictures in his camera are of her.'

'Look at the stars!' Aurora put her head back to gaze at the night sky. 'They're like little diamonds on black velvet. It reminds me of that Thomas Hardy poem where he talks about the full-starred heavens.'

'You see the romance in everything,' said James. 'Honestly, it's like you live your life in some kind of poetic haze.'

'Perhaps it's Henry's literary genes.'

'He's a playwright, not a poet.'

They reached the pool and found the gate closed. 'Oh no,' she said in dismay. 'I wanted to sit in those wicker chairs from yesterday.'

James glanced around. The area was deserted and dark. The only light came from the moon and the stars.

'I'll give you a leg up and we'll climb over the fence.'

'Are you sure?' Her eyes widened. 'What if someone sees us?'

'Be quiet,' he said, 'and step on my shoulder.' He bent down and allowed her to use his body as leverage. With a squeal, she fell over the fence and landed in the shrubbery on the other side. Laughing, James followed and helped her to her feet.

The water shimmered in the light, lapping gently against the tiled edge of the pool. Aurora hiked up her dress, sat down and put her legs in the water. 'Oh wow, this is amazing.'

James watched her put her head back and close her eyes. Her hair was half up and down, its long tresses escaping from the pins that held them in place.

'Borealis,' he said softly.

'Hmmm?'

'Can I take down your hair?'

She opened her eyes immediately. 'Whatever for?'

'It's in no man's land. Let me take the pins out.'

She shrugged. 'Okay.'

He knelt down beside her and took out pin after pin. Her long hair slowly fell around her shoulders in a dark cloud. Without a word, he gently massaged her scalp. 'It must have been heavy holding that amount of hair up all day,' he said, kneading gently. 'Did any of the pins jab into your head?'

'Just a few,' she answered letting his fingers work their magic. 'Wow, James, you're talented.' He moved down to her neck and pressed on the muscles. She felt her body slump in relaxation. 'Where did you learn how to massage like this?'

'I had a masseuse girlfriend at uni,' he answered, pressing on each vertebra individually. 'She taught me all the tricks.'

'Well, put it on your CV and the Beeb will definitely hire you.'

He smiled and pushed her hair to one side. 'Is it hard to manage a mane like this?'

'Not really.' She turned to face him. 'Is it hard to manage a beard like that?' She rubbed his stubble playfully.

'Hey, I'm going for the sexy unshaven look.'

'Well, it's certainly unshaven.' She laughed and splashed the water gently with her toes. 'Wouldn't you love to swim? The water looks so inviting.'

He trailed his finger in the pool and sighed. 'It's lukewarm.'

'No one knows we're here,' she said, standing up. 'Who would know or care if we took a little dip?'

'Christ, Borealis, I don't know. An alarm might sound or something.'

The alcohol had gone to her head and made her feel fearless. Immersing her body in the water was all she could think about.

Surely he wouldn't deny her that?

'Come on,' she cajoled. 'Just for a few minutes.'

James could hold his drink but that night he had mixed wine, beer and cocktails. Looking at her excited face, he hadn't the heart to say no.

'Fine, five minutes.' He opened his shirt and pulled down his pants. 'I'm so glad I wore my Calvin Klein's,' he said, smiling.

She pulled her dress over her head. 'I'm glad I wore my new bra.' She threw the gold dress to one side and faced him. Her skin glowed in the moonlight. Her matching underwear was black and gold lace. James averted his eyes for a moment, unsure of what to do. Then, his eyes moved back to meet hers and they stared at one another.

'Right, let's go!' She lunged forward and pushed him into the water. There was a loud splash and when he resurfaced she was laughing her head off at the edge of the pool.

'Very funny,' he said. 'Hilarious.'

Without a word, she dived into the water, appearing beside him moments later. She smoothed her hair back and smiled. 'Isn't this just bliss?'

Her brown eyes shone as she bobbed beside him. Reaching out, he pulled her bra strap up on to her shoulder, as it had fallen down during the dive.

'Shall we do laps?' she suggested, splashing him gently. 'We could have a race.'

He said nothing. Instead, he reached out and caressed her cheek. Reaching out under the water, he put his hand on her waist. Her lips parted slightly and she allowed him to pull her weightless body closer.

'James,' she breathed.

'*Shhh*,' he said, putting his finger to her lips. '*Shhh*, Borealis.'

They could hear shouts from the street and a door slam. Her breasts pressed up against his chest and he cupped her face with his hand. Throwing her head back, she allowed him to guide her lips towards his.

Then a bright light shone onto the pool and a man started shouting in Italian. Like lightning, James pulled back. 'Fuck,' he said, swimming towards the steps. 'They saw us on CCTV. He wants us out right now.'

He apologised in rapid Italian and grabbed his shirt. Aurora followed and wrapped her dress around her body. Her hair was plastered to her head and she shivered. Barefoot, she followed them to the exit, trying to make out what the man was saying. You could tell from his tone and hand movements that he wasn't pleased. They got to the gate and he pulled out a bunch of keys. When they were outside the pool area, he gestured for them to go back to the hotel. James shook his hand and apologised again.

'Are we in trouble?' she asked wide-eyed.

'Just go to bed,' he replied. 'I'll sort it.'

'Are you okay?' She touched his arm.

He moved back slightly, out of her reach. 'I'm fine, Borealis. Just had far too much to drink. Go to bed. I'll sort this.' He didn't quite meet her eyes. 'Goodnight.'

# Chapter Thirty-nine

Laura zipped up her dress and inserted her feet into her heels.

'It's only four,' said Christian who was lying naked on the bed. 'You got another hour here at least.'

'Goodbye, Christian.' She picked up her clutch. 'Please don't contact me any more.'

'Say again?' He sat bolt upright. 'Laura?'

She walked towards the door and turned one last time. 'Goodbye.'

She turned to go but, just as she opened the door, his strong arm banged it shut.

'What the fuck do you think you're doing?' he demanded, grabbing her wrist and pulling her back to the bed. 'What do you mean "goodbye"?'

'I can't do this, Chris. I can't be second best.' Her eyes filled with tears. 'You have treated me like total shit the last few days. I've never felt as cheap as I did tonight. I hate myself for coming up here with you.'

'Laura, be reasonable.' His brown eyes were warm. 'You're overreacting.'

'No. No, I'm not.'

'You are.' He stroked her arm. 'We get to leave tomorrow and then that's it.'

Her eyes began to flash. 'You see, it's not "it". You'll still put her first. You'll still try to hide me away. Nobody knows about our engagement. What do you say to that?'

'We both agreed.'

'No, we did not! *You* decided! *You* made the rules. I wanted to tell the world.' She held up her bare hand. 'I couldn't even wear my bloody ring. How degrading is that?'

'You know my reasons.'

'But what about me?' She stood up. 'Hurting me should be the last thing you'd want to do. Instead, you're so obsessed with sparing other people's feelings that you stamp on mine.' She wiped a tear away. 'I can't live like this. Goodbye, Christian. It's over.'

She walked towards the door once more, her heart heavy.

Just as she opened the door, he called her name. 'Laura!'

'Yes?' she said, not turning around.

'Stay with me.'

'No.'

'I mean, sleep here with me and let the world see it. Stay with me.'

She hung her head. 'You don't mean that.'

He circled her waist from behind and kissed her neck. 'Stay with me and we'll tell everyone tomorrow. No more secrets.'

'About the wedding?'

'About everything.'

She turned to face him. 'You're serious? You'd do that for me?'

'Why sure. Now close the door and protect my modesty. I'm naked right here.'

Aurora woke with a splitting headache. Laura's bed was unslept in which was no surprise. Reaching for the bottle of Evian on the bedside locker, she drank thirstily. Unused to such large amounts of alcohol, she was even more unaccustomed to hangovers. Slowly the events of the night came back to her: the dancing, the cocktails, the pool . . .

She sat upright and her hand flew to her mouth.

*The pool.*

Her hair was still damp and so was the pillow she had been sleeping on. Her gold dress was in a heap on the ground and she was still wearing her fancy underwear. Lying back, she blushed furiously.

*James.*

Did she imagine it? Was it all a dream? She struggled to think. It all seemed surreal somehow.

*What happened exactly?*

They were swimming and then he pulled her close. He told her to be quiet and she waited for him to kiss her and then . . .

The Italian man appeared in her memory, angry and shouting. He had interrupted them at the last minute and prevented anything from happening.

*What would have happened?*

She buried her face in the damp pillow. He was going to kiss her. She knew that. She could feel his breath on her lips just before they were caught. The thing is, she *wanted* him to kiss her. She wanted him to hold her and touch her and . . .

She closed her eyes in confusion. What happened? It was crazy to even contemplate it. James was her brother. Her much older brother. Her best friend. Her pal. Kissing him was just plain weird. *Wasn't it?*

She swung her legs out of bed and winced as her head began to pound. Slipping on a navy sundress, she combed her hair and brushed her teeth. A cup of strong coffee sounded like just what she needed.

The breakfast room was full of guests. Ignoring the long buffet table filled with hams, cheeses, patisserie and fruit, she made a beeline for Colin and Val who were sitting by the French windows. Colin was nursing a Bloody Mary and was wearing enormous Dior shades.

'Morning,' he said, sipping his drink. 'Sunshine is not kind to my horrendous hangover.'

'Morning,' she said, smiling. 'Have you two seen Laura or James?'

Val looked up from the newspaper he was reading. 'I met James an hour ago in the foyer. He had an early flight.'

Aurora's face fell. 'You mean, he's gone?'

'Yes.' Val shuffled the newspaper and disappeared behind it once more. 'He spoke to Lyd and told her that he'd have the photos in about a week. Great turn around if you ask me. Very prompt for a wedding photographer.'

'Are you taking notes?' asked Colin with a pointed look.

A waiter appeared with a jug of juice and filled their glasses. Aurora's head was spinning. Why had he left without a word?

Laura and Christian walked in, holding hands.

Colin nudged Val and pulled down his shades for a closer look. 'I thought that was a no-no. They look like teenagers.'

Aurora waved at them to join them. Christian ignored her and took a seat at a table for two by the door. Laura walked over, her blonde ponytail swinging from side to side.

'I thought public displays of affection were forbidden,' said Colin, stirring his drink with a stick of celery. 'Do tell.'

Laura beamed at them all. 'I gave him an ultimatum: either we go public and tell everyone about the wedding or it's over.'

'Wedding?' Colin nearly spat out his cocktail. 'Don't tell me you're getting married too?'

'Next month.' She held up her left hand and then groaned in disappointment. 'I keep forgetting that I had to leave my ring in

New York. I wish I could flash it around.'

'Have you told Luca and Lydia?' asked Aurora.

'Yes. We called over to their room this morning.' She shrugged. 'Luca got a bit of a shock, but Lyd was delighted for us.'

'What about Tara?' said Val. 'I presume he told her personally.'

Laura bristled. 'Of course he did. We're not monsters, you know.' Her face fell. 'She was quite put out. She berated him about having a mid-life crisis and that he'd never hold me and that soon I'd be replacing his catheter.'

'*Ouch*.' Colin picked at his fruit salad. 'Although, she has a point. In another ten years, he'll be a pensioner and you'll be in your thirties.'

'Colin!' Val glared at him.

'He'll always be utterly gorgeous to me,' said Laura simply. 'Liver spots and all.'

'Well, all's well that ends well,' said Aurora, taking her hand and squeezing it. 'I'm no longer the clandestine bridesmaid then?'

'Well, not a bridesmaid exactly.' Laura refused a glass of juice from a hovering waiter. 'We just need two witnesses: you and Luca.'

'Luca?' Aurora's eyes widened.

'Look at you,' mocked Colin. 'Who has a thumping crush on my cousin-in-law?'

Aurora blushed. 'I do not!'

'Anyway, it will be the four of us in the town hall and then a posh dinner at the hotel. Then, we're off on safari.'

'Was there a mention of a pre-nup?' asked Val. 'Americans love those when there's money involved.'

'Well, we did have a document drawn up.' Laura looked uncomfortable. 'It's more to protect Luca and Sienna. You know, with Mimi's legacy.' She stood up. 'I'd better join my fiancé for breakfast.'

'Well, congratulations, Laura. We wish you the best.' Colin waved and the waiter appeared straight away. 'Another Bloody Mary, young man. Heavy on the Tabasco.'

# Chapter Forty

Two weeks later, Aurora went for a run in Central Park. The sun was going down over the great trees that lined the walkways and her iPod was on 'shuffle' mode. She'd had a gruelling day at the studio. The director wanted all the takes of Lincoln's speech reshot as he wasn't happy with the lighting. She had to stand for hours as Brad Munroe, who was playing Abraham Lincoln in the show, delivered his lines over and over again. 'Day Lewis is a hard act to follow,' he grumbled, fed up of wearing a top hat.

Venice seemed like months ago as her life had been a whirlwind since then. She had planned on flying to London before returning to New York. Gloria had emailed saying that Henry had been sick with the flu and was still recovering. Then Harry had called when she was at the airport, telling her that the Scarlett audition had been brought forward and she needed to get back to the States right away. Laura and Christian had flown off together so she had made the journey back alone.

She had also planned to track down James in London to clear the air. Despite three phone calls and four texts the morning after the wedding, it had taken him almost a week to reply. Even then, his email was short and curt, a minimal message telling her about his new job in Africa and how he and Claire had made an offer on the house they wanted. Since then, he had barely been in touch.

She stopped at a bench and took a swig of water. The evening was her preferred time to run as the heat of the day had dissipated and the shade of the trees cooled her down. She was anxiously waiting for news on her Scarlett audition, but to date nothing had come through.

Two days after her return from Italy, she had made her way to Harry's office where she met with the director, Carey McGrath. She had practised her lines, singling out the scene where Scarlett refuses to be beaten by hunger and poverty. Facing him in Harry's small office had been nerve-racking. He was the hottest director in town, fresh from an Oscar-nominated film and rave reviews. She was taken aback by his small frame but his blue eyes were friendly and kind and they put her at ease right away.

Instead of requesting an interpretation of a scene, he had asked her why she would like to play Scarlett O'Hara. Biting her lip, she paused and reflected. What appealed about this Southern Belle?

'Well,' she began, 'I admire her strength. I admire how she refused to be beaten and knew how to survive. I like how spoilt she was, even how she manipulated and used people to get her way. Life knocked her down but she got back up again.' She paused. 'She had flaws – real human flaws.'

Carey took notes and smiled encouragingly. 'Anything else?'

She smiled. 'My mother was Irish so I feel a connection to Tara. I love Scarlett's wild Irish side which had to be tamed under the strict societal rules of Confederate America.' She flicked back her hair. 'I'm quite good at the accent also.'

He nodded, writing furiously. 'Thank you.'

That had been nearly two weeks ago. Now, she was waiting and waiting. Harry said he couldn't call it. Carey was enigmatic to say the least and hadn't given any indication of his decision.

Every time her phone rang, her heart jumped. It was always Laura, William or Ophelia, never Carey McGrath. In the end, she gave up. He would get in touch eventually. She just had to be patient.

Bertie was sipping champagne when she arrived at the Four Seasons. He was in town for the weekend and had arranged a catch-up lunch. He kissed her on each cheek and smelt of Paco Rabanne.

'Aurora! It has been too long, my sweet.' His grey hair was slicked back and his manicured nails held a champagne flute from the base. He was dressed as ever in a jacket and cravat.

People were staring from around the bar. He was Albert Wells after all.

'You look wonderful,' she said genuinely. 'How was the wrap party?'

'Oh, the usual – too much of everything. Dom Perignon flowing, cocaine on every available surface. Ended up as a raging orgy of course.'

'Any scandal?'

'Me?' He looked shocked. 'I had a polite flute of bubbly and retired to my bed. My orgy days are over, darling.' He filled a glass and handed it to her. 'Let's toast! To your possible role as Scarlett.'

'It's looking less possible with every passing day,' she said gloomily. 'He could at least let me know so I can get on with my life.'

'Directors are all the same: vainglorious control freaks who play with us like marionettes.' Bertie regarded her for a moment. 'It will happen for you, you know. I believe in destiny. If Scarlett doesn't work out, then it wasn't meant to be. Never stop believing.'

'I suppose.'

Soft jazz played in the background and the bar was half full.

Bertie regaled her with stories about his latest film shoot and she found herself laughing out loud.

'So, my birthday is fast approaching,' he said with a dramatic sigh. 'Age undisclosed, I'm afraid. 2016 has been a dreadful year for my kind, so I'm living each day to the full.'

'I'm still mourning Alan Rickman,' said Aurora.

'Quite.' Bertie refilled their glasses. 'Capital fellow: a wonderful actor and friend.' He clinked his flute against hers. 'I have a request but feel free to refuse.'

'Oh?'

'I'm planning on having a huge party to celebrate my fast approaching old age. It will be a James Bond theme, from costumes to shaken not stirred martinis. I was wondering if you would do me the honour of singing? Just the theme tunes from all the films.'

'Me?' she squeaked.

'Yes, you.' He smiled affectionately. 'Who better to belt out Bassey? I would be delighted.'

Aurora glowed with pleasure. 'I'd love to! I mean, I'd be thrilled. I'd have to familiarise myself with the music but . . .'

'It's in three weeks. I'm hiring a yacht next week and cruising around the Riviera. Then back to London for my little *soirée.* There will be lots of important people there, my darling. I want them to hear your beautiful voice.'

'Oh, Bertie, you're so good to me.'

'Not at all. It's you who's doing me the favour. I'll pay for your flights, of course. Just send me the details.'

'Well, I'll be in Antibes for my sister's wedding the week before so I could just fly back to London afterwards.' She beamed. 'I've been meaning to spend time with Daddy anyway.'

'Smashing. Now, let's go and eat something ridiculously overpriced and enjoy ourselves.'

Two weeks later, Aurora stepped off the plane in France and the heat hit her straight away: that muggy dead heat filled with petrol fumes from the runway. Nice airport was small and she quickly made her way to the main terminal building. Gloria had promised to pick her up as she and Henry had flown out earlier in the week and hired a villa near Juan Les Pins.

Laura had kept her word – it was just immediate family for a very low-key affair. William had declined his invitation, simply because Ella was due to give birth any day. Laura was disappointed but she had masked it well. It was just unfortunate timing. James and Claire had flown out the day before as she had managed to get four days off from the hospital.

Aurora was the last of the family to arrive. She was just back from L.A. after a four-day stint on a film set. She had trained herself to forget about Carey McGrath. Ophelia had sent her some mindfulness exercises to practise. It was all out of her control and feelings of frustration were futile.

Sure enough, Gloria was waiting at the front door of the airport, a parking ticket in her right hand. Her skin was golden brown from the French sun and her hair had streaks of white-blonde. She looked relaxed and happy.

Aurora hugged her tightly. 'It's so good to see you!'

'Likewise. We miss you, sweetheart.'

'How's Laura?' she asked as they walked outside.

'Oh, she's been at the spa all day. She booked every appointment available. Luca and Lydia arrived this morning as well, so we're all meeting for dinner later.'

They reached a BMW coupé and she pressed the key to open the door. As soon as they were strapped in, she activated the air conditioning.

'It's been so hot,' said Gloria, fanning her face. 'Your father has spent most of his time indoors.'

'How's Daddy?'

'He's much better. It was just a nasty cold. Odd time of year to have it, I'll grant you that, but that's how it goes.' She indicated out onto the road. 'I suspect he picked it up on that flight to Singapore last month.'

'Any news from Will?'

'Nothing yet. Her due date is tomorrow so it's intense.' Gloria sighed. 'I'm just not ready to be a granny.'

'A glamorous granny,' corrected Aurora, smiling. 'You look fantastic.'

Soon they were on the motorway. Gloria stayed at a steady pace as cars efficiently overtook her. The roads were smooth and in perfect condition so the car ate up the miles.

'How's James?' Aurora asked casually, fiddling with a bracelet on her wrist.

'Oh, he's fine. He and Claire went on a boat trip today so he could take some photos. She cut her hair again. It's back to the short bob. I'm not sure it's the best look for her.'

'Any news on their wedding?'

'No, nothing. It's odd really. It feels like they've been engaged for years.' She indicated out onto the fast lane to overtake a lorry. 'She's adamant that they buy this semi-detached place near her parents' house. He's not too keen. I guess they're saving all their pennies for that.'

Aurora said nothing. She just stared out the window at the passing hills dotted with houses. She still couldn't imagine James in a semi-detached house in suburbia. It didn't fit.

The Hotel du Cap-Eden-Roc, the luxury hotel Laura and Christian had chosen for their wedding, was situated on the shoreline of the famous Côte d'Azur. It was a large majestic building at the end of a long driveway with an oceanside pool and lush green gardens. It was the hotel Christian had brought Laura to for their very first weekend away together. Gloria pulled up outside the main door and helped Aurora with her bag.

'Go and check in, sweetheart. They're expecting you. The pool is lovely so take a dip and relax. Henry and I will be over later.' She opened her car door. 'We're leaving the villa at Juan Les Pins today so it's hectic. They expect you to clean it and strip the beds.'

'Daddy is cleaning?'

'Probably not. He was working on the second act of his new play when I left.'

'What time will you be back?'

The BMW roared to life. 'Around five. We're staying here for three more nights before we return home. Laura mentioned drinks at the bar at six so we'll see you there. Bye, darling.' She drove off, past the palm trees blowing in the ocean breeze.

Taking Gloria's advice, Aurora checked in and went straight to the pool. She saw Luca first. He was by the pool in small black shorts, his torso brown from the sun. Lydia, who had paler skin, was under an umbrella in a green bikini. Sienna, gloriously chubby, was playing in the sun in a frilly pink swimsuit.

'Hi!' Aurora called, walking towards them.

Lydia smiled and waved. 'Hello! We've been waiting for you to arrive. How was your flight?'

'Oh, you know, the usual. Children screaming and no overhead locker space.' She sat down on the lounger next to Lydia's, removing her black see-through chiffon wrap to reveal a gold bikini. Her long brown hair was wound up into a messy bun and her eyes were concealed behind large Prada shades. 'How was your honeymoon?'

'Sweet,' drawled Luca, 'but I guess that's why they call it honey, right?' He turned around and dived into the water, his muscles rippling as he swam off down the length of the pool. Lydia squirted some sun cream on her belly and rubbed it in. Her diamond ring sparkled in the afternoon sun.

'I love your engagement ring,' said Aurora enviously, gazing at the large solitaire diamond set in white gold.

Lydia held up her hand and squinted. 'The diamond's a bit big for me, but it belonged to Mimi so Luca likes when I wear it.'

'Laura's diamond is bigger,' said Aurora. 'She absolutely adores it.'

'That's Laura all over.' Lydia giggled. 'No surprise there.'

Luca flipped backwards and did another lap, his strong arms making powerful strokes in the clear water.

'How's Luca about tomorrow?' asked Aurora. 'It must be strange for him.'

Lydia shrugged. 'He's not over the moon, but he's adjusting. He never expected his parents to stay together, but I think he finds Laura's age a bit weird.'

'Gloria finds that odd as well.' Aurora stretched out on the lounger and opened the belt of her wrap. 'I, however, think it's wonderful. They're lucky to have found love.'

'Absolutely.'

Sienna poked her mother's leg. 'Pool?' she said, pointing to the water.

Lydia groaned. 'It's Daddy's turn. Look, he's swimming over there. Mama needs some down time.'

'*Pool*,' repeated Sienna. '*Mama, pool.*'

'Ah, Sienna. Back off and plague your dad, will you?' Lydia put her head back and closed her eyes. 'I want to relax.'

'*Mama!*'

'Oh fine.' She got to her feet. 'Just for a few minutes.' She took her daughter's hand and led her over to the steps leading into the water.

In the pool, Sienna splashed Lydia immediately. Lydia pretend-screamed.

'Mama! Mama!' laughed the little girl.

Luca swam up beside them and grabbed Sienna.

'*Dada! No!*' He whirled her around and around in the water, making her shriek.

Then, sitting Sienna on the edge of the pool, he caught Lydia around the waist and ducked her under the water. Sienna clapped her hands in delight.

Lydia resurfaced, spluttering. 'You're dead!' she said, shaking her fist at Luca.

Luca laughed and pulled Sienna back into his arms.

Aurora watched them. The pool brought back memories: memories she didn't want to deal with. Not now. Not when she had to meet him and act like nothing happened. She had never felt more confused in her life.

After a long hot shower, Aurora gave herself a good talking to. There was no need to feel awkward. They had both been drinking and it was all a bit hazy now. Nothing happened. She would just go down to the bar and act like she always did.

She looked at her reflection in the mirror. She had chosen a white dress with a fitted waist and a full skirt. It had short sleeves and a plunging neckline. Simple strappy sandals and a touch of make-up and she was ready. She decided to leave her hair free – it flowed down her back, slightly wavy from the shower. She sprayed some perfume on and, picking up her room key, walked out the door.

The family were seated at a table on an outside balcony, looking out over the blue sea. White parasols lined the railing but they had all been taken down as the evening sun was milder. She scanned the group and was relieved to see that James wasn't there.

Henry saw her first. 'My darling!'

She was instantly struck by how old he looked. Being sick had rendered him thin and wan. He had obviously been avoiding the sun as his skin was lined and pale.

'Daddy!' She hugged him tightly. 'I'm so sorry it's been so long. Work has been so busy.' She breathed in his familiar smell.

'Not to worry,' he said into her hair. 'I'm delighted that it's all happening for you.'

Laura was in a short blue dress and high black heels. Her diamond solitaire dominated her small hand and her blonde hair was slicked back. The day at the spa had worked wonders: she looked relaxed and groomed. Christian was by her side, wearing a white shirt that was open at the neck.

'There's champagne on the table if you want,' he said in his American twang.

Aurora smiled and nodded.

'Isn't this place just heavenly?' said Laura. 'I could stay here forever.'

Luca was playing 'Horsey Horsey' with Sienna who kept saying 'Again, again, Dada!'

Claire waved. 'Hi, Aurora,' she said.

'Hi, Claire. Did you enjoy your boat trip?'

'Oh, it was terribly overpriced.' She made a face. 'Daddy warned me about this part of the world. They're out to rook you from the moment you arrive.'

'Lucky you're not paying for most of it,' Luca drawled, deciding that he didn't really like this new addition to the party.

Lydia poked him in the leg and glared at him. 'So,' she said, changing the subject. 'Thank you for having us.'

Christian shrugged. 'Hey, it's just a dinner. There won't be dancing and speeches.'

'Hallelujah,' said Luca.

'We just wanted something small and meaningful.' Laura took Christian's hand. 'This is the happiest time of our lives.'

Gloria held up her glass. 'Best of luck, darling!'

'*Best of luck!*' they all chorused.

'It's a pity Will isn't here,' said Aurora sipping her drink. 'Any news on Ella?'

Laura's face fell for a moment, but then she smiled again. 'No news. Not even a twinge.' She laughed. 'He asked if we could FaceTime him later as a sort of video link into the family.'

'Oh, do!' said Gloria in delight. She had taken on her role as grandmother-in-waiting with great enthusiasm.

Aurora gazed out at the twinkling blue sea. A huge white yacht passed, leaving a trail in the water.

'Where's James?' she asked as normally as she could.

Claire pointed to the beach below them. 'Off taking photos, where else? Before he loses –'

'The light,' finished Aurora. 'He never changes.'

'Well, I'm fed up of it. He downloads them onto his Mac and we never see them again.'

Aurora bristled slightly. 'He has them arranged into folders. Then he pulls out certain shots for his portfolio.'

'Yes, but not all,' said Claire. 'One doesn't need hundreds of pictures of a rock formation, Aurora. He should choose the best one and delete the rest.'

'But they're not all the same,' she argued. 'Each one has a slightly different angle. Every single one has a different story.'

'Anyway,' said Laura, cutting them off, 'let's go inside. We've organised a seafood buffet.'

Slightly flushed, Aurora got to her feet. She understood exactly why James kept those photos. Each one was original and equally valid in its own right.

The chef had prepared poached lobster surrounded by langoustines and crab claws. Shucked oysters lay on a bed of seaweed and steamed mussels were in a large black *moules* pot. Ice-cold bottles of Pouilly Fumé were on the table with baskets of fresh baguette nearby.

'Just take a plate and enjoy,' said Laura.

Aurora lined up beside Luca and took a sample of each dish. She sat next to Lydia and accepted a piece of bread when offered.

The fish was sweet and perfectly cooked. She closed her eyes in pleasure as she savoured the lobster tail dipped in an aioli. James' seat remained empty so she kept glancing around, hoping to see him.

'Where are the toilets?' she asked Laura after her second glass of wine.

'Out the door, around the corner and to the right.'

She wandered out of the dining room, her dress swishing as she walked. Brushing a stray crumb from the bodice of her dress, she didn't watch where she was going and almost bashed straight into James.

'Oh!' she exclaimed, stepping back. 'James!' she breathed, her cheeks pink. 'We've been waiting for you.'

He stared at her for a moment, his brown eyes unreadable. Then he spoke. 'Hi, Borealis. The beach was so lovely I couldn't leave.'

'Claire was wondering where you were. Especially as the sun went down half an hour ago.'

He shrugged. 'I took my time coming back.' His camera was slung over his shoulder. 'Is there any food left?'

'Oh, plenty.' She smiled awkwardly. 'So, I was just on my way to the loo so . . .'

He nodded curtly. 'Of course. See you in a sec.'

In the end, only Aurora and Lydia remained at the outside bar. Luca had taken Sienna to bed with the full intention of returning but had probably fallen asleep. James and Claire had left straight after the meal, as had Henry and Gloria. Henry's cough was still plaguing him, despite the warm weather and relaxation. Gloria had ordered a hot whiskey and marched him off to bed.

Laura and Christian had left also. She wanted her full eight hours before the ceremony the next day. The family would be free to do what they liked while she, Christian, Luca and Aurora went to the local town hall. Then, the party would begin in the grand dining room of the hotel.

Lydia took off her sandals and rubbed her feet. 'So, Laura tells me that you're on TV now.'

Aurora laughed. 'Not in a starring role. Just as an extra really.'

'You've got to start somewhere. When I first worked at *Papped!* all I did was get coffee for people. Then I got promoted to writing articles. It will happen for you.'

'Perhaps.'

The buzz of French conversation surrounded them and the evening was balmy.

'Did you enjoy my wedding? Your gold dress was just beautiful.'

'Oh, I loved it.' She smiled at the memory. 'Thank you so much for having me.'

'Thank you for singing. Father Colum is still talking about you. He's trying to convince me to post "Ave Maria" on YouTube.'

Aurora blushed. 'It was only a hymn . . .'

'James sent me some amazing photos too. You're such a talented family.'

'Oh?'

'Yes. He caught expressions and moments. Actually, one of my favourite shots is of you. It's in the church. You're standing alone, waiting for your cue to sing. I told Laura to show you.'

'This is the first I've heard of it,' laughed Aurora. 'Typical Laura.'

'Oh, I'll email it to you. It's really nice.' She stretched. 'Right, I'm off to bed. I need my beauty sleep.'

Aurora gave a little wave. 'See you tomorrow, Lydia. Sleep well.'

'Night.'

Aurora didn't move for a few minutes. Instead, she stared at the starry sky and drowned out the noise of the bar. New York was so crazy that sometimes she yearned to just *be*. Closing her eyes, she let her head fall backwards on the cushioned chair.

'*Boo!*' came a voice and she jumped.

It was James.

'You frightened me!' She sat up abruptly and straightened her dress. 'What are you doing down here?'

He had his Mac under his arm. 'I was just uploading photos from today. Claire kept complaining about the light from the screen so I thought that I'd do it down here.'

She ran her fingers through her hair. 'I can leave if you want . . .'

'Please don't.' He opened the laptop. 'It'd be nice to have company.'

His earlier strange mood seemed to have disappeared and he was the James of old. Slowly she relaxed and watched as photo after photo appeared on the screen. There was one of a wave crashing on the shore and another of an old woman standing by a palm tree.

After about ten minutes, he exited out of the folder. 'All done,' he said in satisfaction. 'This place is quite beautiful.'

'I love the peace here,' she said. 'All you can hear are the waving lapping on the shore.'

'How's life? Laura told me that you're very busy.'

'It has been hectic,' she admitted. 'Bertie wants me to sing at his James-Bond-themed birthday party next week so I'm practising all the songs.'

'In New York?'

'No, in London. He's cruising around the Med at the moment on a yacht. I got a text earlier saying that he was docked at St. Tropez and that I should pop down for a drink.' She smiled fondly. 'It will be a pleasure to sing for him. He really is so nice.'

James drummed his fingers on the armrest of his chair. 'Africa was good.'

'Of course, excuse me!' She laughed. 'I'm so self-obsessed!'

'Just a tad.' He grinned. 'Anyway, it was great – Africa, I mean. Two weeks waiting for a mountain gorilla to appear.'

'Did you get the shot?'

'Eventually.' He accessed some photos on the screen. 'There he is. I christened him Ali G. You know, like Ali Gorilla.'

'I get it.'

'Anyway, I need to use the loo. Back in a minute.' He walked away, leaving his computer on the table.

She glanced at the screen. There were hundreds of folders, ranging from Mexico to Nairobi. Maybe he had the wedding on there? Lydia had mentioned how lovely the photos were. She scrolled down through the files. Suddenly she noticed a folder called 'Borealis'. She let the arrow hover over the icon. Surely that photo in the church would be there? She really wanted to see it, especially as it was one of Lydia's favourites.

With a beating heart, she clicked on the screen. Hundreds of photos appeared and every single one of them was of her.

The first one was of her as a child running on the Cornish beach where she grew up. Her long hair was blowing in the wind and her cheeks were rosy from the cold. Then there were shots of her with Henry and Maggie and others of her on stage or blowing out candles on a cake. There were photos of her sitting by the willow tree in their garden at home, unaware that a picture was being taken. There were close-ups of her face, artful shots of her eyes and profile. Some were in colour and others in black and white. Wordlessly, she scanned through them, hundreds of memories flooding her brain. Maybe he had a folder for all family members. She typed 'Laura' into the search engine at the top of the screen. Nothing appeared. Then, she typed 'William'. The same happened. Then she tried 'Lolly' and 'Will', just in case. Nothing appeared. Glancing up, she noticed James approaching through the doors on the right. Guiltily, she closed the folder and resumed her position on the seat.

'So, I hear that you're the bridesmaid tomorrow,' he said. 'Nice to be invited to the actual wedding, I guess.'

Aurora smiled. 'She only wants the bare minimum at the town hall. You know Laura. She likes things short and sweet. Take the opportunity to sleep in or go on a day trip. Count your blessings.'

'Luca's the best man, yeah?'

She blushed. 'Yes.'

'*Woooo!* Look who fancies Christian's son!'

'Oh, stop it. I don't. Anyway, he's totally in love with Lydia.' She didn't dare meet his eyes. 'I just envy them, that's all. They have everything. They're young and gorgeous with a beautiful child. Plus, they adore each other. It restores my faith.'

'In what?'

'The fairy tale.'

Their eyes locked. He reached out and brushed a tendril of hair off her face. 'You and your fairy tales,' he said softly.

'James,' she said breathlessly. 'Why have you a folder of . . .'

'James! I've been looking for you!' Claire appeared with her hands on her hips.

He pulled back instantly. 'Sorry, I got delayed here chatting with Borealis.' He turned to Aurora. 'You were saying?'

'Oh nothing.'

Claire scowled. 'Well, I can't sleep until I know you're back, so . . .'

'I'll be right there.' He winked at Aurora. 'See you tomorrow.'

# Chapter Forty-one

Aurora inserted the last pin into Laura's hair. She had grown her blonde locks especially so that she could put them in a sleek chignon for the big day. Her make-up was subtle. She had opted for an untraditional outfit of a cream Chanel suit and matching heels. Her huge diamond sparkled on her hand and two diamond stud earrings glistened in her ears, but she wore no other jewellery.

'You look like a blonde Jackie Kennedy,' said Aurora in awe. 'So classy.'

'Well, I wanted to look the part.' She took a deep breath.

Aurora checked her reflection in the mirror. Laura had chosen her dress – a short simple silk dress the same colour as her own costume. It was mid-thigh length and shimmered when she walked. She wore her mother's fuchsia necklace around her neck. Her favourite part of the outfit was the shoes: silver Grecian Jimmy Choo sandals with four-inch heels.

'Our car is waiting,' she said, handing Laura a single red rose. 'Let's go.'

Gloria was waiting for them in the foyer with tears in her eyes. 'Oh, how I wish you'd let me come,' she said, hugging her daughter. 'You've always been an odd little thing.'

'Charming,' said Laura, pecking her cheek. 'Look, Mum, it's no big deal. Just a formality really. We don't want a fuss and since Daddy isn't around to give me away . . .' Her voice caught in her throat and she inhaled sharply.

Gloria's expression softened and she rubbed her arm. 'I'm no one to talk. Henry and I did it on the sly as well if you remember.' She smiled. 'Good luck, my love. See you later.'

James, who had gone for an early swim, was walking down the corridor when he heard coughing from his mother's room. As he had just met Gloria having an espresso with Lydia, he concluded that it was Henry. On and on the old man coughed, so loudly that it could be heard on the corridor. James paused and waited for it to subside. Henry hadn't looked well in weeks. Maybe he needed a glass of water? He was surprised to find the door ajar, so he pushed it open and went in.

There he found Henry slumped over on the bed holding a tissue stained with blood.

'Bloody hell, Henry!' He rushed over to his stepfather. 'Are you all right?'

Henry wheezed slightly and tried to smile. 'Quite all right, son. Just a bit of a chest infection.'

James rubbed his back and that set off another violent coughing fit. 'My God, you should get checked out by a doctor. Shall I call Claire? I'm pretty sure blood isn't good.'

'Not at all,' he insisted, wiping his mouth. 'It's nothing, my boy. No need to worry anybody. This is Laura's day, let's leave it.'

'Sit up – that might help.'

James helped him to sit and propped some pillows behind his back. The once tall man was now shrunken and frail. He could feel his bones jutting out through his robe.

James looked him square in the eye. 'How long has this been going on?'

Henry shook his head. 'I don't know, a couple of months perhaps? This week has been bad.' He coughed again. 'There's nothing to be concerned about, son. My GP isn't worried so neither am I.'

'Does Mum know?'

'Of course not. She's been far too busy with the wedding and William's baby.' He took a sip of water. 'I've had colds before. This one is harder to shake admittedly but I'm quite all right. I promise I'll get it checked out when we go home.' He smiled. 'Now, bugger off. I have to get dressed.'

James nodded and vacated the room. He didn't believe him for a moment. Henry was seriously ill. He could only imagine his mother's reaction. And then there was Aurora.

He vowed to badger the old man to get treatment as soon as possible. As soon as they got back to London.

They had a drinks reception on a private terrace by the beach. A waiter stood with a tray of champagne and there were tiny canapés on china plates.

Aurora stood by a palm tree and watched the family interact. Laura had her arm in Christian's as they chatted with Gloria and Henry. Luca was sitting down with Sienna on his lap and she was avidly watching *Frozen* on the iPad. Lydia was chatting to James, her long hair blowing in the breeze. Claire was standing close by, dressed in a short violet dress and black heels. Gloria was right about her short hair – it didn't suit her.

William was notably absent. How she wished he were with them! She needed his flippancy and his wit. There was still no news of the baby. Gloria jumped every time the phone rang but it was never a birth announcement.

James threw his head back and laughed at something Lydia said. His handsome face was tanned and had a slight shadow of stubble. His dark-blue suit looked great on him and his shirt was open at the neck. Ophelia had always claimed that he was 'fit' but she had never taken any notice. Now, she could see it. Now, she couldn't stop staring. The folder of photos played on her mind.

James clinked his glass to gain everyone's attention.

'I know Laura said there were to be no speeches,' he began.

'I meant it, Jiminy,' she retorted.

'However, I feel that I should say a few words in my dad's place.'

The group fell silent.

'Dad was a gentleman: a kind, hardworking man who gave everything to his wife and family. The apple of his eye was his little girl – Lolly or Laura as we know her now.' He turned to his sister. 'I remember him lifting you above his head and twirling you around. You were the first child he would hug after work and the only one he let climb in between him and Mum in bed.'

Laura's eyes filled with tears. 'He would say *shhh* and lift me under the covers before Mum woke up. Then I would stay as quiet as a mouse, cuddled up beside him.'

Gloria let out a sob and Henry pulled her close to him.

'I know that he would be so proud of you today, Lolly. He would have loved to be here to give you away. I'm sure he's raising a glass of champagne to you and Christian somewhere. Let's join him – to Laura and Christian!'

'*To Laura and Christian!*'

Gloria embraced her son. 'Wonderful speech, James. 'Thank you for remembering him.'

James smiled and hugged her close.

Aurora gazed at him and a realisation dawned. Her cloudy mind cleared and she saw the truth.

She was in love with James.

All this time she had loved him and it was only now she could see it. James: funny, caring, kind James. The one who'd always looked out for her: her hero.

A warm feeling flooded her body. Suddenly she ached to touch him. When he looked at her, everything made sense. She was never happier than when he was near.

Sienna jumped up in excitement and started to sing 'Let It Go!' along with Elsa on the iPad. Everyone laughed.

Laura approached her brother, wiping away a tear. 'You're so right,' she said, sniffing. 'He would have loved this hotel.'

'Now, no more tears. Have a few more drinks and enjoy your wedding.' He kissed her forehead and then walked over to Aurora. 'You're looking very lonely over here, Borealis.'

She reddened slightly and gulped her champagne. 'I'm perfectly all right, thank you. I just wish William were here.'

'I know. Me too.' He nudged her playfully. 'Will this brother do instead?' His brown eyes were warm.

For a moment no one spoke. The light breeze blew her hair from her face.

'You'll do just fine,' she said eventually.

'I should have thanked you in my speech. Sorry about that.'

'Thanked me? Whatever for?'

'You're the bridesmaid. I think it's customary to give a shout-out for all your hard work.'

She giggled. 'Hardly hard work, James. The only thing she let me do by myself was organise a drinks party in Soho as a lame attempt at a hen night. She even chose my dress.'

He regarded her short silky ensemble and shook his head. 'Thank God it was a civil ceremony. I can't see you being allowed into a church in a nightie.'

'It's not that bad!'

'I love the Grecian shoes too. Although, you do realise that Aurora was a Roman goddess?'

'I'm no goddess.'

His face became serious for a moment. 'You are. You're beautiful. Don't ever believe otherwise.'

Claire appeared and took James' hand. 'Here you are again. I often wonder what you two find to talk about.'

'Like Gratiano in *The Merchant of Venice,* I talk an infinite deal –'

'Of nothing,' finished Aurora, laughing. 'You're so right.'

'I did *Romeo and Juliet* for my GCSE,' said Claire icily. She tugged his sleeve. 'Let's go for a walk.'

'Where?'

'Just around the grounds. I've had too much champagne already and I feel light-headed.'

'But the party is here . . .'

'Just a short walk.' She tightened her grip on his hand.

'Okay.' He drained his glass and placed it on a table. 'See you in a while, Borealis.'

The whole wedding party later dined on *foie gras* with a cassis foam, noisette of lamb with a delectable ratatouille, and tiny profiteroles filled with caramel cream. Aurora was seated next to Luca who kept filling her glass with Chablis. Initially tongue-tied, she answered in monosyllables. Then, when the wine took effect, she found that he was easy to talk to and soon they were chatting like old friends. She noticed that he watched Lydia constantly. She was seated with Henry and every so often she would laugh and flick her hair.

'I really enjoyed your wedding,' she said, mopping up the sauce on her plate with a piece of bread.

'Yeah.' He filled up her glass. 'I wanted just me and Lyd on a beach but she liked Venice and the lady always gets what she wants.'

'I envy you,' said Aurora genuinely. 'You're so lucky to have found each other.'

'Hey, it wasn't easy,' he argued. 'We had our troubles. In the beginning she wouldn't admit that she loved me. That was hard.'

'But why?'

'She wasn't ready, I guess. Sometimes you can be in love and not realise it.'

Aurora knew exactly what he meant. Her gaze drifted to James who was laughing with his mother.

'You've got to fight for what you want,' he continued. 'If you really believe that person is the one, you've got to tell them.'

'What if they reject you?'

'Then you live in hope.' He shrugged. 'That girl right there broke my heart into a million pieces. I thought we'd never make it, but we did.' His expression softened. 'She's everything I want.'

Aurora sipped her wine in confusion. James was engaged. That night in the pool was a blur. Sometimes she wasn't even sure if it had happened. Yet he had hundreds of photos on his computer – photos of her. Sometimes he looked at her in a way that made her legs weak. Maybe he loved her – in that way – but didn't know it.

Gloria clapped her hands. 'Will is on FaceTime,' she announced, holding up her phone. 'Everyone wave!'

'*Hi, Will!*' chorused the wedding party.

His blond head filled the small screen. Ella blew a kiss from the background.

'Hello, all,' said William. 'Hope your meal was nice. We just had Domino's pizza.'

Everyone laughed.

'Any movement?' asked Gloria.

William shook his head. 'Nothing. That baby is perfectly happy in there. Thank the Lord we have Netflix. It's at times like this that I realise the supreme importance of the humble boxset.' He smiled. 'I miss you all. Where's Lolly?'

Gloria angled the phone so that he could see his sister.

'Congratulations, little sis. So sorry I can't be there. It's all Ella's fault.'

'Hey!' protested Ella from the background.

'Let's go for dinner when I'm back in London,' said Laura. 'Surely that child will have made an appearance by then?'

William nodded. 'I look forward to it. Congratulations to you both.' He waved madly. 'I'll text if we have news.'

'Good luck!' said Gloria. 'Let us know the minute things kick off.' She sighed as she put down her phone.

Christian squeezed Laura's hand. 'I know you wanted him here today. I wish I could have made it happen.'

Sienna threw a piece of bread at Claire and hit her on the cheek. '*Shit!*' she said, giggling.

Luca laughed. 'Hey, sorry about that. She's crazy.'

Claire forced a smile. 'That's no problem at all. At least it wasn't ratatouille.'

Aurora went for a walk after dinner. Her head was spinning and she didn't know what to do. Luca's words played on her mind: she had to fight for what she wanted. The problem was that James would probably reject her. Her head told her to say nothing, but her heart was screaming at her to reveal all.

She was standing on the shoreline with her Jimmy Choo shoes in her hand when James found her.

'There you are, Borealis,' he said, loping towards her. 'Gloria's looking for you. They're having brandies at the bar.'

She stared out at the sea which was streaked with orange from the sunset. Warm water lapped at her feet and the evening air was warm.

'Hey!' he repeated, touching her arm. 'Are you okay?'

The Chablis dulled her senses and gave her courage. She turned around slowly and faced him.

'Why is there a folder called "Borealis" on your laptop?'

He stopped dead. 'Say again?'

'There are hundreds of photos of me on your computer. Why,

James?' Her brown eyes stared at him steadily.

'I just file everything, that's all.' He smiled amiably. 'Now, come on, we need to go back.'

'Do you have files for Laura? Or Will?'

He paused for a fraction too long. 'Of course.'

'No, you don't. I checked.' She stood there defiantly. 'Tell me the truth.'

'What's this about? Are you angry?' He ran his fingers through his hair. 'I don't know why I have a folder of you. I suppose I started it years ago when I took those pictures in Cornwall and it made sense to keep adding to it.'

'Why me?'

'The camera loves you.' He shrugged. 'You're photogenic. Far better to have your face than William's ugly mug.'

Her chest heaved with emotion. 'James, I . . .'

'What?' he asked gently. 'You're acting really weird.'

'I want to say something.'

'So say it.'

'Remember Venice . . .'

His expression changed immediately. 'Not really, no.' He stepped backwards. 'We'd better be getting back.'

*'No!'* She reached out and grabbed his hand. 'Don't leave! I need to say something.'

He shook his head. 'I think you need some water. Luca kept filling your glass with wine at dinner.' He tried to break free but she tightened her grip.

'I'm not a child, James.'

'Come on, Borealis. Gloria wants a family photo.'

Moving closer, she grabbed his hand and placed it on her waist. His eyes widened in surprise. Her flimsy dress was no barrier and she could feel the heat of his fingers on her skin.

'You touched me like this,' she whispered, her eyes huge. 'Do you remember? You pulled me close.' She took his free hand and put it on the other side of her body. 'You were about to kiss me . . .'

'Aurora . . .'

'Admit it!' She reached out and caressed his face. 'You wanted to kiss me. The reason I know is because I wanted it too.'

His face was impassive as he stared at her. She couldn't read what he was thinking but she didn't care.

'I love you,' she said simply. 'Not just as a brother but as something more.'

'Aurora . . . you're just emotional after what happened with that creep.'

'I'm not!' she said angrily. She felt her eyes well up with tears. 'I'm in love with you. I can't stop myself. I need you to kiss me, James. Right now.'

'You need to calm down.' He backed away slightly. 'You don't know what you're saying.'

'Yes, I do!' she said, tears rolling down her cheeks. 'Please don't go all noble on me, James. I can't bear it.'

'Borealis,' he said gently. 'Come here.' He pulled her into his strong arms and cuddled her close. 'You don't know what you're saying. I'm too old for you. Plus, I'm your brother.'

'No, you're not.'

'You know what I mean.' He stroked her soft hair. 'You're so special and beautiful. Any guy would be so lucky to have you.'

'But I don't want any guy,' she said, sobbing.

She rested her head on his shoulder and let him hold her. She couldn't think straight. She had just revealed her innermost feelings to him and she had been rejected. Her cheeks burned with mortification.

'Venice was a once-off. We were both drunk and it shouldn't have happened.'

'*In vino veritas*,' she said in a muffled voice. 'I truly believe that.'

It felt so good to be held. Suddenly she knew what to do.

Moving to the right, she encountered his neck. Lightly she kissed his skin, moving up towards his ear. He smelled so good – so familiar.

'Aurora,' he protested, but he didn't stop her.

She continued to kiss him with small feather kisses up his neck, up as far as his jaw. Boldly, she took his face in her hands and kissed his lips with a fervour and passion she didn't know she possessed. His stubble grazed her skin and she relished it. James didn't react for a moment and she took advantage of his surprise. Wrapping her arms around his neck, she pressed up against him, moulding her body to his. For a few seconds, he responded, his mouth crushing hers. His hands moved around her body and she moaned.

Then, abruptly, he pulled back.

'Fucking hell, Aurora,' he said breathlessly. 'I'm engaged.'

Her eyes glittered and her chest heaved. 'Say you don't feel it too,' she challenged. 'Say it!'

He pushed her away gently. 'That shouldn't have happened.'

Her dress was rucked up to mid-thigh and her hair was tousled. 'It felt good. For you too. You know it did!'

He kicked the sand. 'I can't handle this right now. You need to stop this.'

'Stop what?'

'*You're my sister!*' he shouted. '*This is fucked up!*'

'I'm not your sister! I'm no relation at all. I love you. Why can't you see that?' Her eyes flashed. 'You're just too stubborn to admit how you feel.'

'I need to get back.' He started to walk away.

'James, please!'

'Leave me alone, Aurora. This is not right.'

'You don't mean that!' Her voice wavered.

He turned around angrily. 'Yes, I do. This is impossible.'

'You're lying.'

'I'm not! I love you as a sister – nothing more. You need to find someone your own age and forget about this fantasy. I'm not your hero. You've picked the wrong guy.'

She gasped in horror and stumbled backwards, his words cutting deep. His face looked deadly serious and, for a moment, she thought that she'd pass out. Grabbing her shoes, she ran away.

'*Aurora!*' he yelled. '*Come back! It's not safe on your own!*'

She ignored him and kept running, her heart breaking in two. There was no going back now. James didn't want her and now she had lost him forever.

# Chapter Forty-two

Claire was waiting on the now deserted terrace when he got back. Her eyes were narrowed as he approached, her foot tapping on the flagstones.

'Where were you?' she asked coldly. 'Everyone is asking if you've gone to bed.'

He groaned inwardly. His night had been awful enough without the third degree.

'I just went for a quick walk. Shall we join the others?'

'I saw you,' she said. 'I saw you and Aurora on the shoreline.'

He closed his eyes. 'Oh?'

'What were you arguing about? Why did she run off?'

'Nothing.' He ushered her along. 'Come on, we need to get to the bar.'

'What's going on between you two?' she pressed on.

'What are you talking about?'

'Oh, don't deny it. You've always had a soft spot for her.'

'Stop it, Claire.'

'I'm always finding you two together. Take last night for example. I look for you and there you are, in a cosy twosome with her.'

'You're imagining it.'

'When she's in trouble, who does she call?' She laughed bitterly. 'Then you run like a faithful puppy and do her bidding.'

'Claire, you're being ridiculous. She's my sister.'

'Except she's not your sister, in fact.' Her eyes flashed.

'Stop it.' He grew angry. 'You're out of order.'

'Oh, I'm not. It's Borealis this and Borealis that. When she calls, you drop everything. I'm sick of it.'

'I'm going to the bar. Join me if you want.' He stalked off, but she grabbed his shirt.

'I saw you kiss her on the beach, James.'

He cursed silently. 'I didn't kiss her.'

'It didn't look like that to me,' she spat. 'You're pathetic. I can't believe I didn't see it until now.'

'Stop it, Claire.'

'You're in love with her! Your bloody sister. No wonder you're not keen on a mortgage. You had no intention of marrying me.'

'You've gone mad! Stop this craziness!'

'On the contrary.' She laughed sardonically. 'I've finally woken up.' She stalked off towards the hotel.

'*Claire!*' he called after her retreating back. '*Claire, come back!*'

She ignored him and kept walking.

'*Claire! Bloody hell, you're overreacting!*'

She swung around angrily. 'I'll be in our room.'

James gestured to the barman to fill his glass with Courvoisier. The bar was full of tourists and a mixture of languages could be heard over the soft jazz music in the background. Claire hadn't come back so he guessed that she was in bed. He knew that he should find her and apologise, but a few drinks at the bar seemed more appealing.

Lydia sidled up beside him and smiled. 'Thanks again for those beautiful photos. I absolutely love the one of us on the gondola.'

'It's my job after all,' he said with a grin.

'I'm so glad that you came. You left so early after the wedding, I didn't have a chance to thank you.' The barman placed a full glass of wine on the counter and Lydia took a seat on a bar stool.

'I had to get back. A job cropped up at the Beeb that I couldn't refuse.' He swirled the golden liquid around his glass, his expression sombre.

'Where's Aurora?' Lydia asked stealing a glance sideways. 'I haven't seen her since dinner.'

'I've no idea,' he answered grimly. He was worried about her and wished she would appear. He kept looking over his shoulder, willing her to arrive, but so far there was no sign. He didn't like to think of her on the beach all alone. He should never have left her. His rational side told him that she was probably in her room, but he was still concerned.

'When did your mum and Henry get married?' asked Lydia.

'2002,' he replied. 'It seems like yesterday.'

'Aurora must have been about nine or ten.'

'Ten. They moved to London straight after.'

'Have you two always been close?'

'What do you mean?' he asked sharply.

'I didn't mean anything,' she said, holding up her hands. 'Whoa!'

'Sorry – I'm just on edge.'

'Everything okay?' Her green eyes were kind. 'You've been sitting here all alone for ages.'

He said nothing, his countenance gloomy.

'James, I might be overstepping the mark here, but do you need to talk?'

He sighed. 'I thought I had it all worked out, Lydia. I have a great fiancée. We're looking to buy a house. I thought I was happy.'

'Go on,' she encouraged.

'Now, I don't know anything any more.' He took a swig of brandy.

'It's Aurora, isn't it?' she said softly.

His head snapped up. 'What do you mean?'

'You have feelings for her.'

'*No.*'

She raised an eyebrow. 'I think that you do. You can't deal with it because she's your sister. You think people will think it's strange.'

'You're crazy!'

'I don't think I am,' she argued. 'I saw you two at my wedding. It was as obvious as anything. My sister Molly was convinced that you two were together. And Molly is notoriously perceptive.'

He didn't answer. Instead he drained his drink and banged the glass on the wooden countertop.

'Love is never easy, James,' she said in her soft voice. 'Don't wait too long or it might pass you by.'

'I'm too old . . .'

'No, you're not,' she scoffed. 'Look at Laura and Christian.'

'I'm engaged.'

'Luca was married before we finally got our act together. People make mistakes.'

'It's impossible.'

'Nothing is impossible.' She got up. 'Think carefully about this. We only get one chance.'

He drained his drink and winced as it scalded his throat.

*Aurora.*

He had to find her.

He got up and stalked out of the bar, his face set in a determined line. He would start on the beach and work from there.

An hour later, Gloria jumped to her feet and whooped. '*Ella's waters have broken!*' she shouted in delight. 'Will just texted.'

Luca raised his glass of whiskey in salute. 'Awesome.'

'My word! I wonder if it'll be a girl or a boy,' said Gloria in excitement. 'Imagine if it was a baby girl! I could buy sweet little dresses and bows for her hair.'

'I thought babies had no hair,' said Christian.

Laura arrived back into the bar, having been upstairs changing into a sundress. Her Chanel suit was too formal for the evening and her heels were cutting her feet. 'Did I just hear that the baby's on the way?' she asked.

Gloria nodded, her hand on her chest. 'I hope it goes well.'

Henry patted her arm. 'Of course it will. She's young and healthy. They have a hospital nearby.' His face tightened as he thought of Grace all those years ago. Grace who had been isolated in an old house during a terrible storm. Times were different now.

'I'm just being silly. Oh Henry, I can't wait to have a cuddle. I hope the poor girl has a fast labour. Nothing worse than a forty-eight-hour trauma.'

James went upstairs after searching both the beach and the garden. Despite having phoned Aurora five times, she still hadn't returned his calls. There were three missed calls on his phone from Claire, but he didn't return them. He would deal with that later – his priority now was to find Aurora.

She had to be in her room. She was staying down the hall from Laura and Christian.

He reached her bedroom door and knocked loudly. '*Borealis?*'

he called. '*Open up!*' There was no movement from inside so he knocked again. '*Aurora! Come on! Open the door!*' He rested his head against the door in frustration. She obviously wasn't there. Maybe she had joined the others at the bar and they had just missed each other.

He turned to walk back to the stairway and saw Claire standing there watching him.

'I was wondering where you were,' she said in a shaky voice. 'I rang you over and over.'

'I was at the bar. Then I went for a walk.'

'And now you're here, knocking on her door. What a surprise.' She backed away. 'Why do I bother?'

'Claire!' he called after her retreating back. 'Come back!'

'Piss off,' she said, walking away.

He knew that he should follow her and try to work things out. He contemplated going back to their room and explaining, but what would he say? He had just spent over an hour searching for Aurora. Claire was right – he always put her first.

The family were still in the bar when he appeared a few minutes later. He scanned the group. 'Where's Aurora?' he asked. 'Has anyone seen her?'

'Oh, I met her at reception,' answered Laura. 'She had to leave.'

James did a double take. 'Leave?'

Gloria nodded. 'Harry called. He needs her back in New York as soon as possible.'

'So where is she now?'

'She's gone to meet Bertie. She wanted to go through the song list for his party before she jets off.'

'Bertie?' he repeated stupidly. 'But he's cruising around the Med.'

'He's docked at St. Tropez as we speak,' said Laura. 'She was all apologies about not saying goodbye, but her taxi was waiting.'

'Taxi?' James ran his fingers through his hair. 'So she's gone?'

'About half an hour ago.' Gloria regarded her eldest son. 'Are you all right, my darling?'

But James had gone.

He sprinted out to the main foyer, rushing up to the main reception desk.

'*Bonsoir*,' he said to the small man behind the main desk. '*Bonsoir, je* – I want – *voudrais* – *a taxi*.'

'You would like a taxi, sir?' he answered in perfect English. 'Certainly. For when?'

'Right away. Um, *tout de suite*.'

The receptionist picked up the phone and spoke in rapid French. 'To where, sir?'

'St. Tropez.'

He nodded and finished the call. 'Five minutes. Will that be all?'

But James had rushed out the main door. The stars sparkled in the sky and he immediately thought of her. She loved starry nights.

He willed the car to arrive. If he left now, he might catch her. He had to see her – he had to explain.

Sure enough, a Mercedes pulled up a few minutes later with an Algerian driver. French rap blared from the stereo.

'St. Tropez,' said James, jumping into the back seat. 'Please hurry! I mean, *dépêchez-vous*.'

The driver nodded and the car accelerated down the driveway. James looked out the window at the lights of Antibes, a grim expression on his face.

She had run away because of him. He had to find her and make things right. Claire, his family and Laura were all forgotten. Her image filled his mind and he vowed to find her.

The journey took longer than expected due to the volume of

traffic on the motorway. Nearly two hours later, the taxi pulled up to the harbour.

'*Deux cents euros,*' said the driver, holding out his hand.

James pulled out his wallet and cursed. He only had one hundred in cash. Mercifully there was a bank machine on the corner of the street. He paid the driver and sprinted down onto the marina. Boats of all sizes were docked by the wooden promenade. Many were worth millions with luxurious balconies and plush interiors. He strained his eyes to see if he could spot either Bertie or Aurora. A man approached wearing a navy uniform so he stopped him and tried to explain who he was looking for. The man pointed in the direction of the marina office so James wasted no time. There was an elderly man behind the desk, his half-moon glasses perched on his nose.

'Albert Wells,' said James breathlessly. '*Je cherche Albert Wells.*'

The man shrugged and went back to his Sudoku puzzle.

James banged the countertop. '*Écoutez moi! Je cherche Albert Wells . . . le bateau.*' He pointed to the boats outside. 'Actor! He has a boat!'

The man started to gesticulate wildly, berating him in rapid French. He could tell from his tone that he had no idea what he was talking about and that he didn't appreciate being disturbed.

'*Fine, fine, forget it!*' he shouted running outside. '*Fuck!*' he yelled in frustration.

A blonde woman in a Hermès scarf looked at him curiously from the railing of her cruiser.

He ran down the remaining length of the dock, desperately trying to see inside the boats. Most of them were empty and in darkness.

Suddenly, a small man wearing a sailor's cap and a cravat tapped his shoulder. 'Are you quite all right, old chap?' he asked amiably. 'You look a bit lost.'

James turned around immediately. 'You're English? *Thank God!* I'm looking for Albert Wells, you know, the actor. His yacht is docked here, but I can't find it.'

'Bertie? Why do you want him?'

'You know him?' His face lit up.

'Of course. He's an old friend.' The man looked suspicious.

'Hey, I'm not a crazed fan or anything. My sister is on that boat. I need to find her. Please tell me where it is.'

'Your sister? The pretty girl with the long dark hair?'

'Yes! Aurora. That's her.'

'I saw her earlier having a drink at La Voile Rouge. Beautiful girl.'

James wanted to shake him. 'Where is she now?'

'Oh, they've gone. You've missed the boat, old boy. Quite literally.' He smiled at his own joke. 'Bertie set sail half an hour ago.'

'Set sail? Where to?'

'Italy, I think. He wasn't sure. She was with him. I say, are they an item? If so, I have to commend the old codger. She's quite the beauty.'

But James wasn't listening. Instead, he was gazing out to sea. Taking out his phone, he rang her and just like all the times before there was no answer.

She was gone and he had let her go. If only he had that moment back on the beach. He would never have said such things. He would never have let her run away.

# Chapter Forty-three

Aurora silenced her phone and shoved it under a velour cushion. She was sitting on the plush sofa in the living room of Bertie's yacht, her legs curled up underneath her like a cat. The walls were lined with books and a walnut coffee table stood in the middle of the small space. The boat undulated slightly as there was a slight swell out at sea. She clutched her brandy as tears stung her eyes. He could ring her for a hundred years but there was no way she was answering. He had rejected her and now she had to pay the price for her honesty.

Bertie eyed her compassionately. 'Are you ready to tell me about it now?' he asked gently. 'I hate to see that gorgeous face all blotched with tears.'

'Oh, Bertie,' she said. 'I've made a royal mess of things.'

'I'm sure it's not as bad as you think.'

'It's worse.' She sipped her drink and coughed. 'What is this stuff? It's like petrol.'

'Brandy,' he replied cheerfully. 'I get it from a farmer in Bordeaux. Unregulated of course so I'd imagine that it's awfully dangerous. Huge alcohol content: ideal for getting pretty girls drunk.' He winked at her.

'I'm no fun,' she said dolefully.

'Oh, buck up and tell me what the matter is. I've been dying to know why you turned up on my boat looking forlorn and dejected.'

She bit her lip. 'Okay, I'll tell you now.'

He leaned forward in excitement. 'Don't leave out any of it and embellish all you want.'

She half-smiled. 'I'm in love.'

'Well, that's pretty obvious.' He rolled his eyes. 'Go on.'

'With my brother James.'

'*Ooh!* That's better,' he said, rubbing his hands together. 'I like a bit of good old incest.'

'Except he's not my brother, as you know. Well, not really.' Her huge eyes were sad. 'I didn't realise how I felt until recently.'

'So what happened?'

'I told him. He didn't feel the same. I ran away.' A big tear rolled down her cheek. 'Now I can never face him again.'

Bertie snorted. 'Oh, of course you will. You're family, my darling. It will be impossible to avoid him.' He rubbed his chin. 'Is he gay?'

Aurora gasped. 'No! Not at all.'

'So what's his problem then? You're sublime. He must be crazy to reject you.'

'He thinks that he's too old and that I don't know what I want. Plus he's engaged.'

'Oh, he is.' Bertie raised an eyebrow.

She blushed. 'Yes. Perhaps I should've mentioned that earlier.'

'Well, it certainly changes things.' He got up and filled his glass. 'Why did you tell him? You must have had some indication of how he felt.'

'Well, we almost kissed in Venice and then I found hundreds of photos on his laptop and they were all of me.' She shrugged. 'He's always looked out for me. I suppose, I hoped that he felt the same but I was wrong.'

'*Hmmm*, perhaps not, my child. Perhaps not.'

'What do you mean?'

'You gave him a huge shock. He has a fiancée. Maybe he's in denial. Maybe he wants you too but is having a problem admitting it.' He sat down on the couch beside her. 'Give him time. This is a big step.'

Her phone buzzed under the cushion. She pulled it out. 'That's him again,' she said, glancing at the screen. 'He keeps calling me.'

'That's positive.'

She shook her head. 'He's just worried about where I am. Like all big brothers, I suppose. James has always treated me like a child.'

'And therein lies the problem, my sweet,' he said gently. 'This James can't accept the fact that you've become a woman. He's having a crisis because the little girl he cared for through the years is now a desirable sex goddess.' He rubbed her cheek. 'Give him time. He needs to adjust.'

'Oh, Bertie, if only you were right!'

'Right, enough moping. Give me a blast of some James Bond, please. I've hired an orchestra to accompany you – strings for "You Only Live Twice" and brass for "Skyfall". It will be stupendous!'

The boat travelled across the Mediterranean overnight and docked off Livorno in Northern Italy. They had breakfast on the deck, served by a butler and prepared by a private chef.

Aurora took a bite of a crisp buttery croissant and groaned. 'This is heavenly.'

Bertie nodded in agreement. 'Divine. Fernando is a wizard in the kitchen. Did you sleep well?'

'Oh, wonderfully well. The boat rocked me to sleep like a cradle.'

'The brandy helped too, I imagine.'

'Well, it certainly made me forget.' She sipped her coffee. 'Sorry for my self-indulgent rant last night. It must have been boring for you.'

Bertie snorted. 'On the contrary, my dear. Such drama! And I can never resist a woebegone damsel in distress.' He poured some honey on his granola. 'Has he called since?'

'No.' She sighed. 'I have been expecting a text but there's been nothing. Just missed calls.'

'He's probably waiting for you to call him back.'

'Not a chance. I'm so embarrassed. It's back to New York for me.'

'He might follow you and go down on one knee, proclaiming his undying love for you.'

'Hardly. He made it quite clear how he felt. I'm like a sister to him – that's all I'll ever be.'

'Have you any work lined up?'

She shook her head. 'Not really. I was banking on that Scarlett role but I suspect that it's not going to happen.'

Bertie chewed thoughtfully. 'You know, Justin still hasn't found an Elise Sloane for the Broadway run.'

'Oh?'

'He'll be at my party next week. How about you two have a rapprochement? He's dreadfully sorry for his behaviour.'

She scowled. 'Harry doesn't want me to do theatre any more.'

'Harry has no soul,' said Bertie dismissively. 'I think it would be a terrific idea. You were so good in that role, my darling. It's just until Christmas.'

'I don't think so.' She pushed her plate away. 'Justin doesn't respect me. He frightened and disgusted me. I can't trust him.'

'That was the coke,' he said. 'I keep telling him to lay off the white stuff but he never listens. Look, think about it. You'd see all your old friends.'

She said nothing. *La Morte* was so far from her mind it was difficult to engage with it now. She checked her phone for the tenth time.

Nothing.

What did she expect? She had run away and ignored him. As if on cue, her phone buzzed loudly and she jumped. With a beating heart, she illuminated the screen, hoping that it was James.

'Oh, it's Gloria,' she said, biting her lip in disappointment. She accessed the message and gasped. 'Oh Bertie! Ella had her baby!'

'Who?'

'My brother's girlfriend!'

'Not your *brother* brother!'

'No!' She laughed. 'I certainly wouldn't be delighted about that.' She frowned as she read the details. 'A baby boy, six pound seven ounces. Mother and baby doing well and they're calling it Andrew.' She put her hand on her heart. 'That's so lovely – that was his late father's name.'

'So you're an auntie,' Bertie concluded. 'That's wonderful news.'

'Well, step-auntie, I suppose.' She took another croissant. 'I'm so glad it went well. I'll pop over to visit when I'm back for your party.'

'Would you like to stay with me for those few days?'

'You read my mind,' she said gratefully. 'I can't possibly run the risk of meeting James.'

'I think it's inevitable you will, darling. You can't hide forever.'

'I can until it's all forgotten,' she said with determination. 'A couple of months should do it.'

'I'll tell Miranda my housekeeper to make up the guest suite in grand style for the sumptuous Aurora Sinclair.'

She reached out and grasped his hand. 'You're so good to me, Bertie. I'm so thankful.'

He winked. 'I'm still hoping that you'll realise that I'm the love of your life and we'll take off into the sunset and get married.'

She giggled. 'You never know.'

William threw a soiled baby wipe onto a pile. 'My God, how does a man this small produce so much poo?'

Ella rested her head on a cushion. 'God knows.'

She had never been so tired. He had only been in their lives for six days and already she was sleep-deprived. Oh, how she took those uninterrupted nights for granted! Andrew was gorgeous and cute and adorable but also loved waking up on the hour every hour for a feed. Her breasts ached and she couldn't sit down properly due to the seventeen stitches she had received for a small tear during labour. She had imagined herself pushing her chic buggy around London, full of energy and vitality. Instead, she was a bedraggled mess with lank hair and milk-stained clothes. William had taken two weeks' leave so at least he was around to help. He walked around with Andrew when he had wind and gave her half an hour here and there to sleep or shower. No one had told her how hard it was: no one.

Gloria and Henry had called three days before. Gloria had been hooked from the moment she saw Andrew – if not before. 'I love the name,' she said tearfully. 'Beautiful gesture.' She had rocked him to sleep, cooing and kissing his soft forehead, clearly besotted.

The doorbell rang. William scooped up Andrew and placed him in Ella's arms. Putting the nappy in a scented bag, he expertly threw it into the bin.

'*Coming!*' he called.

James was standing on the threshold with a large bunch of flowers and a present wrapped in blue paper.

'Well, hello, Jiminy Cricket,' said William, hugging him.

'Come and meet Andrew.'

James placed the flowers on the kitchen counter and walked over to Ella. Andrew was sound asleep on his mother's breast, his small chest moving up and down rapidly.

'He's lovely,' said James softly. 'So tiny.'

Ella smiled. 'He's a good boy,' she agreed. 'Except at night-time.'

William took a seat on the armrest of the sofa behind her. 'We're shadows of our former selves, James. He's confusing night and day at the moment.'

'I might be wrong, but isn't that what babies do?'

'Not all babies,' said William. 'You meet some parents who have produced angels. Coffee? Something stronger?'

James shook his head. 'I'm fine. I just came from Mum's place.' He regarded his younger brother. 'Fatherhood suits you, Will. Especially the milk stains on your shirt.'

'Vomit stains,' he corrected. 'Andrew likes to regurgitate sometimes.'

'How was the wedding?' asked Ella conversationally.

James stiffened. 'It was fine,' he said. 'Very short and to the point. Very Laura.'

'Aurora called yesterday and she was gushing about the hotel. She said that the beach was incredible.'

James' face was impassive. 'She was here?'

'Yeah,' said William. 'She's staying with that Bertie bloke. His party's tomorrow night and she's singing at it.'

'Did she say anything else?'

Ella shrugged. 'Not really. She adored Andrew and was very good with him actually. He slept in her arms for half an hour.' She kissed the baby's nose. 'I think she's heading back to New York immediately after the party. Her agent called and summoned her.'

William crossed his long legs. 'She seems to be running around in circles at the moment. One minute she has a job, the next she's singing at parties and weddings. Nothing seems to be stable. Mum is worried about her. She thinks it's no life for a young girl. She's dying for her to meet someone and settle down.'

James said nothing. Instead, he fiddled with the tassels on the cushion next to him.

'Have you seen Henry?' he asked William directly. 'He's been very ill.'

'He called with Mum a few days ago to see the baby. They only stayed a few minutes as he was coughing – Mum said it was the aftermath of some kind of flu.' William shrugged. 'If I'm honest, I barely took any notice. Andrew didn't sleep the night before and we were frazzled.'

'Still coughing?' James was dismayed. 'Will, I found him coughing up blood in France.'

William's face changed. 'That's not good. What did Mum say?'

'She wasn't there. It was the day of Laura's wedding, just before we all went to dinner, and he begged me not to say anything. So I let it go but I made him promise to see a doctor as soon as he got back to England. I assumed he did.' James was suddenly stricken with guilt. He had been so preoccupied with Aurora, he had neglected Henry. 'I should have checked. I'd better contact him.'

'Look, leave it to me,' said William. 'I'll find out and make sure he sees a specialist if necessary.'

'Thanks, Will. I really should have checked. But do it discreetly. He mightn't have told Mum.'

'I will.'

There was a pause, then Ella changed the subject. 'So, is Claire working today?'

James reddened slightly. 'Um, yes, she is. That's why she couldn't make it.' He shifted uncomfortably in his seat. 'She sends her love.'

'So when's your big day?' asked Ella. 'Please give me time to lose some of this weight. All my nice dresses are much smaller.'

'Not for a while. We're saving for a house.'

'Don't leave it too long, Jiminy,' said William. 'You're fast approaching middle age.'

Later that evening, Aurora was in her bedroom at Bertie's, painting her toenails dark-red. The bedroom was like something out of a fairy tale. The bathroom alone was bigger than her old flat. There was a large four-poster bed and a walk-in wardrobe with panoramic mirrors. She had purchased a white full-length gown for her performance and her stomach did flips when she thought of it. Bertie had shown her the guest list and it was littered with famous names. He had invited actors, directors and producers, writers and poets and musicians. A big security firm had been safeguarding his home for the last two days, making sure that it was like Fort Knox. Bertie had given her a plus one for the party and suggested asking James. She had looked at him as if he were mad. Had he forgotten what had happened? And James was engaged. In the end, she asked Ophelia who screamed when she heard.

'*I might meet Justin Bieber!*' she yelled, jumping around her flat.

'I'm not sure if he's invited but you never know,' said Aurora in amusement.

She had refused a dinner invitation at The Ivy with Bertie's ex-wife and her new Italian lover, simply because she wanted to rest her voice. She had a face mask all ready to go, then a soak in the bath and finally bed.

Her phone beeped, signalling that she had a message. Ophelia had been texting all evening so she presumed that it was her. She waited until her toenails were completely dry before pressing the screen. James' name flashed before her. Her heart slowed down and then began to thump loudly.

It read: *Hi, Borealis. Heard you're in London. Can we meet? I want to sort things out.*

She reread it three times.

*I want to sort things out.*

That could only mean one thing. He wanted things to go back to normal. What he didn't realise was, things would never be normal again. She didn't want to hear what he had to say. She could almost predict it anyway: it was all a mistake, there was too much wine involved, he was due to be married soon and she, being young, had the world at her feet.

It was all too raw for that. He didn't realise how she felt – he didn't take her seriously. Like lightning she replied.

*Too busy. See you soon.*

She pressed 'send' and sat back. It was curt, but not too unfriendly. She would see him soon, probably at Andrew's christening. She just needed time to sort out her head. Seeing him now would set her back.

The phone beeped again and she jumped. It was Ophelia wondering if she was allowed to snog Justin Bieber if the opportunity arose. Was there a protocol she had to follow?

Aurora smiled, despite the ache in her heart. She decided to put James out of her mind and concentrate on her upcoming performance.

As promised, Bertie had hired a full orchestra to accompany her. His party-planner Marcel had cleared some bushes at the end of the garden to facilitate the huge number of musicians. There was a silver podium right in front of the conductor's spot where she was due to stand. The repertoire was simple: most of the Bond songs from the start of the movie franchise. She would begin with 'Goldfinger' and go from there. The conductor, a small Russian named Alexei, had arranged slower versions of 'A View to a Kill' by Duran Duran and 'You Know My Name' by Chris Cornell to suit her voice. Her favourite song was Nancy Sinatra's 'You Only Live Twice'. The violin intro with the French horn harmony sent shivers down her spine. She couldn't wait to perform it.

Ophelia arrived at five. She had her red curls piled on her head and was dressed in a green-and-silver mermaid dress with a fishtail. Despite having an invitation, it took her twenty minutes to get past security.

Aurora met her in the foyer and hugged her close.

'You look like Ariel from *The Little Mermaid*, she said fondly. 'I love the dress.'

'Oh, they're all the rage,' Ophelia replied. 'Bloody hard work though. The narrow hemline doesn't give me much room to walk.'

They ventured out into the garden. Bertie was instructing the head waiter on how he wanted things done and men with earphones walked around constantly, monitoring any suspicious behaviour.

'Are you nervous?' asked Ophelia. 'That's an awfully big orchestra for such a little girl.'

'It's strange but I feel completely relaxed,' said Aurora. 'I've been looking forward to this.'

'Bertie went for the Sean Connery look. I was hoping for Daniel Craig.'

'Oh, he's convinced that Connery is the best Bond.' Aurora smiled.

Someone tapped her shoulder and she turned around. Standing there was Justin Debussy, all dressed up in a tuxedo and with a wary expression.

'Hello,' he said in his clipped tone.

Aurora stiffened.

Ophelia, sensing the awkwardness, backed away. 'I'll just get some champagne,' she said lamely, disappearing into the house.

Aurora hadn't seen him since that night in his flat – that night when he was drunk and high and nasty.

'Bertie's looking well,' he said, gesturing to his uncle.

'Very well.'

His blue eyes darted around the room. She could tell that he was nervous. This made her glad – she wanted him to squirm.

'So he told you about my Elise Sloane situation then?'

'Yes, what a shame.' She stared at him steadily. 'Surely there's some up-and-coming American actress who will fit the bill?'

He shook his head. 'Anyone who has auditioned has been wrong. Actresses are ten a penny in this business. Stars are harder to find.' He twirled the stem of his glass between his forefinger and thumb. 'Would you consider . . .?'

'I don't think that's a good idea.'

'Purely professional – no funny business. No one else can play her like you. No one else comes close.'

'I can't.'

'Just a month. Just until November. Let the critics see you and write about you.'

'Harry doesn't want me doing theatre.'

'Bugger Harry! He has you running around doing bits and pieces. This is solid and it will be great for your reputation.' He stared at her. 'Do you want to be a two-bit extra for the rest of your life?'

Her brown eyes widened. The past few months had indeed been bitty. Nothing to ring home about – just small roles that people forget. Maybe a few weeks of Elsie Sloane would be refreshing. She had enjoyed it and she liked the cast. Justin aside, it had been a nice experience.

'Look, I'll call you when I get back to America,' she said. 'I need to think about this.'

'It's the right move, Sinclair, and you know it.' He walked away.

At around nine, Bertie nodded at her to get ready. She ran to her room to check her make-up and do some warm-up exercises.

Ophelia had bonded with one of the bodyguards and was on her fifth glass of champagne. She had forgotten about Justin Bieber and was now concentrating on flirting outrageously with the hunky security guard.

Aurora looked at her reflection in the full-length mirror in her bedroom. In her white dress she resembled Grace in that portrait. Her cloudy dark hair framed her face and her fuchsia necklace lay between her breasts.

'Get me through this, Mummy,' she whispered. 'Guide me through.'

Bertie was on the podium when she got downstairs. There were about one hundred guests milling around. She had already seen Gordon Ramsey, Jeremy Irons, Judi Dench and Paul Weller. She had met Victoria Beckham in the loo and Stephen Fry was holding court in Bertie's study, telling amusing stories about last year's BAFTAs. In a brief conversation, she had told him of Henry's most recent birthday present: the first edition of *Salomé*. He had been very impressed as he was a huge fan of Oscar Wilde and proceeded to tell her a story of a time that he and Henry went fly-fishing together.

Bertie thanked everyone for coming and for their overly generous gifts which he was giving to charity. The crowd applauded. 'Well, except for Elton's all-expenses-paid week in Mauritius,' he added. 'That's just too tempting to forfeit.'

He then told a little anecdote about Ian Fleming and how James Bond had been a major influence in his life since he was a boy.

'Who wouldn't want to be that cool, sophisticated seemingly indestructible spy who could get any woman into bed?' he asked.

'He didn't bonk Moneypenny!' called Ophelia and everyone laughed.

'You're quite right, young woman,' agreed Bertie.

Aurora walked up onto the podium and stood next to him.

She kept her eyes down, her face slightly flushed. It was intimidating to stand in front of such talented people.

Bertie took her hand and kissed it. 'Good luck, my sweet,' he whispered. Then he turned to the crowd. 'So, without further ado, I give you Aurora Sinclair!'

The crowd clapped and the orchestra played a few notes in sync. Then the opening bars of 'Goldfinger' began to play, a spotlight was trained on her and she started to sing. There were a few wobbles at the beginning as she battled with the brass section. But then she found her feet and her voice soared out over the crowd. She never felt as alive as she did on stage. Something happened to her and she was transported away.

The song ended and there were slight murmurs in the crowd followed by rapturous applause. Bertie clapped the loudest. '*Bravo!*' he shouted. '*Bravo, my darling!*'

Aurora blushed. 'Thank you,' she said quietly.

The pianist started to play the intro to 'Skyfall' and she started to sing.

After two encores, she finally got to mingle. Everyone she met congratulated her and shook her hand. People she had never seen in her life were gushing about her talent and wondering if she had ever done musical theatre. Someone put a flute of champagne in her hand and then she was whisked off to meet Tom Cruise. After an hour of small talk, she stole away into the house. She needed to wind down. Ophelia had disappeared with her hunky guard so she grabbed her phone and bag and sneaked off.

Walking down the corridor, she checked her phone, just in case James had texted. There was nothing. She sighed in disappointment and threw the offending phone into her bag. It was odd really. She had told him that she was too busy to meet him, but part of her wanted him to arrive on Bertie's doorstep, whisk her into his arms and take her away with him. Just like her

Barbie Ferrari dream. She was confusing herself at this stage with her mixed signals. Maybe she should meet him before she jetted off. Maybe . . .

The study was mercifully empty so she took refuge in there. The walls were lined with books and journals, some old and frayed. Bertie's desk was overflowing with papers and magazines and a large plant stood in the corner with drooping leaves and dry soil.

She took off her shoes and rubbed one of her feet.

'Hello,' came a voice from one of the leather armchairs facing the fire.

She whipped around. 'Yes?'

A man was sitting there, his dark-brown eyes fixed on her.

'You sang well.'

She couldn't place his accent – it sounded Irish but with British overtones. He looked about fifty, his dark hair slightly streaked with grey, and he had sallow skin.

'Thank you,' she said warily. 'Sorry to disturb. I thought this room was empty.'

'Not at all,' he said, gesturing for her to sit down on the other chair. 'I could do with some company myself. How's Henry?'

'You know my father?'

A shadow passed over his face for a second. 'Yes, I do. We go back a long way.'

'And you are?'

'I knew your mother too.'

She relaxed a little. 'So many people have said that to me tonight. It's been wonderful hearing about her. Daddy doesn't say much.'

'Oh, I knew Grace very well.' He sipped his whiskey. 'You look like her.'

She smiled then. 'I know. There's a portrait of her in my old house and I can see the resemblance.' She sat down and continued to rub her feet. 'No one ever warns you about heels. They have the potential to maim you.' Her long hair fell to the side. 'So, how do you know Bertie?'

'Oh, everyone knows Bertie.'

She laughed. 'I suppose.'

'I knew him in the eighties, before he was a mega star. I directed a play he was in once.'

'Oh, so you're a director.' She sat back.

'Not any more. I write books now. I'm also a poet.'

'Oh, I love poetry,' she said wistfully. 'We had an English teacher at school called Mr. Crowley. He taught us everything from Donne to Kinsella. Are you well known?'

'In my own circle.' He smiled. 'I don't do it for the fame.'

'Nor does Daddy,' she said. 'He hates fuss.'

'I suspect that he's slightly more famous than I.' He focused in on her necklace. 'I like the fuchsia around your neck. Where did you get that?'

She looked at him in surprise. 'You're one of the first people I've met outside of Cornwall who could identify it correctly – are you a botanist too?'

'I live in West Cork, right down the south of Ireland. That little flower is quite abundant down there.' He stared at the pendant. 'Why do you have such a flower?'

'It belonged to my mother,' she explained. 'I like to wear it as it makes me feel close to her.'

There was a loud scream and lots of laughter from outside the window. They could hear a man shouting, '*Get in the pool!*' and then a splash.

Aurora giggled. 'This will get crazy, I think.'

The man said nothing. Instead, he gazed at her unflinchingly. 'So, this Mr. Crowley instilled a love of poetry in you. I commend him. Do you have a favourite poet?'

Aurora paused. 'Gosh, that's a hard question. Poems speak to one in such different ways. Depending on one's mood, of course. For example, at the moment I'm reading lots of Yeats as I can relate to his heartbreak regarding Maud Gonne's rejection.'

'Have you been rejected?'

She nodded. 'Yes.' She met his gaze. 'Quite badly in fact. So, when I read a poem about a similar theme, it gives me solace.'

'Go on.'

'I adore the Romantic poets, Shelley in particular.'

'Your mother loved Lord Byron,' he said.

'Yes, Daddy mentioned that one time. You must have known her quite well.' She eyed him suspiciously. 'You never told me your name – how did you know Mummy?'

He got to his feet. 'You were wonderful tonight, Miss Aurora Sinclair. Congratulations.' He held out his hand formally. 'Until we meet again.'

She shook his hand firmly. 'You're leaving?'

'Goodbye, Aurora.'

And he was gone.

Three weeks later, Aurora stepped off the stage with Paul Lewis by her side. *La Morte* was sold out every night and the American crowd couldn't get enough of the tragic tale. Bertie came to see her during the first week and brought a herd of journalists with him. 'My favourite play in the world,' he gushed to the different newspapers. 'Watch this space.' And they did.

It had been relatively easy to lapse back into character. She had learnt her lines so well for the first run that they were imprinted on her brain. The majority of the original cast had flown out for the run so she met up with Ray Rossi and all her old pals from the lighting and costume department. Laura had recommended an Italian restaurant in Greenwich Village so they went there a lot to wind down after the show. It felt good to be part of a team – her months of freelancing had been exciting but lacked structure. Flitting from one job to the next, she didn't make lasting friends and often felt isolated.

Justin had been impeccably behaved since their reunion. Their relationship was professional and cold and it worked like a dream. Gone was the innocent naïve girl who allowed him to manipulate her. She had grown up since the London days and was not afraid to show it.

Harry, however, was incensed that she was tied up in a play at a small theatre off 44$^{th}$ Street and insisted that she free up her schedule. '*You gotta stay on the screen!*' he shouted down the phone. '*You need exposure!*' She had placated him in her gentle but firm way – she had promised Justin that she would play Elise for a month and she would follow through.

Working six days a week kept her busy and took her mind off James. France seemed like a dream now. She still cringed when she thought of the beach, but she thought of it less and less. He hadn't texted since Bertie's party and she didn't blame him either. She had been bordering on rude in her reply when she refused to meet him. Anyway, he was probably knee-deep in acquiring a mortgage now. Her heart twisted in misery when she thought of Claire and his future. Deep down she truly felt that becoming Mr. Suburbia was the wrong move for him – he would suffocate in that lifestyle. Or perhaps she didn't know him at all. He had rejected her against all her gut feelings and he had walked away.

Laura had come back from a two-week safari trip in Kenya. Christian had gone straight back to the office so she busied herself looking for a job. Even though being a kept woman was always her objective as a teenager, the reality was very different. Being alone in a big apartment with little or no friends was tedious. She loved interacting with others and thrived on witty conversation. She needed to socialise and have a life of her own. Christian came home later and later each night, always with some excuse about a meeting or a client that went over time. Tara's warning, months before, rested unpleasantly in her memory and she vowed not to let their marriage suffer. Instead of berating him for his tardiness, she welcomed him with a glass of wine and a smile. She made a huge effort not to make a scene, but that was proving difficult. Sometimes she wanted to shout at him for putting the firm first; sometimes she yearned to walk out in anger so that he would take notice of her unhappiness. Aurora met her twice a week for lunch or coffee and she enjoyed their little outings as it gave her an opportunity to let off steam. Aurora recommended joining a yoga class or volunteering for a charity. Laura scorned these suggestions. She didn't see herself as one of those wives. Deep down she knew the answer. The solution was simple: she had to find a job.

On a cold Tuesday morning Aurora bought a coffee from her favourite barista on the corner near the theatre. She waved goodbye, her long red scarf trailing down her back, and walked down the street.

Hundreds of people passed her by, all in a hurry. She paused to cross a busy street and waited for the green 'Walk' sign. Taxis beeped their horns and buses whizzed past, emitting fumes of smoke that polluted the air. Sometimes the tall buildings made her feel claustrophobic. It was virtually impossible to see the stars in New York. One had to crane one's neck right back to get a glimpse of the sky and, more often than not, it was overcast and murky.

A man fell into step beside her and she jumped.

It was Carey McGrath: the director.

'Hey, Aurora,' he said with a smile. 'How you doin'?'

She stopped dead and nearly dropped her coffee. 'Hello! My goodness, you gave me a fright.'

'Sorry.' They were just outside the theatre and he pointed to the stage door. 'Can we step in here? It's so damn cold.' He pulled his fleece jacket tightly around him.

'Sure – I have a small dressing room here.'

'Great.'

She pushed in the old door and held it open for Carey to follow. The air smelt musty as they passed through the auditorium.

Why was he there, she wondered. Surely he hadn't met her on the street just by chance?

Once they were backstage in her dressing room, he took a seat and crossed his arms.

'I saw you perform here,' he began.

'You did?'

'Three times.' He smiled. 'You're good. Very good in fact.'

'Oh?' Her heart was pounding. She placed her polystyrene cup on the dressing table.

'We start shooting in January. In Los Angeles. I want you to play Scarlett.'

The whole world slowed down and she felt as if she were falling backwards. It was just a normal Tuesday morning. She had ordered her coffee on her way to work like any other day. She had put Carey out of her head and moved on. Now, he was offering her a break. Not just any break – the biggest break of her career.

'Are you serious?' she asked, trembling slightly.

'I sure am. You got that *je ne sais quoi*. I think you're the one.'

'Are you sure?'

'Of course I'm sure. Would I say it otherwise?'

'Sorry – I just can't believe it.'

'So you want it?'

'Oh, I really want it,' she said breathlessly. 'Thank you so much.'

'And can you do it? No clash in your schedule?'

'No, no – none.'

'Right. So – no more to be said.' He got to his feet. 'I'll get my people to call Harry and we can work from there.'

He walked to the door.

'Oh, and Aurora?' he said on the threshold. 'Don't cut your hair.'

'I won't!'

He disappeared.

She hugged herself in ecstasy. It was her dream role. Who would play Rhett Butler? Would it be epic length like the original version? Her heart filled with joy. This was it! She was going to make it.

Grabbing her bag, she ran out onto the street. A yellow cab stopped when she hailed it.

'Upper East Side,' she said, beaming at the driver.

She had to tell Laura. She would be thrilled for her. Maybe they could go for a boozy lunch and celebrate. The car took off down the busy street and a huge smile was plastered on her face.

Laura and Christian's apartment was on the third floor of a luxury building overlooking Central Park. Mimi had lived there for years and her name was still on the plaque outside the front door: *Mme Marcheline Jacob*.

Aurora knocked loudly. She prayed that Laura was there. She had pilates on a Tuesday but that was in the afternoon. She knocked again.

The heavy oak door moved and a sombre-looking Laura appeared. There was a flicker of surprise on her face when she saw her stepsister.

'Why are you here?' she asked.

Aurora hugged her and shouted, '*I got the part! I got the part!*'

Laura pushed her away. 'What part? Calm down.'

'Scarlett O'Hara! I've made it, Laura! This is my big break.'

Laura didn't react. Instead she looked at her pityingly. 'I think you'd better come inside. I wasn't expecting you.'

Aurora stepped backwards. 'Are you all right? Blimey, Laura, you could be happier for me.'

'Come inside.'

She followed her into the sitting-room area. The décor was still as classical as when Mimi lived there: old Louis XIV chairs and a huge marble fireplace. Aurora scanned the room and gasped. There, standing by the Monet on the wall, was James.

'Oh!' Aurora stumbled backwards. 'What the hell!'

His handsome face looked tired and his brown eyes regarded her compassionately. 'Hi, Borealis.'

Laura took a seat and looked meaningfully at her brother.

'Why are you here?' asked Aurora in confusion. 'What's going on?'

'We were about to come and find you,' said Laura.

'Why?'

James cleared his throat. 'It's Henry,' he said in his deep voice. 'He's dying.'

The world slowed right down. Her heartbeat almost stopped, before speeding up again and thundering in her ears. She looked at them wildly, failing to understand.

'What?'

'He has terminal lung cancer. It seems that he's had it for a while. He's been hospitalised. Palliative care. I'm so sorry.'

'Had it for a while?'

'He didn't tell anyone, not even Gloria.'

Her eyes filled with tears. 'Laura? Did you know?' she demanded. 'We met for lunch two days ago and you never said anything.'

'I didn't know,' she answered quietly. 'James arrived half an hour ago. We were planning on finding you. Then you arrived all by yourself.'

'I didn't want to tell you over the phone,' he added. 'So, I flew out here.'

Her ears began to ring and the noise was deafening. 'But he was fine at the wedding. There was nothing wrong with him!'

James shook his head. 'He's dying, Aurora. I'm here to take you home. To say goodbye.'

'No,' she said firmly. 'It can't be true.'

Laura looked at James helplessly. They had expected a reaction like this. They just didn't know how to handle it.

'Aurora, sit down and we'll have a cup of tea,' she said kindly. 'We have to book flights and get organised. You need to let Justin know.'

'No!' Her brown eyes flashed. 'I'm going back to the theatre. I need to go over my lines.' She stalked off and banged the door.

James caught up with her by the elevator.

'Borealis,' he said softly, pulling at her sleeve.

She turned to him and her eyes filled with tears. 'Tell me that you're lying, James. Tell me it's not true.'

He pulled her into his strong arms and she inhaled his familiar smell. He rubbed her back soothingly and kissed her forehead. Everything that had happened between them was instantly forgotten. It didn't matter as there were far more serious things to think about. The chips were down and she needed him.

'I'm so sorry, I'm so sorry.' He held her close. 'I'll take you back. We need to go back.'

# Chapter Forty-four

The journey back to London passed in a blur. Images of James carrying her bags, Laura's sleeping profile on the plane, untouched food on her table and then a black cab taking her to the hospital passed her by. Her hands were clenched and her face taut as they approached the building. Gloria had rung to say that he had taken a turn for the worst and that the family had been called.

She saw George first. His rotund frame and bald head were instantly recognisable. He was standing by a door, talking in his haughty tone to a nurse. Sebastian was sitting by a vending machine, his blond hair slightly greying now. Cressida wasn't there – the last Aurora had heard, she had left him for a Sikh barrister and was now living in Chester.

Gloria held out her arms and Aurora fell gratefully into her embrace.

'Thank God you're here,' said Gloria in relief.

'How is he now?' Aurora mumbled into her shoulder. 'May I see him?'

Gloria wiped her tears away. 'Of course. The boys have just been in. He's been waiting to see you.'

George nodded curtly in her direction and then proceeded to take out a cigarette and disappear out the door. Seb, who was texting furiously on his phone, didn't even look up.

Laura sat down on the chair beside him and opened a magazine. She would wait her turn – it was far more important for Aurora to spend time with Henry. Sebastian's rudeness didn't matter as it was incidental in the scheme of things.

'Shall I come in with you?' asked Gloria, taking Aurora's hand.

'I'll go with her, Mum,' James said. He took her arm and they entered the quiet room.

Henry was asleep, propped up on four pillows. A machine beeped beside him and there were lots of wires and monitors flashing. Aurora's hand flew to her mouth in horror. He looked so different. In just a month he had transformed. His breathing was rapid, his face thin and wan, his body shrunken. And his blue eyes – those merry warm blue eyes – were closed.

'Daddy?' whispered Aurora, her voice catching. 'Daddy! It's me, Aurora.'

His eyelids flickered slightly and then opened. Focusing on her, he smiled. 'My darling girl. I'm so glad to see you.' His voice was weak and raspy.

She leant forward and kissed him gently. 'I'm here.' A tear rolled down her cheek. 'I'm here.'

James hovered in the background, silent but supportive.

'I wanted to see you,' said Henry breathlessly. 'There's something I have to say.' He coughed feebly.

She sat on the bedside chair and took his hand. 'Don't strain yourself,' she said firmly. 'Just hold my hand. I'm not going anywhere.'

'Yes, but *I* might.' He smiled at his own joke. 'Aurora, there's something you should know . . .' He coughed again and this time his whole body shook.

She rubbed his back in alarm. 'Shall I call the nurse?'

'No,' he answered, shaking his head. 'Listen to your daddy. Listen to me.' He grasped her hand tightly. 'Years ago I made a decision. I did it to protect you. I honestly believed that it was the right thing to do. Please remember that.'

'*Shhh*,' she soothed. 'Don't get worked up. You must rest.'

'I've regretted it since then. I should have told you the truth. Then it was too late and I was a coward.' The old man started to cry.

Horrified, Aurora leant in and kissed his cheek again. 'Daddy! Stop this. Please rest.'

'No, my darling, you must know the truth.'

'What truth? What are you talking about?'

'Aurora, there's a secret. I meant to tell you for so long. Your mother was already with child when we got married. I raised you like my own, but you're not mine.'

The world stopped moving for a second. She felt herself sway.

'Your real father? He wanted to take you away but I felt it was better that you stay with me. Grace would have wanted that. I kept this from you to protect you.'

'I don't understand,' she whispered. 'What are you saying?' She looked around wildly to see James' shocked face.

'You weren't premature, like we said. You were due to be born in the New Year. I should have been with Grace that night. She was so far along, I should never have gone to that party. I've lived with that guilt since.'

'Why did you never tell me, if that's the truth?' Tears began to stream down her cheeks. 'How could you not tell me?'

'I've been so guilty. When you were a child, I excused myself with the fact that you had already experienced so much pain. I didn't want you to be uprooted. Now, you're a young woman and you deserve to know . . . you need to know . . .'

'Daddy?'

'I made a promise . . .' He started to cough harshly. His whole body convulsed and his eyes began to bulge. Then he began to choke, phlegm and blood splattering out from his mouth.

'Keep back!' said James, pulling her away. 'Call the nurse. *Call the nurse!*'

She stumbled over to the door and called for help. Gloria pushed past her and two seconds later a nurse followed.

Laura and Sebastian jumped up in alarm.

'*What the fuck did you do to him?*' roared Sebastian, rounding on Aurora. '*He was fine until you arrived!*'

James shoved him backwards. 'Don't ever speak to her like that again,' he seethed. 'She did nothing.'

'They allow that woman in and not his own sons,' continued Sebastian in fury. 'What if this episode finishes him off?'

George appeared and motioned for his younger brother to sit down. 'They'll settle him, now calm down.'

Aurora couldn't focus. Her brain was spinning and she felt dizzy. Sebastian's angry words didn't register. James, as if sensing her turmoil, led her outside. There was a small garden with a wooden bench. George had discarded his cigarette butts carelessly on the ground and she irrationally bent down to pick them up.

'Leave it, Borealis,' said James, pulling her back. 'Sit down.'

Like a zombie, she sat on the hard bench and started to wring her hands.

'Do you think it was the morphine?' she asked in a shaky voice. 'He's out of his mind. What do you think?'

James said nothing. He stroked her wrist and gave her time to process.

'What did he mean, James? He married Mummy even though she was pregnant? With another man's child?' A big fat tear rolled down her cheek.

'Don't think about that now.'

'But I'm not a Sinclair. Those people in there are no blood relations at all.'

'*Shhh!*' said James in alarm. 'Don't let your brothers hear that.'

'But it's true, isn't it?' She turned to face him. 'Who am I?'

'Don't think about it,' he repeated softly. 'One thing at a time.'

'Did you know?' she asked suddenly. 'Did Gloria know?'

James shook his head. 'I'm as shocked as you are.'

She was crying openly now. 'I'm a foundling – a nobody. I have no claim to anything.'

He pulled her into his arms and let her sob. On and on she cried, her body convulsing. A million thoughts raced around her brain but she couldn't focus. Not when Henry's life was hanging by a thread.

'When Henry's stable again, we can ask him for more information,' suggested James. 'Just try and forget it for now.'

She wiped her nose with her sleeve. 'It might trigger another fit.'

'Yes, but you need to know about your real father. He owes you that.'

Aurora inhaled sharply. 'I can't even imagine it, James. Daddy is my father. He always has been. This seems like a cruel joke.'

'We'll broach the subject later,' he said firmly. 'In private, far away from those awful brothers of yours.'

'Will you stay with me?' Her eyes met his.

'Always.'

# Chapter Forty-five

Later that evening, Henry died.

Laura, James and Aurora had gone to a nearby McDonald's for a bite to eat. William met them there and they ordered nuggets and Big Macs like the old days. 'Remember when Mum would take us all for a slap-up meal on a Sunday?' said Laura, chewing on a chip. 'Our restaurant of choice was McDonald's on the High Street.'

'Well, someone's tastes have changed,' said James winking. 'I can't see Laura and Christian dining out on a Super Saver Meal for fun.'

Then Gloria called, in hysterics. Abandoning their meal, they rushed back to find that it was too late. George and Sebastian were standing by the window. Gloria was sitting by the bed, her head resting on her husband's lifeless arm. There was a strange quietness in the room. It had an eerie quality, almost like time had stopped.

Aurora stood there motionless. Henry's eyes were closed and he looked so peaceful. Gloria had parted his white hair, just how he liked it. His hands lay on his lap, one covering the other.

It was too late. She had wanted to know so much but now it was too late.

Laura yelped slightly and moved backwards out of the room. She didn't know how to handle death. The sight of his corpse made her feel faint. William put his hand on his mother's shoulder in comfort. James took Aurora's small hand in his and held it tightly. There was silence in the room as there was nothing to be said. Henry was gone.

They ordered a taxi to take them back to Oxshott. Gloria didn't want to go home so they left her by Henry's bedside. James hugged her tightly and offered to stay, but she refused. She wanted time alone with her husband. She needed some space.

William escorted them to the main door of the hospital and hugged them all individually. Henry's death brought back stark memories of his own dad. He could tell that Laura was feeling it too. Aurora looked like a ghost – her large brown eyes were glassy and she was shivering uncontrollably.

'I'll be over in the morning,' he said as they piled into the car. 'I have to get back to Ella and the baby.'

The house seemed big and empty. James switched on the light and filled the kettle. Laura disappeared upstairs and returned wearing her old pink pyjamas. Without make-up and with tear-stained cheeks, she looked about fifteen.

James placed three cups of tea on the table and sat down. The only sound was the ticking of the kitchen clock.

'Poor Henry,' said Laura in a shaky voice.

A muscle flickered in James' cheek. His own dad's death came flooding back and he had that same helpless feeling.

Then there was Aurora. Henry's bombshell seemed surreal now, overshadowed by his sudden death. He couldn't even imagine what she was thinking. Not only had she lost her father, she had learned that her whole life had been a lie. She was staring into space, her cheeks deathly white.

'Drink your tea, Borealis,' he said softly.

She didn't even register his voice.

After a while, she got to her feet and disappeared out the door. Laura's eyes met his in alarm so he followed right away. He found her in Henry's study, sitting at his desk. Slowly she reached out and traced the outline of his leather writing pad. Then she gathered up the loose pages and stacked them neatly in a pile.

'Are you okay?' he asked, unsure of what to do.

She started opening drawers in his desk, rifling through the miscellaneous items stored within. What started as a rummage ended up as a frantic search. Throwing things onto the floor, she emptied each drawer, tears streaming down her cheeks.

'Borealis!' He grabbed her arms. 'Stop!'

'There has to be something,' she said. 'There has to be a note or a letter. Something to lead me to the truth.'

'Aurora!' he said firmly. 'Stop this. *Stop!*' He pinned her arms down. 'There won't be anything here. Not after all this time.'

'*Then how will I find out?*' she yelled. '*I need to know who I am!*'

He held her firmly, allowing her to struggle. This was to be expected. She was in complete shock and was reacting to it. Suddenly she slumped in defeat and fell to the floor. Her shoulders hunched and she started to cry.

'Borealis,' he said gently. 'Please don't.' He lifted her into his arms. 'I'm putting you to bed.'

Laura was in the corridor when they emerged, her face ashen. 'Is she all right?'

'Get some sleeping tablets from Gloria's room,' he ordered. 'Follow me up and bring a glass of water.'

He kicked open her bedroom door and deposited her on the bed. She buried her face in the pillow, her body shuddering. Laura appeared with the pills and a large glass of water.

'I'll get a pyjamas for her,' she said.

James forced her to sit up and shook her gently. 'Borealis, you need to swallow these. You need to sleep.'

She didn't respond so he put the tablets into her mouth and tipped the water down her throat. She choked slightly but managed to keep them down.

Laura pushed him gently away. 'Leave while I get her dressed.'

'Of course,' he said flustered. 'Call me when you're ready.'

When he was allowed back in, she was under the covers. Her long hair was fanned across the pillow and her eyes were drooping. He fell to his knees and caressed her head, smoothing the long tresses away from her face. Laura watched him in silence.

'Don't go,' Aurora mumbled.

He kissed her forehead. 'I'm here.' He turned to Laura. 'Get some rest. I'll stay with her.'

Laura gave him a strange look. She had always known that they were close but this was different. It was the way he looked at her.

'I can stay, James,' she offered. 'You should get home to Claire.'

'No.' He waved her away. 'I've got this. I'll stay a while.'

'If you're sure . . .'

He turned his back and continued to stroke her head. Laura closed the door quietly.

'*Freddie Thompson! You get back here right now!*'

Aurora ran after her friend, her small legs struggling to keep up. She could never catch him, mainly because he had longer legs and was extremely nimble. Through the rose garden they ran, past all the bushes and flowers. Mr. Crowley was there, reading a book with his glasses on his nose. Aurora waved at him as she scampered by, but he didn't notice. The big house came into view but it had a conservatory – just like the one in Oxshott. Henry was sitting in his favourite chair and there was a man standing next to him: a tall, dark-skinned man with brown eyes and slightly greying hair. They were arguing and the stranger walked away.

'*Daddy!*' called Aurora. '*What's the matter?*'

Henry couldn't hear. He just shook his fist. The other man stopped and turned.

She got a jolt. She recognised him. She had seen this before and she remembered this scenario. Suddenly, Justin Debussy appeared, eating a doughnut and laughing.

Then she woke up.

Her eyes opened slowly and struggled to focus. For a moment, she thought she was back in Cornwall. She could almost hear the waves crashing on the shore. It was still dark outside so she snuggled down under the blankets once more. Something moved beside her and she jumped. Reaching out, she encountered a warm lump on the bed next to her and she instantly knew it was James. In a flash, reality took its terrible hold and the events of the previous day came flooding back.

*Henry was dead.*

The grief punched her in the gut and she felt momentarily winded. For a few blissful moments, she had forgotten everything. She had been safely cocooned between being awake and asleep, lost in a dream world. Now, the cold grasp of the reality clutched her heart and she curled up into a ball.

She couldn't really remember coming home. There were flashes of William hugging her goodbye and Laura in a pink pyjamas. Then she remembered James by her bedside, soothing her to sleep. His presence next to her meant that he had been overcome by sleep himself. Or had he stayed just to comfort her?

Shifting slightly, she rested her head on his chest, instantly comforted by his steady heartbeat. She didn't care why he was here. It didn't matter. It was lovely to have him close by. His heat and regular breathing reminded her that she was alive.

He moved and swung his arm around her shoulder. Turning slightly, she got into a spooning position, relishing the close contact. His strong arms around her mitigated her misery a little, so she closed her eyes and relaxed. She wasn't ready to face the day – not just yet. Not when her mind was spinning and all she could think of was Henry's shocking revelation before he died.

She woke up to see Laura was standing at the doorway of her room holding a cup of coffee. James was still wrapped around her and she could tell from Laura's face that she was shocked.

'Just checking to see how you are,' she said warily, her eyes travelling from Aurora to James and back again. 'You were in a proper state last night.'

Aurora disentangled herself gently from James' arms and swung her legs on to the floor. Immediately she felt dizzy and slightly nauseated.

'Where's Gloria?'

'She got back around two. I woke up and crawled into bed beside her.' Laura's face fell. 'The last time I did that was when Dad died.'

'It's nice to have company,' agreed Aurora.

'*Hmmm*.' Laura raised an eyebrow. 'Why is Jiminy in here?' she asked directly. 'I thought he'd go home to Claire.'

Aurora blushed. 'I don't know. He must have fallen asleep. I woke up to find him there.'

'He has his own room . . .'

'Ask him when he wakes up.' Aurora got to her feet. She didn't have time for the third degree. 'Is Gloria awake? I need to see her.'

Laura took one last look at James and then nodded. 'She's on the phone to Gordon. Arrangements have to be made for the burial.'

Aurora headed straight for her stepmother's room. She was in bed, her face sad as she spoke quietly to Henry's brother-in-law.

'May I come in?' Aurora mouthed.

Gloria nodded and patted the bed beside her.

'Great, so I'll see you in a few days. Thank you, Gordon. Sure, sure. I'll let George and Seb know. Bye.' She hung up the phone.

'What did Uncle Gordon say?'

'Oh, he's organising the burial plot. Henry will be laid to rest with Marcella.'

'Why?' asked Aurora in shock. 'You're his wife!'

'It's customary to be buried with your first spouse.' Gloria sighed. 'When the time comes, I shall be with Andrew.'

The cup of tea Laura had brought her ten minutes before lay untouched on the bedside locker. She twisted her wedding ring around and around, her face troubled.

'Gloria?'

'*Hmmm?*'

'Did Daddy ever tell you anything about me?'

'He always spoke of you.' She closed her eyes. 'He loved you, darling.'

'No, I mean, something private – something about my mother.'

'Nothing, my love. Why do you ask?'

'No reason.' Aurora's face fell. 'I just wondered.'

Gloria took her hand and stroked it. 'I know this must be so difficult for you, sweetheart. I want you to know that you will always be a daughter to me. I know we're not blood-related, but you'll always be part of this family.'

Aurora said nothing. Instead she closed her eyes in sadness. What did 'blood-related' mean anyway? From what Henry had said she was a stranger amongst them all.

'How was Daddy over the last few weeks? Was he terribly sick?'

Gloria shrugged. 'Not really. His cough worsened and he went off his food. I just thought it was that bloody flu back again. Then William took me aside and explained. I had no idea. Perhaps if I'd known, I could have helped.' She looked stricken for a moment. 'Hot toddies were not the answer.'

Aurora gave her a hug. 'You did the right thing. Daddy loved whiskey.' She kissed her cheek. 'You made him so happy, Gloria. Thank you for that.'

# Chapter Forty-six

The news broke later that day. Social media sites were filled with reports on Henry's death. His long career and critical acclaim rendered his death front page news.

**HENRY SINCLAIR DIES**

**THE CURSE OF 2016 STRIKES AGAIN**

**PLAYWRIGHT DEAD**

Tributes began to flow in from around the world. The phone didn't stop ringing and hundreds of messages arrived from fans and fellow writers. Thousands of people left comments on Facebook and #henrysinclair was trending on Twitter.

Laura kept a note of phone calls and random visitors who happened to pop in to express their condolences. Soon the notebook she had been using was almost full, with names ranging from Mike the gardener to Ralph Fiennes.

Bertie called from Tokyo. He was tied up with an advertising campaign for vodka and couldn't make it back. He sent an enormous bunch of lilies and a personal card to Aurora. Harry Finkelman sent a bouquet, as did Justin and the cast of *La Morte*. Even Carey McGrath sent some roses and a lovely message saying to take all the time she needed.

They released Henry's body three days after his death and so the family packed up and drove to Cornwall. George and Sebastian were *in situ* when the Bentley pulled up outside the old house. Gloria and Aurora had travelled down together as they were chief mourners. James and Laura were due to follow the following day with William, Ella and the baby.

Conny Thompson had organised a group of villagers to come and prepare the house for guests. It had lain empty for so long it was extremely damp and dusty. The sheer size of the old building made their task insurmountable so George instructed them to fix up the main drawing room, the kitchen and his and Sebastian's bedroom only.

'What about Mrs. Sinclair?' asked Conny.

'She can stay at a hotel,' snarled Sebastian.

Caterers were brought down from London and all the paintings were straightened and fixed. Grace, covered for over twelve years, saw the light of day once more.

The first thing Aurora did when she arrived was run into the old drawing room and gaze at her mother. She had forgotten the sheer size of the portrait. It dominated the west gable wall. The fuchsia necklace that Aurora wore daily lay between her breasts.

Aurora stood before her and stared at her mother. 'Tell me your secrets,' she whispered, her eyes filling with tears. 'Tell me, Mummy. Give me a sign.'

Grace stared straight ahead, her beautiful face frozen in time.

'I'm ever so sorry, little 'un,' came a voice from behind her.

Aurora swung around. There, looking smaller than ever, was Maggie. She had a walking stick now and her frame was hunched. However, her wise blue eyes were the same and she held out her arms.

'Oh, Maggie,' sobbed Aurora, rushing towards her. 'I'm so glad to see you!'

'Now, now,' she said gently. 'You cry all you like, my lovely.

Maggie's 'ere to mind you, Maggie's 'ere.' She rubbed her back rhythmically and sang an old Cornish folksong. Aurora recognised it from when she was a child and it was oddly comforting.

'I can't believe he's gone, Maggie.'

'Poor Mr. 'Enry. It was a nasty way to go in the end. Still, 'ee's at peace now. 'Ee's sleeping.'

Aurora rubbed her nose. 'I'm so sorry I haven't been to visit. There's no excuse.'

'Now, now, none of that, if you please.' The old lady looked stern. 'Let's enjoy our time together without all of that. You come with me and we'll 'ave a cup of tea.'

Aurora smiled through her tears. 'I'd like that very much.'

Henry was buried in the old graveyard by the water's edge. The huge tombstone already had Marcella's name carved on it. Grace's grave was on the other side of the yard, standing alone against the howling wind.

Aurora watched as they lowered the coffin into the ground. She wore a simple black coat and a black lace veil which covered her face. George and Sebastian stood by her side, both in black suits and ties. They had requested that only close friends and family attend so the crowd was quite small. However, there was a pile of flowers by the east wall from fans and colleagues. Aurora had never seen its equal. There was a large bouquet from Buckingham Palace – even the Queen had been a fan of his work.

James stood behind her, looking handsome in a black suit. He had arrived with Claire, William, Ella and Baby Andrew, just before the service. Laura had travelled with Christian who had turned up out of the blue the night before. Josephine, his longsuffering secretary, had rearranged some meetings at the last minute, giving him two days to fly in for the funeral. Hiring a Mercedes, they had driven down at breakneck speed directly from the airport.

Mary and Conny Thompson stood with Susie, their daughter, and of course Freddie. His handsome ruddy face was sad as he watched the priest sprinkle holy water on the coffin. Maggie stood by his side, her small frame slightly hunched.

Aurora threw the first sod of earth onto the coffin when it was in place. George threw some more and finally Sebastian. The three Sinclair children stood together, all united in grief for their father. Gloria threw a single red rose and wiped her eyes with a white handkerchief. She looked demure in a black suit with a string of pearls. She too had a lace veil over her face; she didn't want the press taking photos of her tear-stained cheeks.

There was a horde of photographers and journalists by the gates of the big house when the entourage drove by. Aurora stared blankly out the window as nothing seemed real. She and Gloria were in the Bentley and George and Sebastian had opted for a Rolls-Royce. Gordon and Helena were waiting on the front steps when they emerged from their respective cars. Both were white-faced and sad.

'Bloody dreadful,' said Gordon, shaking Gloria's hand. 'Too soon, my girl. Far too soon.'

'Right, tell the waiting staff to earn their money,' ordered Sebastian. 'There will be about fifty people or so.'

They entered the house and were met by a line of men and women dressed in black.

'Wine, sir?' asked one.

'I'll have a scotch,' snapped George. 'A large one.'

William kissed Andrew's nose. Ella had just fed him in the privacy of the kitchen and he was now in his arms, content and sleepy.

'He's quite handsome,' said Laura, stroking his soft cheek. Sipping her wine, she shivered. 'This house is just as creepy as the last time. Remember that New Year we spent here?'

'Not really. I was plastered if you recall.' He looked longingly at the pint of beer on the table by his side. He was cradling the baby on his right arm and was afraid to move for fear of waking him.

'I'm so glad Henry had the sense to move to London.' She watched Christian and Gloria. He reached out, patted her back and she smiled. They seemed to be having an amiable conversation and for that she was glad. If only her mother would love him like she did. It irked her that Gloria didn't quite approve of their union, although she masked it well.

'I'll just pop over and see what they're talking about,' she said, walking away.

William glanced at Andrew. He had fallen asleep again, his eyes fluttering as he slept. He had grown so much already. His blue sleepsuit was straining at the toes. Ella was of average height so he had to presume that that Josh person was tall. It would be a lie to say that he didn't think about the other man. He had been terrified when Andrew was born – terrified that an emotional exhausted Ella would insist on informing the biological father. Instead, she hadn't even mentioned him.

Aurora appeared and William gave her a pleading look. 'Will you hold him for a while? My arm is sore. And I'm dying to drink that.' He nodded at the glass of beer. 'Come on, you were so good with him at our place.'

She hesitated but nodded. 'Okay, just for a while.'

She took the sleeping baby in her arms and kissed his soft head. Softly, she sang the Cornish lullaby Maggie had taught her, rocking him to and fro. Looking up, she saw James watching her. He had a faraway look on his face. Their eyes met and he jumped, pulling himself together immediately.

'Will,' she began.

'Yep?'

'Did you see much of Daddy lately?'

'Not as much as I should have,' he said honestly. 'What with the baby and all, we've been so busy.'

Her eyes shone. 'Me too. I feel guilty.'

'Hey, there's no need for that,' he said kindly. 'You were in another country entirely. He was so thrilled for you.' He took a swig of beer. 'The last time I saw him was about three weeks ago or maybe it was longer. Gloria invited us down for Sunday dinner: a slow cooker stew. It was our first outing with Andrew, you know, with a car seat and all that. It took us about half an hour to get out of the house.'

'How was he? Did he look sick then?'

'Well, I hadn't noticed it before, I must admit. Then James mentioned how ill he was in France.'

She nodded miserably. 'We thought he had a cold.'

'But that day he looked so frail. He barely touched his food. Then this bloke turned up out of nowhere, just as we were eating, and demanded to talk to Henry.'

'A bloke?' She looked up.

'Yes – a tall guy with an Irish accent. They went into his study for ages. Then we heard shouting so Gloria went to intervene.'

'Shouting?' she repeated. 'Why?'

William shrugged. 'We don't know. The man left and Henry said absolutely nothing. He didn't explain or even tell us who the stranger was.'

Aurora desperately tried to make sense of what he was saying. 'Three weeks ago, you say?'

'Yes – just after Andrew was born. Or maybe it was four weeks? Ella will know. She counts that sort of thing.' He grinned. 'I'm useless.'

'Was it the weekend of Bertie's party?'

'You know, as you mention it . . .'

Aurora stood and thrust the baby into his arms. Then she was gone.

She ran outside and took deep gulps of air. The rose garden

was empty and had become overgrown and wild. Pushing open the small gate, she went straight to the bush where Henry had picked her mother's rose each year. The perfumed smell hit her immediately and she almost gagged.

That man. The man she met at the party. He had called to Henry. It had to be the same person. He was friend of Bertie's – a writer, he said. He had avoided telling her his name. Looking back on it, he had known things: about Grace and the past. Oh, how did she miss it? She struggled to remember his face. He had dark skin and brown eyes.

Brown eyes.

*Eyes identical to her own.*

'No, no, it can't be,' she said out loud. 'Please, no.'

'Borealis?' James appeared around the corner. 'Are you all right?'

She put her head in her hands.

'What is it?' He was beside her in a flash. 'Is the mingling too much for you? I can take you back to Maggie's if you'd like.'

'Oh, James, I'm so confused.' She burst into tears.

'Come here,' he said, hugging her tightly. 'Let it all out. Today was always going to be hard.' He held her as she sobbed, rubbing her back soothingly.

'I just can't believe how irrevocably my life has changed in a few days. Everything was going brilliantly. I got that part I wanted and my career is on the up.' She pulled back slightly. 'I didn't get a chance to tell Daddy. I didn't get a chance to tell him about *Scarlett*.'

'I'm sure he knows,' said James. 'He's somewhere right now toasting your success.'

'And now I have that other business to deal with . . .'

'All in good time.'

'I need a drink,' she said suddenly. 'A large one.'

'Of course. Let's go back inside.' He took her hand. 'Gordon has some Rare Midleton if you fancy that. He was saving it for his own funeral but then realised he wouldn't get to taste it.'

She half-smiled. 'I hate whiskey.'

'Wine then.' He smiled. 'Come on, before Laura cleans us out.'

Claire stood awkwardly in the corner, nursing a glass of red wine and checking her phone.

Laura sidled over and smiled. 'How are you?' she asked. 'Long time no see.'

Claire shrugged. 'Things could be better, Laura, but that's how it goes, I suppose.'

'Oh?'

'James and I . . . well, we've been having some problems.' She looked uncomfortable for a moment. 'I'm not sure if we can work them out.'

Laura stared at her. 'Really? What's up?'

Claire stared at the ground. 'He's refusing to commit properly. We fight about the house and then there was your wedding . . .'

'My wedding?'

Claire nodded. 'That was the climax really. I caught him kissing Aurora on the beach. Then, instead of falling on his knees and begging for my forgiveness, he took off to St. Tropez and spent nearly four hundred quid on a taxi.'

Laura did a double take. 'You caught him doing what? Are you quite sure? James and Aurora?'

'I know. Sounds crazy, doesn't it?' She slammed her glass down on the table bitterly. 'Then again, it was obvious from the start. He's in love with her – he has been for years.'

Laura shook her head. 'That can't be true,' she said uneasily, remembering a sleeping James draped over Aurora in bed the morning after Henry died. 'He's her brother.'

'Is he? Really?' The small girl snorted. 'What he feels for her is far from brotherly love, Laura. I'm just kicking myself that I didn't see it. Oh, it was Borealis this and Borealis that. Then, she'd call and he'd drop everything and run. He spoils her and puts her first. It came to a head out in France and he's been so distant since.'

'I'm finding this hard to believe . . .'

'Look!' Claire pointed to the doorway.

James had just appeared with a tear-stained Aurora trailing behind. He had her hand firmly in his and they went straight to the drinks trolley. He filled a glass of white wine and rubbed her cheek. Laura watched him. He had the same expression on his face that last night in her room. It had bothered her then but she had forgotten it due to the stress and grief. Now, she could see exactly what Claire was talking about. In fact, it was like she had always known.

'So, I came today to show my respect for Henry. He was such a lovely man.' Claire straightened her dress and picked up her bag. 'James promised me that he'd take me back to London. I guess we'll have *that* conversation when we get home.'

Laura shook her hand. 'Thank you for coming. I'm truly gobsmacked.'

'So am I, Laura. So am I.'

Aurora gulped back three glasses of Chablis and immediately felt better. The alcohol had a dulling effect – it numbed her senses and made her forget. She drained her glass and held it out for more.

James held his hands. '*Whoa*, *whoa*, Borealis. You'll be on the floor soon. How about some water?'

'No. I want more wine, please.' She faced him defiantly. 'A large glass again and stop babying me.'

He nodded. 'Of course. Coming right up.'

Laura stared at them from across the room.

William ambled up beside her and nudged her playfully. 'You

look all serious, Lolly. Is it the dwindling white-wine supply? I have to admit, it's decreasing at an alarming rate.'

'Look over there,' she said, nodding towards James handing a full glass of wine to Aurora. 'What do you think of those two?'

William gave her a strange look. 'I suppose I like them, as they're family and all.'

'No, I mean, have you ever noticed anything strange between them? I just had an eye-opening chat with Claire. She thinks they're in love.'

'Oh.' William didn't look remotely surprised. 'Maybe she's right.'

'Will?' Laura whipped her head around. 'You're not shocked?'

He shook his head. 'Not particularly. They've always had this thing – surely you noticed it. He adored her, ever since the beginning.' He shrugged. 'I thought everyone knew.'

'Everyone knew what?'

'Look, think about it. He always made it home for her birthday: always. Through gales and earthquakes and freezing conditions. I don't remember him being around faithfully to help you to blow out your candles, Lolly.' He popped a blini in his mouth. 'Then there's the way he always puts her first. I can't say I'm surprised. Crikey, Claire must be in a state.'

'Oh, they're on the rocks. He's taking her back to London in a while so she thinks that will be it. They'll have *that* conversation.'

'Thank God we decided to stay at the pub with Gloria,' said William in relief. 'The journey down was pretty tense. They didn't speak at all.'

'Oh, Chris and I booked in there too.' Laura smiled. 'Let's get out of here soon and avail of the residents' bar.'

Freddie Thompson arrived with Maggie and shook George's hand. 'Sorry for your troubles,' he said, nodding formally. 'Mr. 'Enry was a gentleman, 'ee was.'

'Why, thank you, Frederick.' George smiled tightly. 'I agree – my father was a wonderful man.' He turned away immediately and resumed his conversation with the local magistrate.

James appeared and hugged Maggie. 'Well, hello,' he said, kissing her cheek. 'Any pies for me today?'

'Not today,' she said, beaming. 'You look the same, you do.'

'Hello, Freddie,' said James, shaking his hand warmly. 'You probably don't remember me?'

'Oh, I rightly do, Master James. Sorry for your loss.'

'The little 'un is takin' it badly,' said Maggie. 'She stayed with me last night and all I 'eard was sobbin' from 'er room.'

'She loved Mr. 'Enry,' agreed Freddie. 'It's only natural.'

James face was troubled as he looked at Aurora. She looked lost on her own, drinking wine and struggling not to cry. He wished he hadn't offered to drive Claire now. All he wanted to do was stay by her side. She needed him – she needed stability. Judging by the cold reception from her brothers, she'd need all the allies she could get.

Suddenly Claire appeared and pulled James' sleeve. 'Sorry to be rude, but we need to make a move. I've an early shift in the morning.'

'You want to leave now?' He looked dismayed. 'Really, Claire?'

'Yes, really.' She checked her watch. 'We've been here for hours.'

James knew it was futile to argue. 'Oh, okay. I'll meet you at the main door.'

She walked away, waving at Laura and William as she passed.

''Oo's that?' asked Maggie curiously.

James said nothing for a moment. 'A friend,' he said eventually. 'Look, I must go. Wonderful to see you, even if it was brief. Look after Aurora. I think she's had far too much wine.'

Freddie nodded. 'I'll take care of 'er, Master James. Poor girl

.s mighty upset, she is.'

'Yes, yes, she is.' He blew Maggie a kiss. 'I'll call to see you soon. I'd forgotten how beautiful it was down here.'

'Drive safely, Master James,' she said.

He walked over to Aurora who was standing alone by a large plant. 'I've got to go,' he said gently. 'I promised Claire that I'd take her back to London.'

Her fuddled brain struggled to process what he was saying. So, him and Claire were still together? Of course they were. His presence all day was just the usual brotherly duty – James was being James. The kind rock who always looked out for her.

'Take it easy on the wine, Borealis. You're not used to it.'

She barely registered what he was saying. 'Claire is waiting,' she said vaguely. 'You need to go.'

His expression darkened for a moment but then regained its cheerful expression. Leaning in, he kissed her cheek lightly. 'I'll see you back at home.'

She nodded. 'Sure.'

'James?' called Claire from the door. 'Come on!'

Sebastian stood up and clinked his glass. 'Thank you all for coming here today,' he said in his plummy accent. 'Daddy would have been delighted to see so many faces he knew and loved.'

Aurora threw back her wine and stared broodily at the ground.

'It was wonderful to see him reunited with our mother, Marcella, today.' He beckoned at George to join him. 'She was his one true love and I'm sure he's at peace now, lying by her side.'

Gloria's face reddened and she shrank backwards. The boys had barely spoken to her all day. In fact, they had kept her out of everything. If it wasn't for Gordon, she would have been clueless. She prayed that they would mention her – just once.

Being on their turf, she felt like an outsider. Certainly not the grieving wife.

'This sad day reminds us of Mummy's funeral. We had the reception in the very same room. It seemed fitting to have Daddy's here as well.'

William patted Baby Andrew's back, his face darkening. Surely they would mention Gloria or even Aurora for that matter.

'So, if you'll all raise your glasses,' continued Sebastian. 'To Henry!'

'*To Henry!*' chorused the bemused crowd.

Aurora slammed her glass down. '*Might I have your attention?*' she said in her clear voice.

Everyone turned around and she stood up straight.

'My mother, Grace, was Henry's second wife. Many of you knew her during her brief time here in Cornwall. I think it's only right that she gets a mention.'

'*Hear! Hear!*' said Gordon.

'Also, Daddy's widow Gloria. My lovely stepmother.' She gestured to where Gloria was sitting. 'A truly beautiful person who welcomed me as one of her own. I think it's important that we acknowledge her loss today. Indeed, all our loss.'

Sebastian glared at her but George said nothing. He just sipped his whiskey with an impassive face.

'You see, Henry Sinclair was not just a fine playwright and loving father, he was also the kindest man I've ever known.' Tears began to roll down her cheeks. 'He loved us all so much and did everything he could for us.'

'Thank you, Aurora,' said Sebastian, giving her a pointed look. 'That's quite enough.'

She ignored him. 'You see, he was so generous and kind that he even took in a child that wasn't his.'

She looked around at all their bemused faces.

'You see, Henry wasn't my father. My mother was pregnant

when he married her.'

There were horrified mumblings amongst the guests.

Sebastian made a move to grab Aurora, but George held him back. 'Let her finish,' he said silkily.

'He told me before he died: how he raised me as his own and protected me from further heartbreak.' She was crying openly now. 'I loved him. He was the best father anyone could ask for.'

'Except he wasn't your father,' said Sebastian nastily. 'What a revelation.'

She turned on him. 'I can see exactly what's going through your narrow little mind. How this affects your inheritance. That's all you think about, isn't it, Seb? Because your life is so pathetic, it's all you have.'

'Well, it certainly changes things,' he said. 'If you're the illegitimate brat of that Irish whore you have no claim to his estate. I think that has made my day.'

There were gasps from the crowd. Laura looked at William in alarm. Aurora was clearly drunk and needed to be stopped.

Gloria got up and grabbed her arm. 'This is an entirely inappropriate conversation,' she said in her ear. 'Come on, my love. Let's go.'

Aurora ignored her and faced her brothers head on. 'Don't fret. I don't want a penny from you. You two can have the lot.'

George remained silent but she could see his eyes gleam.

'All I want is my mother's portrait.' She pointed to the painting of Grace on the wall.

Sebastian laughed. 'We'll see about that, my dear. We need to get it valued. If it's worth money, than you can buy it at auction.'

'*No!* I want that picture. That's my mother.'

'And of course, there are all those first editions he gave you over the years,' he continued. 'We'll have them back too.'

'Never,' she said softly. 'You'll never get your hands on them.'

George interjected. 'Let's discuss this later,' he said smoothly.

'Our guests are not interested in this petty squabble.' He smiled at the horrified occupants of the room. 'Make sure your glasses are full. It has been an emotional day.'

Sebastian grinned at Aurora. 'I always knew you were an imposter. This has made my day. We can finally cut ties with your gypsy tramp of a mother and regain some respectability.'

Aurora raised her arm and slapped him hard across the cheek. The sound resonated through the room. Then she raised her other arm to slap the other side, but he was too quick for her. His strong arm grabbed her wrist. 'I wouldn't do that if I were you,' he said menacingly, twisting her arm.

'*Ow!* You're hurting me!' she said, squirming.

'You're lucky I don't break your neck.'

'Seb!' George pulled him away. 'Let her go.' He stared contemptuously at Aurora. 'I'd like you to leave, Aurora. Get out of our house.'

'Gladly,' she answered bitterly, 'but I want that painting.'

Sebastian snorted. 'Not a chance.'

'Oh, I'll have it,' she said, her eyes glittering. 'I'm pretty sure Henry's will is quite favourable on my part. He must have taken measures to ensure that I got my fair share. If you don't give me that picture of my mother, I'll take you to court and fight you to the end.'

'You wouldn't dare,' scoffed Sebastian.

'The portrait.' She stood her ground.

'Fine,' said George, ignoring protests from his younger brother. 'We'll have it sent up to London. Will that be all?'

'No, that's not all.' She raised herself up to her full height. 'I think you're the most despicable human beings I've ever encountered. I hope we never meet again.'

Turning on her heel, she stalked off.

Freddie was waiting for her at the door. 'You're coming with us, Sinclair,' he said, taking her arm. 'Maggie is waiting.'

'*Aurora!*' called a tear-stained Gloria. 'My darling, we need to talk.'

'Not now,' said Freddie. 'She needs to rest, Mrs. Sinclair. I'll get her to ring you in the morning.'

# Chapter Forty-seven

Maggie sipped her tea. 'So, Mr. 'Enry told you that, did 'ee?'

Aurora nodded miserably. 'Just before he died. He didn't mention a name. He never told me who my father was.'

Freddie held her hand in his. His palms felt rough to touch. 'It won't be too 'ard to find out, Sinclair. Not in this day and age.'

'I think I have an inkling.' She blew her nose. 'Did Mummy ever mention a director? An Irishman?'

Maggie got to her feet. 'I think it's time you saw this,' she mumbled, disappearing into the back room.

Freddie glanced at Aurora. She shrugged.

Maggie reappeared with a notebook. She blew some dust off its cover and placed it on the table. 'This was your mother's,' she said quietly. 'Mr. 'Enry told me to destroy it after she died, but I kept it. I thought you might like it someday.'

Aurora traced its edge with her finger.

'It's a diary of sorts,' said Maggie. 'She wrote about different things when it took her fancy.'

'A diary?' Aurora sat up straight. 'From when?'

'From just before she died.' The old lady gave her a compassionate look. 'It might be difficult for you to read but I think it's important.'

'These are my mother's words and thoughts?' said Aurora in disbelief. 'She wrote about her life here?'

'This was long before computers and social media, little 'un,' answered Maggie. 'It kept 'er occupied, I expect.'

Aurora got to her feet. 'I think I'll look at this in my room, if you don't mind.'

'You do that.' Maggie's wise old face betrayed nothing. 'I'm out 'ere if you need me.'

Aurora closed the door of the little bedroom and sat on the edge of the bed. Opening the book, she read:

*Friday 16$^{th}$ October 1992*

*So lonely down here. The weather is incessantly bad and it prevents me from going outside. I miss my walks by the shoreline. Henry says the winters here are grim. I'm not surprised.*

*The baby keeps moving around. It feels so strange! Sometimes a hand or a leg can jut out and take me by surprise. The women in the village are convinced it's a girl. They say when you're very sick in the beginning and the bump is high, that it's definite. That would be lovely – a little princess for me to love.*

*Oh, come out, little one! I yearn to meet you and hold you and kiss your soft skin. It feels like I've been waiting for years to meet you. Not too long now. Maybe then the heartbreak will ease. Maybe then I'll forget.*

Aurora flicked forward a few pages. She scanned the contents which consisted of updates on the progress of the pregnancy, notes on a book she was reading and stories about the villagers. Then she stopped.

*Tuesday 15$^{th}$ December 1992*

*I can't believe it! It's as if my dreams have been realised. S appeared as promised. We walked on the beach and he's serious about our plan. He looks just the same. I was so shocked I could barely talk.*

*He'll write with all the details. I know it seems so disloyal to Henry – good, kind Henry – but I can't live without S. My life made sense again today, for the first time in months. He explained why. He made me understand. My heart feels light. Everything is falling into place.*

Aurora flicked on.

*Thursday 24th December 1992*

*Henry is thinking of staying at home on New Year's Eve. He feels it's too close to the baby to go away. May God forgive me but I convinced him otherwise. He cannot be here. When S comes, it would be easier if he wasn't here. My heart breaks at the thought of hurting him. I wish there was another way.*

Then an envelope fell out. It was addressed to Grace. With a beating heart, Aurora opened it, pulling out a neatly folded piece of paper. It read:

*My love,*

*It's all arranged. I will be there on the 31st and we'll leave right away. Then we'll be settled in London by the time the baby arrives.*

*Don't fret. I know this feels wrong, but it's so right.*

*We're meant to be together, Grace. If your predictions are correct and it is a girl, I think we should name her Aurora. She will be a symbol of our new beginning – our new life. The goddess of the dawn.*

*Keep walking 'in beauty like the night, of cloudless climes and starry skies' . . .*

*Love forever,*

*S*

Peering inside the envelope, Aurora noticed a splash of colour. Tipping it upside down, a dried flower fell out and floated onto the bed: a fuchsia.

She closed the notebook, unable to read any more. It was like someone had assaulted her brain. It throbbed with information overload and she struggled to make sense of it all. Her mother had planned to leave Henry, just before her birth. She had planned to take off and start a new life. One side of her was angry – how could Grace have broken Henry's heart like that? What kind of person would do something that cruel? Then another side of her understood – love was complicated and required courage. Her mother was miserable without this S person who was clearly her real father. So why had she left him in the first place?

Maggie appeared in the doorway. 'Are you all right, little 'un? I 'ave a pot of tea waitin'.'

'What was his name?' she asked bleakly, her head hanging. 'What was my father's name?'

There was a pause. She could hear the waves crashing on the shore and the raucous call of the gulls.

'Silas,' said the old lady quietly. 'Silas Walsh.'

Maggie wisely left her alone for a while to gather her thoughts. The first thing she did was google his name. Links to his books and plays appeared instantly. She clicked on Google Images and the face of the man she had met at Bertie's stared back at her. Wiping a tear from her eye, she typed in Silas Walsh and Grace Molloy. Reviews of *Salomé* appeared along with *My Fair Lady*. '*She's my muse*,' was a quote from one. '*Grace is simply the greatest actress the world has ever seen.*'

Then she saw photos. He had longer hair and she looked young and happy. There was one of them outside the Abbey Theatre. He had his arm slung around her shoulders and she was beaming into the camera. There was another of them on stage where he was holding her shoulders and talking intently. She was gazing up at him, listening to every word he said. They looked as if they belonged together.

She flung the phone on the bed, her mind reeling. Why had Silas rejected her? If he knew she was his daughter, why then did he leave her behind? Or had Grace left him? Hot tears stung her lids once more. She didn't know how to feel.

She went back to the kitchen. Two cups of tea later and her head still felt muddled. The old lady opposite her had known all along yet she had kept it from her. Maggie, her surrogate mother, had been privy to all of this for years. She felt confused and betrayed, resentful and hurt. It was like everything she had ever known had disappeared and now she was rootless and wandering, unsure of whom she was.

'Have you met him?'

'I 'ave, my lovely. A few times over the years.'

'Where is he now?'

''Ee lives in southern Ireland.'

'Are you in contact?'

'Not any more.'

'But you were.'

Maggie nodded. 'I sent him pictures and things over the years. He made a promise to Mr. 'Enry, you see. To leave you be. Maybe it was wrong, but I felt sorry for 'im. 'Ee pleaded with me to keep 'im informed. 'Ee so desperately wanted to know about you.'

'What happened, Maggie? Why didn't they run off together?'

Her face grew sad. 'There was a storm that time – a terrible storm. It lasted a few days and he couldn't travel. The boat wouldn't run, you see. Then Mr. 'Enry was in London and your mother got pains. The rest you know, my darlin'. I won't bring all that back up.'

'So Mummy died and I survived.' Her tone was bitter. 'Why then didn't he come for me?'

'You need to ask 'im yourself. It's not my place, little 'un.'

'But why didn't he and my mother stay together in the first place, Maggie? If they loved each other so much?'

'You need to go to 'im and ask 'im about all of that, little 'un.'

'To Ireland?'

Maggie nodded. 'I 'ave 'is address.'

'So you won't tell me any more?'

'I don't rightly know much more,' she admitted. 'All I do know is that 'ee 'ad an arrangement with Mr. 'Enry. It was to protect you. You 'ave to give 'im a chance to explain.'

Aurora put her head in her hands and moaned slightly. 'I can't believe this is happening. I just can't.'

'All will be well, my darlin'. Trust in God. It doesn't change 'oo you are. You will always be Aurora Sinclair. Don't forget that.'

'Walk on the beach, Sinclair?' asked Freddie the next morning. 'I just fed the animals so I 'ave some time.'

Her eyes were red-rimmed from crying and her hair was unkempt. Maggie had asked Freddie's mother for a loan of some clothes and she had dropped over some black leggings, a large sweatshirt with Snoopy on the front and thick woolly socks. 'They belonged to Susie years ago,' she explained. 'And 'ere are some boots.'

'Okay,' she said with a sigh.

Anything was better than moping around the house. Gloria had called, telling her to be ready to leave by five. She had some business to attend to in the village first and would pick her up later.

The wind was as cold as ever as they trudged through the thick waterlogged sand. The waves crashed on the shoreline and the spray wet her face.

'Bet you miss this,' he said, linking arms with her. 'There's no place in the world like this.'

'You're right,' she said wistfully. 'Remember all the days we spent down here? Telling stories and finding treasure.'

'Yep,' he answered, smiling. 'You believed all those porkies I told you about pirates and smuggling.'

'Porkies?' She nudged him playfully. 'I truly believed that there were ducats of gold in that cave.'

'You were always dramatic.'

They stopped by the rock pool. She sat down on a rock and stretched out her legs.

'Are you happy, Freddie?' she asked.

He nodded. 'I am, Sinclair. I love my farm and my family – I don't want much more.'

'Have you ever been in love?'

He chuckled. 'Oh, I thought I was in love with you. You broke my 'eart when you left.'

'Me?' She gave him an incredulous look. 'Really?'

'Of course. We were only kids but you were so beautiful.'

Her face softened. 'You were my best friend, you know. Back when I was so lonely.'

He took her hand. 'I'm always 'ere for you, you know that.'

'You're not still in love?'

'No!' He laughed loudly. 'I got over you, I did. Now I'm sweet on Corey Jones' youngest – Gwen. She's the girl I want to marry.'

'Oh, Fred, that's wonderful.' She hugged him tightly. 'I'm so happy for you.'

He blushed. 'She loves pigs, she does, so that's a bonus. We've been together on and off a few years.' His freckled face was crunched up against the wind. 'You must sing at our wedding, if I ever get the courage to ask.'

'Of course I will.' She snuggled up closely to him. 'Anything you want.'

'What about you, Sinclair? Any love story?'

Her heart constricted. 'Not really. He's taken, I'm afraid. I'll just have to find someone new.'

'It's not that director from that play I saw you in a few months back?'

'God, no. Not him.' She reddened slightly. 'In fact, it's James.'

She expected Freddie to be shocked but instead he chuckled softly. 'That's no surprise at all.'

'What?'

'It's as obvious as day.' He pulled his coat tightly around him. 'I wouldn't give up 'ope yet either. I see the way 'ee looks at you. Sometimes people get 'urt, Sinclair, where love is concerned. It's not nice but it 'as to 'appen sometimes.'

'Oh, it's been a long-drawn-out disaster. He's engaged to another girl and sees me as his baby sister.'

'Are you sure about that?'

'Pretty sure.' She trailed her finger in the water of the rock pool. 'Things have been so crazy lately, I haven't had time to think about him.'

'That's only natural, Sinclair. I don't think you 'ave room for any more drama right now.'

'You're so right.' She smiled. 'My priorities have changed a tad.'

'It will all work out, my lovely. Just take one day at a time.'

# Chapter Forty-eight

James' Golf pulled up outside Maggie's house. He knocked on the door loudly and eventually she appeared. 'Master James!' she exclaimed in delight. 'You're back!'

'Laura rang me this morning. She told me about Aurora's revelation last night. Where is she?' He ran his fingers through his hair. 'I drove down as quickly as I could. Did those vile brothers of hers upset her, Maggie? I should never have left.'

'She went to the beach with Fred,' said the old lady. 'Would you like a cup of tea?'

'No, not now.' He turned and headed down the lane. 'Thank you though,' he added over his shoulder, blowing a kiss.

He ran towards the cliffs. It was still as overgrown and wild as ever, with large mounds of grass and sand.

On the way he met Freddie who raised an eyebrow. 'You're back, Master James? Already?'

James nodded breathlessly. 'Where's Aurora?'

'She's below still,' he answered. 'Down by the shore.'

'Thanks.' He headed away.

Freddie smiled to himself. Find someone else indeed. It was as plain as the nose on his face. This engagement she spoke of was a farce – Master James was mad about her. Anyone with two eyes could see that.

James' shoes sank deep into the damp sand. Soon, the bottoms of his jeans were saturated. Aurora was standing on the shore. She had her back to him and her long hair was blowing in the wind. For a moment, he was transported back to when she was a child, standing in a similar position.

'*Borealis!*' he called.

She didn't hear so he quickened his pace.

'*Aurora!*'

She turned around this time and her face lit up. 'James?' she said incredulously. 'You're back?'

He reached her and pulled her into his arms. 'Laura rang me and told me what happened. Are you all right? I drove here as fast as I could.'

She could feel his beating heart.

'I'm fine. I got a bit drunk and made a fool of myself, but it feels oddly liberating. I don't have to deal with my brothers any more.'

'I'm sorry I left. I should never have left you behind.'

She buried her face in his jacket, feeling a sense of calmness wash over her. 'I'm all right now,' she murmured. 'I'm so glad you're here.'

She idly wondered about Claire and if she knew that he had turned around and driven back down. It was on the tip of her tongue to ask, but then she didn't. She had no room for any more emotional trauma – he was here and that was all that mattered.

'Let's go somewhere and talk.' He wrapped his arm around her shoulders and they walked back towards the marram grass.

'James?'

'Hmmm?'

'Will you come with me to Ireland?'

He stopped short. 'Ireland? Whatever for?'

'I'll explain on the way,' she answered, 'but we need to go now.'

'Is this to do with your father?'

She nodded. 'I have to go. I have to meet him and find out the truth.' Her eyes filled with tears. 'I just don't want to go alone. I understand if it's hassle with Claire and all . . .'

'It's perfectly fine,' he said, cutting her off. 'Claire and I, well, we're not together any more.'

'You're not?' She felt her heart soar.

He shook his head. 'It's been bad for a while.'

'Oh?'

'For a long time, in fact. We just couldn't admit it.' His eyes burned. 'So, I'm all yours.'

She felt her stomach jump. 'So you'll come with me?'

'What do you think?'

Maggie wrote out Silas Walsh's address on a piece of paper. He lived on an island off the south coast called Cape Clear. It was a haven for writers and artists apparently, a quiet untouched place of great beauty. He had moved there permanently five years before. Aurora had googled it and it indeed looked amazing. She scrolled down and saw that you could get a ferry from a place called Baltimore and it was just under an hour from there. Baltimore? That sounded familiar. Then she remembered Lydia saying her family home was there.

They touched down in Cork at five the next day. Laura, on hearing of their plans, had given Colin a ring and asked if he would put them up for a night. Lydia and Luca had taken Sienna to New York, so their apartment was locked up.

'Oh, it's like a posh hotel,' said Laura. 'Just keep it clean – he's a neat freak.'

If she thought it was strange that James was accompanying her, she didn't say. Aurora didn't care what she thought – all that mattered was that he was with her, carrying her bags and holding her hand.

Colin even drove out to the airport to pick them up. Laura had given him the bare details of Aurora's story and he was fascinated. 'It's like an episode of *Dallas* or something,' he mused. 'Affairs, lost love, different fathers. I'm all over it.'

His apartment was indeed as lovely as Laura had said. A white couch stood in the middle of the room and expensive art hung on the walls. The kitchen gleamed and there wasn't a hair out of place.

Colin gestured down the hall. 'So, I have one bedroom so you can fight over it.' He blushed. 'Unless you both want to . . .'

James shook his head. 'Not at all. I'll take the couch.'

Aurora felt a pang of disappointment but she brushed it away. He was right, of course. In the public's eyes they were still brother and sister. It would look very odd if they bunked in together at their age. She still couldn't gauge his feelings. He acted like a perfect gentleman, making sure that she was looked after. Her muddled brain couldn't even contemplate anything else and it was as if he knew it.

Colin cooked a fabulous dinner of bouillabaisse washed down with Pouilly Fuissé and, for dessert, a delectable *crêpe soufflé* with a caramel sauce. 'Well, I love to cook,' he said modestly when James had seconds of everything. 'It gives me great pleasure to see others enjoy my food.'

Val had thrown his eyes to heaven at that point. 'We normally have Dolmio days,' he whispered.

'We do *not!*' shrieked Colin indignantly.

At two in the morning, Aurora woke. Despite the soft sheets and comfortable mattress, she felt ill at ease and jumpy. Opening her bedroom door quietly, she padded down to the sitting room.

'James?' she whispered.

'Yeah?' he answered immediately.

She breathed a sigh of relief. He couldn't sleep either. His head was propped up on a pillow and his chest was bare.

'You okay?' he asked as she sat on the edge of the couch.

'I can't sleep.'

'Me too. This sofa is as hard as a rock.'

She bounced up and down. 'Blimey, you're right. It's awful.' She bit her lip. 'Do you want to sleep with me? The bed is huge and . . .'

'Are you propositioning me?' he asked in mock horror. 'Borealis!'

'No, no.' She blushed furiously. 'I just mean that it's a waste and we need our sleep and . . .' Her eyes grew sad. 'I can't think of anything but Silas Walsh at the moment. I'm so nervous.'

'I know what you mean.' He smiled. 'I like the left side if that's okay.'

'That's okay,' she answered.

Minutes later, they were lying on the soft mattress with the heavy duvet on top.

'You definitely got the better deal,' said James. 'This is bliss.'

'I felt sorry for you out there . . .'

'Oh, you did.' He pulled her body close so that they were spooning. 'Is it okay to hold you like this?' he whispered into her ear.

Aurora closed her eyes. It felt amazing. All she wanted was his presence. She couldn't handle anything else. Just to know he was there.

'Yes.'

'Sleep well, Borealis,' he whispered, kissing her head.

Colin eyed them suspiciously when they emerged the next morning. Val had already left so he was sitting at the table on his own.

'Was the couch uncomfortable?' he asked innocently.

James poured himself a cup of coffee. 'We got talking and I must have fallen asleep. I woke up in my clothes.'

'I don't remember dropping off,' added Aurora. 'You came to say goodnight, wasn't it, James? Then the next thing we knew it was morning.' She avoided eye contact and sat down.

'Oh, I see,' said Colin who looked like he didn't see at all. Stirring his coffee, he changed the subject. 'I'm heading down to see Auntie Helen later so I'll give you a lift.'

'We can get a bus, Colin,' said James. 'You've been far too generous already.'

'Not at all. I've been meaning to visit for weeks. I loaned her my fondue set months ago and I need it back.' He took a big bite of granola. 'Plus the ferry leaves from where she lives. Her house is five minutes from the pier.'

'If you're sure?'

'Oh, I'm sure.' He smiled. 'I think I might have some news.'

'Oh?' Aurora buttered some toast.

'Have you ever heard of a barm brack?'

'A what?' said James.

'It's a fruit loaf we eat here at Halloween. It's no ordinary bread though. It has items baked inside it: items that decide your destiny.'

'Such as?' asked Aurora.

'A pea for poverty so no one wants that. A stick means you'll beat your spouse and a bean means that you'll be rich.' His eyes glowed. 'The most coveted slice contains the *fáinne:* a small gold ring. If you get it, it means that you'll be married within the year.'

James laughed. 'Are you still obsessed with that?'

Colin ignored him. 'So this year, I bought a loaf and decide to have a slice with butter. I grabbed the bread knife and was about to slice the crust off when I got a rare moment of wild impulsiveness and I slashed through the middle.' He fanned his face. 'Crumbs flew everywhere which totally freaked me out so I went to get my mini-hoover. Then I noticed something on the table: the *fáinne!*'

Aurora gasped. 'You got the ring!'

'It wanted me to find it. It led me to it. Like Arthur and the Sword of Truth!' He held up his hand to show them a small gold ring on his pinkie. 'It's not the most expensive ring in the world,' he admitted, 'and it leaves a horrible green stain. However, its symbolism is everything.'

'Did Val get the message?' asked Aurora.

'I think so! He said he has to start saving as he knows I'd be super-picky about a ring.' Colin glowed with pleasure. 'And he'd be right.'

Colin dropped them at the pier in Baltimore.

'Are you sure you won't come up to Auntie Hel's for a cup of tea?' he said, yanking their bags out of the small boot of his Audi TT. 'She lives just up the road.'

Aurora shook her head. 'No, thanks, Colin. I'm anxious to get out there.'

'I understand,' he said his brown curls blowing in the wind. 'Good luck with finding your daddy.'

According to the timetable, the ferry was due to leave at two. James had booked a guest house for them both which was just near the harbour and reasonably priced.

She could feel her stomach do flip-flops over and over. Cape Clear Island didn't look very big therefore it should be easy to track down this Silas. She zipped up her coat and they took their place in the queue which was forming. A man with a peaked cap helped her on board and James lifted the bags on. Soon they were out at sea, the boat moving up and down on the large waves.

The scenery was magnificent. She could see the green hills of Sherkin Island with dark caves underneath and the white waves crashing on the shoreline. Ahead was open water: a vast expanse of murky blue that stretched as far as the eye could see. An old lady sat on an upended fish crate, her white hair covered with a green scarf. Her lined face looked weather-beaten and wise and she reminded Aurora of Maggie. A young woman sat on another crate with a small boy on her lap and bags of shopping at her feet. No one batted an eye when the swell increased and the boat rocked from side to side.

James pulled his beanie hat over his ears and rubbed his hands together in an effort to keep warm. She, however, didn't feel the slightest chill. Breathing in the salty air, she felt invigorated and alive. She could face this. One conversation and it would all be over.

Just under an hour later, the ferry docked at North Harbour. The man with the peaked cap threw a big thick rope onto the pier where another man fastened it in place. The crowd disembarked quickly until only James and Aurora were left.

With a heavy heart, she stepped onto the pier and looked around. There was a shop and a café nestled at the bottom of a steep hill.

'Let's go to the shop and ask for directions,' suggested James.

Aurora nodded. 'I feel sick,' she said, clutching his hand. 'It's just like the time I was waiting for my A-level results.'

When they reached the shop, a small red-haired man greeted them in Gaelic. Aurora waved, unsure of what to say.

'Oh, you don't speak Irish,' he said smiling. 'That's no problem at all.'

'I was wondering if you could help me,' said Aurora in her clear voice. 'I'm looking for a man called Silas Walsh. He's a writer.'

'Sure, I know Silas. He lives up on the hill.' He pointed upwards. 'Go halfway up and take a sharp left. Then continue on for about ten minutes and his cottage is the small one on the left.'

'Has it any defining feature?' asked James. 'A specific colour or shape?'

The man scratched his beard. 'It's a greyish colour with a large potted plant outside the door. Oh, and a big fuchsia bush. You'll see that all right.'

Aurora smiled. 'Thank you.'

They walked out into the winter sunshine. The hill was almost at a right angle to the pier and after about two minutes they were breathless.

'One would be very fit living here,' she said, stopping for breath.

'Smoking would be a definite no-no,' agreed James.

They turned left as instructed and the gradient eased slightly. The small lane way was overgrown and wild. Orange and blue wildflowers dominated the hedgerows and there was no sound except for the seagulls flying overhead.

'It's beautiful here,' she said wistfully. 'Look at the view.'

They gazed out at the blue sea glistening the fading light. The mainland was visible in the distance, dominated by mountains. On and on they walked until they reached a group of small houses. One was a two-storey with white walls and Velux windows. Then there was a stone cottage with vibrant window boxes full of flowers. Finally, on the left was a grey house with a large bush outside it. The red-and-purple flowers danced in the breeze.

'This is it,' she said. 'This is the one.'

James dropped the bags and faced her. 'Do you want me to wait out here?'

She nodded. 'I think that would be best. I need to face him alone.'

He leaned over and kissed her lips gently. 'Best of luck.'

Her eyes widened for a moment. 'Thank you,' she said with a warm glow inside.

She knocked on the door loudly – three loud raps. No one answered so she knocked again.

James leaned against a wall and watched. 'Maybe he's gone out?' he suggested.

Disappointment flooded her body. She had geared up to face him and now she felt deflated. Knocking one last time, she rested her head against the door.

*Please answer . . . please.*

Suddenly, the door creaked and opened slowly. She fell backwards in surprise and held her breath. There, wearing a black woollen jumper, stood Silas Walsh. He looked the same as that time at Bertie's party: tall, sallow-skinned and with slightly greying hair. A brief look of shock flashed over his face, but he regained his composure almost immediately.

'Aurora,' he stated.

'May I come in?' She held her head up high.

He nodded and opened the door wide. 'Please.'

The cottage was small and modest. A wooden table with four chairs stood in the middle of the flagstones and a small stove was burning in the corner. The shelves were filled with books and papers were strewn all over the floor and on a small couch.

'Have a seat,' he said, clearing a place on the couch. 'Sorry about the mess, I wasn't expecting anyone.'

'It's quite all right.' She sat down stiffly. 'I'm sorry for arriving unannounced.'

He regarded her thoughtfully. 'Henry told you before he died, didn't he? He promised he would.'

She nodded. 'On his deathbed, in fact. It was quite a shock.'

'I'm sorry about that.' His face tightened. 'We should have told you years ago.'

'Why didn't you?' she asked directly, the hurt evident in her voice.

He looked out the window, his broad back inhibiting the

light. For a moment he said nothing, he just stood there deep in contemplation.

'Time passed by,' he said in his deep voice. 'The initial fervour faded.' He sighed. 'By the time you were grown, I felt it was too late.'

'So what changed? Why did Henry reveal the truth?' Her chest heaved with emotion.

'I felt the time had come. You had grown up and I wanted to know you.'

'You wanted? *You* wanted?' Her eyes flashed. 'What about me? What about my needs and my feelings?'

'I'm sorry.'

'What happened, Silas? Why did you and Mummy lead separate lives?'

He took a seat at the table. 'When I met Grace, my life was very different. I was married to a woman called Jessica. I met her at Trinity in Dublin and we got engaged in our final year. Her father played golf with my father and it was a suitable match. Our wedding was a merging of two great Dublin families and all was how it should be.' His face tightened. 'Then Jess lost our first baby and then the second. She grew depressed and distant. I knew she was unfulfilled but there was nothing I could do. We drifted apart as my work in the theatre took me to London a lot.'

'Is that where you met Mummy?'

'Yes. She was playing Rosalind in *As You Like It*. I had never seen anyone like her. I had always scoffed at the idea of love at first sight, you know, that *coup de foudre* moment, but I swear it happened then. I was entranced.'

'But you were married,' she said reproachfully.

'Yes, I was. I'm not proud of that, Aurora. I didn't set out to hurt anyone – you've got to believe that.'

'So why didn't you leave your wife?'

'She was very depressed. She even attempted suicide. I was

trapped. We were like strangers and I was miserable at home. Grace was everything I wanted.'

'So why did she marry Henry?' she pressed on. 'If you were so in love, why did she marry Daddy?'

'Jess became very ill. I was forced to go back home and care for her. I broke all ties with Grace as I was desperately guilty about our affair. I felt it would be better to separate.' His face changed. 'She came to me and asked me to run away with her. I refused. I told her that it was over and not to contact me again.' He closed his eyes. 'I had to, Aurora. My wife needed me. So Grace went away. I'll never forget the look on her face.'

'You sent away a pregnant girl? How could you?'

He shook his head. 'I didn't know about the baby – about you – not until much later. Henry was waiting in the wings and they got married. I read about it in the newspapers and I was heartbroken. I felt that I'd lost her forever.'

'But you arranged to run away with her. I saw your letter.'

'Yes, I couldn't forget her. In fact, I was pining for her. I drove to Cornwall and we met on a beach. She was about eight months gone by then. The minute I saw her I knew the baby was mine.'

'And that changed things?'

'Yes, of course it did.' His eyes flashed. 'I should never have left her go. Then when I realised how miserable she was too, I knew we had to run away. There was no point ruining both our lives. So we arranged everything.'

'I know the rest.' She wrapped her arms around her body protectively. 'She died and you left me with Henry Sinclair.'

'Left you? I came for you. I heard of your birth and came for you. Henry pulled out the big guns and threatened legal action. He told me that I was in no position to raise a child. My work was unstable and my wife even more so. He insisted that you stay with him and be raised as a Sinclair. I was so devastated about Grace, I let him convince me.' He banged the table with his fist.

'Left you? If only you knew. I watched you grow up. I saw you from the distance all the time. Maggie sent me pictures and updates. I tried to take you back on numerous occasions, but Henry wouldn't allow it. On Grace's tenth anniversary, I visited him. I had read about his new wife and his plans to move to London. I pleaded with him to tell you the truth but he forced me off his property. He claimed that you were happy and had a whole new life to live in the city. I didn't believe him until I saw you with those other children. You were at the park with the stepsons. The blond one was pushing you on the swing and you looked so happy. It was then I realised that Henry was right – you had a loving family which was something I could never give you.'

'That was when I was a child,' she said. 'You could have introduced yourself to me a million times over the past few years. Why leave it until now?'

Silas cast his eyes down. 'Lots of reasons. I was afraid to approach you. You seemed so happy and successful – why would you believe me? I also didn't want to betray Henry. I felt he would be the best person to tell you the truth.'

She said nothing. She struggled to understand but it was difficult.

'I saw all your plays,' he said softly. 'I was at the opening night of that last one. I thought it was your best.'

'You came to my plays?' Her hand flew to her mouth. 'So it *was* you who left the bunch of fuchsias. You left them at my dressing room door.'

He nodded. 'I picked them from that bush outside. Again, it was in homage to your mother.' His face relaxed as he remembered. 'Grace and I came down here for a week at the beginning of summer. We rented a house on the other side of the island. We hired a boat and went to Schull.' He pointed to the mainland. 'It's the village over there. I bought her a necklace in a craft shop. She promised me that she would never take it off.

You're wearing it now.'

'The fuchsia.' She held it up. 'You gave her this?'

He nodded. 'She loved that flower. It reminded her of here.'

'Maggie gave it to me for my tenth birthday.'

'I know. I told her to. You see, when your mother died, Henry had her body laid out in the big house for a couple of days. Hordes of people came to show their respects. I, however, wasn't welcome. Henry knew about our affair and didn't want me around.'

'I called to the house but he wouldn't let me in. I was desperate to see Grace, just one last time. Henry refused and told me never to come back. He was deranged with grief. Afterwards I realised that he felt guilty for leaving her alone.'

'She insisted that Daddy go to that party,' said Aurora defensively. 'The poor man was not at fault.'

'I know that,' he said. 'I never blamed him for anything.' He got up and started to pace the room. 'Maggie left me in after dark. She understood that I had to see her.' His face softened. 'She looked like an angel, all dressed in white, with her hair around her face. I remember gazing at the body and wishing that it was me instead of her. She had so much to offer, so much talent and beauty. I couldn't believe the injustice of it all. I couldn't comprehend why she was taken. She wasn't wearing the necklace so I asked Maggie to find it and keep it for you. I wanted you to have a link to her: a link to me.'

'She never said.'

'I asked her not to. I told her to give it to you when you were older. I felt it would be a connection. Grace would have loved that. You see, she wanted you so much. All she talked about was the baby. In her letters, she wrote about her excitement and love for you, Aurora. No one expected what happened.'

She felt something clutch her heart. The injustice he spoke of assaulted her being and for a moment she couldn't breathe. Death had taken her mother and denied her so much. Tears welled up in her eyes but she blinked them away.

'You're from Dublin, Maggie says,' she said, changing the subject. 'Why do you live here?'

Silas shrugged. 'Jess died seven years ago. The city served its purpose when I was a young man. It was vital and current, perfect for my work at the theatre. Then I began to seek simplicity: a life without emails and noise and parties. I was drawn to here. It gives me the space to write and it also reminds me of a happy time.' He smiled. 'I had a vain fantasy of becoming that "wise and simple man" that Yeats talked of.'

'"The Fisherman"?' she said immediately.

'Exactly.' He laughed. 'You're no joke, Aurora. Not many people I know are so familiar with Yeats.' He took her hand. 'When I met you at Bertie's party, I was struck at how articulate and bright you were. You look like Grace but I could also see myself in you.'

'The poetry?'

'Yes. I was so delighted to think that you loved it as much as I.'

'Did you know that I'd be there?'

'Of course. Bertie sent me an elaborate invitation, covered in guns and martini glasses. I almost threw it away until I saw your name. I booked my flight straight away. It was fate, I'm sure of it.'

'Did you hear me sing?'

'Every song.' He ruffled her hair. 'Dare I say it, but your voice is even more angelic than your mother's. You took my breath away. Then I tried to talk to you but there was always someone in the way.'

'Did you visit Daddy?'

'The next day. I knew that there was no going back. I had to meet you again and get to know you. Despite not growing up in my presence, you were clearly mine. I could sense it the minute we talked. Gives evidence to that nature v nurture debate, doesn't it?'

'Did you upset him?' Her large eyes filled with tears. 'I hope you didn't shout at him. He was so ill.'

'We had a civilised conversation after the old man had calmed down.' He squeezed her hand. 'I could tell that he was very sick. I asked him to tell you himself. I felt it would be better. I didn't want to turn up out of the blue and claim that you were my daughter. You didn't know me from Adam. I felt that he owed me that. To my surprise, he agreed. He seemed tired.'

They stared at each other with identical eyes. Even though her mind was spinning, she felt a strange peace. It was like it all made sense. All her life she had felt like an outsider, putting it down to George and Sebastian's dislike of her mother and refusal to accept her. Then, when she moved to London, she was always deemed odd. Beautiful, talented but like a child from another time, so Laura said.

Maybe deep down she had always known. Maybe a sixth sense was telling her that she didn't belong. The only time she ever felt truly happy was when James was around. He was the constant in her variable life. Now, the pieces had slotted together. Sitting opposite her was her father: a man she knew nothing about. Yet that would change. He was a symbol of a new beginning and it gave her hope. Life would go on and she still had a family.

'Are you okay?' he asked in concern. 'You looked so far away.'

She nodded. 'The past few days have been so bizarre. My poor brain is struggling to process it.'

'I understand.' He patted her back. 'I want to show you something.' He got up and disappeared into a back room.

She got up and walked about, surveying the room. There was

an unfinished painting of a bird propped up on an easel by the window, three books by Paul Durcan with multi-coloured tags on random pages on the table, and used mugs of coffee on the windowsill.

Silas came back holding a piece of worn paper. 'Read this,' he said softly. 'I wrote it a long time ago.'

She took the piece of paper and unfolded it gently. It was a poem.

*Filia – Daughter*

*New beginning*
*New life*
*But alone.*
*Tiny, helpless yet powerful*
*You survived*
*Your birth, her death, a terrible quid pro quo*
*The pain, the sorrow, the joy . . .*
*Goddess of the Dawn, may you begin again*
*Rejuvenation*
*Hope*

Aurora clutched the page. She read it again, her eyes blurred with tears.

'I love it,' she whispered. 'I love it.'

He stood back, watching the emotions flit over her face. 'I never published it,' he said. 'I kept it all this time and imagined your face when you read it.'

'You loved me,' she stated.

'More than you know.' He held out his arms. 'More than you know.'

She fell into his embrace and hugged him tightly. He smelt of turf and musk. There were no words necessary. She allowed him to hold her and she savoured it.

'Is your young man still outside?' said Silas, minutes later. 'The poor boy must be frozen.'

'Poor James!' she exclaimed, pulling back. 'I forgot about him.'

Silas opened the door and gestured for James to come inside. 'Excuse us, son. We got carried away.'

James had his camera around his neck. 'It's quite all right. I've been taking shots of the landscape. This is some place you've got here.'

They shook hands and Silas smiled. 'You're Henry's stepson, am I right?'

James nodded. 'The eldest.'

Silas ushered him inside. 'Right, I want to cook something. You must be starving. Now, my supplies are limited but I'm sure I have enough to whip up a chilli con carne.'

'We can go to the café on the pier,' protested Aurora. 'You weren't expecting us. I wouldn't dream of imposing.'

'Please.' His brown eyes were warm. 'I'm no Jamie Oliver but I do a mean Mexican.' He turned to James. 'There's beer in the fridge. Help yourselves.' He disappeared out the back door.

'All okay?' mouthed James.

Aurora nodded and smiled. 'Yes. Unexpectedly, yes.'

After dinner, Silas suggested that they go to the local pub where there was a session of traditional music. 'I play the *bodhrán*,' he explained. 'It's a drum that you beat with a stick.'

'Oh, yes, I've seen that on TV,' said James. 'Excellent.'

There was a small crowd sitting around the open log fire when they arrived. The pub was small and dark, with pictures of Gaelic football teams on the wall. Nautical paraphernalia like anchors and compasses were haphazardly displayed on shelves.

'Evening, Silas,' said the barman.

'Michael, this is Aurora and this is James – all the way from London.'

'*Céad míle fáilte romhaibh,*' said the barman.

'A hundred thousand welcomes,' Silas translated.

'Thank you,' said Aurora, smiling.

'Guinness, Silas?'

'Yes, Michael. A pint for me.' He turned to the other two. 'Would you like some stout?'

'Sure,' said James.

Aurora made a face. 'I'll have some white wine.'

'Coming up,' said Michael.

James pulled Aurora aside. 'Our guesthouse is two minutes up the road. You stay here and I'll drop our bags off and get a key.'

'If you're sure.'

'Of course. Bond with him. You have so much to catch up on.'

She watched Silas converse with the barman. He had a calmness about him that put her at ease. He didn't try too hard nor did he expect anything. He just allowed her to be and come to him on her terms.

There was a man playing a fiddle and another with an accordion. She watched them in fascination as they played, perfectly in tune with each other. The flames of the fire flickered and shadows danced on the walls. Sipping her wine, she waited for the reel to end. Silas had his drum under his arm and was waiting for an opportunity to join the others.

James arrived back and picked up his pint of Guinness. 'Cheers!' he said, smiling, taking a long drink. When he had finished, there was white residue on his upper lip. Aurora laughed and wiped it away with her forefinger.

Then Silas began to play.

Aurora knew of the *bodhrán* but had never heard it live. Using a small stick he beat out a rhythm, his head bent down in concentration and his eyes closed. There was something primeval about it – something tribal. The fiddler played a melody and then a man on a flute joined in. The lively music resonated around the room and she felt her feet tapping on the barstool. The weather had changed since their arrival. The darkness had brought a howling wind and smatterings of rain. It only added to the warmth and comfort of the fire and she relished its cosiness.

After a while, the musicians took a break. Silas took a huge gulp of his stout and joined Aurora and James at the bar.

'There's nothing like it,' he said. 'That music speaks to me like nothing else.'

'I understand,' agreed Aurora. 'It's the like all the magic and history of Ireland is in every note. It transports me.'

James raised an eyebrow. 'It's nice but I've got to admit I don't get it like you two.'

Silas smiled. 'It's the Irish. The beat of the *bodhrán* is in our blood.'

Cocooned in the small pub at the end of the earth, Aurora felt content. Henry's death, *Scarlett* and her old life seemed to be a distant memory. She didn't want this interlude to end.

Silas drained his drink. 'Will you sing?' he asked her directly. 'Just one song?'

She blushed. 'I don't know many traditional Irish songs.'

'You must have one,' he said. 'Come on! The boys would love it.'

'Go on,' urged James.

'Oh, all right.' She got to her feet. 'Bear with me. I may forget the words.'

The musicians smiled encouragingly and sat back.

Closing her eyes, she began to sing 'She Moves Through the Fair'. Her pure voice soared over the assembled crowd. James watched her intently. When she sang, she was mesmerising.

When she finished, there was silence for a moment and then thunderous applause.

Aurora curtseyed. 'Thank you,' she said shyly.

Silas felt a pang. She reminded him so much of Grace. Picking up his drum, he began to tap it lightly. 'How about a hornpipe?' he suggested.

The musicians nodded. Soon the little pub was full of music once more.

James and Aurora left the pub an hour later. Silas tried to convince them to stay but Aurora refused. The trauma and stress of the funeral and their meeting had rendered her exhausted. James took her hand and they walked up the road to an old bungalow. He took out a key and opened the main door.

'It's pretty basic,' he warned.

Aurora shrugged. 'All I want is a bed. It's been a tiring few days.'

They climbed the stairs and he stopped outside a white door.

'Is this my room?' she asked sleepily.

He lifted her chin with his finger, his dark eyes smouldering. 'It's *our* room,' he said. 'I just booked one. I hope that's okay.'

Her pulse quickened. 'That's okay.'

He opened the door and led her inside. A large double bed stood in the centre with plywood lockers on either side. Blue woollen blankets added a splash of colour and a small sink stood in the corner.

'We have to share the toilet with the others,' he said. 'It's down the hall.'

'Others?'

'Well, I haven't seen anyone but . . .'

She stood motionless, unsure of what to do. Her heart was thumping so loudly it rang in her ears. The last time he had looked at her like that was near the pool in Venice: the night she had gone for a swim. Crossing her fingers, she prayed that he wouldn't get a bout of conscience again. She wanted him. She wanted to touch him and have him hold her. She didn't want to be alone any more.

He took off his jacket and threw it on the bed. With wide eyes, she watched him walk towards her. They could still hear music from the pub, carried over the wind. He reached out and traced her full lips with his finger. 'You're so beautiful,' he said in wonder.

'Kiss me,' she said urgently. 'Please, James.'

He cupped her face with his hands and took possession of her mouth.

Eagerly she kissed him back, arching towards him. 'I've waited so long for this,' she moaned. 'Please don't stop. Please don't run away.'

He ran his finger through the long tresses of her hair and his hands roamed around her body. She pressed her breasts against his broad chest and he groaned.

'I'll never run away again,' he said hoarsely. 'I just wasn't ready. I wanted you but I didn't know it.' He yanked her top over her head and gazed at her black-and-gold bra. 'You wore this in Venice,' he said, fingering the strap.

'Yes, I did! How did you remember that?'

'It was imprinted on my brain,' he said drily.

'Really? I would never have thought.'

He reached behind and unclasped it with one hand. Then he pulled it down and let her breasts fall free.

Immediately she reddened and hung her head in embarrassment.

'Hey, what's wrong?' he asked in concern. 'If you want me to stop, just say.'

'Oh, no. I don't want you to stop,' she said fervently. 'It's just, I've never done this before and I'm not sure . . .'

'Done this?' he repeated, amused.

'Been with a man.' She put her head in her hands. 'I'm a novice – a neophyte. Sorry.'

He burst out laughing. 'Borealis!' he exclaimed. 'Do you really think I'd mind?'

Her eyes met his and they burned with intensity.

'This makes it even better,' he continued. 'It makes me wa to beat my chest and throw you over my shoulder.' He pulled he close. 'It means you're mine.' He kissed her tenderly. 'I love you,' he said gruffly. 'You're everything to me.'

He lifted her into his arms and laid her gently on the bed. 'Now, I'm not sure how good a teacher I am . . .'

She giggled.

'Or if I'll measure up to the famous Mr. Crowley . . .'

'Oh stop!' she chided. 'That's not funny.'

'But I'll try my best.' He kissed her again, more urgently this time, pressing his body against her soft frame. Lifting her knees, he wrapped her legs around him.

Her insides melted and she urged him closer.

'I won't hurt you,' he murmured. 'Don't be afraid.'

She ran her arms over his muscular back. 'I'd never be afraid with you,' she said. 'Ever.'

Later they lay entwined on the bed, her head resting on his bare chest. She traced her finger up and down his arm and sighed in contentment.

'How do you feel?' he asked, kissing her forehead.

'So good,' she said, stretching languidly. 'I can't believe that I waited this long to feel like this.'

He laughed. 'Well, I've got to say that I'm glad that you did.' He flipped her over and lay on top of her, his face inches from hers. Holding her wrists above her head, he kissed her neck and her shoulder, before moving down to the underside of her breast. She squirmed in delight, pushing her body upwards.

'It's crazy,' he said, releasing her. 'I feel like I've discovered America or something.'

'A pioneer,' she said, smiling.

He caressed the curve of her waist. 'It's pretty mind-blowing. You're a goddess, Aurora Sinclair.'

She turned her face away. 'Don't call me that.'

'What?'

'Sinclair. That's not my name.'

'Of course it is. Don't be silly.' He pulled her upright. 'I know you may not be Henry's biological daughter, but you're never going to be anything but a Sinclair.'

'Really?'

'Really,' he said firmly.

He wrapped his arms around her and kissed her thoroughly. 'I love you,' he said quietly. 'I know you better than anyone. I can't imagine being without you.'

Her mind filled with images of her future: a life where James was around all the time. She envisaged herself baking a cherry pie with her hands caked in flour. He appeared, kissing her neck and helping her to roll out the pastry. They were laughing in this vision and happiness flooded her every cell.

Aurora called to Silas's cottage the next morning. He was drinking coffee on the stone wall outside, his tall frame hunched over from the biting wind. She tapped his shoulder.

'Silas?' she said softly.

'Are you leaving?' he asked, warming his hands on the china cup. He didn't turn around.

'I have to,' she explained. 'I'm needed back in America. I just got a big part in a film and I need to rehearse.'

'Will you come back?' He kept his back to her.

'You know I will.' She pulled at his arm. 'I want to know you – I want us to be close. You've all I've got left.'

'I think you have a back-up over there,' he said, gesturing to James by the gable wall.

'You know what I mean.' She forced him to look at her. 'Thank you for making us feel so welcome. It can't have been easy.'

He shrugged. 'It just feels cruel that we have found each other and now you have to leave.'

Her brown eyes were compassionate. 'The world is a small place now. We can keep in touch quite easily. You could always come to New York.'

'I don't like cities.'

'Or I can come here.' She smiled. 'We can make it work. We just have to try.'

He placed his cup on the wall and pulled her into his arms. 'I'm sorry,' he mumbled into her hair. 'I'm sorry for all that I did.'

'Don't,' she said tremulously. 'Don't say sorry. Let's just start again.'

'Don't stay away too long, Aurora.' He handed her a fuchsia that he had plucked from the bush nearby. 'Come back.'

'I will. I swear that I will.' She broke free and rubbed the tears from her eyes. 'Write me a new poem,' she said meaningfully, backing away.

Silas nodded. 'A happy one this time, one that looks to the future.'

The man with the peaked cap threw the rope on the pier and helped Aurora onto the ferry. James stashed their bags in the crew cabin and joined her at the stern of the boat. She bent over the edge to see the swirling backwash of water as the engine roared to life. The big boat turned three hundred and sixty degrees and headed out of the harbour. She pulled her coat tightly around her as the wind whipped past.

'What are your plans when we get back to London?' she asked casually, not daring to presume anything.

James wiped some spray from his face. 'Oh, I can think of a few things I want to do.' He grinned. 'Namely take you to bed for as long as possible.'

'What will Gloria say?' Aurora blushed. 'She'll die of shock.'

'She'll get over it,' he said sensibly. 'Laura's sugar daddy surprise was far worse.' He wrapped his arm around her shoulders. 'Don't give anyone else a second thought. All that matters is that we're together.'

'You know I have to go back to New York,' she said quietly, not daring to meet his eyes. 'I have to finish that run of *La Morte* before flying to L.A. to meet Carey.'

'Well, someone once told me that she imagined me in a studio apartment in New York,' he said. 'It's not a bad idea, all things considered.'

'You'd move to America?' she gasped. 'For me?'

'Mainly for you, but also to feed my artistic spirit. I need to start exhibiting again – I need to feel part of the world. The last few months have been mundane and stifling.'

'I rent a small place near Greenwich.'

'Ideal.'

She kissed him hard on the lips. His stubble grazed her cheek and she felt herself melt inside. It was crazy how she wanted him again – it was as though a dam had burst. All the feelings and desire she had felt for so long finally had an outlet. She kissed him furiously, channelling all her emotions, then snuggled in close.

'You were always my Prince in the Barbie Ferrari. You rescued me, James. I'm yours forever.'

The boat moved up and down on the waves, sending the occasional spray of seawater over its occupants. James kept his arms around Aurora to protect her from falling, whispering in her ear and making her laugh.

A woman in white watched them from the clifftop as the boat passed by. Her long hair blew in the breeze and her beautiful face was smiling. Turning around, she walked away and disappeared into the morning mist.

**THE END**

Now that you're hooked why not try

*Indecision*

also published by Poolbeg

Here's a sneak preview of chapter one.

# Chapter 1

'How does five hundred a month sound to you, ladies?'

Lydia bit her lip. This was the flat! She just knew it. Sure, it was in bad condition, but the location was fantastic. Five minutes from campus – only ten minutes from the city centre.

'What do you think, Sam?' Lydia turned to her best friend.

'I don't know,' said Samantha, screwing up her nose distastefully at the peeling walls and threadbare carpet. 'It's so dreary! Look at those grey walls.'

Lydia laughed. 'We are on a budget, you know. Come on, it's so central. You could walk to work from here.'

Samantha looked doubtful. 'I suppose.'

Michael McCarthy cleared his throat. He owned five apartments just like this around the city. These girls should realise that their answer really didn't matter. He could fill this flat twice over if he wanted to.

'Look, ladies, I'm a busy man – are you going to rent it or not?' He tapped his foot impatiently and glanced at his watch.

Lydia crossed her fingers. *Please say yes, please say yes,* she pleaded silently.

Samantha threw up her arms in defeat. 'Count me in, I suppose.'

Lydia clapped her hands in delight. 'I've a good feeling about this, Sam. A few books on the shelves and some pictures on the wall will make a big difference.'

She turned to the landlord and smiled.

'We'll take it,' she said.

He shook their hands. 'Good choice, girls. Trust me. This one has a nice view of the college.'

Lydia took some cash out of her bag. 'Will a month in advance be enough?'

Michael pulled out a receipt book. 'Yes, that'll be fine. I'll need a deposit of a month's rent as well. Then I'll collect rent on the first Friday of every month.'

Samantha counted out a wad of notes. 'Any hope of a paint job? I really hate the colour of the sitting-room area.'

'If you want to paint it yourself, go ahead. Any decoration that doesn't cost me anything is welcome.' He handed them a receipt and a bunch of keys. 'My wife will email you the contract later today. Once that's signed, it's all official. Now, I'll leave you to it. Good luck!'

He turned on his heel and exited the room, banging the door loudly. Seconds later they heard the roar of an engine.

'And he's gone!' Lydia laughed.

'Still, it seems like we can do what we like to the place and he won't care.' Samantha smiled. 'I bags the room on the left.'

Lydia shrugged. 'It doesn't matter to me.'

She walked into her new bedroom. It was quite small with a window looking out on the busy street. The violet walls gave it a feminine feel; it was lucky that purple was her favourite colour. A dusty mahogany wardrobe stood in the corner, next to a matching dressing table. A lamp with a lopsided shade stood precariously on the edge of the bedside locker.

Samantha popped her head in the door and made a face. 'Is

that dry rot by the window?' she asked, pointing to t windowsill.

Lydia shrugged. 'Maybe. Give me a chance – I'll spruce this place up in no time. Now, enough of the negativity.'

'Okay, okay, calm down. I'm going to head to the shop for some basics. Do you need anything?'

'No, I'm all right. See you in a while.'

The door slammed shut.

Lydia hugged herself.

After graduating with a French and English degree, she had enrolled to do a post-graduate diploma in education with Samantha. But after an intense year of teaching teenagers, she was positive that she never wanted to be a teacher. So she decided to do a Master's in English and pursue her dream of becoming a writer. Her parents had agreed to bankroll her for another year, but after that she was on her own. They couldn't understand why she didn't go into teaching like Samantha. 'It's a fine dependable job,' her father had said a million times. 'Aren't you trained now and all?'

Lydia screwed up her nose. No way, she thought. Life has other plans for me.

She unzipped her bag and started to pull out some clothes. Opening the wardrobe, she coughed as a cloud of dust blew everywhere.

This place needs a good clean, she thought, grimacing. Not her favourite job in the world, it had to be said. Dominic always teased her about how messy she was. He couldn't believe that she didn't know how to use a washing machine.

Dominic. Her expression softened.

It's going to be so weird without him, she thought sadly, looking at the enormous bed she would have to fill alone.

Dominic and Lydia had met when she'd fallen off a gate while protesting against the possible introduction of college fees. He

·ad helped her up and offered to buy her coffee. It was then, while he gently massaged the inside of her sprained wrist, that Lydia had a *coup de foudre* moment.

They had been inseparable for the past three years. An unlikely match to say the least, she an Arts student and he a newly graduated doctor, yet somehow it had worked. Then Dominic finished his internship with a burning ambition to be a surgeon. This dream had led him to Dublin, over two hundred and fifty kilometres away.

The prospect of Dominic not being around was unthinkable, but Lydia knew it was the best thing to further his career. She loved him too much to create a fuss.

Anyway, she thought, he will be down most weekends. And absence is supposed to make the heart grow fonder.

'*Lyd? Are you ready?*' Samantha called. '*Want to get some pizza before we head home?*'

'*I'd love to, coming now.*'

Lydia grabbed her bag and closed the door of her new room.

Samantha's battered Golf pulled up outside Lydia's family home, an old stone house partially covered in green ivy. Both girls had grown up here in Baltimore in West Cork – a small seaside village on the south coast and over an hour's drive from the city.

'Thanks for the lift, Sam.' Lydia hugged her friend. 'See you Sunday evening?'

'Sure thing. Enjoy your last days of freedom.' She smiled broadly as Lydia exited the car.

'Oh, I will. Colin texted me earlier saying that he's coming down for the weekend. God help me!'

Samantha laughed. 'Give him a big kiss for me. Talk on Sunday.'

She waved and drove off down the street.

Colin McCarthy was Lydia's first cousin. A fellow English

student, he adored hanging out with Lydia's mum, his favourite aunt. Born and raised in Dublin, he was the only son of Helen's older and extremely successful sister, Diana. Classically good-looking, spoilt but totally adorable, he had never wanted for anything in his life. His parents had a house in Killiney the size of a small country and Colin had sucked the silver spoon dry.

'Hey, Mum!' called Lydia, walking into the kitchen and dumping her bag on the counter.

Helen Kelly walked into the kitchen, closely followed by Lydia's dog Toto, a brindle Cairn Terrier who was the image of his famous namesake.

'Hello, darling! Hungry? Dinner's in the oven.'

Lydia melted into her familiar embrace, loving the smell of perfume mixed with Shepherd's Pie.

'Sam and I had pizza a little while ago, so I'll give it a miss.'

Helen shook her head. 'Won't you be eating enough of that rubbish next week, young lady? I have a lovely pie made from yesterday's leftover lamb.'

Lydia shrugged and smiled. 'You should have texted me.'

'All the more for me, Auntie Hel,' came a voice from behind and Lydia jumped.

'Colin! I thought you weren't coming until tomorrow?'

'No, sugarplum. I decided to jump in my car and avail of some home cooking and *America's Next Top Model* with Molly.' He kissed her lightly on the cheek. Kitted out in black Armani chinos, coupled with a purple Dolce and Gabbana shirt, he looked his usual immaculate self. His brown curls had unfamiliar streaks of blond which danced in the bright light of the kitchen.

'New hairdo?' enquired Lydia, amused.

Colin beamed. 'Felix was doing the usual trim and suddenly he screamed and told me that I just *had* to get these highlights.' He paused in front of the microwave and peered at his reflection. 'Are you impressed?'

'You look gorgeous, Col.' Lydia giggled. 'Beautiful.'

Colin gave her an arch look. 'How genuine of you! I really feel it. Molly loves it, anyway. She has taste.'

Lydia's younger sister Molly walked into the kitchen at that moment, her hair wet from the shower. A seventeen-year-old version of Helen Kelly, she had a shock of blonde hair and twinkling blue eyes.

'Did I hear my name?' she asked, towelling her hair. 'Who was talking about me?'

*Moi*,' said Colin, pouring himself a glass of wine from the fridge. 'We have a date to watch TV later, right?'

'I'll be there,' said Molly. 'Hey, Lyd, did you find a flat?'

Lydia nodded. 'It's not exactly beautiful or anything but it is right next door to college. The pros and cons sort of balance each other out.'

'How much?' asked Helen, her half-moon spectacles perched on her nose as she read a recipe for pavlova.

'Five hundred a month.'

'God, I wonder what it's like to pay rent,' said Colin, wide-eyed.

Lydia punched him playfully in the arm. 'Watch it, rich boy.'

When Colin had decided to study in Cork four years before, his father had purchased an apartment for him. It was situated by the college, looking out on the river. Lydia privately thought that his flat was more akin to a show house. Spotlessly clean, it looked like something from a magazine. Colin was incredibly house-proud and prided himself on his pristine white couch and gleaming marble floor. Lydia had once put a glass of wine down on his coffee table without using a coaster and there had been a meltdown.

'Did Dom ring?' she asked her mother as she poured herself a glass of juice.

'No, honey, not yet. Go into the sitting room now and take

Colin with you. I have to bake and his constant chatter will drive me mad.'

'Gee, thanks,' said Colin, following Lydia out of the kitchen. 'So, cuz, how's Dom doing in the big smoke?'

'Okay, I think. He's always so tired when he rings. I really miss him, Col. I mean we lived in each other's pockets for three years and now I'm back to an electric blanket and girls' nights out.'

'*Boo hoo!* At least you're not me! Do you know how hard it is to find a monogamous gay guy in Cork? In Ireland for that matter? My youth is passing me by, Lyd.' He rolled his eyes dramatically.

'Oh, you're ancient all right, Col. Really past it.' Lydia laughed. He always cheered her up. 'Come on, *EastEnders* is on soon. Let's get the couch before Molly.'

Dominic rang just as Lydia was snuggling down under her duvet. His familiar ringtone pulsated through the room.

'Dom,' she murmured, settling into the pillow. 'How are you doing, baby?'

'Exhausted. I love every second of it, but it's hard work. I assisted in a gall-bladder removal today.'

'Yuk, how was it? I would pass out if I saw that much blood.'

'It was amazing, Lydia, totally incredible. I got great feedback from O'Leary – remember I told you about him? The head guy?'

'Oh yeah.' Lydia's tone was flat, but Dominic didn't notice.

'Anyway,' he continued, 'he said that I can observe a triple bypass next Wednesday, but only from behind glass.'

Lydia didn't know why, but she felt her skin grow cold. Of course she was happy for Dominic – he was living the dream, fulfilling his ambition. It just felt like he was telling her about a world far beyond her imagination. He would be playing golf with O'Leary in the K Club while she'd be drinking a skinny latte in the student centre with Colin. He would be experiencing life-changing operations while she'd be getting to grips with the *Norton Anthology of Poetry.*

Lydia, said a small voice inside her head, calm down. Far away hills are greener. He's missing you just as much as you are missing him.

She shook her head and started to tell him about her new flat and Colin singing Beyoncé at dinner.

He laughed when she related how her dad had told Colin to zip it or lose a limb. She pictured Dominic lounging on the couch, his brown hair flopping over his eyes.

Fifteen minutes later, she hung up the phone. Closing her eyes, she tried to block out that niggling, uneasy feeling. The idea that Dominic was slipping away from her into a new exciting life that didn't include her.

Lydia Kelly, get a grip, she scolded herself. This is Dominic you're talking about. He loves you to distraction. One more year and everything will be different. You'll be back together and, who knows, you might have a job in RTÉ as an investigatory journalist.

Lydia drifted into a dreamless sleep, while hundreds of miles away her boyfriend lay awake thinking about her.

Dominic had been bowled over the first day he had helped her to her feet. He was intrigued by this fiery, passionate young girl. Jolted, he had bought her coffee and boldly massaged her injured wrist.

He realised how lucky he was to have a girl like Lydia. She was genuinely a special person. He hated being away from her, but he knew that he had to follow his dream.